CROWN OF
SERPENTS

ᒍᒥᖅ ᒍᐅᐅᖸ ᒥᐁᐳ ᐸᒥᒥᐁᒐ ᐅᐁᐅᒍᐣᐊᐳᐁᒐ

PRAISE FOR CROWN OF SERPENTS

CROWN OF SERPENTS is a compelling novel deeply rooted in the history of the Six Nations Iroquois. It takes place in contemporary times with fully developed characters and a powerful narrative; its author is well versed in the complexity of modern Iroquois life. Far more than a simple mystery the book follows the path of Tony Hillerman's Navajo based novels by providing the reader with remarkable insights into the culture and traditions of the most influential Native nation east of the Mississippi.

— *Doug George-Kanentiio, editor, columnist, author from Akwesasne Mohawk Nation*

CROWN OF SERPENTS is a page-turning story with a creative plot backed up with incredible historical tidbits from the author's extensive research. Karpovage's careful crafting throughout compares him very favorably with others in the genre such as Follett and Ludlum.

— *Sue Lofstrom, Associate Professor of English, Georgia Perimeter College, Atlanta, GA*

I thought: Indiana Jones meets the Godfather! Read the entire book in two sittings. Had to pause occasionally during the first eight-hour read-a-thon to catch my breath. One of the best novels I have ever read!

— *Paulette Likoudis, Finger Lakes Times columnist, Lodi, NY*

The plot is very intricate but well conducted by the author, the characters are well developed and the narrative is fluent. This mystery thriller grabs the reader and does not let go of him until the end.

— *Bruno Gazzo, editor, PS Review of Freemasonry, Genoa, Italy*

I thoroughly enjoyed this book. I couldn't put it down from the moment I picked it up, until I finished the last page. Karpovage is a name to watch for in future writings…right up there with Dan Brown. I am anxiously awaiting his next novel!

— *Brother Alan Johnson, Stone Mountain Lodge #449, Stone Mountain, GA*

CROWN OF SERPENTS is a bombshell of a book! Precise maps and historic manuscripts help lend credence to a compelling scavenger hunt that burns across the reservations of Western New York.

— *William P. Robertson, Bucktail novelist, Duke Center, PA*

Michael Karpovage's character Jake Tunundu is fascinating and displays the amazing qualities of a Seneca Indian, an American soldier and true Freemason. The author, being a Freemason, was able to weave the Craft in and out of the story so well that it didn't appear forced and complemented the plot well. He was also able to describe some small secrets about the Craft which only Freemasons would recognize and stays true to any obligation, which is a great accomplishment.

— *Brother Jeb W. Carroll, Kenilworth Lodge #29 GRA, Edmonton, Alberta, Canada*

MICHAEL
KARPOVAGE

ALSO BY MICHAEL KARPOVAGE

Flashpoint Quebec
www.flashpointquebec.com

This is a work of fiction. Names, characters, places, and incidents either are
the product of the author's imagination or are used fictitiously, and any
resemblance to actual persons, living or dead, business establishments,
events, or locales is entirely coincidental.

Published by
Karpovage Creative, Inc.
322 Fernhill Court
Jonesboro, GA 30236
www.karpovagecreative.com

Publishers Cataloging-in-Publication Data
Karpovage, Michael.
Crown of Serpents / Michael Karpovage
ISBN: 978-0-615-28110-0
1. Tununda, Jake (Fictitious character) — Fiction
2. New York (state) — Fiction
3. Mystery fiction.
I. Title
PS3611.A7 C7 2009

Printed in the United States of America
Second Edition

Cover / interior book design, maps (except where noted), and illustrations by
Karpovage Creative, Inc.
designer • map illustrator • publisher
www.karpovagecreative.com

For my sons Jake and Alex...

AUTHOR'S NOTE

Although *Crown of Serpents* is a work of fiction based on pure speculative narrative, and all the present day characters are creations of my imagination, some of the historical figures in this book are real people. They existed and left records of themselves, some more abundant than others. I tried to be faithful to their actions and encounters as best I could determine from historical sources. For anyone interested in the historical background of the story within the novel, a time line of events is provided in the back of this book. For more in-depth information, including source notes on the Boyd-Brant-Butler Masonic affair, plus a photo gallery that follows the story, please visit **www.CrownofSerpents.com**.

— Michael Karpovage

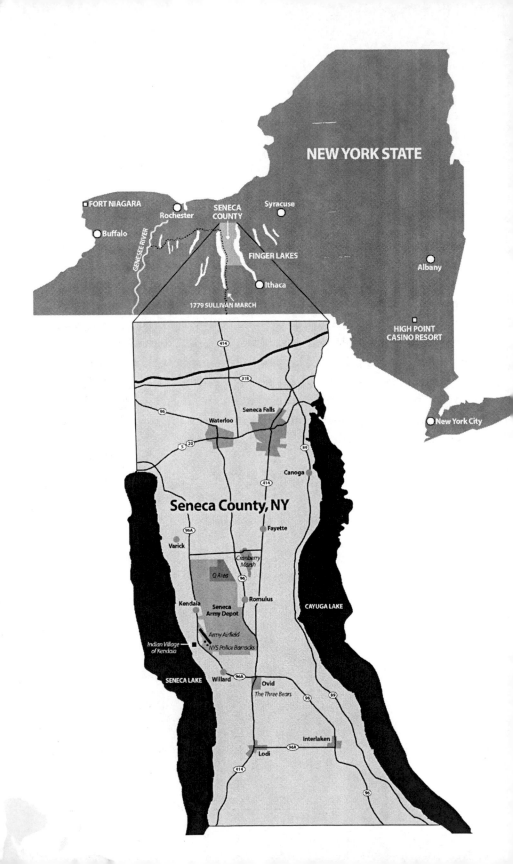

NEW YORK STATE

FORT NIAGARA

Rochester

SENECA COUNTY

Syracuse

Buffalo

GENESEE RIVER

FINGER LAKES

Albany

Ithaca

1779 SULLIVAN MARCH

HIGH POINT
CASINO RESORT

New York City

414

318

96

Seneca Falls

Waterloo

5 20

89

Canoga

414

Seneca County, NY

96A

Varick

Fayette

Cranberry
Marsh

96

Q Area

Romulus

CAYUGA LAKE

Kendaia

Seneca
Army Depot

Army Airfield

Indian Village
of Kendaia

NYS Police Barracks

SENECA LAKE

Willard

96A

Ovid

The Three Bears

96

89

Interlaken

96A

Lodi

414

96

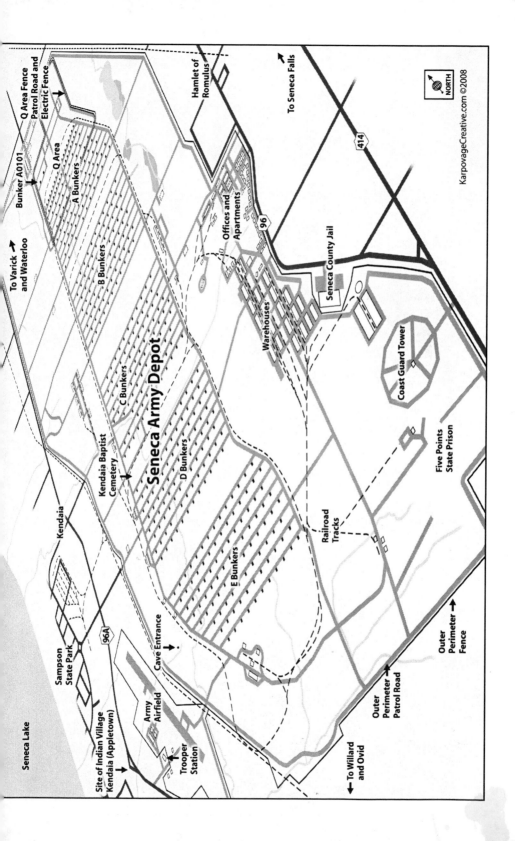

CROWN OF SERPENTS

PROLOGUE

Monday, September 13, 1779. Seneca Nation territory between Genesee River and Conesus Lake.

LIEUTENANT THOMAS BOYD wrenched his head back as a heavy wooden war hammer passed by his face. The momentum of the missed blow threw the attacking Iroquois Indian off balance and gave the young rebel officer the chance he needed to counterattack with his sword. With a horizontal slice, Boyd opened the Indian's bare tattooed chest. The warrior screamed and looked down at the gaping red gash across his abdomen. He dropped to his knees and bent over on his hands. Boyd finished him off by plunging his sword deep between the Indian's shoulder blades. The hard thrust slammed the warrior flat against the ground. With a boot on his victim's back and a twist of his hand, Boyd extracted his blood-smeared sword and readied himself for the next onslaught.

Movement from behind a tree.

A lone British Ranger, his musket fitted with a dreaded bayonet, charged directly at Boyd. The Ranger made it to within seven feet when a rifle cracked to the officer's right. The Ranger grunted, dropped his musket, and clutched at his face. He stumbled past Boyd and slumped to the ground — dead. Heavy gray smoke drifted over the British trooper, enveloping the officer's next would-be killer.

Boyd, a veteran of the Continental Army under General Sullivan, glanced to his right to see which of his trusted scouts had made the shot. It was his Oneida Indian guide, Honyost Thaosagwat, a courageous fighter from the only breakaway Iroquois nation supporting the American rebellion. He received a wide-eyed nod from Boyd. Thaosagwat gave him a nervous smile in return and took cover behind a boulder to reload his weapon.

Through the wafting battlefield haze, not fifty paces away, a British officer barked the command to fire. Several shots of lead whistled by Boyd's head as he sought cover behind a tree. The volley of enemy musket fire cut down what was left of his small scout detachment. Hugging the tree, he felt a searing sensation rip through his side as a musket ball penetrated his deerskin coat and impacted above his hip. Boyd grimaced and dropped to a knee. He grabbed at his waist, blood oozing between his fingers. Nausea and dizziness immediately swept over him.

"Lieutenant's been hit!"

Boyd looked to the shout. One of his soldiers crouched toward him, scout rifle and powder horn in hand. It was Sergeant Michael Parker.

"We've got to get you out of here, sir."

Through labored breathing, Boyd managed a response. "No, no, it went straight through. Stay in the fight. They'll be coming again."

Parker nodded, "I won't leave your side Lieutenant." He knelt and popped open his horn, poured black powder into his rifle's barrel, reloaded another shot, and then rammed it all home with his rifle rod. His actions were swift and practiced. He then moved to a nearby tree and rested the rifle against the trunk to steady his aim.

Boyd squeezed his eyes shut, pressed his wound tighter, and willed himself to fight on. He looked beyond Parker, wondering how many of his men were still alive inside the grove of sapling trees where they had sought protection. The pressing attack by the British and their Indian allies had nearly decimated his detachment of twenty-nine scout riflemen. And it was completely his fault.

Guided by youthful cockiness and overconfidence, he pushed too far when he deliberately made contact with three Seneca Indians earlier in the day. Thinking he could take their scalps as trophies, Boyd ordered his marksman to open fire while the Indians ate over a campfire. His men killed two, but one had made his escape. Boyd ordered pursuit of the lone

Indian against his Oneida guide's recommendation. They pursued their prey through the woods and mistakenly ran into an ambuscade made up of the fiercest combination of wilderness fighters the rebellion had seen. He had led his troops directly into the jaws of four hundred British Rangers, Tories, and Iroquois warriors led by the notorious pair of Colonel John Butler and Mohawk Chief Joseph Brant.

Boyd could clearly hear the specific orders of his commander now ringing inside his throbbing head. The night before, General John Sullivan had ordered him not to make contact with the enemy. His was supposed to be a recon mission only.

The British and Indians had immediately surrounded his men and commenced the ambush. Boyd's marksmen fought back with utmost precision, shooting behind good cover. They felled many but Butler and Brant's sheer numbers ultimately proved too great. The slaughter took its toll after three heavy volleys from the British crack troops. Boyd knew he had no choice but to get his men out. After several unsuccessful organized attempts at breaking through the enemy lines, he had become separated and lost all means of control over his scouts. Each man was on his own.

Now shot through the side and panic-stricken, he looked around as the end closed near. Smoke shifted and he watched brutal hand-to-hand combat rage on his right flank. The famous Virginian marksman Timothy Murphy, the best shot in his detachment, had just beaten down an Indian. Boyd's close friend and Brother in the Freemasons, Sergeant Sean McTavish, waved Murphy over as he and several others made one more desperate attempt to break the enemy lines for escape. The battlefield haze shifted across Boyd's vision again and the rest of his scouts vanished.

Parker fired his rifle bringing Boyd back to his immediate surroundings. Parker then moved up, disappearing into his gunpowder-filled cloud. Boyd's vision blurred, his eyes burning in the smoke.

The violence of the battle suddenly subsided.

Two British Rangers emerged from the thick haze to Boyd's front, their bayoneted muskets at the hip. Boyd heard more movement behind him. Turning, he observed a half dozen shirtless, sweat and blood stained Iroquois warriors jump from tree to tree. Donning distinctive war paint, feather headdresses, and decorative jewelry, they clutched war hammers, tomahawks, and hot muskets. Using his sword as a crutch, Boyd staggered to his feet to face their final assault. He knew he was a dead man either way, whether it was the two Rangers at his back or the Iroquois pack of wolves to his front. He could only hope the end would come swiftly.

Instead, time stood still.

The battlefield grew strangely quiet.

Boyd blinked through watery eyes.

A war whoop shattered the silence as a young Seneca Indian made a dash straight for Boyd. But another Indian cut the youngster off. Clad in a fine red cape over a ruffled white blouse with a silver gorget about his neck, there stood their leader. His arm was stretched straight out, blocking the scalp-hungry young warrior from gaining his trophy.

Boyd recognized this man from when he first laid eyes on him at the Battle of Newtown last month — the feared Mohawk chief, Joseph Brant. A captain with the British Army responsible for several massacres against the colonists, Brant was the great persuader who had convinced the other Iroquois nations to ally with the British instead of staying neutral.

Brant strode to within several feet of Boyd, a blood-smeared tomahawk in one hand, a pistol in the other. His plumed headdress swayed atop his closely shaven, battle-tattooed head. His warriors shouted encouragement in anticipation of the kill.

Fear gripped Thomas Boyd's entire body, intensifying all of his senses. He could feel the warmth of his own life-blood spreading across his wound. He became dizzy again. His hands shook. His knees trembled. With a pounding heart ready to burst from his chest, he suddenly remembered Brant's stature as the very first from the Iroquois Confederacy to become an English Freemason. He remembered that Brant had helped two other rebel soldiers escape death back in 1776 at the Battle of Cedars. He knew now there was but one slim chance for survival. Since he and Brant belonged to the same secret fraternity, he could only hope his so-called Brother would honor the ancient obligation of a Mason in distress — and spare his life.

He must make the sign.

With the tip of his officer's sword planted in the ground, Boyd let go of the hilt and watched it swing away to drop at Brant's feet. Surrender. Boyd then raised both arms, made the secret magical gestures only a fellow Freemason would interpret, and lowered his arms back down to his side. He finished by whispering a single word to Brant. The communication was delivered.

A confused murmur rippled through the group of Indians. The two British Rangers looked at one another then over to Brant. Brant narrowed his eyes and hesitated. He inspected Boyd from head to bloody boot then calmly scanned the battlefield around him. Boyd followed his gaze.

Off to one side, Boyd noticed his battered Sergeant Parker resting on his knees, head silently bowed as the two British Rangers stood over their prisoner with muskets ready to fire. Brant then looked in the opposite direction and became transfixed on several Iroquois warriors just beyond some rocks. Boyd too looked that way.

His Oneida guide Thaosagwat was being held by two other Indians as a third spat in his face. A fourth Indian then snuck up from behind Thaosagwat and buried a tomahawk in the back of his skull. The crunch was crisp. Thaosagwat's legs buckled and he collapsed face first to the ground. His scalp was immediately and thoroughly sliced and peeled back from his head. It was held high in victory.

War whoops echoed through the woods.

Brant turned back and locked eyes with Boyd. They held each other's gaze for several seconds. Boyd never flinched, even as the blood drained from his body.

"Brother, your life is under my protection," Brant finally declared in perfect English. "Should you survive your wound, I'll transport you to Montreal for a prisoner exchange."

With relief, Boyd promptly passed out.

Brant directed his war chiefs to take both Boyd and the other surviving rebel soldier into custody. He then turned and ran off into the thick woods, a group of his warriors at his heels. A Ranger grabbed Boyd's sword before the Indians could get to it, but once they pounced on the unconscious prisoner, the savages stripped him of all clothing and possessions, like vultures on a fresh carcass.

The young Seneca warrior who had been denied Thomas Boyd's scalp as a trophy, was one of the Indians pillaging the victim for items of value. He came away with the rebel officer's shiny belt buckle, his hunting knife, powder horn, and a small leather booklet. The youngster fanned the English language pages inside the book and frowned. He had no idea it was Boyd's personal campaign journal. He stuffed the booklet into his pouch thinking he could barter with it later. He then kicked Boyd several times in the ribs to awaken him for the march back to their village. The Seneca warrior still felt the officer's scalp was rightfully his and that he would not be denied taking it again.

He did not have to wait long.

His trophy would come the very next day.

1

Present day. November. Early Monday morning.
Cranberry Marsh. North of the Hamlet of Romulus, N.Y.

THIRTY FEET DEEP inside a rock fissure, U.S. Army Major Robert "Jake" Tununda gained his footing on a ledge, gripped his rescue rope tight, and hugged the stone wall to catch his breath. As he inhaled, the stench of fresh human excrement rose from below and filled his nostrils. He shook his head, the odor somehow triggering a suppressed memory he had stored away for many years. His eyes glazed over for a moment and he remembered himself back as a young infantry captain leading an assault into a shit-filled al-Qaeda underground bunker in Afghanistan. The scene in his head ended in an atrocity he would never forget — his black moment in an otherwise illustrious combat career. Jake pressed his eyes shut and filed the thought back where it belonged, refusing to let it cloud the attempted rescue he was performing. Only now, he thought, as he crinkled his nose, there would probably be a dead body instead to recover below.

It had been about twenty minutes since he had turned north up Route 96 out of the central New York State hamlet of Romulus to continue his early morning rural drive. He had left his home in Carlisle, Pennsylvania and was in route to Rochester, up on Lake Ontario. Deciding to kill the early hours of boredom, he had eavesdropped on his portable police and fire scanner, and to his surprise he had caught the tail end of a local emergency dispatch, complete with Global Positioning Satellite coordinates. The female dispatcher described a man trapped in a well or hole in a marsh.

Upon her repeat page of the GPS coordinates Jake was ready with his Chevy Tahoe's on-board navigation system. He typed in the sequence of Latitude: 42 degrees 47'28.04"N and Longitude: 76 degrees 49'51.12"W and found out he was right around the corner from where the victim was supposedly trapped.

Suffering not the slightest hint of hesitation, the 37-year-old former commander of highly trained combat infantrymen, moved into action. Attempting to rescue a stranger in a bad predicament was the embodiment of Jake's personal make-up.

After following the directional waypoint on his navigation system monitor, he motored down a dirt road off 96. It was labeled Marsh Road on his screen. As more chatter filled the radio, Jake heard that the victim's location was apparently on an island in the swamp and next to some old Indian grave.

Bringing his sports utility vehicle to a grinding halt, he jumped out, ran to the rear, and raised the back hatch. Unzipping his handy emergency duffel bag of gadgets and gear he switched his Army dress shoes for a pair of zip-up waterproof boots. He then pulled out his hand-held GPS unit and typed in the same coordinates to guide him through the marsh. Slinging his equipment bag over one shoulder, he followed the directional arrow on his hand-held unit and stepped foot into shin-deep muck.

After quickly trailblazing his way through a combination of marsh and brush, he entered a line of woods and soon arrived at the small island that matched the GPS coordinates. He was first on scene. He then located the supposed well, thought it looked more like an earthquake fissure, and tried to make initial contact with the victim, all the while anchoring his rescue rope to a tree.

Now, resting on the ledge after his climb down inside the shaft and his mind reset on his self-imposed task, he unclipped an already illuminated flashlight from a carabiner. He directed the beam down into a shimmering puddle of soupy red mud. Floating in the muck was a crosshatch of rotted wood, swamp grass, and several pieces of shale that had tumbled in from the surface.

"Anybody down here?" Jake shouted. It was the fifth time. He received the same response — echoed silence. He shifted his body and moved the flashlight beam further into the hole. He saw a black baseball cap partially submerged in the muck. Embroidered on the hat was a recognizable NASCAR logo alongside a familiar slanted white number three. Floating next to the hat was the top half of a shattered cell phone, its LCD panel grayed-out. Jake's eyes followed the trail of liquid into a wider cave-like room. He bent down on the ledge to get a better view below.

There, lying face down in about four inches of muck was the motionless body of the man who had no doubt placed the call to 9-1-1.

"Son of a bitch," Jake grumbled.

He let go of his safety rope and dropped into the water, the scum splashing his starched green uniform pants tucked into his boots. He slogged over to the body and squatted down as the flashlight beam centered on the back of the man's head. Chips of bone and brain matter were pressed into wet hair where the top of the skull had been crushed. The man's legs lay twisted at irregular angles. The smell of feces was heavy. The backside of the victim's pants was stained with brown discharge. Jake swallowed back a gag. He knew it was useless to even take a pulse, but he'd go through the motions anyway.

Setting the flashlight on a rock so the beam illuminated the back of the cave, his eyes scanned the chamber — solid limestone walls, low ceiling, and a pile of rocks in a corner oddly shaped like a human figure. He looked down at the victim, grabbed hold of a shoulder and hip, and rolled the body onto its back.

The man's wide-open eyes were frozen in a glazed death stare as bloody water rolled off his battered face. He wore a teeth-shattered grimace. Jake sized him up quickly. Unshaven, weathered face with sunken cheeks, mid-forties. A long gash over his eye revealed a thick mixture of blood and mud. The guy definitely took a beating on his tumble down the hole. Jake looked away, adding the dead man's image to the mosaic of deceased in the storage cabinet of his mind.

He peeled off his rappelling gloves and set them next to his flashlight. Placing two fingers under the man's jaw, he checked the carotid artery for a beat. There was none, of course. He pulled his fingers back and wiped them on his uniform pants before glancing down at the man's abdomen. Plaid shirt covered with a black denim vest, a busted arm with a clenched fist across the stomach. Jake's eyes narrowed as he noticed something clutched in the man's hand.

He grabbed the wrist, turned it over, and exposed the palm. Prying the man's fingers open, he revealed the bottom half of the cell phone. Shaking his head, he closed the hand back up. Then he saw something shiny — halfway out of the vest side pocket — some type of circular item bordered by elongated white wampum shells. He recognized the wampum right away as a common decorative addition to jewelry he had seen growing up on the Seneca Indian reservation.

He carefully pulled the item from the pocket and held it in the flashlight beam. A little larger than a half dollar, the shiny disk was clearly made of old hammered silver. Paralleling the outer wampum border was an inner border of small decorative holes — definitely an Indian motif he had seen in many past artifacts. And in the middle of the circle was a barely noticeable engraved outline of a buck with a full antler rack. Inside the deer's body was a little squiggle with a head and eyes. It reminded Jake of a snake. Separately, the deer and the snake symbols were familiar enough, but arranged in this odd manner was a configuration he had never seen before. He turned the disk over to reveal a pin and clasp made of old materials. Still clinging to the pin was a shred of rotted green cloth.

He concluded the old item was a broach used to hold together the collar of a shirt or coat — quite common as a Native American dress accessory. Did this guy snatch it from the Indian grave above?

"Hello! Hello!" an excited woman shouted from topside, her voice echoing in the chamber. "Anybody down there?" A flashlight beam bounced into the fissure as Jake looked back up.

"Yes! Hello," he shouted back, shielding his eyes.

"Are you okay? We're here to help. Just stay calm," the woman offered. "Are you on this rope line?"

"Yes, I'm fine. Thanks for asking. But the guy who was trapped down here is already dead!"

"What? Say again. Couldn't hear you."

"The victim is dead. The guy who called and said he was trapped, he is *dead*!"

"Who the hell are you then?"

Jake paused, then shouted back. "Jake Tununda, U.S. Army."

MICHAEL KARPOVAGE

2

Same time. High Point Mountain Casino and Resort,
West of Kingston, Ulster County, N.Y.

IMMACULATELY ATTIRED in a black, custom-tailored Italian suit, fifty seven year-old Alex Nero, one of the wealthiest and most powerful men in New York State, stood alone on his penthouse balcony suite overlooking his mountain entertainment complex. He leaned over an iron railing and puffed on a Churchill-sized Cuban cigar. A single silver serpent attached to a necklace dangled from his open collared shirt. With troubled eyes, he gazed down upon the blue waters of Ashokan Reservoir spread out below. He then shifted to the distant beauty of the surrounding Catskill Mountains. A cool early morning breeze fluttered his shoulder-length gray hair as he watched the sun rise from the mist. The view had always lifted his spirits.

Not this morning.

Nero exhaled the nutty flavored smoke of his cigar then looked closer at the sprawling entertainment complex below. He nodded in somewhat self-reassurance at his greatest accomplishment to date.

Named High Point Mountain Casino and Resort after the mountain it sat atop, Nero's gambling facility had just beaten Howe Caverns as the second most visited tourist attraction in the state, behind Niagara Falls. It even rivaled some of Las Vegas' best gambling resorts and certainly put to shame any of the other Native American gaming venues elsewhere in New York. Located just west of the Hudson River near Kingston, this architectural wonder catered to New York City customers and high rollers from all over the world — mostly Saudi Arabian princes, Japanese executives, and European playboys.

An eighteen-hole golf course, a top-notch winery, a private runway, and a spa graced the base of the mountain along the reservoir road. Up on top sat the casino, the hotel, and a members-only, exclusive adult-entertainment club. Named Bucks & Does, the club catered to celebrities, athletes, politicians, and VIPs. Nero stocked it with the finest looking men and women money could buy. It's where he did most of his political lobbying and where he had spent most of the previous night with a contingent of Seneca County officials from whom he would be purchasing 8,000 acres of land on the abandoned Seneca Army Depot.

Along with his core businesses at the top of the mountain was his personal museum named the Haudenosaunee Collection. This collection was ranked as one of the best in the world and where he spent most of his time in search of rare northeastern Native American artifacts. Nero had even constructed his summit facilities in a luxurious mountain lodge style of architecture reminiscent of the ancient Iroquois culture that once ruled the area.

High Point, he mockingly mused with a grunt, was an appropriate name for his flagship business. He had fulfilled his personal climb to the pinnacle of wealth, women, power, and political influence. He had everything a man with his ambition could hope for in a lifetime. But still it was not enough to quench his thirst.

Nero coveted a permanent place in history, just as his Onondaga warrior forefathers had done in defense of the ancient Confederacy. He too wanted that essence of historical immortality, to be known for ages to come. That would be the true High Point legacy, he thought — to never be forgotten in history. That was his ultimate goal.

And his path was almost complete. In the most recent Confederacy election, he had finally won the coveted title of Tadodaho or Head Chief of the Grand Council of the Haudenosaunee Confederacy. It was a spiritual position he had sought for years. Granted he had to put some key people on his payroll, but he gained his desire. Always had.

The Tadodaho was a figurehead position held only by an Onondaga. It was a rubber stamp position to the chiefs of the other tribes and their outdated traditionalist beliefs. But Nero had grander plans. He aimed to change the position into the true dictatorship it once was. He sought complete control — authority over all the separate Iroquois nation-tribes, in and out of the state.

His ancient bloodline demanded it.

Securing his place as the rightful ruler, he would set in motion his ultimate objective of retaking all Iroquois lands stolen by the U.S. and New York State governments. He would centralize the pathetically weak and splintered tribal nations back into the powerful empire they once were and deserved to be again. He would wreak cultural and civil havoc, and claim a true sovereign confederacy right in the heart of the Empire State.

Yet he frowned. Because there was one elusive item that would help him gain the unstoppable power to defeat his foes and he still had no solid clues as to where it resided.

The item was called the Crown of Serpents. It was once owned by the most powerful ruler of his tribe, Nero's ancient Onondaga forefather named Atotarho. This shaman had perfected the crown's abilities to suppress his enemies and heal his friends many centuries ago. Supposedly, the relic held legendary powers, not only medicinal, but also more importantly, of complete mind control. And then it disappeared. It had actually been stolen from Atotarho then hidden away and never seen again.

Generations of Nero's clan members had sought to find the crown ever since, but they were poor, scattered, and did not have the means to conduct serious searches or excavations. The ignorant uneducated tribal members even questioned the legend to begin with. But ten years ago, Nero's late mother had made a breakthrough discovery.

During one of her magical black arts sessions, the old medicine woman unveiled a prophecy that centered on Alex Nero himself finding and using the artifact. She had said a sign would reveal itself to him, that he was the rightful bloodline recipient, that the spirits beyond the sunset had predicted it, but that he should respect and use the crown with great care, never to abuse it. The most important clue his mother had gleaned from the paranormal world of spirits she communicated with, was the symbol of the guardian cult that supposedly had kept the crown hidden for so long. The symbol she had envisioned was that of a silhouetted white buck, and inside of the buck's belly was a snake.

Until her death two years ago, she had headed up his Haudenosaunee Collection, and with him had spent countless hours pursuing leads to find remnants of the lost cult and its symbol. They had focused their efforts in the area between the two largest Finger Lakes of Seneca and Cayuga — because of the link with the famous white deer herd there and the location of the lost Seneca village of Kendaia, once a spiritual Mecca of the Iroquois. But they had come up empty. The main obstacles to their search were the U.S. properties of Sampson State Park and the abandoned 10,000-acre Seneca Army Depot.

Up until now.

The Depot had been put up for sale by Seneca County, a real estate transaction Nero jumped all over. Money was not an issue. Local politics were. And keeping the sale anonymous until the last moment was paramount to his transaction. Unfortunately, word had leaked out that an Indian was interested in the sale. Now the local waters were rippling with fear, anger, and resentment.

Everything, up until now, was working out for him. He could see the path to the top. His goal was near. He wasn't upset with the media leak. He could deal with that with extortion and bribery. His problem was if he didn't reach his pinnacle within six months or less, he'd be six feet under.

As of last week and several professional second opinions later, the diagnosis of full-blown, stage four throat cancer had been confirmed. The doctors had given him less than six months to live if he did not seek treatment immediately.

He shook his head in utter disbelief, taking yet another puff on his cigar, still defiant of the possibility that he might travel beyond the sunset before he could culminate his final ambitious acts. He ground his teeth together with a screech.

Six months.

Nero looked down and angrily tapped the ashes from his long cigar.

It would be his greatest challenge — to beat the white man's disease. He watched the ashes float away, disintegrating above the throngs of his white scum customers filing in and out of the main entrance to his casino. Near the valet-service he also noticed his black Hummer waiting for him.

Two of his hand picked bodyguards stood by the vehicle pacing rather impatiently. After all, a carved-up body stuffed in a barrel in the back of the SUV surely weighed heavily on their minds. It was Nero's top pit boss, caught in an elaborate plan to bilk him out of millions of dollars. The *missing* Indian was waiting to be sunk in the reservoir under Nero's personal watch. After that, he would catch his flight to Buffalo later in the day.

On tap in Buffalo was his first meeting with doctors at the Roswell Park Cancer Institute to discuss surgical options and his regimen of treatments. It was a trip Nero had not wanted to make. He had never believed in western methods of healing, but now his choices were limited. If only his mother were still alive she could have conjured up one of her ancient remedies and fixed everything, or so he had hoped.

There was one glimmer of good news though. Late yesterday, his new collections director had surprised him with a short-notice acquisitions opportunity at Old Fort Niagara. She told him there were several recently discovered items from an American Revolutionary War officer and he would be given a full viewing with a chance to purchase them. One of the items that piqued his interest was the officer's scalp. It was taken by Seneca Indians during the American campaign of 1779 to destroy the Iroquois homelands. It would make a fine trophy for the Confederacy — a priceless highlight for his private Scalp Room deep within his mountain museum.

Nero took another pull on his cigar thinking it would be a good diversion after his Roswell meeting. And probably would be the last scalp he'd ever add to his collection.

Cranberry Marsh. Thirty minutes later.

UNDER LEAFLESS TREES backlit by a slate gray sky, Jake stood shivering in his filth-covered Army dress shirt and slacks. He had just crawled out from the clammy hole after securing the victim's body for the local fire department. He hadn't wanted to put any of the volunteer firefighters at risk since there was only room for one person in the tight shaft anyway. It was the least he could do to spare them the same disgust he had waded into. The adrenaline rush of a possible rescue had long since worn off. All he wanted now was a hot shower and dry clothes. He heaved a sigh of relief as the final phase of the body recovery came to a close.

The rescuers had lowered a wire Stokes body basket, a portable radio, a digital camera, and an evidence collection bag to him shortly after they arrived on the scene and determined who he was and how he had climbed down there. Under cramped quarters, Jake had lifted the body up and strapped it into the basket, the blood and mud soiling his uniform. He was then directed to take pictures and recover as much evidence as possible by the woman who had first shouted down to him.

She had adamantly made it known she was a New York State Police investigator and wanted him to follow her direct orders since he was messing up her scene and compromising evidence. He had gathered the broken cell phone pieces and the silver broach, placed them in the bag and then took multiple photos of the scene and victim. When finished he took the victim's baseball cap and placed it back on his head. He wondered what the loud-mouthed investigator would think of that once the body returned topside.

Upon emerging from the hole, Jake returned the evidence bag, camera, and radio to the fire captain he had been in contact with during the operation. Several more firefighters greeted him with a pat on the back for his efforts. The captain and a South Seneca Ambulance paramedic checked Jake for injuries and then, shaking his hand, thanked him for a job well done. Jake assured the medic he was fine and was left with a gray wool blanket which he wrapped around his shoulders.

The captain asked Jake to stand back before giving the order for the recovery team to haul the body up. The captain then walked the evidence bag over to a woman in a dark blue baseball cap squatting down at a mound of earth. Three law enforcement personnel flanked her. Long auburn hair swayed through the back clasp of her hat. Jake read the words *State Police* on the back of her blue field jacket. She spun around, caught his gaze, slowly looked him up and down, and frowned. Jake turned back to the recovery.

Four firefighters in yellow bunker gear and helmets pulled for several minutes on a utility rope to extract the victim. The body, with a skewed racing cap on his bashed-in head, finally made it out. The rope team set down their line as the basket surfaced next to the hole. The captain announced on his radio that the body had been recovered. A static-filled voice of a woman on the radio affirmed his message.

One of the volunteers on the team, an overweight, sweat-soaked young man with a scruffy goatee, looked toward Jake, eyeing him with genuine disgust. Jake stared back until the volunteer glanced away, fumbling with his equipment. A large, red circular sticker decorated the side of the volunteer's helmet. *Don't Sell Our Lands* it blared, a red slash through an Indian head profile.

In a barely audible sarcastic tone, Jake heard the young man say to his fellow firefighter, "Another noble savage to the rescue. Low life red faces are popping up everywhere these days." He then chuckled. The other firefighter walked away telling the kid to grow up.

Many a quick judgment had been made about Jake before. He had heard the whispers of lower ranked soldiers denounce his warrior ancestry or his intimidating zeal to lead from the front. He had heard the nicknames but had not been bothered. The nicknames actually were a form of flattery. But when it came down to an outright racist provocation he confronted each individual head-on and never backed down. This pudgy volunteer was certainly no exception.

With a pulsating jaw, Jake walked up on the lone volunteer and stepped into the kid's personal space. "You all pissed off that some red face got here first and stole your glory, eh hero?"

"What the f—!" The volunteer jumped back in surprise. He then angrily folded his arms across his chest. "I didn't say a thing, man. You must be hearing shit. Besides what your kind doing out here anyway?"

Jake's blood went hot. "My kind?" he questioned loudly. He stood nose to nose with the young man. Several heads turned their way. Jake pointed over to the body basket. "My *kind* was trying to saving that guy's damn life."

"We don't need no Indians out here, trying to take things from us."

"Take things from you?" spat Jake. He advanced a step forward, forcing the volunteer back. "You got a screw loose in that so-called brain of yours?"

The volunteer recoiled. "I mean threatening to steal our rightful county property over at the Depot. What did your tribe do, call you in since you're with the Army or something? Them lands belong to taxpaying people of this county. Not some so-called sovereign Indian nation that's going to put up another casino, another gas station, and another cigarette store and not pay taxes on any of it!"

Jake tossed his head back and mockingly laughed. Now he got it — the pending sale of the abandoned Seneca Army Depot lands, a sprawling weapons storage facility not a mile to the west. He should have known this was coming out of left field. The volunteer's anti-Indian helmet sticker said it all.

"Listen," replied Jake, with a wry grin and tepid tone. "You seriously must be on meth or something to make a leap like that. I just happened to be driving through, heard the radio call, and acted. So next time, before you soil my race and my uniform, you better think twice about wagging that little tongue of yours."

The volunteer's upper lip curled. His jaw muscles twitched. He was just about to spit something back when the captain walked up.

"Get your ass back to the truck now!" barked the fire officer. He wore a stone cold expression on his face. The volunteer immediately huffed off into the swamp without saying a word.

The captain turned to Jake, hiding his eyes under the rim of his red helmet. In a low voice of utter embarrassment, he said, "I apologize about firefighter Owens, sir. He does not represent the views of our department."

Jake shook his head. "Captain, all I have to say is good timing because his jaw was as good as broken with one more piece of bullshit coming out of his mouth."

The captain looked up. "Sir, I wish you would have. I wouldn't have stopped you. None of the cops would have either. Tommy Owens is our resident no-brains jackass. Every department has one. Problem is we need all the vollies we can get because of manpower shortages. And sometimes they aren't the brightest crayon in the box."

"Listen, I hear you," replied Jake. He cooled his tone with a light chuckle. "You should see some of the loose nuts we recruit in the Army. Believe me, a high school diploma is a terrible thing to waste." He smiled and shook hands with the captain indicating no harm was done.

"Thanks Major. I appreciate your understanding. Listen, the state police investigator said to not to leave the scene until she gets your statement."

"Figured that."

The captain walked off, wishing Jake good luck with everything. But inside Jake still simmered at the volunteer's ignorance. He knew the broken treaty land claims, in reference to property the Iroquois lost after the American Revolution, had been a hot button issue in New York State for decades, but he had never come face to face with the emotions it had brewed. Tempers on both sides of the fight had always been high, especially on the issues of sovereignty, tax collection, and gambling. At one boiling point years ago, riots even had to be suppressed by the State Police on the

Onondaga Nation south of Syracuse. And eventually, lives were lost during a Mohawk tribal stand off up in the Adirondacks. Finally, cooler heads had prevailed, and in 2006 all land claim lawsuits were put to rest with a Supreme Court ruling *against* the Indians. But now the pending sale of the interior of the abandoned Seneca Army Depot raised the slumbering political beast back to the surface once again. It was a story Jake had been following off and on simply because of the military history attached to the famous Army facility.

Constructed in the 1940s between the two largest Finger Lakes, the sprawling 10,000-acre base had served the important role as a storage installation for every piece of weaponry and ammunition in the U.S. Army's arsenal since World War II. The Depot, as locals named it, later became the transshipment point for nuclear bombs and missiles servicing the entire eastern theater of military operations. The Department of Defense, however, never officially confirmed nor denied the existence of nuclear weapons at the installation. Unofficially, investigators had shown beyond a reasonable doubt that weapons were there.

But after fifty years of distinguished service, the Depot's mission shifted and Congress shut it down in the mid-nineties. It was then turned over to county officials for re-development. The Seneca County Industrial Development Agency immediately solicited new investors to take over the land and pre-existing structures in order to reinvent the base into something beneficial to the local and state economy. In just a few short years, private corporations bought up most of the main structures on the eastern side near the hamlet of Romulus. There, a state prison and a county jail were constructed while on the far western side, near Seneca Lake along the southwest perimeter adjacent to the defunct airfield, a new State Trooper sub station and a fire-training facility had been added.

But it was the huge, fenced-in, 8,000-acre parcel of the interior of the base that had remained abandoned for years. It had served as an ecology-tourism attraction and wildlife habitat and had thus become overgrown with weeds and cracked pavement as it aged. This inner area contained all 519 weapons and ammunition storage bunkers, some operations buildings, unique wetlands, and in the middle of it all the world's largest herd of white deer. Just the sheer magnitude alone of managing the famous deer herd and repairing the twenty-four miles of chain-link perimeter fencing that contained them was sucking the county coffers dry. The county had needed to sell the unused land and when an anonymous individual offered to buy it all their prayers seemed answered.

Apparently, what was getting the locals all fired up again wasn't the fact that the land was being sold at all, but instead to whom. A media leak just a week ago revealed the anonymous buyer as a very wealthy Iroquois Indian philanthropist. As a result, a majority of local residents immediately speculated worse case scenarios. Some feared if the Indians started buying Depot lands then next on the list would be laying claim to their own homes and private property and rekindling the old lawsuits again as the Cayuga tribe did years back. Others concluded that an Indian-owned casino would immediately be built on the base, disrupting their tranquil, rural way of life by adding traffic and crime to the area. Small business owners added to the fracas by noting that several of their tax-paying, American-owned gas marts recently had to shut their doors because of the tribal competition spreading in the area. They figured an Indian-owned Depot would spur even more tribal-owned businesses directly stealing away customers, especially with the incentives of tax-free Indian gasoline and tobacco products. In fact, when driving through the hamlet of Romulus earlier Jake had even recalled a sign in front of a boarded up convenience store that read *Another Business Lost to the Indians*.

The dramatic leap of racist judgment from the volunteer was a result of legitimate arguments and fears, Jake now realized. On the other hand, he also knew the continued transition of the government-owned Depot to the private sector was already an economic success story that had benefited taxpayers by adding more jobs and expanded economic growth for the area. If this Indian philanthropist, whoever he or she was, could provide that same entrepreneurial leadership, the situation could be a win-win for both sides.

Not only had Jake taken an interest in the Depot from its historical role in the Army, but he also had an interest in that unique white deer herd from an ancestral point of view. The deer had been fenced in, managed, and protected by the U.S. Army since 1941. What would be their fate now should a private owner come in? What tribe did this owner represent? Was he or she from an estranged out-of-state tribe or a New York based tribe? The problem was that Jake's own Seneca Indian ancestors and their neighboring Cayuga tribe had held the white deer herd sacred as far back as the founding of the Iroquois Confederacy. From the legends he learned as a child, he knew a white deer was a symbol of protecting the peace between the original five tribal nations that formed the confederacy. On several occasions when he was much older and driving past the Depot with his beloved Uncle Joe, Jake had even caught a rare glimpse of the white deer — behind the perimeter fencing on Route 96A along the west side of the base. Their natural beauty was simply astounding. But because of their stature, they were also considered an elite trophy in the world of sport hunting.

What Jake was hearing about their fate disturbed him. Speculation held that if the land was sold, the new owner could charge an admission fee to hunt the white deer on his private 8,000-acre wildlife preserve. The owner could market it as containing the best stock in the world regardless of the herd's historical significance or its sacred roots.

Jake shook his head. He didn't know the answer. There were too many variables. Ultimately, these local political issues were out of his control. He was just an outside observer. Despite his best intentions, he couldn't solve all of the world's problems. Heck, serving as the world's police force in the U.S. Army taught him that. Trying to save a fringe deer herd in a remote rural county was best left to someone else.

It wasn't his mission.

He looked down at his watch. "7:20. Good." This side escapade he had gotten himself into still allowed him time to issue his police statement, get his uniform cleaned, and not miss his appointment in Rochester for his afternoon lecture at the Army's 98th Division Headquarters. But first he wanted to check out something most interesting to him before packing up — the Indian gravesite. He salivated at what contents might be inside.

Walking toward the mound, he noticed a group of emergency officials already huddled together. They included an African-American State Trooper in his gray uniform and ten-gallon Stetson hat, and two Seneca County sheriff's deputies — one older and bigger, one obviously a young rookie and much skinnier — both in their dark blue uniforms and matching caps. The female state police investigator stood there too, speaking and pointing to the opening of the grave. Jake quietly approached the group from behind and leaned against a tree to listen in. The older deputy sheriff, a large-boned, pot-bellied, rat-faced man smoking a cigarette, turned as Jake's presence was felt. He wore a scowl on his face. Pulling the butt from his lips, he exhaled and folded his arms across his chest, nodding Jake a greeting. Jake returned the gesture noticing the deputy's nametag as *Wyzinski*.

What Jake overheard from the group of cops was that the victim had apparently stepped into the Indian grave by mere accident as he had claimed over 9-1-1, but then proceeded to ransack it — as evident by the silver broach Jake had found on his body. The investigator concluded, based on footprints, that after the theft occurred when the victim was backing out, he had fallen right through some loose shale and into the limestone shaft. He held on long enough to call 9-1-1 and for them to get his GPS coordinates, but then lost his grip and plunged in. To his death. Or as the investigator put it, blunt force trauma to the head.

Deputy Wyzinski immediately spoke up. "Good riddance. The guy was a piece of dogshit anyway." He tossed his butt on the ground and stomped it out. Jake noticed the investigator flinch, her eyes glaring at the cigarette butt.

The big black State Trooper added a remark. "Chalk this one up as a praiseworthy accidental death." He smiled with bleached teeth.

The other deputy, the pencil thin mustached young man, chimed in too. "What was he drinking? Old Milwaukee? What'd they say in that commercial? *It doesn't get any better than this!*"

The three male cops snorted with laughter.

The female investigator ignored them and peered into the grave mound. She rubbed her chin, still not realizing Jake was behind her. She then glanced over at the hole in the ground. "I'm not sending anyone back down there. Too dangerous. Our would-be rescuer did a good enough job already. I have enough to go on."

Jake grinned.

The cops grunted their agreement, then as a group, trudged away toward the body basket for some more derogatory comments. The female investigator split off, picked up the extinguished cigarette butt discarded by the veteran cop, and headed over to the on-scene emergency commander — the fire chief — as denoted by his white helmet ranking. Jake was left alone near the Indian grave. It was obvious the victim and local law enforcement had several run-ins. To blatantly show such lack of respect for a dead person, the victim must have committed some major crime.

Wrapping the wool blanket around him a bit tighter, Jake bent down to peer inside the grave mound. Under a partially collapsed ceiling of weeds, mud, and a framework of rotted wood, there sat an upright skeleton wrapped in deteriorating green and blue cloth. The Indian's skull, still with strands of long gray hair attached, was cocked sideways and sticking out from under its shroud. The bottom jaw was missing. The jawbone, cracked in half but still having some teeth rooted, lay on the ground near several pottery items, beads, and flint arrowheads. How ironic, Jake thought. Here might have been an important chief or even a clan mother from his own Seneca tribe or possibly from the Cayuga tribe that once shared this land. And he was now the one getting crapped on for even setting foot back on his ancestor's old grounds.

On the far side of the skeleton lay a dirty deerskin wrapping. Upon closer inspection he found the fur wasn't the typical brown but actually white. He scratched his temple, his mind spinning. A link to the sacred white deer herd, maybe to the symbol on the broach? But why bury the body in the middle of a marsh on a tiny remote island? Was there even a marsh here way back then? Did the white deer herd once roam this area too? Was this some sacred or spiritual location? Was there a connection to the well? Was it really a well or just some type of natural ground fissure, say from an ancient earthquake?

Replaying what he saw in the hole, Jake remembered the pile of rocks at the back wall of the cave. It seemed out of place, as if someone had deliberately stacked them there — again wild speculation. And also when the shaft became properly lit with rescue lights from above, he couldn't help but notice there were several rock ledges or steps that made climbing back out much easier. The ledges almost acted as a natural staircase. Were they carved that way? And the crosshatched rotted wood that had fallen in from the surface seemed strange too. Could it have been a concealed trapdoor on the surface at one point? It was definitely man-made. Or maybe the well was just some sort of ancient salt mine. He did know that Indians at one time had gathered salt in the area, especially around marshes.

Jake sighed. He could ponder the possibilities for days. He wanted to investigate more, but realized, after checking his watch again, time was growing short. He needed to get washed up and back on the road. He definitely planned on returning on his time off though, maybe hooking up with an excavation team to find out more. He stood up and sauntered toward the group around the body basket as two new firefighters emerged from the swamp. They carried a piece of plywood over to the ground hole and covered it up. Their captain barked an order, and the other firefighters picked up the body basket. He instructed them to carry it out through the marsh to the Seneca County Coroner's van parked at their staging area. Several of men griped about the notoriously lazy old coroner who had refused to walk through the swamp to officially pronounce the victim dead. Grunting their disapproval, they stepped off the island and struggled to get their footing in the murky waters.

Watching the men carry away the body, Jake realized that once again he found himself at the center of the action. It was the story of his life — right place, right time. Scratch that, he corrected himself, the wrong time this morning.

He stole a glance at the fire chief who was just ending his conversation with the woman investigator. Dressed in full bunker gear, the chief turned and faced Jake. The man was an obvious leader in physical presence alone. Tall and barrel-chested, he wore a handlebar mustache and spectacles. Jake estimated his age to be late-fifties. The chief pulled a portable radio out of his coat pocket and turned his back on Jake. Jake read the large white letters on the back of his coat, *Fire and Rescue*, and his name at the bottom, *Bailey*.

"Cranberry command to county dispatch?" the chief broadcast in a slow deep voice.

"Go ahead chief," the radio hissed back in a faster female voice Jake recognized as the original dispatcher he heard in his SUV.

The chief keyed the transmit button. "All units leaving the scene and heading back to the staging area at Hirschman's Farm. We're sealing off the well too. The state investigator will be out here a while longer to finish her report." As he spoke, his fire captain placed several large rocks on the edges of the plywood to weigh it down over the hole. The chief gave him a thumbs-up and motioned him to head back.

The radio crackled again, confirming the chief's report. "Affirmative. The well is sealed. All units back to staging area. Investigator still on scene. 7:42. KED-758 out."

Pocketing his radio, the chief turned around and deliberately settled his eyes back on Jake. With a stern glare, he approached. The way the chief swaggered over, Jake figured another sparring match was in the making. The chief glanced down over his spectacles at Jake's Army rank and nametag.

"How do you pronounce your name Major?" he slowly asked.

"TUNUN-DA."

The chief smiled widely and surprisingly extended his right hand. Jake gladly accepted and gave a bone-crushing squeeze in return.

"Hoo-ah, Major Tununda. I'm Chet Bailey. Just wanted to personally thank you for your effort down there in that God-for-saken shit hole. My captain says you'd make a great member of his rescue team."

Jake cracked a grin, catching the *Hoo-ah*, Army slang for a job well done when addressing a fellow soldier. "Thanks chief. But it was your crew who had to haul the basket up. I just secured it tight to make their job easier. Hey, so when did you serve?"

Bailey snorted, took off his glasses and started to clean them. "Early seventies. 82nd Airborne. Was in that jungle clusterfuck of 'Nam.' Couldn't wait to get the hell out."

"Can't blame you," Jake nodded, knowing full well how politicians screwed up that past war. He could relate. In fact, politicians usually screw up everything they touch.

"Yourself? When'd you get in?"

"Signed up at seventeen years old," Jake replied. "ROTC at Cornell. Been with the 10th Mountain for the last twenty years. Tours in every hotspot. A hell of a rollercoaster ride let me tell you."

"I'll be damned," said the chief. "An Ivy-League university trained combat officer." He winked.

Jake grinned back. "A rare breed indeed. Just don't tell Senator John Kerry that." They both laughed.

Fresh from college with a bachelor degree in American history and a Reserve Officers' Training Corps commission as a second lieutenant, Jake had been assigned to one of the busiest divisions of the Army — the 10th Mountain — up at Fort Drum in Watertown, New York. The soldiers of the 10th were renowned for their high level of physical agility, their ability to foot-march for long periods of time, their proficiency in combat tactics, and their will to close with and destroy the enemy in some of the most treacherous climates conceivable. The 10th gave him all the combat experience he had longed for and more.

But after twenty years of constant deployments to the Balkans, Afghanistan, and Iraq, he needed a change of pace that didn't require him to kill somebody or be killed in the process. Coupled with the incessant bullshit politics the higher he advanced in rank, the rigors of combat had worn him down psychologically. He had been surrounded by death in a never-ending cycle of human conflict. And history told him that despite his best intentions of trying to make a difference, the inherent gene disposition of humans killing humans would never end. He felt he had given enough to the world and now it was his time to settle back — to start a new chapter in life — and to enjoy it.

"My last job was Executive Officer of the 2-14th Infantry Battalion, 10th Mountain," explained Jake. "Experienced a lot of twisted shit out there in the field." A career move had been definitely in order for Jake, but not out of the military. A year and a half ago he decided to pursue his other passion — military history — and enrolled in an accelerated master degree program. "I just landed a nice, non-combat role with the Army's Military

History Institute based out of Carlisle, Pennsylvania."

"I've heard of MHI," the chief acknowledged, sliding his glasses up his nose. "You guys do some interesting work. Hey, so lemme ask you, how the hell'd you get on-scene here so quickly?"

Before replying, Jake noticed the state police investigator inch her way over within earshot of their conversation. He raised his voice slightly so he wouldn't have to re-explain the events to her again later. He told the chief he had left his home in Carlisle some five hours south, where MHI is based, and decided to take the more scenic route through Ithaca and then up through the Finger Lakes for his afternoon appointment further north in Rochester. He deliberately passed by the old Seneca Army Depot trying to catch an early morning glimpse of the famous white deer. Not seeing any deer, he continued north through Romulus and, just out of sheer boredom, happened to turn on his police and fire scanner. The event in the hole unfolded simply as a result of him picking up the GPS coordinates on his scanner and finding himself right around the corner from the victim. "Dumb luck, I guess you could say," Jake offered with a shrug of his shoulders.

The chief praised the benefits of the GPS cell phone tracking software.

"Worked great," agreed Jake. "My hand-held led me right to the shaft. Almost fell in myself. Didn't matter though. Poor guy must have slipped down after he made the original 9-1-1 call. He knocked his head on a rock or something. Was all busted up. Dead on arrival."

"If only you knew that poor bastard," replied the chief as he shook his head. He pointed to a few objects sitting in the weeds next to the Indian mound Jake hadn't noticed before. Three empty Old Milwaukee beer cans sat next to a rusted leg trap used to catch muskrat.

"His name's Derrick Blaylock. Well known here in south Seneca County. Was doing some illegal trapping and some early morning drinking, looks like. Same crap he pulled two months ago."

"What did he do then?"

"Shot a white deer on the Depot lands."

Jake paused, blinked a few times and said, "You know there's a well documented story out there that anyone who shoots and kills a white deer will soon meet a similar fate."

"Yep, I heard that one too. There's been a number of Army personnel over the years that killed the white deer on the base and one way or the other something bad happened to them too. It's sort of a local mystery. Hell, there's lots of mysteries surrounding that old Depot."

Jake nodded. "But how did he find an Indian grave out here in the swamp?"

"According to the investigator he basically stumbled on it by accident. Then got his own ass trapped in the hole. Listen, this guy was what we call a real woodchuck, a real piece of white trash. He was a level-three sex offender who liked young boys. Add grave robbing to his list too. All said, he won't be contributing his talents to the community anymore."

Jake shook his head. No wonder the cops practically spit on his body. He told the chief he had found the Indian broach in Blaylock's vest pocket, confirming that the victim did steal it.

"Yep. My captain gave that jewel to the investigator and she made a match to the same cloth that Indian skeleton is wrapped in. Plus, Blaylock had some arrowheads in his pants pockets and a small piece of jawbone and tooth that just so happens to match the missing piece off the skeleton." The chief's radio suddenly squawked in his coat pocket. It was one of his firefighters. He acknowledged the call. "Cranberry command. Go ahead."

"Chief. We've got a News10Now reporter here at the Hirschman Farm staging area. She won't take no for an answer. Says you owe her one."

"Ah damn, I know who it is. Tell her I'll be there shortly," the chief replied.

"10-4," finished the firefighter.

"Major, I've got to fend off the vultures. Do you need an ambulance? Get you checked out?"

Jake assured the chief he was already looked after, that he was fine, just dirty, wet, and cold. The chief responded with an open invitation for a beer next time he was passing through. He then sloshed back in the swamp leaving Jake alone with the New York state police investigator.

She immediately closed the gap and planted herself squarely in front of him, hands on hips, jaw jutted forward, apparently ready to give him a piece of her mind. Despite her aggressive demeanor, she had an air of powerful attractiveness about her. No make up, she was a natural beauty. She looked a bit Hispanic, maybe a touch Asian. He admired the sizzle in her green eyes and how they tapered off at the corners as her fiery gaze met his. Although her lean body stood a bit shorter than his five-foot-ten inch frame, she made up the size difference with the look of scorn.

"You botched my crime scene," she snarled.

Jake arched one of his black brows. A wry grin formed at the corner of his mouth.

"Next time you try being a hero, mister, make sure you follow certain rules. Number one," — her long slender index finger popped up in his face — "let the professionals handle the job. Number two," another finger. "If you plan on climbing into a hole anytime soon, call 9-1-1 so we know we're rescuing two people. Number three—" The third finger never came up.

"Can the lecture!" Jake retorted with a slight smirk. Taken aback, the investigator gave a head wiggle. Now it was Jake's turn. "Number one, I am a trained professional rescue specialist. This was a cakewalk. No one had to rescue me. Number two. I was closest when the call went out, so sorry to rain on your parade, lady. Number three—" He never finished.

"Oh no. You will address me as investigator, don't ever call me *lady*, understand?"

"Fine. Investigator. Do you have an actual name that goes with your fancy title?" He noticed a small pin on her collar showing the rank stripes of sergeant.

She blinked twice. "Name's Rae Hart."

"Well then, Investigator Rae Hart, you will address me as Major Jake Tununda since I outrank you."

Rae rolled her eyes and gave him another comeback. "Pulleeze, this is my turf, soldier." Her eyes quickly summarized Jake's weathered face. Cheekbones high, nose prominent between light brown eyes with crow's feet. Graying temples blending in with shortly cropped black hair. Not bad, she thought, for a split second. "Being the Good Samaritan is not always the best option," she said, her voice wavering ever so slightly. "Leave it to the locals next time."

"And never taking a risk in life is the greatest failure," Jake countered.

She gave him a condescending head to toe body scan, noticed no wedding band and was about to bite on his bait but instead turned and walked away.

Jake shrugged the blanket up his neck and shook with feigned coldness. "Brrrr. Now that was a chilly reception."

She ignored him.

He'd play her game. Turning his back on her, Jake walked over to gather his duffel bag. Stuffing his gear back in, he could now suddenly feel her stare digging into his back. Dropping the blanket, he pulled off his soiled dress shirt and his sweat-stained under shirt and tossed them into his bag. He stood up and stretched out his naked, well-defined, wedge-shaped back, then rolled his arms and shoulders to work out the kinks in his muscles.

Rae's eyes inspected every inch of him as he bent over and pulled a gray hooded sweatshirt from his bag. He turned around as he pulled it on, exposing a tattooed shoulder, chiseled chest, and cut biceps. He wrestled into the sweatshirt as his six-pack abs rippled. She could feel her face warm.

She couldn't help but give him one more dig. "You always come that prepared?"

"Yes ma'am," he said rather curtly, pulling the sweatshirt down to reveal stenciled gold and black letters of the word *Army*. "You never know when you might end up being shafted." His last word he timed perfectly as he zipped his duffel bag shut with a tug. He then stood upright and flung the bag over his shoulder readying to exit the scene.

Rae's mouth fell open. She then pursed her lips and finally smiled. "Major Tununda, listen, I still have to get your contact information and have some questions for you before wrapping up the investigation. And actually since—"

Jake spun around with a grin. "Hey, call me Jake."

"Touché Jake. Listen, I overheard you saying you work with the Military History Institute. You're a historian?"

"That's right, a traveling field historian," he said, taking a few steps closer. "Kind of a battlefield detective, if you will."

"You've got some Native American in you," she stated while tucking a loose fall of hair back behind her ear. "Are you Iroquois by any chance?"

He wasn't sure where she was leading but definitely caught the subtle flirtation of adjusting her hair. Now he took the bait. "I like to think of myself as a full-blooded American first," he said. "Half Englishman and half of Haudenosaunee ancestry, specifically from the Tonawanda Band of Seneca Indians. Grew up on the reservation over near Akron."

"You know I've heard that term Haudenosaunee used before but never understood the difference between that and Iroquois," Rae confessed.

Jake was more than happy to oblige her with an answer. He went on to explain that the traditionalist Indians in New York liked to refer to themselves as the Haudenosaunee, or the *longhouse people*, based on the original wooden structures they used to build. They didn't care for the Iroquois label, as that was a term given to them by their enemies. *Iroqu* came from the Algonquin tribe who had battled the Haudenosaunee for many generations. It meant rattlesnake. When the French arrived on scene they added the *ois* to make it plural. Either word was acceptable though, he assured her.

"You're certainly versed on the subject. Maybe you can help me out here," she said, gesturing toward the grave. "This is an Iroquois Indian, right? I mean based on first observation at least. Like what the corpse is wearing, the artifacts, the location here in the original homeland, and the grave structure itself. It all adds up, correct?"

Jake stepped over to the grave. "Pretty safe to assume. Could be from the Seneca or Cayuga tribe. This was the border between the two." He lifted crime scene tape and bent down to peer inside the mound where Blaylock had collapsed the roof. "It fits a typical Iroquois burial chamber, from what I've read." He pointed out to Rae the distinct structure of an ancient Iroquois gravesite. There was an outer frame made of bark — now rotted and covered in moss, an inner box or coffin-like chamber made of warped wooden planks, and then the actual body itself, wrapped in heavy cloth and skins and placed in a sitting position against a rock.

Jake stood up. "I'm no archaeologist but…" The biting morning breeze sent a true shiver through his body. "From a historian's perspective this is one amazing discovery. Keep in mind this is a sacred site too. It's already been desecrated. Technically, it belongs to the Iroquois. You are going to inform them, right?"

"Technically, this site belongs to the land owner, a Mennonite farmer named Martin. But yes, I intend to contact the proper Iroquois authorities. I've never come across anything like this before. I mean a corpse this *old*. By law I have to consider this a crime scene, but the case is pretty well closed. So, I do want to contact the right group and get this off my shoulders. I'm honestly not sure who I should call first. Was wondering if you could offer some guidance."

"I charge by the hour but will cut you a deal over dinner and a fine bottle of Finger Lakes Riesling?" Jake offered.

Rae rolled her eyes. "Negative, Major."

"Wow, it sure is frigid out here."

Rae paused then looked down, reconsidering. "Tell you what. You're cold and you stink. Head over to our Troop E Romulus station. It's just on the other side of the Depot, near the old Army Airfield off 96A south of Kendaia. There are locker rooms for fire and police trainees where you can get cleaned up. Then I'll get your official statement."

"You're right, I do need to shower before our date tonight," Jake answered with a sly, gleaming smile.

"Cut the crap," she replied with stern lips. "This is business. See you in a few."

"Okay then," said Jake. "Since you operate by the book I do have one request in return for my expertise."

"Shoot."

"I want a picture of that silver broach that Blaylock stole. It has some very strange symbolism on it I'd like to do some research on."

"I'll think about it back at the station," said Rae, stepping into the swamp. "And please don't try rescuing anyone on your way over."

Same time. High Point Casino and Resort.

ALEX NERO HEARD the sound of his private elevator door opening behind him. He puffed on the last inch of his cigar.

"Sir?" a woman's voice announced.

A snarl formed on his face as he exhaled. He had made specific instructions not to be disturbed. He turned around. It was the director of his collection, an unassuming, unnatural blonde named Anne Stanton. As the fifth director in the two years since his mother died, she had lasted the longest. It was her resourcefulness in landing new additions to his collection that had kept her steadily employed in the high-turnover, high-demand position. Dressed in business attire with contemporary black eyeglasses, she stood nervously with notepad and pen in hand. Nero demanded an explanation for her appearance.

"I apologize sir, but this is breaking news I wanted you to know before you left for Buffalo."

"Better be good Miss Stanton," Nero said in his trademark raspy voice. He pulled on his cigar and deliberately exhaled smoke into the woman's face.

She looked down at her notes and stifled a cough. "News10Now out of central New York just reported an accident in Seneca County."

"Go on."

"Apparently, a hunter discovered an old Indian grave on an island in some swamp. The hunter then fell into a limestone fissure and died before rescuers could get to him."

"Continue," Nero said, interested by the mention of the Indian grave. He couldn't care less about a backwoods hunter dying.

Stanton spoke rapidly. "The reporter quoted an emergency official who said that a piece of old jewelry was found on the Indian corpse in the grave. It was made of pure silver and had a symbol on it." She looked up at him. "I thought immediately of another addition to your collection, sir. And with you as the head of the burial committee, I thought you'd be in a good position to, you know, guide the committee again. That's why I wanted to let you know before heading out."

"Was this symbol described in the report?" Nero asked.

"Ah, yes," said Stanton. She looked back down at her notes. "I remembered everything you've said about pursuing leads associated with white deer representations, so this fits. It was a stag with a snake inside of it, engraved on the piece of silver. And there's more about the actual grave too, which is described as—"

Nero tuned the woman out, waving his hand to silence her. He had heard enough. He was speechless. His heart raced. Could it be the sign at last? He grew dizzy and supported himself against the railing. His cigar dropped at his feet in a shower of red sparks.

Was this the first real hard evidence after all the years of collecting artifacts — sometimes stealing them outright — in search of just one clue that would lead him to his ultimate obsession? Could this be the moment he had been waiting for — actual proof that the guardian cult who protected his prize had even existed? But it comes upon notice of my death. It must be true. The prophecy was in motion. If only Mother were here.

He was simply blown away. He wiped a clammy hand across his sweaty receding hairline.

"Mr. Nero, are you okay?" Stanton asked. She placed a comforting hand on his elbow.

"I'm fine," he growled, his mind spinning, hands shaking. He shook her hand off his arm. "We must move quickly on this. Take notes."

"I'm ready."

Nero paced. "Get me a transcript or a video of that report. I want pictures of this piece of jewelry and the symbolism on it. I want to see it. I want to purchase it. Set up an appointment immediately. Find out about the Indian grave, its exact location and if anything else was found inside. You stay on this story. Drop everything else you're working on. I want a full report by the time I get back tonight."

"Of course. I'll get everything you need. My pleasure."

"Fine work young lady. Very fine work."

Stanton smiled nervously at receiving such a rare compliment. "Thank you, sir." She then bore a cold face and forced herself to say, "And good luck with your appointment at Roswell today. You can beat this, sir."

Nero stomped out the smoldering cigar, ignoring her. He walked over to the elevator for a quick trip down to the lobby.

Through the casino and out the front entrance he snapped his fingers at his bodyguards and entered his Hummer. As his driver raced down the winding mountain road toward the reservoir, Nero reached inside of his coat. He placed a call to his special contractor, an Onondaga Indian named Ray Kantiio, nicknamed *The Mouth*. It was he who had taken care of the disloyal pit boss the night before.

"Mouth? Where are you? Who's that in the background?"

A groggy Kantiio answered. "I'm up in the Adirondacks now. Took off after I sealed the barrel. Got a cutie with me on my vacation time."

"Finish up with her. Grab some coffee. Get on the road. You're going to Seneca County tonight to do some sniffing around for me."

"Jesus, I need some time off after the gig last night. That was some nasty work I did."

"Shut the fuck up. We're on our way to sink the barrel right now, then I've got a flight to catch. Here's what I want—"

MICHAEL KARPOVAGE

New York State Thruway.

AFTER SETTING THE cruise control and adjusting his cell phone's hands-free earpiece, Jake settled back in his SUV's bucket seat. He had just merged his white, government-issued truck onto the New York State Thruway at the Waterloo entrance ramp. He looked forward to an uneventful hour ride up to Rochester for the day's first appointment. Stiff-arming the steering wheel, he rehashed in his mind his meeting with the investigator. Considering the rough start they had back at the swamp and her all-business attitude, he felt he parted company on a very promising note.

Back at the Trooper station Jake had showered and changed into his spare set of his civilian clothes. A cup of coffee later and he was dictating his official statement of events upon finding Blaylock's body in the shaft. Afterward, he and the investigator discussed the handover of the gravesite. Jake suggested she make two phone calls. One should be to the Haudenosaunee Standing Committee on Burial Rules and Regulations, which was composed of all the chiefs of the Confederacy — the Mohawk, Oneida, Onondaga, Cayuga, Seneca, and Tuscarora. He did not know who the current chairman was but informed her that in the past the committee had been very successful in the repatriation of sacred items and newly discovered Indian remains. They would surely work out the bureaucratic technicalities.

The second call he recommended was to Dr. Bruce Burke at Cornell

University, one of the best indigenous archeologists on Iroquois studies. He would definitely ensure proper site excavation. And since the burial site was only a half hour away from Ithaca, Burke would jump at the chance. Jake mentioned the good fortune of studying under him while attending Cornell.

Before leaving the station, the investigator allowed him to take photographs of the silver broach. She left him with her business card, but not before scribbling her personal cell phone number on the back. After stopping in the village of Waterloo for a rush dry-cleaning service on his soiled uniform, he changed into his official Army attire and was now back on the road watching a luxury sedan blow past him in the left lane.

A series of sharp ring tones from his cell phone startled his thoughts. He looked over to its dash-mounted holder, the face of the phone displaying an incoming number he recognized from MHI. He keyed his headset to answer.

"Tununda here."

"Happy Monday Major," said the jovial, static-filled voice of his newly appointed supervisor. It was Collections Manager Dr. Stephen Ashland. "Murphy's Law is on tap again. Your itinerary has changed."

"Really?" Jake replied in a bit of a nervous laugh. An itch developed along the battle scar on his left forearm. Wish he hadn't mentioned Murphy's Law — shit happens with the best-laid plans — thought Jake, knowing full well that eventually the big battle tank he was riding strong with his new career was sure to throw a track. "Where's Murphy got me going now, Doctor Ashland? My morning has already been quite fulfilling as it is."

"I just received an urgent e-mail when I got in. We have an enormous opportunity to acquire some rare items for our collection. If they're within our budget. And this is right up your alley too, so to speak."

Jake speculated as to what was right up his alley, so to speak. Even though he was still getting used to working for Ashland, it was these witty little clichéd phrases like *up your alley* or *Murphy's Law* that started annoying him. Overall though, Jake thought Ashland was impressive, at least on his resume. Obviously the director of MHI, Dr. Paul Jacobson, thought so too or Ashland wouldn't have landed the coveted position.

Ashland was a little over forty, smart, thorough, and enthusiastic about heading up MHI's entire collection. He too was hired on recently, about six months after Jake, so they were still feeling their way through their new working relationship. Things seemed to be going rather smoothly so far. No micromanagement. No interference. He left Jake alone to operate as an independent. But something nagged him about his new boss. There was a veneer there and he couldn't place what it was covering up.

"Ever hear of an American Revolutionary War officer named Thomas Boyd? From the Sullivan-Clinton campaign of 1779. He was captured by the Iroquois—"

Jake finished Ashland's sentence. "After his scouts were ambushed near the end of the offensive. Boyd was then brutally tortured to death the next day. Yep. He's certainly a well-known historical figure. At least because of the way he died."

Jake's mind whirled on. The book was now open. The Sullivan-Clinton military offensive was a campaign he had studied in-depth to say the least. While earning his master degree, Jake wrote a series of articles on General George Washington's reason to order the offensive. It was published in the Army's top professional journal, *Military Review*, and generated much praise in the field.

The campaign resulted from events in 1778 in the wilderness frontier settlements of New York and Pennsylvania. Rebel families and businesses were under repeated attacks from the combined forces of British Colonel John Butler's Rangers and Chief Joseph Brant's Iroquois warriors. They raided and destroyed countless villages that had provided food and supplies to Washington's fledgling army.

The brutal attacks not only saw the burning of houses, barns, mills, livestock, and crops, but also the massacre of the American settlers. No one was spared — men, women, the elderly, even infants. Torture, dismemberment, burnings at the stake, and even the enslavement of prisoners within the tribes were common forms of the heinous terror tactics the British and the Iroquois used against the rebel colonialists. Jake thought for a moment that Hezbollah and al-Qaeda probably studied

Iroquois history.

Hardest hit was Cobleskill and German Flats, New York. Then came the major massacres in Cherry Valley, New York, and Wyoming, Pennsylvania. As a result of these raids, George Washington decided to mount a campaign that following spring. He would take the fight to the Iroquois homeland in what is now upstate New York.

The campaign, headed by Generals Sullivan and Clinton, was deemed a complete success in destroying over 40 villages supplying the Iroquois base of operations. It also proved to be the beginning of the end of the Confederacy — Jake's people, so to speak. Maybe that's why this was up my alley, he thought.

"Where are you right now?" asked Ashland. His voice became garbled.

Jake told his boss he was westbound on I-90, coming up on the Geneva exit. Ashland instructed him to stay on the Thruway, that he'd already taken the liberty to reschedule his Rochester appointment for tomorrow morning. He informed him he would instead be headed to Old Fort Niagara in Youngstown on a four o'clock appointment this afternoon.

So much for not micromanaging him, Jake thought.

"We are on an expedited request for assessment," continued Ashland. His voice faded in static. "The executive director there contacted a handful of institutions and individuals late yesterday. She wants a value placed on the items with the intention of selling them. We landed the first slot because her late husband had served with Dr. Jacobson."

"What am I assessing for the RFA?"

"They found Thomas Boyd's campaign journal, his powder horn—"

"Whoa! Boyd's journal? You're kidding me? It was assumed lost when he was captured and killed."

"That's not all. They also found his knife, a belt buckle, a note pertaining to his officer's sword, and lastly what appears to be his—" Ashland paused, then quickly added, "his scalp."

Jake's right eyelid twitched. His eyebrows creased and his nostrils flared. He gripped the steering wheel tighter and closed his eyes. Finally, he forced the dark battlefield memory from his mind.

Ashland continued, his voice fading again. "These items were found in a box discovered by an archaeology team from the State University of New York at Buffalo just two days ago. They had been excavating an area in the parade ground near an old barracks building and—"

"A box found underground?"

"About three feet down," Ashland said. "You can see the exact location on the fort's website. They have a web camera in the hole. Listen Major, this could be a huge public relations bonanza for the institute if we can acquire these items for our collection. We can tour the nation with this!"

"Tell me about it. I'm already making plans. Just the journal alone is going to be incredible. Listen, I'm starting to lose you."

"I'm going into a meeting with Dr. Jacobson to see how far we can stretch our acquisitions budget. I'll let you know. The discovery is still being kept confidential at this point. It hasn't been broken to the media. There's a gag order in place at Old Fort Niagara. I'll shoot you a copy of the e-mail, there's more specifics in there."

"Wait, I've got a question," said Jake. "Why does Fort Niagara want to sell? I know they have a really nice museum there. Why wouldn't they keep this for their own collection?"

In a barely discernible response, Ashland explained how the fort was in a severe financial bind due to their former director embezzling most of their operating funds. "They either have to sell to raise money or face closure."

"Face closure?"

"Listen, I've got to run. I'll send you that e-mail. Drive safe and I'll talk to you soon."

"Okay. Goodbye," Jake terminated the connection and gunned his SUV's engine. "Looks like my tank is still on track. Sorry Murphy."

MICHAEL KARPOVAGE

Approaching Old Fort Niagara.

HAVING BEEN LISTENING to jazz music for most of the ride west to Old Fort Niagara, Jake switched to news talk radio. He soon became irritated at a local college professor's ramblings on how effective the United Nations had performed in the last decade. Jake knew from first-hand experience how impotent, bloated, and corrupt that organization had become, and if it only had a backbone to all of its rhetoric then maybe a lot of bloodshed would have been avoided. Instead of getting himself all worked up he simply changed the station, catching the tail end of a newsbreak segment.

"...and finally an odd story out of the Finger Lakes that is once again spurring rumors of a subterranean waterway connecting Seneca and Cayuga Lakes. Apparently, a dead lake trout was discovered in Cayuga Lake bearing the tag of Geneva's Hobart and William Smith Colleges biology department. The fish was found by a man walking his dog near Sheldrake Point. He immediately informed college officials who took possession of the fish. According to HWS spokesman Mitch Sanford, this particular specimen, along with fifty others, was tagged and released two days ago in Seneca Lake as part of a student research project on board the school's aquatic research vessel. Sanford claims the rumor of a direct underground river connection between the two lakes was an absurd scientific impossibility based on geological fallacy and persistent pranks. He said the college would be conducting toxicology tests and a dissection of the fish to determine its cause of death."*

Jake rubbed his chin. He clearly remembered his Uncle Joe Tununda telling him a similar story when they had gone fishing once on Seneca Lake, back when he was around ten years old. They were just off from Sampson State Park on the eastern shoreline when Joe told the story of a woman riding in a delivery wagon, losing control of her horse, and plunging off a cliff into the lake. Her body was never found. But several days later her horse's body washed up on the shore of Cayuga Lake — eight miles overland to the east. They knew it was her horse because a piece of wood with her delivery company's name on it was still attached to the reigns wrapped around the carcass. The speculation was that the horse's body must have traveled underground in some type of river. Joe then said there were many more stories like that dating back to ancient pre-Confederacy times, but there had never been any real hard evidence of the subterranean river's existence.

Uncle Joe had always been full of old-time Indian legends, some of which were hardly believable. Most of his tall tales revolved around Seneca Lake and the heartland of the Iroquois empire. One was the famous story of the Seneca Drums, as they were called. His uncle described them as low distant rumbling sounds of the ancestors' evil spirits. He said many of the locals along the lake claimed to have heard them over the years — referring to them as cannon blasts of a distant naval battle. Later, as a Cornell student, Jake read an article that attempted to explain this booming sound in more scientific terms. It noted that the sound came from natural gas escaping from fissures deep on the bottom of the lake, bubbling up, and hitting the surface with thunderous burps. Upon hearing of the academic explanation Jake's uncle merely had a hearty laugh.

But the most colorful legend of all that Jake had never forgotten was that of the spirit boatman paddling the southern end of the lake on moonlit nights. This boatman was a fallen Seneca warrior who sacrificed himself to a vanguard of General Sullivan's Continental troops so others in his war party could escape. While he fought off the Americans, his fellow warriors climbed down sheer cliffs to waiting canoes. Located near Hector on the south end of Seneca Lake, these beetling cliffs were later painted with strange symbols to commemorate the bravery of that great warrior.

The cliffs were afterward named the Painted Rocks. Jake and his uncle had even boated by the symbols while fishing. The tale certainly churned imaginary thoughts of a distant skirmish in a young boy's mind. It was the seed of a scene that had spurred Jake on to seek more knowledge in his later years.

What Jake had found was more than just another romantic Indian legend. During his master degree studies on the Sullivan campaign, several of the existing soldier's journals alluded to a pair of American scouts discovering something much more valuable in that cliff ambush.

Gold.

British Paymaster gold.

Apparently, it was the bankroll funding for the entire British and Indian wilderness campaign and it never made it out of Catherine's Town in time. In fact, there was so much of it that General John Sullivan himself allegedly had his officers fill an entire cannon full. It was stated in one soldier's journal that Sullivan then deliberately plugged and sunk the cannon in the lake. The big mystery however, after all of these years, was why? Why sink the gold? And where exactly was the cannon sunk? These two questions had persisted in Jake's mind for years upon years.

And now a lost journal of one of those Continental scouts appears out of the blue, Jake thought to himself. Maybe it would shed some more light on what truly happened. He was always up for a good adventure. And this was definitely a good one in the making.

Little did he know, however, that some history was best left hidden in the past.

7

Old Fort Niagara. Youngstown, N.Y.

JAKE PARKED HIS truck in the main lot outside of Old Fort Niagara. Excitement had ruled the day already and he hoped this new assignment would be the icing on the cake. He took a deep breath. The Sullivan-Clinton campaign, and more specifically the fate of Thomas Boyd and his scouts, were his areas of expertise. The thought of reading Boyd's lost journal caused his arm wound to tingle again. He scratched the sensation then reached for his cell phone. He fired off a quick text message to Dr. Ashland announcing he was on site and entering the assessment. He stowed the phone in his tote briefcase which contained his laptop computer and digital camera. He then exited his SUV.

Standing tall in his full dress uniform, he grabbed his black beret and cocked it at an angle on his head. Pinned on the left chest of his dress coat was a rainbow of colored service ribbons and medals showing military campaigns in which he had participated, specialized skills achieved, and awards for bravery. They included a Silver Star, and a Purple Heart with an Oak Leaf Cluster for two wounds sustained in combat. High on his right shoulder sleeve was the Ranger tab denoting advanced intelligence and warfare training. Below that hung his past unit patch of the 10th Mountain Division. On his left shoulder sleeve was his current unit patch of the MHI and pinned on top of each shoulder was the single gold oak leaf insignia of his officer ranking of Major. But on his collar was a tiny unofficial pin that went unnoticed to most. It bore the letter G surrounded by the symbols of a builder's square and measuring compasses. Jake looked impressively crisp, official, and definitely had an aura of confidence around him.

Next to the parking lot, in the partially renovated administrative offices, he met the elderly executive director of the Old Fort Niagara Association — Marge Hibbard. After a formal greeting, she informed him they would be viewing the Boyd items in a private room at the original castle fortress across the main parade ground so that he could experience the full flavor of the fort complex. What a sell, Jake thought. He played along, mentioning he hadn't visited the fort since his youth. She was pleased at his interest and guided him ahead toward the main South Redoubt gatehouse entrance.

As they strolled past spiked-top log perimeter fencing, Jake looked up at the fortified gatehouse structure. It was designed with classical Roman arched doorways in its formidable stone wall. Several narrow windows doubling as musket ports lined the face of the wall. A low profile log roof capped the open-air top floor. Several tourists hung over the top ledge snapping pictures.

Under the British coat of arms and past the ticket taker's counter, where Hibbard nodded to the attendant, the two emerged upon a faded grass parade ground. At the end of the main gravel walkway in the far north end of the fort, sat the dominating French Castle. Proceeding toward the castle Jake asked Hibbard about her organization's mission and the severity of their funding situation.

In short prepared statements, she explained that the Old Fort Niagara Association was responsible for preserving, restoring, and maintaining the site and its structures, which comprised about ten acres of land at the mouth of the Niagara River. Included in the site were the main castle fortification and six 18th-century buildings, the outer walls, cannons and fencing, archaeological remains, and even an old cemetery. Hibbard explained that even though it was a registered state historic site, they did not receive any taxpayer funding whatsoever. All of monies necessary to operate the site fell under the association's umbrella with about ninety percent of their revenue coming from admission ticket sales.

As they walked past an old cannon and stack of cannon balls marking the main pathway intersection in the middle of the drill-yard, Hibbard's expression turned sour. She told him of the association's funds being completely wiped out by an embezzlement scandal two years ago by the former director. He had cleaned them out of millions of dollars through an elaborate scheme. She said he was now in jail serving a long sentence, but that the money had disappeared.

"What a dirty, rotten—," said Jake, shaking his head, deliberately not finishing his sentence.

"Tell me about it, we had to lay off half our staff because of him," Hibbard replied. "It had taken us four years to come up with the funding for the new museum and visitors' center and now that whole capital expansion is on hold. And our main collection cannot even be displayed. It's all under lock and key because of lack of security funding."

They walked past two young male re-enactors dressed in 18th century British red coats and white britches, each cradling muskets. A group of tourists had gathered around as the soldiers explained the various attributes of their uniform.

"I remember years ago an incredible display of relics on the top floor of that fortress," said Jake, pointing. "Is it no longer up there?"

Hibbard's jaw tightened. "It's completely empty now. The public was stealing our pieces. It was despicable. Priceless silverware, even a Brown Bess British musket like that soldier is holding." She motioned to the weapon as the re-enactor explained to a tourist the significance of the royal blue regimental lacing on the front of his coat. "An original Brown Bess was valued at over sixty thousand dollars. We only use replicas now. The originals are in a vault. We didn't have the proper security measures or the personnel to monitor the displays. Let alone pay for it all."

"I'm sorry," replied Jake.

Hibbard nodded. Leading him on, she elaborated that with her successful financial background in fundraising she was appointed by the association's board and given emergency authority to save the site by any means possible. She was authorized to sell current relics in their museum and even freshly unearthed items of value. She was not happy about giving up any of the fort's property, but as she said, she wasn't hired to make friends. Instead, her role was to save the fort.

Her biggest loss to date was the selling of the enormous oversized American flag that flew over the fort during the War of 1812. The association had purchased the flag from a private collector a few years back for over nine hundred thousand dollars. Although she sold it off for a profit, she took no pride in the act. She had no choice.

Just in front of the French Castle, Hibbard stopped and showed Jake the rectangular excavation dig site where the SUNY Buffalo archaeology team had unearthed the *Boyd Box*, as she dubbed it. She explained that this was the foundation of an old soldier's barracks used by Seneca Indian warriors during the brutal winter of 1779-1780. The box was hidden in the stone wall behind a large boulder. Obviously forgotten. Perhaps the original owner had died, she speculated, as many did that winter.

Upon discovery she personally took possession of the box and conducted a quick overview of the contents determining she could fetch a considerable amount of money on the market. She admitted that she had not had time to read the journal contents in its entirety. Unsure of the true value of the items, she decided to send out an exclusive RFA to determine its worth.

She told Jake that the Military History Institute's appointment was the first one of only two that day with six major organizations competing in all. She divulged to him that the parties included two Ivy-League universities and three wealthy personal collectors. She had chosen MHI because her late husband had served with Director Paul Jacobson during the Korean War. She then asked him to follow her into the main castle. Jake took off his beret upon entering.

She explained the castle's history as they entered. The castle, the oldest building in the eastern interior of North America, was the lone permanent structure of the original strategic promontory at the outlet of the river into Lake Ontario. Built in 1726 by the French to resemble a large trading post — to calm the hostile Iroquois fears — the stone structure was in fact an imposing citadel capable of resisting enemy assault. She said it sat three floors tall with an attic level that provided defensive positions for muskets and light cannons through its machicolated or overhanging dormers. Hibbard led Jake into the main vestibule and up a set of worn wooden stairs to the second floor.

On the second floor Hibbard paused. "In 1759 the fort was taken over by the British after the French and Indian War and used during the fur trade. It was held throughout the Revolutionary War and used as a base for the British and their Iroquois Indian allies to raid the New York and Pennsylvania frontier until America took it over in 1796. The British then recaptured it during the War of 1812, during the fort's last armed conflict. In 1815, it was ceded back to the U.S."

Jake nodded. Impressed.

Hibbard turned left down the narrow main corridor. He followed. At the far end she unlocked a tall oak door to a room once acting as the original commandant's office.

Leading him into the room, no bigger than a modern day jail cell, she shut the door behind them then proceeded to the window. Sliding back an iron bolt, she hauled open the heavy wooden shutters allowing the late afternoon light to flow in. A heightened view of Lake Ontario's shimmering blue waters lay below, the brownish sediment of Niagara River emptying at its mouth. To her right was another locked door leading to the commandant's bedroom, one of the few rooms on display for the public. Jake heard hushed tourist voices on the other side through cracks in that door.

Hibbard had Jake take a seat at an old wooden table in the center of the room. The table held a box of white linen handling gloves. Grabbing a pair for herself, she unlocked a floor-to-ceiling cabinet off to the side, entered it, and reappeared with a corroded leather box in her gloved hands. It was slightly larger than a shoebox.

"Major. Here's what you came for," she announced in a business-like tone as she set the box on her side of the table. She looked directly at Jake and handed him a pair of gloves. "Please adhere to normal handling procedures. Here are your gloves. You may take digital photos, no flashes. You may take notes by pencil only. Do you need a pencil and notepad?"

"Actually — I apologize. I have the notepad but forgot a pencil. Do you have an extra one?

She pulled a sharpened number 2 pencil from some hidden back pocket and handed it to him. He wouldn't make that mistake again. She was serious now, Jake observed. Not a relaxed bone in her body, but then again, considering the financial distress she was under, he couldn't blame her. He rested his beret on the table, extracted a notepad and a credit card sized digital camera from his tote, put on his gloves, and looked up at the director.

"Are you ready?" she asked.

"Yes ma'am."

Hibbard took a seat, lifted the top of the box and set it aside. "These items, the best I could conclude from my research, belonged to Lieutenant Thomas Boyd of General John Sullivan's Continental Army during the campaign in the summer of 1779. There are six items in the box — just the way it was found. I'll take them out one at a time. We have just one hour scheduled for you to conduct your review. Feel free to ask questions at any time. I'll start with his knife."

Hibbard reached into the box and carefully lifted out a wooden handle rusted blade typical of the Revolutionary War period. She placed it on the table in front of Jake pointing out Boyd's name carved on the handle. He photographed it at several different angles, handled it carefully, and took copious notes.

He repeated this procedure with Boyd's black powder horn and a brass belt buckle — both engraved with his initials. The buckle contained the raised symbol of the letter G surrounded by a compass and square to form a perfectly symmetrical triangle. The symbol for the Freemasons. Jake touched it lightly with his index finger.

Next came a handwritten letter on parchment paper pertaining to Boyd's sword. The letter read:

Buffaloe Creek 14th September 1779
Brother Brant,

I write to you in response to your displeasure of the fate of the late Rebel Scout Lieutenant Thomas Boyd. I was unaware that he had given you the Universal Hail Sign of Distress of a Worthy Brother in Need upon capture with his Sergeant, a one Michael Parker. I had not been informed that you had accepted the Sign and the Word, promising his Safekeeping. He did not present the Sign, nor the Word to me, knowing me full well also to be a fellow Traveling Man of the Craft. Boyd was a brave leader of his Scouts. There is no doubt. He fought us hard during the Ambuscade, even after being wounded in his side. Had I known of your intentions that he was under your Personal Protection, I would not have interrogated him, but in my interpretation at the time, he was the Enemy and thus my duty and my responsibility to the King that I examine the Rebel for intelligence. You should know Boyd refused to divulge any information of General Sullivan's army under thrice repeated threat of death. But the non-Mason Parker gave me everything I needed. Had you not departed on unrelated matters, you might have saved Boyd's life after I was done with him, for I could not control the Anger possessed within Little Beard and his clan of Seneca under your command. They sought revenge for the destruction the Rebel Army had laid upon their villages and crops. Little Beard inflicted torture practices I have never witnessed before. I could not stop them. Such a young man at the age of twenty-three, Boyd was truly a brave soul, even during the pure agony leading up to his death. He never begged for mercy once and died with his dignity intact much to the displeasure of Little Beard. Parker was summarily dispatched with similar techniques. In honor of your initial Obligation to help a Worthy Brother in Need, I've directed the bearer of this letter, a runner from Little Beard's clan, to present to you the sword of the Lieutenant Thomas Boyd, confiscated by my sergeant before your warriors stripped the man. Keep it well. I shall meet you in Niagara.

Fraternally,
John Butler

Jake blinked several times. He stammered for words. "Unbelievable! A letter to Joseph Brant from Colonel John Butler. And completely shrouded in Masonic mystery."

"I'm sorry Major. I don't understand what the letter pertains to."

"Butler and Brant were famous figures," answered Jake. "Or infamous, I should say. The Americans despised them and placed a bounty on their heads. Their actions during several massacres in the Wyoming and Cherry Valley led to Washington's decision to destroy the Iroquois homeland. What you have here is an amazing artifact of history. This letter alone will fetch a pretty penny."

Ms. Hibbard's demeanor changed at the mention of money. "Is that right? Go on."

Jake took several minutes to explain to her the magnitude of the correspondence. Colonel John Butler was the leader of Butler's Rangers, a British detachment based out of Fort Niagara. Chief Joseph Brant was a Mohawk Indian who led a contingent of Seneca, Cayuga, Onondaga, and Mohawk Indians. The Rangers and the Indians were undeniably the fiercest combination of guerilla warriors in the Revolutionary War. Brant had persuaded many Iroquois to ally with the British instead of staying neutral. And because of this stance many Iroquois looked down on Brant and labeled him a *monster* for getting them involved in the war and thus destroying their Confederacy. He and Butler were co-commanders in the western New York and Pennsylvania wilderness and often did not get along. Although they distrusted each other and vied for power, they did work for a common cause — to kill rebels.

During their reign of terror, their soldiers murdered many American settlers and burned countless villages in a brutal land grabbing campaign to oust the Patriots, yet they blamed each other for the atrocious acts of the troops under their command. Jake interpreted the letter, rife with Freemasonry terminology, to be sort of a *gotcha* moment or *I told you so* for Brant harboring rebels against the King's will, even if they were Brother Masons. It added to the mystery surrounding Thomas Boyd's last hours of his life.

Rising from his seat, Jake began to pace, arms folded behind his back.

He went on to explain that Chief Brant was raised and educated in British Tory schools. He was the epitome of the *noble warrior* and had even visited the King of England in 1776. It was there he was initiated into the ancient fraternity called the Freemasons and had the distinction of having his Masonic apron given to him from the hand of King George III himself. The reasoning behind the letter, Jake thought, revolved around the notion that Masons always helped out their Brothers, even when on opposite sides of war, or of different ethnicities or political persuasions. The Brit John Butler was a Freemason, as were the Patriots Thomas Boyd, his General John Sullivan, and even their superior George Washington.

Jake stopped and turned to the executive director. "Now here is the real interesting part that has Freemason historians mystified to this day. It was upon Boyd's capture after he was ambushed that he communicated the secret signal of distress to his captor, Chief Brant — knowing him to be a fellow Mason. It is a highly secretive hand gesture given from one Mason to another when you think you're going to lose your life and you need help. You see, Brant had already proved to be a worthy, quote-unquote Brother, in Boyd's eyes because he had helped two other rebel Masons escape execution after the surrender of American forces after the Battle of the Cedars in 1776. Anyway, Brant took Boyd's signal to heart. He felt obligated to save Boyd's life and assured him he would have safe passage to Montreal for a prisoner exchange. But that's where the official history became muddled."

"How so?" asked Hibbard. Her eyes alight and engaged in Jake's tale of Freemasonry on the battlefield.

"Well, Brant had to take temporary leave before he could help Boyd after his capture. Boyd ended up in the care of Butler," said Jake, thoroughly enjoying his presentation. "Butler took that opportunity to interrogate Boyd himself — he called it an *examination* in the letter. He gained the intelligence on Sullivan's army, and then deliberately handed him over to the Indians so they could exact their revenge. He claims the Indians took Boyd by force in this letter, but I've read other witness accounts that his act was deliberate. If this were so, then Butler would be in direct defiance of the sworn obligations of a Freemason to never deprive a fellow brother of his life or property."

Jake rubbed his chin thoughtfully. Hibbard made a humming sound. He walked over to the window, looked out, and continued speaking. "But it was also known that Butler never did play by the rules and saw only one loyalty, and that was to the British monarchy. He had supposedly justified his actions by saying that any Masonic obligations were overruled by the duty of an army officer to serve his King, and must not be invoked to protect rebels. His letter clearly states he was unaware of the arrangement Brant had made, that it was his duty to interrogate, and furthermore was not in control of the Indians afterward." He turned and faced Hibbard again. "But I think it's a farce." He pointed to the letter.

"What? The letter?"

"No, no. Not the letter itself, but Butler's content, his explanation to Brant within the letter."

"Why?"

"Because I've personally read a contradictory letter by Colonel Butler to *his* superior at Fort Niagara on that same September 14th and it was anything but this explanation. He claimed that Boyd was escorted under protective guard and sent forward to Fort Niagara, but while passing through the Genesee Valley an old Indian rushed out and tomahawked him. Obviously a bold-faced lie."

The director leaned forward, a puzzled look on her face.

"You see, given the history of confrontation between Butler and Brant, I think the letter we have here might have been a ploy on Butler's part to claim innocence in the whole execution and at the same time stick Brant as being responsible for another atrocious act to tarnish his record. He then slaps him in the face by presenting the sword of the one he was supposed to protect."

"Oh, I see now," said Hibbard. "It was personal. Very interesting."

"Very interesting indeed as almost a year later in Pennsylvania, Boyd's sword was taken off a wounded elderly Seneca Indian. How it ended up in this other Indian's hands and not Brant's we'll never know."

Hibbard nodded thoughtfully. "Which means we could possibly conclude that the Seneca runner who was given this letter and the sword intended for Brant never fulfilled his delivery for Butler. And thus this letter sleeps in a box with Boyd's other possessions."

"Right," said Jake. He pointed his index finger in the air. "And like you said earlier, this runner hides this box away here at Niagara, for whatever reason, then simply dies that same winter from starvation or disease like so many others did."

"And the rest of Boyd's story dies too."

Jake pursed his lips. "A sad ending because the way he died was one of the most atrocious acts of murder against an American Patriot in this country's history."

"How so?"

"I'll spare you the gory details, but basically he was tortured to death for hours in every way thinkable."

"I see," said Hibbard, with a frown. She then glanced at her watch. "Oh dear Major, your time is running short and we still have his campaign journal."

"Yes, I'm sorry to ramble like that. This is a truly remarkable discovery. You could write an entire book based on this letter alone."

Hibbard extracted a small leather bound booklet out of the box and set it in front of Jake as he sat back down in his chair. She retrieved the letter and replaced it back in the box.

"Like I said, I had not read much of the entries but Boyd's writing was most terrible." She smiled as she watched Jake open the cover.

He read a little, turned to a random page inside, read some more, saw a few illustrations on a page with a torn corner, then flipped to the last page, noted some odd lettering and that the page had a similar ripped corner as the previous one. He looked over to Hibbard.

"Apparently this is one of several journals from Boyd," explained Jake. "This indicates it was the last in a series. The entries here start on September first. The final entry was dated Sunday, September twelfth, the day before his capture. I wonder what happened to the other journals?"

"Interesting."

"There's a lot here and I noticed several small illustrations and strange lettering too. How much time do I have left?" Jake asked.

"Only about ten minutes, I'm afraid. I cannot go over the limit. My next guest is a very wealthy collector. He demands promptness."

"Okay, I'm just going to photograph each page then read the contents later. Could you assist me by holding the pages down flat while I photograph them? I don't want to damage anything."

"Certainly."

After snapping pictures of the cover and every single page thereafter, Jake checked his watch. "Okay, I'm finished. I believe we have one more item, correct?"

Ms. Hibbard returned the booklet to the box and pulled out an oval patch of skin with brown hair attached to it. "Yes, I'm afraid it's rather unsettling. This is apparently Thomas Boyd's scalp. At least that's what the indications are on the underside."

"Ma'am, there is no need to go any further," Jake said, looking directly into her eyes. "I thought about this on my ride up here and I will not, on matter of principle, try to place a value on his scalp. It is a body part, his remains, and it must be buried in his grave or at least an effort must be made to track down his ancestors and return it to his family. I recommend you take this out of the items to be sold and do the right thing. He was an American soldier and for me, for the institution I represent, to purchase this and put it on display, would not reflect good judgment."

"Major, I understand where you are coming from," she replied in an almost relieved voice. "I too didn't quite know what to do."

"If you do the right thing I'm sure you will get more value out of it than money can buy. You could even garner major publicity for your actions and for your association. I know for a fact that Boyd's remains are buried up in Rochester at Mt. Hope Cemetery along with his sergeant, Michael Parker, and their Oneida Indian guide Honyost Thaosagwat. There is even a Masonic monument up there dedicated to the ambush of his scouts. I would suggest contacting the Grand Lodge of Free and Accepted Masons of the State of New York should you need any help."

"Thank you Major. Thank you. I think I'll do just that." She placed the scalp back in the box. "By the way, how do you know so much about the Freemasons?"

"The foundation of this great country was built on Masonic principles, therefore one takes an interest."

"Indeed. Well, I am sorry but it looks like your time is about done, so please excuse me, I need to lock everything back up. You are free to walk around and explore the rest of the fort if you'd like. Please keep the gloves. Oh, and I took care of your admission fee too."

"Thank you," said Jake. He peeled the white handling gloves off and placed them in a pocket. "I want to digest those journal entries first and then report back to MHI. We'll get you our assessment as soon as possible. Oh, do you have wireless Internet access here at the fort?"

"In fact, we do. We won a grant recently and installed the system to attract more visitors. The main hub is in the museum shop along the riverside wall. But you can get an excellent connection anywhere in the fort."

"Great. Thank you for your time and it was a pleasure meeting you."

"And the same to you Major Tununda. Goodbye."

Jake grabbed his beret, shouldered his tote, and opened the door to let himself out. Instead, he found himself staring into a pair of sinister-looking dark eyes.

Standing directly in his path was an older man about his same height, definitely an Indian, definitely not happy. Wiry gray hair pulled back in a ponytail, a square strong jaw, pockmarked face with hollow cheeks. He reminded Jake of someone beset with sickness. He was broad shouldered and had the lean frame of a boxer. He was dressed in a stylish black suit with a starched white shirt open at the collar. His neck revealed a silver serpent on a necklace.

There was movement from beyond the doorway. Two larger Indians stepped in behind their apparent leader. These were presumably a security detail the way they carried themselves. Jake made firm eye contact with each of them. One, an ugly brute, even had traditional facial tattoos under each eye — streaks of blue — as Iroquois warriors would wear during battle to intimidate their enemy.

Jake settled back on the man blocking his way. "Excuse me," he stated in a casual voice, leaning to one side to pass by. He watched as the man's eyes finished sweeping Jake's nametag, ribbons, and insignia. The man refused to budge.

In a scratchy voice, the man asked, "Is Marge Hibbard in here?"

Jake raised an eyebrow. "Yes, she is. I was just leaving. Excuse me." He moved close and the man finally gave way to let him by. They bumped shoulders. Upon contact, the two bodyguards made a threatening motion forward. Jake ignored them both, turned and walked down the hall.

One of the guards closed up on Jake's heels. "Don't ever touch the merchandise again," he threatened from behind. "Ever."

Jake spun around. It was the tattoo-eyed thug. "Ooh, I'm shaking in my shoes." The man's facial expression turned to instant rage. He looked like a snarling pit bull ready to bite.

But then from around the corner they heard Ms. Hibbard greeting the new guest. "Ah, you must be Mr. Alex Nero. Right on time."

"Get back to your master, Clown Face," Jake spat. "You're out of your league." He turned his back on the bodyguard and simply walked away. He could hear the man panting behind him.

Outside the main castle.

ADJACENT TO THE MAIN CASTLE, Jake had taken a seat on a stone bench inside a circular memorial overlooking both the lake and the expanse of the parade ground. He opened his laptop computer, plugged in his digital camera, and downloaded all of the images. After just thirty seconds the transfer of files was complete. He now had each item from Boyd's Box digitally catalogued for his review. He would be selecting the best images to send, with his initial report, in an email to Dr. Ashland, but first he couldn't wait to delve into Boyd's journal entries. He double tapped his finger touchpad and opened the first page of the journal. Zooming in on the image to get clearer readability, he scrolled down.

Wensday, Sept. 1st – Reach'd French Catherine's Town or Cheoquock at about 7 o'clock in the evining after considerable difficulty traveling thro a much horrid thick mirey swamp. During reconnoyter found fires burning and every other appeerence of the Enimies having just depart'd moments before. This town consists of 30 houses and a number of fruit trees and corn fields.

Jake knew that Catherine's Town would be present day Watkins Glen, situated at the south end of Seneca Lake. Sullivan's campaign would swing up the east side in the days to come. To get a bigger picture he decided to log onto the Internet and visit one of his bookmarked research web pages on the campaign. He found the map section taken from other officer's journals and picked Colonel Dearborn's campaign map for the Continental Army. It was deemed by far the best sketching of the route the main army had made between Seneca and Cayuga Lakes. Jake kept the window open showing the map next to Boyd's journal entry.

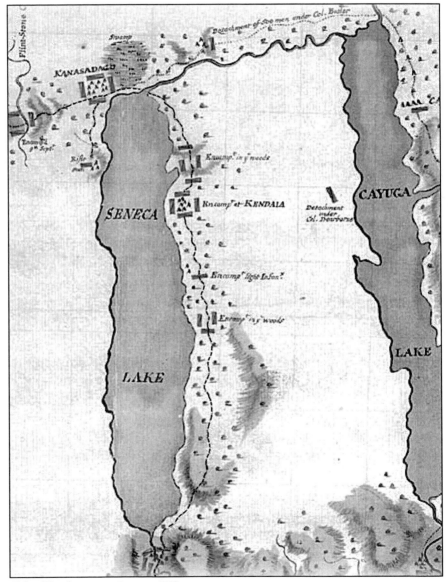

Colonel Dearborn campaign map, 1779.

Thursday, Sept. 2d – General Poor's orders, early morning sent to indeavor to overtake some of the Indians and Rangers who left this place last evining. Accompinied by my Most Trust'd Sergeant Sean McTavish at the vanguard of our riflemen. Travill'd a mile up ridge on east side of Seneca Lake and ambush'd Indian spy at top of cliff. McTavish snuck on him and tomahawk'd the old Savage, now his nineteenth scalp taken. Observ'd 10 Savages and the Colonel of the Rangers – Butler, escaping in canoes at bottom of cliff. Shot at them with no effect. Could not pursue. Much plunder found in small gun powder keg on Indian's horse. Contents reveal'd King George III gold Guineas. Belong'd to Regimental Commander Colonel John Butler's Paymaster, bas'd on accompanying paperwork. Was meant to fund the Tory and Indian allies operating from Catherine's Town. Upon further examination we find five more boxes of British coinage hidden in the woods on a broken wagon. Monies ranging from shillings to Guineas. We informed General Sullivan, our Worshipful Master of the Lodge, but not before secretly securing our own keg. Good fortunes this day. We shall see what the disrespectful Miss Cornelia Becker thinks of my endowmint now when I return home. The General order'd the rest of the pay to be filled and plugged inside one of our disabl'd cannons for easy transport. To our dismay the horse pulling the cannon became spook'd and both cannon and animal roll'd off the cliff into the lake below, sinking the great fortune deep. No matter, the General had us mark the spot so we could somehow retrieve it upon the return march back.

"Holy shit!" Jake blurted out loud once he realized the discovery. The Painted Rocks Indian story and Sullivan's gold cannon legend really happened. What he now had in his hands, in digital form at least, was evidence of what really took place — a historical description that could bring validity to the unsubstantiated claims.

He read it again.

And again.

A whirlwind of questions whipped through his mind. So Sullivan confiscated John Butler's gold but then lost it by accident from a horse gone bonkers. But did Sullivan ever recover the gold on his return journey home as Boyd alluded? How could he if it sank deep as Boyd described?

And what was this secret mark at the location where it sank? Was Butler's interrogation of Boyd really all about troop strengths or was it in fact really about who had King George's gold? So many questions. Jake shook his head clear and went on with the next excerpt.

Friday, Sept. 3d – March'd at 7 o'clock to-day. Passed fine beautiful land. Incamp'd about 4 o'clock near a small Indian settlement, fires left burning in their houses. Our right flank discover'd another Indian spy, who ran off and disappeer'd.

Saturday, Sept. 4th – March'd at 9 o'clock this day. More pleasant level land. Our light troops are ahead of main army about 3 miles such. Caught two fine Enimy horses.

Sunday, Sept. 5th – Much strange excitiment here on this very fine day and more fortunes gained for Brother McTavish and myself. Came upon old Indian town call'd Kendaia or Apple Town. The finest Indian village yet with about 20 well-finish'd houses. Much apple and peach orchards within a half mile of Seneca Lake situat'd on a level ground with a brook running thro it. Some apple trees look ancient in growth. We count'd over 100 trees.

"Kendaia," said Jake, remembering the little hamlet he drove through this morning after leaving Rae Hart's Trooper station. He then looked back at Dearborn's map drawing.

About three quarters of the way up Seneca Lake he found the clearly labeled Village of Kendaia. Dearborn had even illustrated several small buildings and a series of dots in rows, possibly indicating the orchards. He went back to Boyd's entry.

We find 3 Indian Chief's vaults in their burying grounds. One of these was some great man and was bury'd in this manner; his body was laid on the dirt in a shroud or cloth vail. Then a large box made of hewn bords made very neat about 4 feet high was built around the body. The box was paint'd of very curious deer symbols in a variety of coulours. In each end of the box was a small hole where the friends of the Chief could look upon it when they pleas'd. Around this box was built a large shed of bark so as to prevent the weather from damaging it. We later burn'd these vaults to the ground. We burn'd it all down, the orchards, the cornfields, the village. This was for Wyoming.

Jake's stomach knotted. The burnings were a clear indication of the severity of the destruction and what the Americans did to his people long ago. It's why they named George Washington *Town Destroyer* for giving the orders to completely ravage the Iroquois homeland. But then again, his Indian ancestors had brought this on themselves from their rampant scalping, dismembering, and burning of American men, women, and babies. Jake was torn.

Reading of the wholesale destruction, especially the burning of the chiefs' graves, struck him as a tough judgment call. What went through Boyd's mind when he lit the fires? Did he have any remorse? Or was he a cold-hearted, revenge-minded SOB like I've been in combat?

As history would have it, Boyd ended up paying for his actions, experiencing the most heinous death of all of the American troops. Boyd's torturous death was even worse than what Jake saw the Taliban regime and terrorist group al-Qaeda do to their victims in Afghanistan and Iraq — at least they were quick with a beheading. Boyd was tortured for hours upon hours and kept conscious to experience the full pain inflicted. Jake read on.

We also rescued a captive, Luke Swetland, taken prisoner by the Savages near Nanticoke in the Wyoming Valley in the summer last. He was most overjoy'd at making our acquaintance.

Jake remembered many references in other soldier's campaign journals he had studied about this man being repatriated. Luke Swetland had slipped away from his Indian captors the night before and made it back to Kendaia hoping to meet the approaching Army. When he was found in a house by the lead American scouts, he was beaten and almost shot because of a case of mistaken identity. Both he and the scouts were dressed in the same wilderness attire consisting of deer skin. Swetland thought the scouts were British Tories come to take him prisoner again and the two scouts who found him thought he was an Indian spy waiting to ambush them. It had all worked out for the best when other scouts approached later who were from the Wyoming Valley, recognized who Swetland really was, and could vouch for him.

Brought to this town he was given to an old witch who kept him as her adopt'd son. He said she curs'd him from leaving. His starv'd body prov'd that. He show'd us her village's sacred secret in a nearby ravine, a ten minute walk east. Much to explore here. We see a sight never encounter'd before. A pure White-furred Deer. Swetland warns that evils await those who kill a white deer. McTavish shoots at and misses the trophy much to Swetland's relief. Swetland says much about Butler and Brant and dispisition of the Enimy's men.

Cool, thought Jake. A historical report of the white deer back then too. The passage caused him to stare off toward the waters of Lake Ontario. He pictured how it would be to approach the Indian village as an American scout, rescue the captive, to see the ancient homeland untouched in its true wilderness setting, and to see the famous white deer for the first time.

After finishing the page, he loaded the next image, noticing it was one of those oddly torn pages. He zoomed in and started with the wording at the top.

Kendaia plunder illustrat'd below, along with directions to Swetland's Indian cave, so we may re-visit and further examine one day in hopes of finding more fortune.

"Swetland's Indian cave? What the—," Jake whispered. The place in the ravine, the witch's sacred secret? The first illustration catching his eye was a small circle with a dotted border around it. He zoomed in even closer, blinked, stared again, and then almost dropped his laptop. It was an exact match of the deer and snake symbol on Blaylock's stolen broach at the marsh well this morning.

"What in the hell is going on here?" he asked himself.

A tiny caption below the drawing read:
Silver and wampum neck clasp given to us from Swetland. He found it in the cave. Old squaw made him wear it to protect the cave.

Jake's heart raced. A silver broach? Swetland found his in a cave? Wore it to protect the cave?

Jake's eyes shifted to the next illustration. It showed a crude drawing of a long cylinder or tube with an end cap.

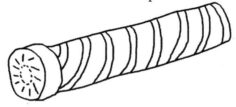

The caption below it read:
Hickory map case, ancient map of Swetland's witch cave passages, quill, and ink inside.

Jake's eyes narrowed. "A cave map too? Unreal!" Out of the corner of his eye, he noticed a young boy glancing at him as he and his father strolled by. Jake winked at the kid who smiled back. He looked around to see if anyone else noticed him talking to himself. No one was around. The fort seemed to be emptying out. He looked back at his screen.

Could Swetland's cave be the same as the one this morning? He swung his head over to Dearborn's map. Kendaia was on the lakeshore. Boyd's entry said Swetland's cave was in a ravine, after a ten-minute walk.

Blaylock's marsh cave, he knew, was way further inland, separated by about five miles — definitely not one and the same cave. But were they linked, was the greater question.

With a slight shake to his hand, he scrolled the page image down to the fragmented lettering at the bottom — the apparent directions to the cave. Upon first glance it looked to be some sort of cryptic code.

Obviously the repetitive characters and their special relationships indicated words arranged in some form of a secret message, but other than that it could have been Arabic for all Jake knew. What in the world was this Lieutenant Boyd hiding, he asked himself.

The words trailed off where the corner of the page had been torn away. It looked deliberate. Then he noticed, in extremely small script, a note written vertically along the gutter of the book. He zoomed in with the magnifier tool and slowly read,

Missing half of cipher is deposit'd in Butler's payroll keg.

Confirming his speculation, Jake realized the page had indeed been deliberately torn off to hide the rest of the cipher. He nodded. This was Boyd's security measure so no one would find it. With a sparkle in his eyes that he had made a major discovery, he moved on to the next image.

From September sixth through the eleventh, Boyd had made brief, one-sentence entries on the next page. Based on his inscriptions, the campaign was in continuous march, his scout detachment being heavily relied upon, loot plentiful and theft among troops common. In one instance, Boyd described a famous Indian killer in his detachment, a Virginian named Tim Murphy. He put a ball in the back of an officer in Butler's Rangers just outside present day Canandaigua. After looting the victim Murphy traded with Boyd the officer's corset, compass, and gold match case.

Boyd's writings overwhelmingly reflected exhaustion. They were marching over ten miles per day through the wilderness and shadowed by Indians who took potshots at them. Jake knew from his own studies that the army would now be in the area just south of present-day Rochester, marching toward the Genesee River Valley and crisscrossing between some of the smaller western Finger Lakes. The troops were at the end of their supply chain and facing severe shortages.

He uploaded Boyd's last journal entry, the other page with a similarly torn corner and cryptic message.

Sunday, Sept. 12th — Much thunder and rain last night. Army left most provisions at Honneyayeu garrison to march with only what will be necessary to reach Little Beard's Town or Chenesee Castle (25 miles) and back again. McTavish and me kept our fortunes close to our person. March'd at 9 o'clock in morning at the vanguard once again almost 2 miles ahead of main army. Mostly rain'd today. Pass'd thro many hills. Travell'd 11 miles and incamp'd a mile north of abandon'd Indian village call'd Kanaghsaws. The troops destroy'd the town of 25 houses and large corn fields. Our camp situat'd atop the flat hill overlooking the swampy inlet and head of a small lake. Much fatigue'd and thirsty.

Most exciting news this night brings. General Sullivan summon'd me to his tent and reward'd me personally with command of a special early morning mission to reconnoyter ahead to our final objective. Says as a Brother of the Craft he knows I can be trust'd and that I've provin my worth in courage, service, and duty. Order'd to pick 4 of my best riflemen. No contact with the Enimy should be made. This could be my step upwards for promotion to full Capt'n. I intend to do the job with utmost success. Must gather my men and provisions.

Jake noticed Boyd's handwriting had become much harder to read — an indication he was in a rush before his mission.

Writing again before reconnoyter. Upon refilling our water pouches at the parallel streams near the village, McTavish and me slipp'd away to have our fortunes bury'd for it prov'd too heavy a burden. We will come back for it on our return journey after reaching objective. Plunder in our keg is inventory'd as such: Butler's 200 Guineas and bear claw necklace taken from his Indian spy; location of Sullivan's sunken cannon of gold near Catherine's Town; Swetland's silver broach, cipher directions to his cave and case containing his cave map; 3 silver rings, 7 pipes, 5 knives, 2 wampum belts; a British Ranger Officer's corset, compass and gold match case.

"Holy crap," Jake uttered. The page finished with the following message along with more cryptic lettering torn at the bottom right corner:

Craft cipher indicates directions to bury'd keg. For purposes of secrecy the other half of cipher is deposit'd in my Most Trust'd Craft Brother's Most Trust'd Trade Tool.

"What the—"

That was the last of Boyd's entries. He would die the very next day. Jake looked up and exhaled. His heart raced with excitement as to the importance of the find. Buried treasure, sunken cannons, secret ciphers, silver broaches, caves, and a map? He didn't know where to begin or how it all fit together. But he certainly recognized a once in a lifetime opportunity at his fingertips. An adventure he wished, an adventure he was granted. With Director Jacobson's expertise and Dr. Ashland's assistance the team at MHI could piece together the puzzles and get started on a new investigation. This is what his new job was all about and he was jacked up to jump in.

Yanking his cell phone from the tote, he called Ashland but received an out of office recording. He left a message for him to check his email as soon as he got in. Jake turned to his laptop, clicked some icons and drafted the email. He attached one digital image each of the horn, buckle, Butler's letter, and the journal page of September the twelfth. He also explained what he told Ms. Hibbard about his thoughts on the scalp. He then hit the *send* button.

Just over his screen, at the entrance to the castle, Jake heard the main door swing open. He glanced up as that Alex Nero fellow strode out in a determined gait, his two Indian bodyguards shadowing him. The bodyguard who had issued the warning to Jake not to touch his boss held something in his hands that he couldn't quite see. He watched him until he came into view then caught sight of the item.

Jake blinked. His eyes grew wide.

The Boyd Box.

Another flurry of questions ran through his mind as he continued observing the men exit toward the front of the fort. He slammed his laptop shut, stowed his gadgets in his tote, and quickly walked back into the main castle. Double-stepping up to the second floor, he found Ms. Hibbard in the hallway. She smiled gleefully.

"What happened to Boyd's Box?" questioned Jake. "Is everything okay? I saw your last guest walking out with it."

"Oh everything is just fine," she said, her teeth gleaming. "He has the box because, well, he owns it now. And I'm sorry, he insisted on purchasing the scalp too. He made the association an offer we couldn't refuse. He is a man of enormous wealth. He immediately wired the funds into our account. We have all of the financial assistance we need to get us out of our hole and then more to cover us for years to come. He is a wonderful man that Alex Nero." She clapped in delight.

"But what about the RFA? Don't all parties get a fair chance to bid on the items? I thought that's how it worked. Six parties view the items, assess them, and bid on the purchase? Not a first come, first serve basis."

The smile left her face. "Mr. Nero made an offer. I acted in the best interests of keeping this fort alive. I terminated the RFA process. It is my right."

"But…"

Hibbard cut him off. "Mr. Nero is our saving grace. Now, if you will excuse me." She turned and proceeded down the stairs.

Jake stood dumbfounded. He felt as if he had just gotten his foot on the playing field at the Super Bowl only to have his legs cut out from underneath him. The profound sense of loss was immediate and deep. In fact, this was the second strike today, he thought. He was too late in rescuing the trapped victim and now a major historical discovery was squandered before his eyes. Murphy certainly threw his track off now! He shuffled over to a window and rested his hands on the ledge, drooping his head and letting out a sigh. He peered out across the drill yard and soon watched Hibbard walk back to South Redoubt to disappear under the gatehouse.

After a minute of stunned silence he held his head high knowing what needed to be done. Exiting the castle he quickly headed back across the empty grounds only to find one of Nero's suits turning the corner from the gatehouse and walking directly toward him. Jake instinctively knew something was up. This guy's pace advertised he meant business.

When they met in the middle of the drill yard, near the old cannon, Jake noticed it was same tattoo-eyed pit bull bodyguard from earlier. As he approached Jake he asked in a gruff voice if he was the Major.

"No, I just dress in Army uniforms for shits and giggles," replied Jake, sidestepping the ruffian without losing his stride.

"Hold up there, buddy."

Jake increased his pace.

"I got a message from Mr. Nero." A large hand then clutched Jake's left shoulder to spin him around.

The instant the bodyguard's hand grabbed him Jake clamped down on it with his right hand, and bent his assailant's wrist outward in one quick motion. The man tried to pull away but Jake moved like a cat and had already cranked the thug's arm behind his back. Now standing behind him with his left hand squeezing the man's opposite shoulder for support, Jake jammed the man's arm up the middle of his back to the point of breakage. The man cursed in agony and dropped to his knees in front of the cannon.

"No one touches me, punk," Jake seethed in his ear. "And I'm in a real pissy mood today so what's your message?"

"Ease off! Ease off! You're gonna break my goddamn arm."

Jake loosened the arm slightly but repeated his question.

"Mr. Nero wants to talk to you. He's in the parking lot. He just needs a minute of your time, okay? You win."

Jake dropped the arm and gave him a shove. "You really shouldn't touch the merchandise," he snickered. "You haven't earned the right." He then jogged off towards the gatehouse.

The kneeling bodyguard took a moment to gather his composure then realized his target had disappeared into the tunnel up ahead. He jumped up to catch him.

Jake's battlefield tactics kicked in. Before approaching hostile territory, a thorough reconnaissance always proved beneficial. When he first entered under the South Redoubt gatehouse with Hibbard he remembered thinking from a military standpoint it offered a heightened view outside of the fort's walls — a perfect sharpshooter's position. Now it would act as a simple observatory to what this Nero fellow might be up to in the parking lot. Next to the ticket taker's window was a steep stairwell leading to the upper levels. He scrambled up the steps and reached the guardroom, checked a musket port to see the trailing bodyguard running his way from the parade ground, then bounded up the next set of stairs to the roofed look-out platform.

Just beyond the outer walls and earthworks, in the parking lot, a long black limousine caught Jake's eagle eyes. Nero's other bodyguard stood outside the vehicle glancing back and forth. That man then approached Jake's parked SUV, stood behind it, bent down for a moment out of sight, stood up then wrote something down on a piece of paper. It looked like the guy was taking his plate number, Jake thought. The bodyguard then approached an open window in the rear of the limo and spoke to a gray-haired man Jake recognized as Nero. They both turned and noticed their counterpart exiting the fort. Clown Face shrugged his shoulders and threw his hands in the air then walked up to the limo. The other guy jumped into the limo and drove it forward, blocking Jake's SUV in.

Not one to be toyed with, Jake bounded down the gatehouse stairs and double-timed it to Nero's vehicle. The tattoo-eyed bodyguard stood at the rear, glaring at him as he approached. The driver remained behind the wheel. Jake walked up to the closed rear window and with his fist rapped loudly on the glass.

The power window dropped halfway and Nero peered out.

Jake spoke first. "Mr. Nero I presume? Your little puppet here said you had a message for me. Make it quick, and move your ride because I've got a tight schedule to keep."

"A tad ticked off are we Major?" replied Nero in a raspy voice.

"Flash enough cash and the little old ladies just drop their panties for you," stated Jake, slinging his laptop tote behind his back while folding his arms across his chest.

"Couldn't have said it better myself," replied Nero with a bit of a grin. His eyes darted behind Jake as his lead enforcer walked up stretching out his arm and shoulder.

Jake glanced back and smirked. The thug's face turned red.

"So, as you know I now own the Boyd Box."

Jake remained quiet, not sure what this character wanted from him.

Nero cleared his throat. "I just want to talk to you."

"So talk," Jake fired back.

"The director informed me you were the only other person beside herself that viewed the contents of the journal. I understand you even took pictures of every single page."

"That is correct," Jake answered. "Part of my governmental duties."

"Well, this concerns me greatly," said Nero, his voice harsher. "I would now like to sincerely ask you to immediately delete those pictures you have of my property. It's a simple matter of copyright infringement."

Jake laughed. "Copyright infringement? You're joking, right? Listen, I don't know who the hell you are, but ..."

"Excuse me, Major. *You* listen very closely," Nero snapped back, pointing a finger at him. "My sincerity was a one-time offer. Do not play hardball with me."

Jake noticed Clown Face inching closer. The driver also exited the limo.

"Hand over your camera now and we'll be on our way. No questions asked," ordered Nero in a deep tone.

"Go screw yourself. You're not touching government property. And tell your driver to move this hunk of shit out of the way. My business is finished here."

Nero flicked his head. The thug behind Jake grunted to catch his attention. Clown Face opened his coat to reveal the handle of a black pistol in his waistband. The driver, having already walked around the back of the vehicle, also showed off his weapon.

Jake's blood boiled as he sized up the situation. An escape plan started to develop but quickly fizzled as Nero displayed a Glock 9 mm and pointed it at Jake's chest.

"Give me the camera and you get to live another day of being an Army of one," said Nero. "Try anything funny and I'll tie a concrete block around your neck and dump your body in the Niagara River."

Jake's eyes locked with Nero's and he knew in an instant this guy meant what he said. Nero's eyes seemed a window to his soul — and what stood on the other side rattled him.

Suddenly Jake remembered he had a copy of every journal page image transferred from his camera onto his laptop. "You win, hotshot. I'm going to reach in my bag for the camera. Put the weapon down. I'm cool."

Nero kept the pistol raised as Jake fished out his digital camera and tossed it through the window. Nero placed his weapon on the seat next to him, picked up the camera and turned it on to review the photos.

He erased everything.

He then took out the tiny memory card and broke it in half, dropping one half of the card and the camera on the pavement at Jake's feet. Then with a crude smile, he snapped his fingers. The window motored up and both thugs walked to the other side of the limo to get in. In a moment the vehicle screeched away, leaving Jake standing in a cloud of gray smoke from burnt rubber.

A vein throbbed in his forehead.

Just then, his phone rang. He snatched it out of his coat pocket and punched the *talk* button.

"Tununda here!"

"Major? What's wrong? You sound alarmed." It was Dr. Ashland.

"Damn right," Jake said, picking up his camera and inspecting it for damage. "Some asshole with a Roman emperor's name of Nero just purchased the Boyd Box from underneath our noses. Walked out with all of it."

"Alex Nero, the Indian billionaire? He bought it all? He was there?"

"Yes, the Indian. You know this guy?" The camera turned on fine and functioned properly. Jake placed it in his briefcase.

"Not personally, but I've read quite a bit on him. He's the Chief and CEO of the Onondaga Nation and was just voted in as the Head Chief of the Grand Council of the Haudenosaunee Confederacy, not to mention being the owner of High Point."

"Oh. And what is High Point?" Jake quietly replied, somewhat embarrassed his new boss from California knew more about Iroquois happenings than he did.

"The gambling resort in the Catskills. Nero is one very powerful casino magnate. Don't tell me you've never heard of him?" said Ashland in a condescending tone.

"I don't follow Native American politics, nor gamble for that matter."

"Jake, I meant that he owns the most extensive private Iroquois artifact collection in the world. It's called the Haudenosaunee Collection. I'm really surprised, since you both are Native American," Ashland chided.

"Give me a break already. A few things like Bosnia, Afghanistan, and Iraq kind of got in my way of keeping track of who has the largest arrowhead set. Did you get my e-mail?"

"Sorry. Yes. Quite astonishing isn't it?"

"Yes, and gone too. All of the items, Butler's letter, the journal. They contained so much incredible history that needs to be investigated. And the cipher codes, the illustrations. We could have had a shot at owning it but Nero bullied his way in and flashed his cash. I won't let this happen. There's something we can do."

"What are your thoughts?"

"In that September 12th journal entry I e-mailed you, I think I can identify who Boyd was talking about when he referred to the other half of the code being hidden in his craft brother's trade tool. I'm pretty sure he was referring to his sergeant, a Sean McTavish. They were Brothers in the Freemasons and that's how fellow members refer to each other."

"Okay, I'm listening."

"Now, if we can track down genealogical records of this McTavish and what his trade tool is, then that's where the second half of that odd lettering is. Maybe we can then decipher the whole message. Which would lead us straight to Boyd's buried war loot and then onto General Sullivan's sunken cannon of gold! We can make a positive out of this negative loss. We can make history out of this whole ordeal. It's what our mission at MHI is. All of our discoveries will belong to the institute. Do you know what this will do for public relations? Plus we'd screw Nero in the end."

Jake waited for a response but none came. There was a long pause. "You there?"

"Slow down there Indiana Jones," Ashland said with a condescending chuckle. "You want to go off on some wild treasure hunt? What is this, a sequel to the movie *National Treasure*? You want to screw Alex Nero too? First of all, your reaction is quite inappropriate to want to screw over one of the most powerful men in our field. MHI doesn't need this headache and quite frankly, neither do I. The Boyd Box is gone. It was bought fair and square. Let's just accept it and let it go. We win some we lose some. It's the nature of the business. Now, I've got to make a phone call to the director to break the bad news. You just take it easy. Get some rest, okay? You've had a long day." Ashland trailed off, wanting to end the conversation.

"W-what?" said Jake, stunned at Ashland's rebuke. "The deal was not square. Nero snatched it before anyone else could place an assessment on it. He bent the rules and we will too. My God. We've got all the clues at our fingertips. This is a once in a lifetime opportunity for a historian and you just want to cut and run and appease him by saying we win some, we lose some?"

"Insubordination!" Ashland blurted. "You may have cut the corners on the battlefield Major, but you will *not* break the rules under my watch. MHI is on a new bus ride to excellence under my supervision and you have to make the decision whether you want to be a passenger on that bus or leave your seat for someone else. I am ordering you to LEAVE IT ALONE."

Jake fumed inside. He had enough of the politically correct clichés. "Oh, grow some balls for Chris-sake!"

His boss gasped. The phone clicked dead.

"Ah, Jake, you stupid hothead," he scolded himself. And now another stupid phrase his uncle always told him crossed his mind. *Even a fish wouldn't get caught if he kept his mouth shut.* He had botched his first assessment, put his job in jeopardy, and had a wealthy collector pull a weapon on him and the damn day hadn't even finished yet. Some icing on the cake this assignment turned out to be.

Tonawanda Band of Seneca Indian Reservation, near Akron, N.Y.

PHONING AHEAD TO his uncle to say he was in the area and stopping by for a visit to unwind, Jake turned off the Thruway at the Pembroke exit and headed north on Route 77 to Indian Falls, the southern entry point into the Tonawanda Band of Seneca Indian Reservation. The waning light of dusk was setting in as he made the left turn near Tonawanda Creek and entered his old stomping grounds. Just up the road, he passed by a state historical marker off the shoulder. Pulling over, he couldn't help but be drawn in. Gobbling up historical tidbits was a habit he just couldn't resist.

He had already read this particular marker countless times, but never grew tired of it for it provided the impetus for him joining the ranks of the warrior class. It was one of his historical role models — one of the most famous Seneca Indians his nation had produced and a distant relative to his own clan. Faded yellow text set against a dark blue background told of the log cabin birthplace of Ely Parker, a Seneca Indian who volunteered in the Union Army during the Civil War. Parker had risen in rank to become General Ulysses Grant's secretary and ultimately helped draft the surrender terms of Confederate General Robert E. Lee at the end the war in 1865. Parker was later commissioned a Brigadier General before retiring from the U.S. Army. Scorned by his tribe for joining the white man's army, he died a controversial figure in Iroquois history.

Jake smirked. He too had heard the same opposition from certain members of his clan upon his announcement of joining Army ROTC. One old crabby clan mother — Miss Lizzie Spiritwalker — told him never to come back. But his Uncle Joe had stood in support. Jake shook off the bitter memory and read the last sentence of the marker.

Never fully appreciating it until recently, that sentence simply stated that Ely Parker was a Freemason. Jake nodded. He had read and absorbed much over the years on the subject. Freemasonry was an incredibly influential organization that had roots as far back as the Middle Ages. As the most ancient esoteric fraternity in the world, its stated goal was to make good men better in their morals, character, and pursuit of knowledge. It had even shaped the founding of the United States in its beliefs of equality, tolerance of religion, and separation of church and state. All men in the fraternity were considered brothers despite their religious or political beliefs. But brotherly love, especially in times of war, was another matter, Jake thought as he gripped the steering wheel. Just look at the outcome of the Boyd, Butler, and Brant affair. They were all Masons.

Punching the gas pedal, he sped up Hopkins Road into the heart of the reservation. Motoring past several modest homes and harvested farmer's fields split by copses of woods, he had a satisfied feeling that the reservation still maintained a semblance of its rural flavor.

The feeling didn't last long. Up past the railroad tracks he noticed a definite change for the worse. It started with the cigarette and gasoline signs along the road, each hawking low prices up ahead. Then came the first of the many makeshift gas and smoke shops — no more than trailer homes turned into mini-flea markets. They had spread like weeds since his last visit a couple of years back. Some had gas pumps installed right in their front yards while others tried to win over customers with a bit more cleanliness by actually paving their driveways. Their customers, mostly non-Indian locals from the neighboring American towns, didn't care one way or the other. They were lined up bumper-to-bumper like crack heads seeking their weekly fix. All they were interested in was cheap tax-free gas and cigarettes — anything to beat the soaring prices in the state.

Jake's uncle, Joe Big Bear Tununda, his mother's brother, also had an enterprising gas and tobacco business like these, but his was much more polished and professional. It had been the very top moneymaker on the reservation for many years and Joe was always generous in spreading the wealth to his clan.

Uncle Joe had taken on a more important role early in Jake's life though. Joe became his surrogate father after both of his parents died in a fiery car crash. Drunk driving was the cause. They had just won the jackpot at a Batavia bingo hall and the drinking and driving celebration afterward had cost them their lives. As tribal custom dictated, the mother's brother would be left the children. Joe gladly accepted. He welcomed his young nephew into an already large family and raised him as his own.

Near Bloomingdale Road, Jake pulled into the busy parking lot of a two-story wood frame building that housed Joe's gas station, smoke shop, and grocery store on the first level. A five room family residence was on the second — Jake's home as a youth. The complex was called Big Bear Gas, Grocery & Smokes. It was a mainstay of the reservation where everyone would come from miles around to fill up their tanks, buy cartons of tobacco products or to just catch up on the local gossip and politics. Jake parked and took a few minutes to reminisce as the people shuffled in and out of the main entrance.

He knew early on in life that working in a business like this was one of the few options he had if he stayed on the reservation. But he could never picture himself making ten dollars an hour, becoming old and overweight and one of those miserable people who said, *I wish I had done things differently.*

He instead yearned for adventure greater than the *rez* could offer. When he was old enough to read and learned of Ely Parker's significance as an Army officer from the birthplace marker, Jake started asking questions of the clan elders of other warriors of the tribe. He soon found out his own Seneca Indian roots derived from some of the most courageous war captains in all of the Iroquois Confederacy. His clan members had also fought for America in her Civil War, World Wars I and II, Korea, Vietnam, and the Persian Gulf. And through a genealogy search of his deceased father's British roots he traced his American ancestry as far back as the War of 1812. His inner fire had been stoked. Through his self-investigative historical research young Robert Jake Tununda decided to join the path of the warrior. He wanted to prove to himself on the battlefield that he too could live up to his glorious past and in the process become a man.

When his uncle discovered his true intentions, he gave Jake just one recommendation. He urged Jake not to go in the Army as a private — the low-level grunt at the bottom of the ladder most often used as cannon fodder. Instead, Joe pressured him to develop his leadership skills first, earn a college degree, study history, sociology, and geopolitics, and enter the service as an educated officer who would be in on the decision-making process during conflicts — one who could influence the outcomes of the battlefield and the men he would be responsible for. Jake ran with his uncle's recommendation. It proved a wise decision. He landed a Native American scholarship and attended Cornell University, just a three-hour drive from the reservation.

Donning his black beret head cover and checking his uniform coat, he jumped out of his SUV and walked into the crowded smoke shop. Next to a young lanky Indian clerk, there, behind the counter, as always, was his beloved Uncle Joe. A large smile appeared on his uncle's wide, double-chinned face.

"Jake, how are ya, son?" he said. "Billy, my new clerk here, said you called. Couldn't believe it." Flipping his black braided ponytail over his shoulder he rose up to greet his nephew, his hefty midsection pressing tightly against a food stained white t-shirt.

Jake smiled warmly, taking off his beret and walking behind the counter to give him a bear hug. "It's good to see you Big Bear."

"Come on, let's go in the back room, get out of this riff-raff," offered Joe, leading to a quiet lounge behind some curtains. "Sit down. Relax," he continued. "Looks like you picked up some more medals since last time you stopped in. It's been quite a while. You really should come home more often. We all miss you here."

"It's been tough," said Jake, plopping down on a well-worn sofa. "I've been on non-stop tours of duty. They had me in all sorts of task forces and intel ops. Didn't get much R and R. Rest and Romance."

"Hey, I got your last e-mail about your new job announcement.

Congratulations," said Joe with a grin. "I don't think you'll be getting injured anymore now that you're a big historian." He walked over to the lounge's refrigerator.

"Other than a paper cut here and there," replied Jake with a laugh. "I tell you what, twenty years of infantry was pure adventure but I was fried. We did one hell of a job in rebuilding countries, saving lives, and spreading democracy — good stuff I'm proud of. But a lot of sacrifice and a lot of screw-ups came with it, on top of the corruption — mostly from our own Congress. The politics were the worst part of it. Lost too many men because of political appeasement."

"I hear you," sympathized Joe, leaning on the open refrigerator door.

"I needed a new direction. Working for MHI will be a whole new adrenaline kick. Ah shit, listen, enough about me. How's life treating you out here? Looks like you've got some competition knocking on the door."

"Same old crap, different day as they say," replied Joe, turning around. "Those start-ups come and go. Can't maintain themselves. They spend all their profits on booze and gambling up at the Indian casinos in Niagara Falls. They never learn. Hey, can I get ya a pop or something? Or a Snapple, I know you like that."

Jake nodded. "Snapple."

"I tell ya Jake, the damn tribal politics are becoming cut throat out here." Joe rattled some glass bottles inside the fridge.

"Oh yeah?"

"We've got us traditionalists hotly debating the Neo-Iroquois, I call them, on whether we should get into the gambling racket like all the other nations." Joe grabbed two iced-tea drinks. "But I'll fight it all the way. Gambling is against the Handsome Lake Code of our religion." He walked back to his nephew and twisted the caps off, handing his nephew his drink.

"No booze, no gambling, no bad music," Jake mentioned. "I know the code. Well, at least I don't gamble, right?"

Joe smiled and gave him a *cheers* to seeing him again. They clicked bottles and swigged down half.

Jake smacked his lips. "Ahhh, that hits the spot. I loved it when you sent me this stuff in Iraq."

Joe plopped down onto the couch beside his nephew, the cushions hissing under his weight. "So, what brings you up this way?"

"Well, got a real nutsy story to tell you. Was wondering if you could help me out."

Jake went on to explain about how he was traveling through Seneca County earlier in the day when some crazy stuff started happening. Joe mentioned there had always been strange going-ons in that area. But when Jake retold the story of the trapped hunter, the shaft, the discovered Indian grave in the marsh, and the silver broach with the odd symbolism, his uncle sat in a stupor.

Setting his drink on a table, Joe looked at his nephew. "What's this symbol look like?"

"Well, I've got a picture of it — a photograph that the investigator let me take. It's on my laptop in the truck but I can draw it for you. It's pretty simple."

Grabbing a napkin and a pen, and with his uncle peering over his shoulder, Jake drew the outline of a buck. He then scribbled the snake inside.

Joe grabbed the napkin and tore it up in tiny pieces. He cautiously glanced around the room as if someone were watching.

"What's wrong?" Jake asked. "You see a ghost?"

"Almost. That symbol is ancient. It's a forbidden secret."

"But Joe—"

"No, just trust me. It has significance with that hole and that gravesite. Oh Great Spirit, I wish that hunter never found it." Joe took a deep breath and then grabbed a pack of cigarettes out of his pocket.

Jake watched him fumble to light a cigarette. He had never seen his uncle act this way. "That's not the only one I found today."

"What!" muttered Joe, butt hanging out his mouth.

"That same symbol appeared in an American Revolutionary War officer's journal up at Old Fort Niagara. They just discovered it after being buried in a box this whole time. This officer was in the same area near Seneca Lake when he found one of those same broaches, back in 1779, during the Sullivan campaign."

Joe turned to his nephew and quickly inhaled the cigarette smoke. He spoke, letting the blue-gray smoke swirl out of his mouth and nostrils. "This cannot be happening. I cannot believe this is happening. Go on Jake. Tell me everything you know."

For the next twenty minutes Jake told him of the Boyd Box discovery while Joe chain-smoked half the cigarette pack. But when he mentioned in the end that Alex Nero bought the box outright, Joe, who had just taken a sip of his drink, gasped and dropped the container on the tiled floor, shattering the glass.

Joe ignored the mess, stood up, grabbed a land line phone. He dialed. "It's Joe. I'm coming over right now. My nephew Jake has a white deer story for you." He paused then nodded "Yes, Robert Jake, the army officer." He then hung up.

Jake was cleaning up his uncle's mess and looked up. "What does Nero have to do with any of this? And who the heck did you just call?"

"Soon you'll know everything. Come on. We're going to Miss Lizzie Spiritwalker's house. Remember her?"

"Oh, how could I forget her? She's that batty old ball-buster that gave me so much shit twenty years ago when she found out I was joining the Army." Jake stood up and threw away the glass shards. "I'm surprised she's still alive."

"Yep, and sharper than ever. She's the eldest clan mother we have now, the nation answers to her as the matriarchal head. She's also the best source of Iroquois history in our entire Confederacy — the most respected Faithkeeper there is. Just be patient with her and your puzzle pieces will fit together."

Ten minutes later. Tonawanda Reservation.

Jake followed his uncle's maroon Ford F-150 pick up truck up a little-used dirt road that led them to a remote section of Tonawanda Creek. The road was narrow and full of deep ruts making it hard to drive in the darkness. They finally emerged at a run-down old Victorian style house partially hidden in the woods. Jake parked, grabbed his laptop and a New York State topo map book. He jumped out but stopped and stared at the front porch.

Dim lighting filtered out from open windows, drapes fluttered in the cool night breeze. Several bamboo wind chimes knocked together in a rhythmic mellow tune while the trees rustled with a groan. Jake remembered this place giving him the creeps as a kid. Some things never change.

With a rap on the front door and an announcement, they entered to find Miss Elizabeth Spiritwalker Canohocton or Miss Lizzie as Joe called her, sitting in a rocking chair in the center of the living room. A heavy blanket was thrown across her lap. A pet Chihuahua was tucked inside, fast asleep.

Lizzie smiled a toothless, wrinkled grin at Joe, her light brown eyes gleaming in the warm light cast from a single table lamp. Long, straight white hair hung from her tiny head. Soft flute music and a steady drumming played from a portable CD tune box in a corner. Jake studied her. The term *walking dead* came to mind.

"Ah, young Robert Jake Tununda," her high-pitched voice wheezed. "My what a handsome man you turned out to be. I've heard much on your exploits out there in the white man's world. Come closer. Don't be shy. I won't cast any spells on you." She extended her hand in greeting and coughed. "Not yet at least."

Jake shook her skeletal-like hand. "Miss Lizzie, it's a pleasure to see you again. It's been a long time."

"Turned one-oh-three last month. Still haven't eaten my most favorite strawberries yet, as they say when you get closer to the sunset. Getting more and more visitors wondering what my secret is. Your father here, I mean your uncle, has kept a good watch over me." She looked over to Joe.

"I can't thank Big Bear enough. Now sit down and tell me about this story you're so upset about."

"Lizzie, Jake has some pictures that go along with his story. He has here a laptop computer to show us and a map book. What happened is he found a silver and wampum broach this morning — two of them to be exact. He'll explain. But you'll recognize what's on them right away. If all of this is true, I fear what will happen. Jake, please tell her everything and she'll make sense of it all."

Jake sat down on the couch beside Lizzie and flipped open his laptop. As it booted up he looked around her living room. It was a treasure trove of old Seneca Indian artifacts. On the wall hung several carved wood and cornhusk false-face masks with their twisted noses and demonic faces. Off in a corner was a genuine water drum and on a table were smoking pipes, beads, jewels, and various sundry items from years past. Joe cleared his throat.

Jake blinked and nodded then began retelling the story of the morning event at the marsh. He opened the topographical map atlas of New York State, turning to the page showing Seneca and Cayuga Lakes, and pointed to the location of Cranberry Marsh — just northeast of the old Seneca Army Depot.

As he spoke of the Indian grave and the victim he had found in the bottom of the hole, on the computer screen he pulled up the silver broach image the investigator had let him take. Lizzie's eyes widened. Her lips pressed together and she flinched. Her Chihuahua opened its large eyes in a panic and scampered off her lap.

"Choo-Choo, come back little girl," Joe urged as the dog shuffled off into the kitchen.

"Jake, was there anything at the bottom of this hole?" Lizzie asked.

"Not much, just a pile of rocks near the wall. A few inches of water."

"Water?" questioned Joe, a bit excited. "Was it flowing water? Like a stream?"

Jake laughed. "No. No. There was no underground river there. I remember that story you told me as a kid. But you know what was kind of odd was when I climbed out of the well it seemed as though there were little footholds carved out of the stone, almost like steps."

"Wait, go back. There was a pile of rocks you said?" asked Joe.

Jake shrugged his shoulders. "Yeah."

"But you didn't see any type of tunnel or an opening down there where the cave went on further?" asked Lizzie.

"No. It was just an open pit at the bottom of a limestone shaft. I'm thinking maybe it was an old salt mine. Salt was usually gathered by the Indians around marshes."

"Very interesting indeed," said his uncle. "Now tell Lizzie about what you found at Fort Niagara."

Jake rehashed the story of the Boyd Box discovery. He showed Lizzie and Joe all of the photos he took, explaining in minute detail the items and their historical significance. He caught himself lecturing the two before getting back to the core of his story, of when Lieutenant Thomas Boyd entered Kendaia. In the topo book, he showed them the location of Kendaia along Route 96A paralleling Seneca Lake's eastern shore — on the opposite side of the Depot. He then pulled the laptop in front of him and started reading out loud the journal excerpt from September 5th, how Boyd and McTavish entered the village first and found the captive Luke Swetland, how Swetland took them to a sacred Indian location and a cave and how they spotted a white deer and that McTavish shot at it.

"Now listen to this part," said Jake, reading very slowly. "Kendaia plunder illustrated below, along with directions to Swetland's Indian cave, so we may re-visit and further examine one day in hopes of finding more fortune." He displayed on screen the indecipherable lettering ripped in half at the corner. They studied the monitor closely. Joe asked Lizzie if she had ever seen lettering like this before.

"I think I have. Not sure where." She shook her head. "This is supposed to be directions to this so-called witch's cave?"

"Yes, and he hid the other half of this cave location in a buried keg of loot," explained Jake. "Check this out. This here is the other cipher that refers to where the keg is located and what it contains." He pulled up Boyd's very last entry from September 12th, showed them the second cipher of lettering on that ripped page and then read the caption accompanying it.

"Craft cipher indicates directions to the buried keg. For purposes of secrecy the other half of cipher is deposited in my most trusted craft brother's most trusted trade tool. So, the second half of this message he deliberately hid in his friend's trusted tool, whatever that is."

Lizzie cleared her throat. "Craft cipher? Craft brother? I know that lettering now. It's from the Freemasons. They also call themselves members of the Craft. It's the Freemason's Cipher. I'm sure of it."

Joe leaned back. "Freemason's Cipher?"

Jake too was perplexed and embarrassed. "Dammit, I should have known that. Craft. Cipher. The answer was right there in front of me! Makes sense now. Boyd was a member of the Freemasons. So were the British Colonel John Butler and the Mohawk Joseph Brant. Most men in those days were. So it does fit."

"Brant was the very first Native American to become a Freemason," added Lizzie.

Jake nodded. "At least I knew that! So, we know then this Freemason code leads to Boyd's buried loot. He even listed the inventory to contain, among other things, the payroll gold taken from Butler, the second half of the cave directions, a map, and the silver broach given to him by the captive Swetland. And here is a drawing of that broach."

"That broach was stolen from Swetland. Not given," said Lizzie. "I've read Swetland's memoirs after his repatriation and —"

Jake sat up straight. "God, now that you mention it, I remember reading that too when I was researching Sullivan's campaign a couple of years ago. Swetland's memoirs were published by an Edward Merrifield I believe."

"You are correct!" exclaimed Lizzie. "And you know," she continued, "Swetland specifically mentioned in his narrative that the two American scouts stripped him naked and beat him thinking him an Indian spy. They were going to kill him."

"Turns out we now know it was Boyd and McTavish who were those scouts," offered Jake, caressing his chin, staring ahead.

"But they somehow extracted the location of the cave from Swetland too," said Joe. "Even claiming he gave them the broach."

Lizzie interrupted. "Swetland was in fear for his life he said in his memoirs. Those scouts thought he was preparing an ambush on them. So maybe he gave up the cave location to prove he wasn't a spy but rather truly an American who had been kidnapped and needed rescuing."

Jake showed them the ink drawing in Boyd's journal, zooming in on the deer and snake symbol. He also placed the photo of the broach Blaylock found side by side with Boyd's drawing.

Lizzie and Joe leaned forward and compared the two images. Their mouths hung open. Lizzie pulled back, bent her head down, and placed a hand over her eyes, rubbing the bridge of her nose.

Joe read the caption below the drawing. "Silver and wampum neck clasp given to us from Swetland. He found it in cave. The old squaw made him wear it to protect the cave."

Barely audible, Lizzie whispered, "The last of the guardians. She cursed this Swetland for finding one of the legendary cave entrances. She forced him wear the broach to protect its location."

Jake slowly turned toward her. "What? Come again? Last of the guardians of what?"

Lizzie met his gaze. Her eyes glimmered. "Today the spirits have spoken to you Robert Jake Tununda, so I have no qualms about revealing the name as I know you will perform well. The guardians I speak of were from a highly secret cult within the government of the Confederacy. They are called the White Deer Society."

"Huh? White Deer Society? Who?" Jake shook his head. "And no spirits have spoken to me today. Finding these two broaches is all just a strange coincidence."

Lizzie cackled. "Oh, you are so out of touch with your faith young man. Don't you know that coincidence does not exist? We meet people and are placed in situations for reasons, for meaning, for opportunities that only you must decide to act upon."

Joe nodded his head in agreement.

Jake eyed them both. The flute music and slow drum beats caused him to reflect on how different his beliefs were as opposed to their mystical traditionalist religion. His was based on the hard core reality he studied in military history — of death, destruction, power, and politics.

"What's this other drawing of?" asked Lizzie, looking at the illustration next to the broach drawing. "I can't read the caption."

Jake pointed. "That's the map case."

"Map of what?" she asked.

Jake read the caption for them. "Hickory map case, ancient map of Swetland's witch cave passages, quill, and ink inside."

Lizzie gasped. "The map exists! Oh Great Spirit! It cannot be. The White Deer Society has guarded this for centuries."

Jake blinked in frustration. "Would someone please tell me what the hell this White Deer Society is?"

The two elders looked at each other. Joe nodded then turned to Jake. "Before we do, please tell Lizzie who now owns the Boyd Box."

"Some billionaire Indian named Alex Nero," said Jake.

Lizzie covered her forehead with her hand. She looked up and closed her eyes, then whispered, "It is true then. The evil is revealing itself. It wants to walk the surface again."

"Listen, what's going on here? Nero and I had a run in this afternoon over that box."

"You spoke with him? Why didn't you tell me that before? What did he say?" asked Joe.

"Well, the pistol aimed at my chest did all the talking. He made me turn over my digital camera then erased all of my photos. I had taken all the pictures of the journal with it. I had no choice. He didn't want any duplicate records out there. Said the journal contents were under his copyright. But what he didn't know is that I had already made copies on my laptop from the camera before he erased them."

"It has started." Lizzie bent her head down, her white hair tumbling in front of her face. "The revelation has started."

"I ought a give that little excuse of a man a piece of my fist for pulling that gun on you."

"Calm down Big Bear, I think the gold is all that fellow is really after," explained Jake. "It's pretty obvious."

"No Jake," Lizzie hissed. "Nero is not after gold. He already has enough riches. He's after something much more valuable. Something the White Deer Society has kept hidden, kept secret for centuries. Something that dates way back before the birth of the Haudenosaunee Confederacy."

"Well, what is it?" asked Jake, drumming his fingers.

"He wants what is called the Crown of Serpents," Lizzie cut in. "The actual crown that the evil wizard Atotarho wore. It is hidden underground somewhere between the big lakes of Seneca and Cayuga."

"Wait. Wait. Hold on," Jake stifled a laugh. "What? The ancient evil medicine man Atotarho, with hair made of serpents? With all due respect, Atotarho's serpents were just an analogy," he continued. "We all know it was a reference to his evil thoughts. A so-called crown of evil thoughts. Not a real crown of snakes."

Joe shot him a hard glance. "That's the story we tell the children to teach them moral lessons of right and wrong, but there's another version you've never heard before."

"Right," quipped Lizzie. "It is one of the most frightening stories of our people's oppression and rebirth. And now, since the ancient signs are revealing themselves and Alex Nero is involved it takes on new meaning."

Jake leaned back on the couch thinking Uncle Joe and the old medicine woman seemed to be laying it on a bit thick — a real serpent's crown hidden in a secret cave system under Seneca County? This day was getting weirder by the minute. He looked down at his watch wondering if he really wanted to hear anymore. He had to be in Rochester, a half hour back east, to check into his hotel. Dr. Ashland had rescheduled his meeting with the 98th for the morning and he wanted to be fresh for his speaking engagement.

"Jake! This is serious business. Listen to us," demanded Joe.

"Sorry. I'm here. I'm listening," Jake responded out of respect. He figured he still had time for their story. Heck, another Indian legend always made for entertaining listening anyway. He would soon find out this story was nothing to be laughing at.

10

Same time. High Point Casino. Haudenosaunee Collection Room.

THE SNAP OF FINGERS reverberated from the open entrance door
to the Haudenosaunee Collection room. Anne Stanton lifted her head
from her late night work. She glanced over at the arrogant head of security,
a suited Indian with face tattoos, leaning against the main doorway. He
thumbed her to hurry up. Their boss was ready to see her.

Moving a strand of her blonde hair out of her eye's way she looked back
down at her work. She had been performing routine cleaning on a rare 15th
century Mohawk ceremonial turtle rattle. Giving the tiny mummified mud
turtle a shake with its wood handle, two cherry pits rattled inside. The old
artifact still worked well she thought with a satisfying smile, then placed it
back in its glass display next to several others. Sliding the case's panel door
shut she locked it then picked up her notepad and made her way toward the
exit. She passed a multitude of displays of other priceless Iroquois items,
ranging from wampum belts to weapons of war to a bark canoe. There was
even a full-sized replica of a traditional longhouse entrance, which she now
passed under to make her way out of the room.

In the hallway Stanton turned and locked the collection room door
behind her. She then walked by two full-sized bronze Indian sculptures of
warriors. They served as flanking welcoming sentinels to those fortunate
enough to visit Nero's below ground private collection.

"Move it woman. He hasn't got all day," snarled the bodyguard, his
arms folded across a wide chest.

Stanton shook her head. "A please would be nice, Mr. Rousseau."

Kenny Rousseau rolled his eyes. A half-Mohawk, half-French Canadian, he was the epitome of a bull headed thug, but one of Nero's closest confidants too. Dressed in an expensive dark blue suit with a High Point Mountain Casino and Resort logo embroidered on his breast pocket, the head man led her to Nero's office just down the hall on the left. He wore his black hair in a long braided ponytail and she could tell by the bulge in his coat he carried some type of weapon. They all did here.

As she strode behind him, placing her eyeglasses on, she looked down the hallway to the elevator entrance back up to the main casino floor. Another bodyguard stood there, dressed and looking the same as Rousseau. He received a nod from Rousseau. Arriving at Nero's office door they were greeted by a grotesque false-face medicine mask hanging on the front. Hand-carved from hardwood, the dark red painted mask screamed in captured agony, its mouth a gaping black hole, its bulging eyes colored yellow, and its hawk-like nose twisted and bent. White hair draped over its sharp, high cheekbones.

Rousseau knocked twice. Stanton heard an electronic unlocking mechanism click to allow them access. "Get in there," whispered Rousseau. "He's pissed off as it is. The cancer is even worse than they thought."

Stanton sighed. That means he'd be doubly degrading to her. It was late and all she wanted was to get back home to Kingston, not deal with more of his abuse. But maybe she should show some sympathy — after all he *was* dying. She pushed the door open and stepped inside the lavish subterranean office of Alex Nero.

On a slate floor stood custom-crafted wood, glass, and leather furniture dotting the spacious room. The furniture shared an aesthetic pattern derived from various North American snakes. A chieftain's headdress, crowned with buck antlers and eagle feathers sat atop one of the tables as a centerpiece. Lit with warm spotlights, several portraits of Iroquois warriors lined the smooth rock walls in an eerie glow. Tomahawks, knives, bows, arrows, war hammers, rifles, pistols, and swords hung between each painting. And among all the artifacts sat her boss behind his large mahogany desk. Surprisingly, she thought, he wore a melancholy look on his face. At least he's not smoking another damn cigar, she thought.

"Mr. Nero, I've got that follow-up report on that Indian grave case."

Nero waved her over to take a seat across from him. As she approached, he gingerly closed a very old leather booklet and placed it inside a worn box of the same deteriorating material.

"Would those be the Thomas Boyd items you acquired at Fort Niagara?" she asked eyeing the old box.

Nero smiled. "Indeed they are young lady. Indeed they are. You did very well in setting up that meeting. As if it was preordained."

Stanton adjusted her posture upright. "Thank you sir." What's with all the accolades lately, she thought. Is the cancer actually bringing him back down to earth? She then noticed two maps open across his desktop. One was of Seneca County and another a blueprint of the Seneca Army Depot that dominated the same area where the Indian grave accident had occurred.

Nero placed a hand on top of the leather box and patted it softly. "The journal in here happens to contain some key historical information that may pertain to that Indian grave and broach that was discovered this morning. But first I'd like to hear your report." He leaned back into his high-backed luxury leather chair.

Stanton raised her eyebrows at the revelation, then cleared her throat, and crossed her legs. "Certainly. First off, I tried to arrange a personal visit for you tomorrow to view the broach, but was turned down by the state police investigator — a Miss Rae Hart. She's the one handling the case."

Nero uttered a gritty, sandpaper cough. "Spell her last name?"

"H-A-R-T. Why? Do you know her?"

Nero's eyes narrowed. "I'll ask the questions."

"I'm sorry."

"Go on."

"Well," said Stanton, tiredly. "I let her know that I represented the head of the Burial Rules Committee, but she still needed some more time before scheduling a meeting. Said she had to consult a Cornell archeologist first."

"Miss Stanton," said Nero. "As you know, my time is short. Make the meeting happen with her before any of those academic liberal do-gooders come snooping around."

"With all due respect sir, we may not need the meeting. I managed to come across some video stills showing the actual broach. It was posted on a news web site."

Nero leaned forward and glared in Stanton's weary eyes. "This hit the news? It went public?"

She extracted a color copy from her folder and handed it across the desk to him. "Unfortunately, yes. Competition to acquire the piece will now increase. The picture is pretty grainy, but it's not a bad close-up. You can clearly make out the engraved outline of a doe—"

Nero studied the print in depth. His smile reappeared. "A buck."

"Right. A buck. And what seems to me to be a snake form inside of its body."

"Ah yes, it sure is," he said, his grin growing wider.

Stanton looked at him funny. She had never seen him so giddy. Was there something she was missing?

Nero looked back down at the color copy. His smile was gone. "Where is this broach actually being kept at the moment?"

"At a state trooper station in Kendaia. Probably in the evidence lock up room."

"Kendaia?" Nero stated, an inquisitive look on his face. "Interesting. Most interesting."

"Want to hear how the actual accident took place?"

"Sure."

Stanton read the entire accident report from a printed transcript obtained on the news web site. She finished up with, "… and the motorist who tried to rescue the victim was identified as, ah, as a Major R.J. Tununda of the U.S. Army. He's a traveling historian with the Army's Military History Institute. He happened to—."

Behind the color copy Nero flashed his teeth in anger. "Tununda. Our paths cross again."

"Excuse me?"

He lowered the paper. "I want a background check on him. Go on with your story."

Great, she thought, more digging up dirt on other people. It was the part of her job she liked the least. Nero had her do it on many occasions as she had all the right contacts and knew where to extract public information on the fly. She shrugged her shoulders and finished reading the article. She even offered to pinpoint the general location of the accident site in Cranberry Marsh explaining that the investigator declined to give out the GPS coordinates.

But Nero already knew where the marsh was, his eyes falling on the Seneca County map. He tapped the spot on the map to the north east of the Depot. "Up here."

"Correct." She then pointed south of the hamlet of Kendaia, down near the Depot's airfield on the southwest corner of the base. "And here's where the broach is being kept. The Trooper's station lies between the runway and Route 96A."

"Ah, such coincidence cannot be missed, Miss Stanton. Did you know that our friend Boyd here," explained Nero, tapping the leather box, "passed through that same village of Kendaia in the year 1779?"

"Really?"

He nodded, then circled the lands to the east of Kendaia — the Depot, with its east-to-west parallel roads containing hundreds of ammo bunkers. "Yes, and here lies a secret somewhere under this former Army base that our Mr. Boyd knew about. It's linked to that symbol on the broach. And now all the land inside of the Depot will soon be mine to crack this mystery."

He snatched up his cell phone and placed a call to his lawyer. He allowed Stanton to listen in as he increased the purchase price on the Depot lands on condition the county close the deal within the next few days.

Stanton wondered why her hands shook. Nero ended the call, fumbling with the cell phone keys then turned back to his collection's director.

"Starting tomorrow morning you will be conducting special research for me based on information gleaned from the Thomas Boyd journal."

She took off and pocketed her eyeglasses. "Yes sir."

"It is a plethora of clues that I'm putting my trust in you to solve. When you do, it will lead to a prize that my Onondaga people have long coveted. It will be the greatest discovery of our lives, my dear. It will make you incredibly rich and famous. That is of course if you accept this task."

Stanton's brows creased. She fidgeted in her chair and ran her fingers through her hair.

"Well, of course sir. It's part of my job."

"No, this task requires your complete loyalty. There is no turning back once you accept. You will become a member of this family, and once you are in, there is no backing out. You understand?"

"Completely sir. I'm not dumb and you know that. I knew what I was getting into when I decided I wanted to work for you. So, yes, I do accept. No question."

"Very well Miss Stanton. To whet your appetite as to the prize we are seeking, I'd like you to join me in the Scalp Room." He rose from his chair and motioned to a doorway behind him. On that door hung a scalp stretched on a wooden hoop. "Come. Let me show you."

Upon entering Nero's highly coveted inner chamber, Stanton's head turned on a swivel. She had only been in there one other time, upon her hire. It still amazed her that these war trophies once belonged to actual people. And it also truly sickened her.

Displayed in various shapes, sizes, hair colors, hair patterns and lengths, the collection of centuries-old scalps were all mounted on small wooden hoops with the skin stretched over like a tambourine. Most of the hairpieces looked neat and combed while others had deteriorated with age. Each had an accompanying wall plaque explaining the time period they had originated from, information about the victim, and the circumstances surrounding their taking. Some were even dated back to the Beaver Wars of the 16th century although most originated from the French and Indian War and the American War for Independence. There were hundreds.

Stanton shook her head. "I still can't believe how many there are."

"With the addition of Thomas Boyd's scalp the count comes to three hundred and thirty three."

The two walked to the front of the rock walled chamber where a stone table and a large hand-carved chair sat. The chair reminded her of an emperor's throne, perfect for a man whose ego led him to name himself after one of the most brutal dictator's in all of history. She even took notice that the same snake design pattern, most prominent in his office, had carried over into his seat.

Nero motioned to the corner of the room, allowing Stanton to proceed in front of him. Stanton flinched and her eyes widened. A life-sized silver bust of a ferocious looking Iroquois warrior-shaman mounted on a column sat under a recessed yellow spotlight. The sculpture's hair was formed of long silver snakes reflecting brightly under the display light. And jutting out of the snake-infested head ornament was a set of buck's antlers and eagle feathers.

"Do you know who this is?" asked Nero in a scratchy voice. He stood by Stanton's side.

Stanton brushed her fingers along her chin and thought for a moment. "I would have to say, based on the snakes in his hair and the headpiece depicting an important chief that this might be Atotarho, the ancient leader of the Onondaga. Am I right?"

"You know your history well," smiled Nero, admiring the piece. "It is a representation of my blood descendant, the Onondaga shaman Atotarho.

The sculptor finished it and installed it just last week in the middle of the night."

"It's beautiful."

Nero replied, "Priced at a few million, it should be." He then walked over to his throne chair and sat down. "Truly an amazing display of noble savagery wouldn't you say?"

"*That*, is an accurate description," replied Stanton, still standing in front of Atotarho's bust. She reached out and lightly stroked the snakes.

Nero watched the young woman touch the piece, then spoke. "On his head he wore an elaborate crown of silver serpents. Some think the crown was merely an allegory – a symbol of his wisdom and power. I happen to think his crown actually existed."

Stanton's jaw dropped. She turned and looked at her boss.

"That crown, Miss Stanton," he pointed, "is what we're after. And I've concluded it's hidden somewhere under the Seneca Army Depot. Thus my pending purchase of the property."

"Holy–"

"Of course I expect you to keep this information confidential."

"Absolutely sir. You think this crown really exists?"

"I do. And you're going to find it for me. If it's the last thing I see on this earth. I'll see you tomorrow bright and early. We'll talk more then." He ushered her away.

A weak-kneed Stanton composed herself and made for the door. All she could utter was a simple, "Yes sir."

11

Same time. Tonawanda Reservation.

LIZZIE ASKED JOE to make some tea as she knew her throat would irritate her once she began telling the story. As Joe heated water in her kitchen, Lizzie closed her eyes and relaxed her body before beginning.

With eyes still shut, she started. "What I am about to reveal to you are deeply held secrets. You are under privilege from me as the elder Faithkeeper. I'm giving you this information for you to act on only because it was you who has been approached. Now, I shall begin."

Jake rolled his eyes.

"Atotarho's Crown of Serpents involves the birth story of the Haudenosaunee Confederacy — the beginning of true democracy in the year 1142 A.D."

"So you believe 1142?" already interrupted Jake. "Most scholars believe The Great Law of Peace was established between 1450 and 1500, not 300 years previous."

Lizzie's eyes shot open and she snapped at him. "And most modern-day scholars believed Christopher Columbus was the first to discover America in 1492! But keepers of our oral history have known it was the Norse Vikings who visited here first. And that was in the 1100's! Next came Irish monks, Celtic Druids, Scottish traders, and Basque fishermen. This was hundreds of years before the brand name explorers claimed our land for their kings and queens. Bet you never heard that version before!"

Jake's eyebrows rose at her feisty reaction. "Point taken."

She wasn't finished. "Young man, our oral history is more accurate than any American textbook could ever explain. Example, the academics like to say the Iroquois were peaceful once the five nations united. A crock! They were only peaceful to their sister tribes within the Confederacy. All others who disagreed with them were butchered or taken as slaves. What do you think happened to the Huron and the Algonquin? How about the Erie and the Mahican? All killed by the war mongering Iroquois as they expanded their empire under the Great Law of Peace. So, don't kid yourself boy."

Joe chuckled from the kitchen. "Oh Jake, now you've really set her off. Lizzie, your tea is coming right up."

She continued, quieter. "The time before the five nations united was a troubled time of blood revenge between tribes. An eye-for-an-eye. Our people considered it normal to kill those who had killed our loved ones. When an offender was taken captive he was tortured slowly while being burned at the stake. This was the common practice in order for the tribe to absorb that person's spirit — and in turn end the mourning inside the clan. This cycle of violence had no end. Terror and oppression ruled the lands. Cannibalistic rituals and atrocities against one another were our early forms of religion. And in this period of chaos emerged the most terrifying and powerful of all the dictators — the wizard Atotarho of the Onondaga Nation."

Joe arrived with a cup of tea and set it on the reading table next to Lizzie. He plunked down in a chair across from Jake.

Lizzie reached for her tea. "He ruled with a brutal war hammer and quick tomahawk. He controlled the pre-confederacy tribes of the Seneca, Cayuga, Oneida, and Mohawk. His territory stretched across New York State's present day borders but was centered near Syracuse."

"Wait, I thought he was a renowned charismatic leader, a courageous man and a heroic warrior," stated Jake with a wave of his hand.

Joe piped in. "He was to his own Onondaga people. They turned him into a superhuman figure — kind of like a George Washington — but that was only *after* he allowed his nation to join the Confederacy. We're still talking about the years *before* the unification — the time when we were killing our fellow neighbors. The truth was Atotarho was a tyrannical Saddam Hussein to his own people. Those who challenged him were executed or simply disappeared. But most of all though, he brutalized our Seneca ancestors."

Lizzie interjected. "Your Cornell University education taught you the sanitized, don't-hurt-my-feelings version of our history. That's what I'm hearing from you, young Jake. Truth is, Atotarho had oppressed our people and our neighbors, the Cayuga, for so long that no one would stand up to him." She leaned forward, pointed her finger in Jake's face, and spoke in a low, dry voice. "But his true power came from that crown. The snakes weren't just a saying, but part of an actual ancient relic that he possessed."

Jake pulled back, not sure he believed her. As a youth he had learned the general history of his ancestry, but he was more interested in trying to get off the reservation rather than wholeheartedly embracing Iroquois beliefs and culture.

Lizzie coughed aloud. She urged Joe to explain where the crown came from. Her little pet Chihuahua tap-danced over and jumped back up on her lap.

Joe turned to his nephew. "The Faithkeepers tell us that a young Atotarho went on a rite of passage journey with his top Onondaga war captains to seek out a fabled empire inland past the Western Door of Seneca lands. They followed the Ohio River west until they came to the Great Mississippi. Thereabouts, they made contact with the most sophisticated society of prehistoric North America. We know them today as the Cahokia Mound Builders."

"I've read of them," nodded Jake. "Archeologists have discovered over 100 of their burial mounds. Their ancient city had tens of thousands of inhabitants before it was mysteriously abandoned."

Joe nodded. "This was a peaceful, spiritual nation — at one with earth — farmers, not warmongers. As visitors, Atotarho and his war party were invited into the city. But Atotarho saw this invitation as a stepping-stone to gain personal prominence. One day he observed the tribe's eldest clan mother or queen in a secret dream ceremony. She wore a silver crown molded with snakes. This crown was all-powerful. It allowed her to maintain mental control over her people and to heal them with supernatural forces."

Lizzie cut in. "This crown was said to have originated from an even older civilization native to the American southwest, from what the Faithkeepers could determine from the story. The serpents were a universal symbol of wisdom and knowledge, not just of evil. They had dual meaning but it depended on the wearer's intentions."

"Okay," said Jake, in a tone marking that he still wasn't convinced.

"And Atotarho wanted it," said Joe.

Jake grunted. "Of course."

Joe ignored him. "He wanted to wield its power, to take it back home and conquer the blood-thirsty tribes threatening his Onondaga people. In a fit of greed he slit the great queen's throat as she slept and stole the crown, then he and his war party slipped away."

"Not so courageous was he?" asked Lizzie, rubbing her pet dog behind its ears.

Jake played along with their story. "No, sounds like a true coward. But then again it depends on who is writing history." He didn't dare look at Lizzie.

Joe shifted in his seat. "The Mound Builders went into decline after the theft of their most sacred relic. By 1400 the civilization was gone. Their history was over."

Lizzie took over. "When Atotarho returned to Onondaga territory he brought with him a fearsome reputation. Of those in his war party who made it back, only his closest friends survived. The elder chiefs had mysteriously died along the journey home — at the hands of Atotarho it is said. Thereafter, he took immediate control of the tribe using the powers of the crown to perfection. He turned into an evil sorcerer, a wizard, because of the things he could do with the silver snakes on his head. All opposition to him in the Onondaga tribe withered away. He then set about to conquer the neighboring nations."

"How did this crown let him do it? How did it work?" asked Jake, a bit interested now.

Joe was about to answer when Lizzie held up her hand to silence him. In a raspy voice, she explained. "It gave him the magical power to read your mind and interpret your dreams when you slept. First he would knock you unconscious with a powerful blast to your mind, then in your incoherent state he would pull the thoughts out of your head. This technique was used not only for the extraordinary medicinal and healing purposes —" She paused then coughed hoarsely before going on. "But also to enslave your living spirit to use as he saw fit. And then after you entered the world beyond the sunset — death — he could still conjure up your spirit when he wanted to." Lizzie gurgled in her throat and could not speak any further.

Jake seemed a bit confused at her explanation.

Joe looked into Lizzie's teacup to check on a refill then picked up where she had left off. "This mind mapping, I call it, only worked when the subject was in sleep paralysis. With the crown on, it was said that Atotarho would then press his hands upon your head and go into a deep clairvoyant state where he would pull out and interpret your exposed subconscious inner thoughts and dreams."

"Sort of like a medium," offered Jake.

Joe angled his head. "Sort of. These thoughts are the things that make up the core of a person, exposing the spirits that reside in your body and determining what those spirits want the most. By knowing your soul's desire Atotarho had the power to fulfill or take away those desires. It acted as food for the mind. Once he tapped in, he could control your supply and demand."

Jake stared straight ahead, lost in a past action — Afghanistan. Some spirit definitely tapped into him when he did what he did.

Joe lifted his big frame off the chair and scooped up Lizzie's empty teacup. He started toward the kitchen but instead turned back to his nephew and lightly smacked him on the shoulder. Jake jumped.

"Jake, it's based on our traditionalist beliefs that all natural forces contain immortal spirits. It's why we worship the sun, moon, stars, trees, animals, and fire. It's why we believe in a life beyond the sunset. It's classic orenda, a person's unique aura or charisma about them. Possessing more orenda turns you into a great leader or warrior, versus otkon, the evil energy or bad thoughts. A normal human being always wants to find and keep orenda and expel otkon. Atotarho instead, reversed it. He tapped into the evil and used it for his own means. You get it?"

Jake tipped his head. Joe turned and walked in the kitchen for the tea refill. There was silence among the three. When he returned, he sat down on the couch next to his nephew and continued with the story. Lizzie gulped her fresh tea, seemingly relieved.

"Atotarho always wore the crown," explained Joe. "It became his identity. The crown was said to have had hideous twisted snakes made of pure silver and painted to look real. He let his hair intertwine with the snakes for added effect and even added buck's antlers and eagle feathers to pronounce his monarchy."

Lizzie grunted in a hoarse voice. "It was a silver crown of power, once used for healing and wisdom, but turned into an evil vessel of hatred and deceit."

"And as his power grew, his spirit became embedded in the crown. The crown then transformed his body as a result," added Joe. "His own hair turned silver and seemed to literally mesh with the snakes. He became grotesque looking, misshapen, his face disfigured. Now can you see how otkon took hold of him, how the myth and the truth merged as legend?"

Jake was sufficiently mesmerized. "Okay, you've captured my attention. There's a lot to digest here, but how does this crown fit in with the White Deer Society and the symbols on the broach that I found today."

Lizzie arched an eyebrow. "Remember this Jake, you did not find the broach. It was never lost. It was simply revealed to you at the right time."

"Yes ma'am."

"Good," replied a satisfied Lizzie. "The White Deer Society formed in the time when the three great founders of the Iroquois Confederacy emerged — Deganawida, Hiawatha and Jecumseh. It starts when Atotarho murdered the family of Seneca chief Hiawatha — his wife and seven daughters — over a hunting ground dispute. Afterward, Hiawatha went into depression and lived a hermit's life in the forest."

"Some say he lived near the present day Irondequoit Bay up near Rochester," stated Joe.

Jake agreed, familiar with the creation story of the Confederacy. But as Lizzie started up again he checked his watch then cut her off to save time. "And a Huron named Deganawida crossed Lake Ontario in a white stone canoe, met Hiawatha and pulled him out of depression. They came up with the concept of a unified democratic confederacy of peace to stop the cycle of violence. They were joined by Seneca Clan Mother Jecumseh, and the three of them traveled to the other tribes to convince them to band together."

"Well, it all worked out great," picked up Joe. "They had the approval of the four nations under Atotarho's rule. They needed one more to form the confederacy, his — the Onondaga. When they approached Atotarho and his nation with the idea, he wouldn't have any of it."

"Of course," said Jake.

Joe agreed. "But Atotarho was facing a coalition who now surrounded him and the pressure to join was intense."

Jake knew the tale. "And this is when Hiawatha persuaded Atotarho to join him — by singing a calming song and acting like a psychiatrist to comb out the evil serpent thoughts from his hair. I've always been amazed he could forgive the murderer of his entire family to join his cause."

"Wrong!" spouted Lizzie. Her pet dog twitched. "He never forgave him! The truth is they hatched a plot to steal his crown to make him capitulate power — to force his nation to join. And they did it! They drugged Atotarho and stole the crown when he slept. Ironic, isn't it?" Lizzie gave a disturbed cackle.

"That's when the White Deer Society was formed," prompted Joe. "The three founders escaped back to Seneca territory in the area where the sacred white deer lived. They secretly hid the crown deep underground in a cave network that follows a subterranean river. Our ancestors knew every inch of the aboriginal territory and knew of every entrance to this underworld. They knew where to hide the relic and once it was concealed the society was formed to guard against a resurgence of Atotarho's otkon power so it never returned to the surface again. They extracted silver from the crown and created a series of jewels or broaches with the guardian's mark. Thus, the symbol of the white buck — the good — eating the snake — the evil, was born. Conversely, it could also be a symbol for the purity of the white buck encasing wisdom — thus a vessel of the good or orenda."

Lizzie grunted then quietly spoke. "The White Deer guardians were the most ancient and secretive of all the false-face societies. And true to the maternal tradition of our people, Jecumseh was appointed leader of the guardians. Clan mothers chose those who got in just as they elected who would be chief of their nations." Her voice started giving out. She looked exhausted.

"It's even more ironic if you ask me, that the most ancient of fraternities, the Freemasons, have unwittingly kept this secret hidden for the most ancient of Iroquois societies," said Joe.

Jake glanced at him. "Yeah, go figure. So, this Crown of Serpents is hidden underground somewhere in Seneca County, somewhere between Seneca and Cayuga Lakes?" He shifted in his seat. "And the broach I came across, err, I mean that was revealed to me early this morning, was of the White Deer Society's mark?"

"Exactly," said Lizzie. "There are many jewels out there. Lost. Thomas Boyd came across one and was deemed unfit to bear the burden. He met his cruel fate at the hands of our forefathers. And then today this hunter Blaylock came across one and he too was unworthy."

Joe nodded. "And also met his fate."

Jake glanced at Joe and Lizzie then cracked a nervous smile. "I held the broach. I touched it. Let's hope I don't meet the same fate too."

"If your mind has pure intentions and filled with orenda then you are safe," Lizzie answered. "Like Luke Swetland."

Jake looked down at the floor in silence. After a sigh he asked. "So when Atotarho found out his crown was stolen, what happened next?"

"He lost his power. The three founders made him beg for mercy," answered Joe. "They exorcized the demons from his mind. He fell apart. Broke down. Gave in. The Onondaga Nation finally joined the Haudenosaunee Confederacy or League of Five Nations, under Deganawida's Great Law of Peace. This is why the three figures are held in such high honor as the founding figures of our confederacy. They stood up to the evil against all odds. During the exorcism it was said that Atotarho confronted the spirits of all his victims and he was a changed man. An army of lost souls descended upon him, and he had seen the light and orenda once again. He was made a figurehead of penitence, unity, and acceptance. That's when the honorable attributes were placed on him, only *after* he lost his power and reformed."

Lizzie chimed in. "In Deganawida's address to the Five Nations, he said these exact words, *So now we have put this evil from the earth. Verily, we have cast it deep down into the earth.*" Her voice strengthened and became crisp. "*So, I Deganawida, and the Confederate lords now uproot the tallest pine tree and into the hole we cast all weapons of war.* You see, all the clues have been there, they always were. It's just that history warped the story so that the mainstream would accept it. But we Faithkeepers know the real truth. We have kept it guarded for centuries. And now you know the truth."

Jake exhaled loudly and blinked his eyes. Lizzie and Joe's whole story closely paralleled the mythical creationist version but theirs was definitely more convincing, more true to human nature. He wasn't sure what to think now. He stood up and started pacing, his hand on his chin in thought.

"Who runs the White Deer Society now? Are there present day guardians?"

Lizzie and Joe looked at each other. She sat back in her chair and in a quiet voice explained that the society withered away when the Americans came through in 1779 and destroyed all remnants of the guardians and the knowledge of the entrances to the cave network.

Jake could attest to that fact just by reading Boyd's journal entries on how the Continental troops looted, burned, and desecrated villages and sacred grave sites, destroying with them any possible evidence of the White Deer Society. The winter of 1779 and the starvation and diseases that followed wiped out the rest, most likely including Swetland's adopted grandmother who was probably a guardian. Jake's pacing stopped.

He realized the gravesite and the fissure in the Cranberry Marsh had survived that destruction most likely due to its remote uninhabitable location in the middle of a swamp. It went unnoticed for over two-centuries. Just as Boyd's journal had remained hidden. And now they have both been revealed and a connection made.

Was there a cave entrance at the bottom of Blaylock's pit? And what of

Boyd's reference to Luke Swetland's cave and the secret directions leading to it? Jake now realized why Lizzie and Joe were so upset that the cave system might be discovered. He was surprised to find himself getting all worked up too.

"Alright, tell me about Alex Nero," said Jake. "Why does he want the Crown of Serpents?"

Same time. Cranberry Marsh.

AFTER CAREFULLY PICKING his way through the dark marsh with nothing more to guide him than a mini-flashlight and a GPS receiver, the heavy-set man finally arrived at the dry island where the Indian grave was located.

Stepping up into weed-infested grass, his leather boot slipped on a root. He fell forward to his knees, dropping the metal gas can and small dead dog he had lugged in. Cursing, he picked himself back up and examined his hands. To his relief, the latex gloves he had on to protect against fingerprints had not been ripped.

Snatching the gas can, he inadvertently sloshed some of the liquid onto his dark coat causing him to issue another expletive. He then grabbed the white-furred, West Highland terrier by the nape of its strangled neck and flung it over his shoulder. Stepping up onto the island, he scanned with his flashlight until he found the grave mound.

Clenching the flashlight between his teeth, the man unzipped a side pocket of his coat and took out a short length of rope. After checking the wind direction, he searched for a suitable tree limb and found an old oak at the island's edge. Letting the dog drop on the ground, he flipped the standing end of the rope over the branch. He then tied an overhand knot around the dog's hind legs, pulled tight, and raised the dead animal up about five feet off the ground. He knotted the running end of the rope around the trunk to secure the dog in position. Placing the flashlight upright in the weeds for illumination, he reached into another pocket and pulled out a red-capped spray paint can. Popping the top off and flinging it in the grass, he gave the can a couple of shakes and proceeded to spray paint the dog's shiny white fur with red spots.

Admiring his clever handiwork the big man grinned, revealing yellow, smoke-stained teeth. To include the dog would send the right message to keep the authorities off his tail. He threw the expended spray can off into the swamp when he was done. Glancing back at the dog's face — its clouded eyes bulging out of their sockets, its faded pink tongue hanging out of its snout — he was reminded of how quickly he had dispatched the animal, how easy it was to squeeze its poor little neck and watch the color fade from its eyes.

He had always found that moment, when life froze at the point of no return, rather exhilarating. Especially in his line of work. But in a rare show of sympathy, the man wondered how the dog breeder, from whose run he snatched the animal, would react to the sight of his cute little pet now. It was collateral he coldly concluded — a sacrifice that had to be made now that the Indian grave was discovered. It had to be done to send the right message that his people would fight back.

Walking over to the Indian grave, he positioned his flashlight in the crook of a nearby sapling so the beam struck the mound opening just enough for him to conduct his final business. The man hefted the gas can and poured most of the contents over the skeletal remains inside. He scattered more fuel on top of the mound, saving just enough to leave a trail back to the edge of the island.

Grabbing his flashlight, he backpedaled and poured out the rest of the gas before tossing the container off into the marsh. He peeled off his latex gloves, dropped them onto the gas trail, and lit the gas with a cheap convenience store lighter. At the first flicker of ignition he turned and entered the swamp at a hurried pace, tossing the lighter in the water.

Five seconds later a loud whoosh ripped through the air.

The concussion knocked him forward into a tree, slamming his elbow and ripping off a small piece of his gas-stained jacket. A bright glow lit up the woods. He never felt the pain in his elbow, never noticed the rip in his coat, and never turned back. In a few minutes he reached Marsh Road.

The exhausted man gave a glance around for any movement or approaching vehicles. He walked to his truck, concealed in the brush, jumped in, and started it. As he inched out onto the dirt road — headlights off — he finally looked over to the barely visible light filtering between the marsh trees. He smiled, reached for a cigarette, punched his headlights on, and pressed the accelerator.

MICHAEL KARPOVAGE

13

Same time. Tonawanda Reservation.

L IZZIE JUMPED AT the chance to speak of Nero. "Alex Nero has been a man possessed with an insatiable appetite for all things illicit — smuggling, bribery, extortion, theft — and because of this he naturally found his voice in the business of gambling. The wealth he has generated has given him the power to turn his very sadistic cravings into reality and he will stop at nothing to keep his needs alive."

"Wow, that's one hell of an endorsement," said Jake with a sly grin.

Joe cleared his throat. "He has so perverted the Haudenosaunee with his casino in the Catskills that a cultural civil war has resulted and traditionalists, like our Tonawanda Band, are stuck on the losing end."

"High Point, right?" asked Jake.

"Correct," answered Joe. "Sits on top of a mountain. It's his personal fortress and playground. His thugs run the place. He rules like a dictator, according to our inside people who are employed there. He is a racist manipulator who loves gambling and stealing people's hard-earned money. When he was Chief of the Onondaga and was persuading the tribe to turn their government into his company-run conglomerate, he promised to give back to those members who were less fortunate, but he merely gives out crumbs. Just drive through the Onondaga Nation today south of Syracuse and you'll see what I mean."

Jake was getting fidgety. "Alright, listen I know you two don't like Nero or his business of gambling. I just want to know why he really wants this crown?" he asked, trying to get them back on track. "Is he after it just to add to his collection?"

Shifting in her chair, Lizzie spoke up. "He is a direct bloodline descendant of the Onondaga wizard Atotarho. He claims to be the rightful owner of the crown. He's been searching for it for years, as did his late mother, and generations of their Turtle Clan before that."

"How do you guys know all this?"

Joe frowned. "We've been watching him and following him during his rise to power. When he was born his mother announced that he was the direct male descendant of Atotarho. At that time our clan elders took notice of him as a precautionary measure."

"Listen, maybe his mother made the whole Atotarho bloodline thing up as a political ploy," suggested Jake.

Lizzie answered, her voice wavering. "We thought so too but his mother offered clear evidence of direct matrilineal descent that was backed by the other nations. It was undisputed. She and I were once very close and she revealed to me her intentions of finding the crown, but we had a falling out because I predicted her young son would only use the crown to harm people not help them. My predictions came true. Nero is for real. This is why he is such a threat if he gets a hold of it."

"Come on you two," chastised Jake. "Anyone can claim descent. Unless you had a clear DNA match then you have no real evidence."

"Not in the Confederacy!" Lizzie growled, clearly fed up with Jake's attitude. The little dog jumped off her lap and scampered off into the kitchen. "We hold matrilineal evidence to an even higher standard. Family trees recorded over the ages act as our DNA. We saw the Onondaga evidence with our own eyes, so did other nations. Nero is the one."

Jake pursed his lips.

"His evil path started early on," Lizzie continued. "As a young man he led the Onondaga Warrior Society. They smuggled cigarettes, drugs, all kinds of weapons, and even illegal immigrants in from Canada. They worked with the Mohawk Warrior Society in the St. Lawrence River region. The state police finally broke up the gangs and he served many years in prison."

Jake was unimpressed. "I remember all the crap going on in the 80s and 90s between the nations and the state, but I never heard of Nero."

"Well, his real clan name is Alex Tortoaha," instructed Joe. "But in prison his power grew and he started a ruthless Neo-Iroquois gang who beat, stabbed, and raped many other prisoners. It was also rumored that he even ordered the death of a State Trooper although no one could prove it. That's when he took on the name of Nero. He adopted it from the greatest warrior of the Onondaga Nation, a war-captain during the 1600's named Aharihon who was called Nero by his French enemies because of his cruelty in comparison to the brutal Roman emperor Nero."

Jake blurted out. "This bonehead thinks a lot of himself to adopt a name like that."

"He also landed a freakin' business degree behind bars too!" said Joe, disgust marking his face. "A Yale bachelor's degree online. Hah! The American correctional system, it never ceases to amaze me how good the criminals have it."

Lizzie told more. "When he got out he used his mother's influence, appeared to reform himself, and set out to become chief, all the while keeping his thugs ready to use as he saw fit."

"The Onondaga clan mothers then elected him chief," mentioned Joe. "It's an automatic seat on the Grand Council. That's when we really started getting nervous. We knew his mother convinced him to seek the crown but some of the things he spoke about made us look harder at him. He wanted to declare war on New York State. He was a real rogue. He introduced gambling into the Onondaga tribe against their wishes. He set about suppressing the traditionalists within his own nation, and then consolidated his forces through bribes, evictions, character assassination, and violence. Anyone who disagreed with him or the notion of gambling was punished one way or another."

Lizzie cut in. "His pro-casino forces then voted in a new Onondaga Provisional Council and changed their form of government. The U.S. Bureau of Indian Affairs approved the government change and the mothers turned him into a corporate CEO. That allowed him to pursue the casino deal. At the time, there was a previous lawsuit against the state covering

4,000 acres of ancestral Onondaga lands. It did not claim the lands back but instead wanted the state to clean up major pollutants throughout the area — like the third worst polluted lake in the U.S. — Onondaga Lake near Syracuse."

Joe added. "Then Nero negotiated with the last state governor, another corrupt bastard, and he offered to drop the lawsuit for land in the Catskills suitable for a casino. Nero used a well-intentioned tribal lawsuit of environmental cleanup and twisted it into a gambling racket for himself. He now sucks most of his money from New York City folk. His personal wealth has skyrocketed."

"And the pockets of his backers bulged in return, including some of the most powerful state and federal lawmakers who granted him the deal," said Lizzie.

"Then he started that sham museum, the Haudenosaunee Collection, with his tainted wealth," said Joe, folding his thick arms across his chest and resting them on his belly. "He claims to be collecting artifacts for the good of our confederacy but his real goal is to find any clue that will lead him to that crown. His collection is somewhere deep within his mountain. He only lets high-rollers in to show it off. We've made several requests for a viewing but have been turned down every time."

Jake rubbed the bridge of his nose. "I don't know—"

Joe grew louder. "Jake, if he finds the crown then the combination of his ruthlessness, his political power, and his wealth will sow chaos and destruction for all of us. He's already a raving megalomaniac who has divided our confederacy and seeks to reunite it under him. Especially now that he is Head Chief of the Grand Council. Giving him a legendary vessel of untold powers will turn him into a genocidal madman. This is why the crown must remain hidden. This is why I got so nervous and had to tell Lizzie."

"There is a prophecy that we fear the most," Lizzie quietly announced. "That an evil will resurface once again and destroy our lands, and all that reside on them. This is an evil that corrupts, that does not show mercy on any physical human being, be it a child or an elder. The discoveries that have revealed themselves to you today and the fact that Atotarho's spirit lives in Alex Nero is evidence that this evil no longer lies dormant." She looked into Jake's brown eyes. "The crown has awakened and seeks its master. It calls Nero. He now has the keys to unlock its whereabouts. And you were chosen to stop him!"

Jake stood up, shaking his head. "Me? What are you talking about? I'm not involved in any of this!" He glared down at his uncle and the old witch. Were they drinking something funny in their tea? The notion that all of a sudden, as of today, Jake Tununda was supposed to stop the elected head of the Iroquois Confederacy from finding some ancient evil crown he never even knew existed, was absurd. And besides, the events of today happened by sheer luck.

Or did they?

As if Lizzie was reading his mind, she also rose from her chair and grabbed his wrists with her frail hands. "Don't you realize that you are at the center of all this. You must start now where the lost White Deer Society left off. You must now be *our* guardian, for those of us who are too weak to fight back. It's up to you."

Jake removed her hands. She plunked back down on the rocking chair with a sigh.

Joe pressed the issue, holding his palms out for acceptance. "Listen to me Jake and let me finish, please. I've never steered you wrong in life and you know that. Okay?"

"Okay."

"We know Luke Swetland discovered one of the cave entrances when he was adopted into the tribe after being taken prisoner. Even Boyd wrote down that he saw the cave himself. A map was even made of it. It exists. But where the exact location is, we don't know. We do know it's within a ten-minute walk from Kendaia near a sacred burial area. We do know Boyd's cipher in his journal contains directions to it? And it's stashed in his buried keg along with the cave map. And the other cipher code leads to where that keg is. Which is hidden in his partner's trusted tool, whatever that is."

Jake found himself nodding, following along with his uncle's thinking.

Joe went on. "So, it's clear that finding this *trade* tool and the missing piece of the code, and then breaking the code is a must if we are then able to find the buried keg, the other half of the cave location code, the map, and then hopefully go down underground and secure the crown!"

"Right," said Jake. It was the same adventurous spark he had proposed to Ashland earlier in the day, albeit without a crown involved. And Lizzie had even given him a good lead that the cipher had its origins with the Freemasons. But to go further and find the cave and be some sort of guardian isn't what he expected. He just wanted the buried keg and its contents for MHI. Nothing more.

Joe stood up out of his chair, face-to-face with Jake. "Putting all that aside, the immediate thing we can do is go back to the Cranberry Marsh well. There was a guardian buried there. There must be some kind of link to the cave system underneath, so the marsh hole needs to be explored further if anything, even if we cannot find all the other pieces of the puzzle that lead to the Kendaia cave entrance. I would guess there's a tunnel behind those rocks you mentioned. If there is, then it must be secured, concealed, collapsed. Whatever it takes to keep someone out of there."

Jake shook his head. "The proper Haudenosaunee Burial Rules and Regulations committee should excavate that site. Not me. I'm not going into any more caves and I'm not the long lost savior of the White Deer Society. The committee can take care of everything. I'm just interested in the buried keg contents for historical purposes."

"Guess who just got elected chairman of that committee?" whispered Lizzie. "Alex Nero. If he gets hold of the crown he will have the power to talk to the spirits, and if that happens then untold evil will encompass all of us."

"I'll go back in there with you Jake," pleaded his uncle. "Let's do this together."

There was a long silence. The drum beats and flute music had long since played itself out. Lizzie stared at the ceiling. Uncle Joe stood facing him. Jake knew his uncle was physically unfit to go into the well but he also didn't want to let him down. Jake remembered how the clan had treated him when he announced he was joining the Army, how they even called him a traitor to his face and Joe was the lone person who stood by his side and defended him. Although the mission did sound incredibly exciting, he made a decision to stick to his guns and serve MHI first.

"I'm sorry. I think you two are wrong about me. This crown business is not my fight. I've done enough fighting in my life. I'm really only interested in the keg and its historical contents for MHI. That I *may* pursue. I haven't made up my mind yet. I've got a meeting in Rochester tomorrow, then I'm going back home to Carlisle to think this whole thing over."

"No, you are wrong!" shouted Lizzie, giving him a sinister stare.

"Jake, you've never been one to give up an important mission to help others, to stop evil," pleaded Joe. "This is a different form of evil. Take this on. It's in your own blood, son."

Jake avoided his gaze. He started gathering his items. "It was good to see you both, but I've got to run. It's late. I'll think about it is all I can say."

Joe stared at him. "Just think about it."

Jake bid them a traditional farewell. "Ascungehhi, may you be guided by Kanikariio," — Until we meet again, may you be guided by the good mind.

"Ascungehhi," replied Lizzie in a low voice. "Sleep well."

Jake paused to raise an eyebrow then bolted out the front door, jumped in his truck, and sped off.

14

THE WHITE-FURRED, ten-point buck turned its head and stared at Jake. Its dark eyes scanned him, pinkish-gray nose sniffing, searching for clues as to who the invader was. The deer raised its tail, lowered its head, and stomped its front foot, his milky white hoof crunching into the leaves. Jake raised an old rifle and aimed the long barrel at the deer's heart. The pull of the trigger felt natural, something he had longed for. The rifle fired with a loud report echoing through the woods. A cloud of gray smoke blew from the barrel, followed by the recoil which he absorbed in his shoulder. But the buck remained standing. The shot had missed. Snorting in defiance, the buck stared at him again, and stomped its hoof. It turned its body to face Jake head on. Jake dropped the rifle and reached down to his waistband, realizing for the first time he was dressed in Indian deerskins. Somehow he knew that he was Red Knife, the great scout warrior from whom the Tununda clan had descended. He pulled out an antique pistol and held it in his right hand, noticing for a moment how exquisite the craftsmanship was — almost a replica of George Washington's pistol. He aimed at the buck's head this time and fired. Another miss! But now the buck made a motion to charge. It leapt towards Jake. But as it landed, it was swallowed up by the earth. Jake ran over to the hole where the deer went in and saw that it slithered with silver and black snakes. He bent down to push the snakes aside with his pistol, but was suddenly attacked as the snakes reared up and wrapped themselves around the pistol barrel and his wrist. Jumping back, he tripped on a root, banged his head on a tree behind him, and hit the ground. The snakes swarmed over him, biting and squeezing as they covered every inch of his body. He rolled over to get them off but blackness enveloped his vision. He screamed but his voice was silent. Snakes covered his head and face. He couldn't fight them off. They dug into his head and tore off his scalp with excruciating pain. His body went limp. And all he remembered was Lizzie Spiritwalker's cackling laughter as he faded away.

Jake awoke facing the red numbers 6:59 A.M. on the night stand clock. His heart pounded. He blinked several times to make sure that he was still alive. He even reached up to make sure his scalp was still attached. Trying to recover from the shock of the dream, he watched the numbers hit the top of the hour.

The phone blared.

His heart skipped a beat. "Son of a bitch!" he yelled. It was his morning wake up call.

He picked up and set down the phone receiver, then flipped onto his back and stared at the ceiling. His chest heaved as he tried to make sense of the dream. He knew for a fact he had never been that close to a white deer before to clearly remember every detail of it. How did I know? The pink of the buck's nose, its dark brown eyes, the pure white fur covering lean muscles, its milky colored hooves as it stomped the leaves. And the weapons he had fired, and the way he was dressed — most definitely from the Revolutionary War period. Was a past spirit present inside of his mind? Did Lizzie cast some sort of spell on him?

After a few minutes of clearing the cobwebs, he logically pieced together the cause of the dream and relaxed. He convinced himself it was just a strange meshing of Boyd's journal entries and his uncle and Lizzie's ravings from yesterday. Now this whole white deer and snake bullshit has infested my head, he thought wearily. He told himself he would have none of it, but he still couldn't help the nagging feeling that he should do something.

Shaking the dream off and switching gears to his upcoming appointment later in the morning, he pulled his naked body out of bed and walked into the bathroom.

He showered, shaved, and pumped out forty push-ups before dressing in his full uniform. Looking in the mirror, he inspected his uniform and was satisfied. He pocketed his vehicle's keys from the dresser table, slung the laptop tote over one shoulder and the travel bag over the other. Finally, he grabbed his cell phone, powered it on and checked the display. He noticed a new e-mail message in the in-box. It was dated from last night.

He checked the message and saw that it was from his boss, the collection manager, to the MHI senior staff of which he had been sent a copy. Dr. Ashland had come down with a fever and was taking the following day off to recuperate. Today. Jake deleted the message, thinking nothing of it. He grabbed his beret and headed for the door.

A hard knock greeted him before he could turn the knob. He flinched then bent down to peer in the security hole to see who it was.

A silver New York State Police badge reflected back at him. He pulled the door open and was surprised to see Investigator Hart standing there, her slanted green eyes cutting through him with intensity. She was dressed for business in a blue blouse, tight black slacks and an open black overcoat revealing her service pistol holstered at her shapely waist. Her reddish-brown hair, now pinned up, accentuated her strong neck and rounded face. He found himself not only wondering what she was doing at his room, but also very intrigued at how great she looked. He soon found out she was anything but thrilled to see him.

"Major Tununda, I need to ask you a few questions before you leave."

"And a good morning to you too, Investigator Hart. Great to see you again. I must say you're looking incredibly sharp."

Rae blinked, but in an instant composed herself and put on her investigator's face. "Major, this isn't a social call. I need to know where you were last night around ten."

"O-kay," replied Jake, stepping back in the room and setting his bags down. He placed his beret on the dresser. "Come on in. You can still call me Jake, just like yesterday. Now would you like to tell me what this is all about?"

Rae walked into the room but blocked the door open with her foot. She pulled a notepad and pen out of her back pocket. "Mr. Tununda, please answer the question if you don't mind."

"Yes ma'am. Ten o'clock? I was at an old witch's house on the Tonawanda Indian Reservation visiting with her and my uncle. That good enough?"

"Their names?"

"Joe Big Bear Tununda and Miss Lizzie Spiritwalker Canohocton," said Jake, frowning.

"Can these two individuals corroborate you were in fact there at that time?" Rae asked, writing down the names.

"Ah, yes they most certainly can. In fact, other people at my uncle's smoke shop saw me too. Now want to tell me what's going on here, please?" Jake wondered how it was that this attractive woman could swing from being so inviting at her station yesterday to being so cold-hearted twenty-four hours later.

"What were you wearing last night when you made your visit?"

"Same clothes I have on now," Jake replied, shaking his head. "Class A Dress Uniform. I had just come from an appointment. You didn't answer my question." He noticed she was checking out his hands.

"Do you have an extra set of clothing in your suitcase?" she asked, taking notes, ignoring his demand.

"Yes, one set of civilian clothes. Same ones I had on when I changed at your station. I brought two sets of clothes, my dress uniform and a civilian outfit of jeans and a shirt. I only planned on one night in Rochester. I'm headed back to Carlisle today. You want to rifle through my personal effects to see for yourself? Feel free." He bent down to unzip his suitcase.

"Won't be necessary. Do you have any other coats?"

"Yes ma'am, my black leather jacket. It's out in my truck. Wanna see that?"

"Won't be necessary," said Rae. "I saw it in there already through the window. Just confirming."

"Now how about you tell me what this is all about."

"Have you done any research on that Indian's broach symbol you took a picture of yesterday?"

Jake's brows drew together. He raised his voice. "What the hell is going on here? You better start elaborating a little more or I'm not going to answer anything."

Rae looked up from her note pad and placed a hand on her hip near her sidearm. "Calm down. I'll let you know after you answer the questions."

"No, I am not going to calm down," he barked. "Why did you ask about the broach? What happened last night at ten? Why are you worried about what I was wearing? I'm not answering a damn thing until you show me some courtesy. And remove your goddamn hand from your weapon. That's totally uncalled for."

To her surprise she complied with his last request, taking her hand away from the holster. She then deliberately took a more innocent approach, letting her good looks soothe his anger. She cocked her head slightly and stared directly into his eyes. It was a technique she had mastered on many occasions.

"Jake, listen," she said in a throaty voice. "Something serious happened last night at that the gravesite in the marsh. Someone got hurt really bad, okay? I've been up all night and this morning trying to establish motivation, and you seemed to have the most interest in the grave and that Indian's broach yesterday. I'm here hoping to clear your name. I just have a few more questions and then I'll explain everything, okay?"

Jake took a breath. "Fine. Okay."

That was easy, she thought with an inward smile. "Now, have you found out anything significant about that broach? You said yesterday you wanted to look into it further. Does that symbol mean anything?"

Jake gazed at her, not saying a word. *Does it mean anything*, he thought. *She's going to think I'm a nut job if I tell her what it means.*

"Ah, well, yes, I did find out a few things."

"And?"

"Well, the symbol is from an ancient esoteric Indian cult that protects against something evil," he said hesitantly.

"Details please."

He sighed. This woman was relentless. He checked his watch. Guess he'd be skipping breakfast. Shifting his body weight he leaned against the wardrobe and faced away from her. He chose his words carefully.

"Well, legend has it that the corpse in the grave was some type of guardian for a powerful relic that is hidden somewhere in that area of Seneca County. Apparently, this cult kept guard over the sacred lands of my people. It had ties to the white deer herd out there now trapped inside the Army depot. I really don't know much more about it other than that. It seemed pretty farfetched to me."

Rae could tell he was holding back. "What was this powerful relic?

"I guess it goes back to the beginnings of my people when they warred amongst themselves. I was told its powers could be used for good or evil but that it had been abused and was deliberately hidden, that's all."

"Did these guardians have enemies who wanted to find it?"

"Everyone has enemies," Jake replied. "I suppose they might have been looking for it. I don't really know to be honest."

"So, I'm interested to know," said Rae, toying with him. "Would *you* like to get hold of this legendary relic? Make a historical discovery for your new job? Impress your peers? After all, it's what you do for a living."

"You're pretty good," Jake lashed back, shaking his head at her provocation. He folded his arms across his chest, then leaned in and faced her in all seriousness. "No, Investigator Hart. I do not have an interest in finding this relic. Don't play games with me. I don't believe in hocus-pocus crap, okay? I know what you're getting at. I left the reservation around ten-thirty last night. Checked into this hotel a little after eleven. Call the front desk. Call my uncle. Call the old witch for all I care. I was nowhere near that marsh!"

"I already checked with the front desk. Eleven was about right. Another question I have for you is that you told me yesterday you had a lecture up here in Rochester at the 98th Division Headquarters, but you never showed. I called and they said you cancelled and rescheduled for this morning. Why did you cancel?"

"Nice try again," he remarked in a condescending tone to his voice. "My boss rescheduled the Rochester appointment right after I got on the Thruway. I did not. You want his name too? It's Doctor Stephen Ashland. He's in charge of the entire collection at MHI. Is that good enough yet?"

"Where did you go if your lecture was cancelled?"

"I was at Old Fort Niagara and met with the executive director there.

I drove from Seneca County all the way to Youngstown yesterday. Write that down in your little notepad. Her name is Marge Hibbard. She can verify that I was there on business. Hell, I even had a bite to eat in a local restaurant there. Want the freakin' receipt as proof? I've got it in my wallet."

"Won't be necessary," said Rae.

Jake wasn't finished. "You want to tell me what the hell is going on now?"

"Okay, fine! You're all cleared," she said holding up her hands to calm him down. "I believe you. I had to be thorough that's all." She let the door shut behind her and entered his room. Putting her notebook and pen in her back pocket, she leaned against the wall and started to tell him of the ordeal last night at the Indian gravesite.

"An arsonist hit the gravesite about ten, poured accelerant all over and lit it up. There's nothing left. It's a total loss. The fire also spread to several trees downwind before the volunteers got in. They had a hell of a time putting it out — middle of the night, middle of the marsh." She paused.

Jake's lips parted. He shook his head in disbelief.

"But there was a fire official seriously injured," Rae said quietly. "I know him well. Name's Ed McMann. He's the county emergency coordinator. The nicest guy you'll ever meet. A tree collapsed on him. He has a severe head injury, multiple broken bones, and second degree burns. If it weren't for his helmet and bunker gear he'd probably be dead. He's still in the ICU at Geneva General."

"Good God," said Jake. "I'm really sorry."

"We are pursuing this as an attempted murder case because when an emergency worker gets injured during arson the law states we can apply the charge."

"Son of a bitch," Jake said slowly. "Who the hell would want to torch the—, I mean, how did— damn, and you thought I was a suspect? Attempted murder?"

"You're cleared. Okay? Can you help me now? Do you have any idea who would do something like this?"

"No, it doesn't make any sense," he answered, running his hand through his short hair. "What about the actual hole? Was that damaged in any way?"

"No, it was untouched. The plywood wasn't even moved," said Rae. "But no one's getting in there ever again. The chief realized it was a safety hazard with all of his guys walking over it and replaced it with a heavy iron plate. Brought it in with the farmer's four-wheel Gator. Then they covered it up with dirt and branches to hide it from curiosity seekers."

Jake was silent. There goes Uncle Joe's chance to check for a cave.

"The whole thing is just odd," said Rae thinking out loud. "Why target the grave so drastically, what's the motivation?"

"That's what I'm wondering too. Why destroy an Indian skeleton? Maybe it's just based on pure hate? Oh, wait hold on. There was one firefighter named Owens — an overweight younger guy with a goatee — he got in my face about the Depot's land being sold to, ah, an Indian. You might want to interview him? Hate motivates people to do stupid things."

"I think I remember him," said Rae, retrieving her notepad and jotting down the lead.

"He was on the rope team who hauled the body up. Ask the fire captain. He called him the jackass of the department."

"Nice memory. But get this, there was one big clue deliberately left behind that might explain the suspect's intention. It was strategically placed upwind so it didn't catch fire. Maybe you can help explain it. I kind of came here seeking your expertise too, ya know." She raised an eyebrow.

"What was it?"

"A dead dog hanging from a tree. Had red spots painted all over it. Got any idea what it means?"

Jake was floored. He knew the meaning. "How was it killed?"

"Strangulation."

"What color fur did it have?"

"White. It was a West Highland white terrier according to the breeder who reported it missing last night. Why?"

He closed his eyes momentarily, trying to think how best to explain the meaning. "It's an ancient Iroquois ritual of thanksgiving when you sacrifice or immolate a white-haired dog on a newly kindled fire. It was an offering for success in war or the battle yet to come. It required that the white dog be strangled to death so as not to ruin its perfection."

"What?" Hart retorted.

Jake nodded. "It's true. The ritual also required the dog be painted with red dots and decorated with many ribbons, feathers, and wampum. And that a pouch of tobacco be burnt along with it. Were there any decorations on it? Any evidence of tobacco?" he asked with a frown.

"No," she answered in a confused look. "Nothing like that. I scoured the whole area. Found a multitude of good evidence." She ticked off her fingers as she named them. "A gas can to carry the fuel in, ripped fabric from clothing, remnants of a latex glove, a lighter, and a spray can complete with a red cap. The arsonist made sure there were no fingerprints but just didn't give a shit about leaving it all behind."

"Seems like an amateur to leave it all behind," speculated Jake.

"Yeah, but they took the care to wear latex gloves. That's not an amateur," countered Rae. "It's this dog message that just doesn't make sense to me. You're saying whoever did this was giving thanks? For what, finding that damn grave? For Derrick Blaylock's death?"

"No, not in that sense," explained Jake. "Not since they destroyed the grave. I'm thinking maybe the message means the arsonist was looking for success in a future battle to come. Maybe sending a warning?" Jake shrugged his shoulders in confusion. "But whoever did this must have been Indian. Couldn't have been that volunteer, well, although he could have done it, not impossible. But you see only Indians can perform the ritual." *Was it Nero?* Jake thought to himself. "Obviously they knew how to do it, but they kind of screwed it all up."

"How so?"

"Well, the dog wasn't decorated properly, no tobacco burned off, and you said the dog itself wasn't destroyed in the fire as is required," he explained. "An amateur had to do this."

"Listen, when you were down in that hole, did you see anything unusual?" asked Rae. "Anything significant that would explain why the guardian's grave was located there? That would maybe give some motivation for this arson?"

"Nothing. It was just an empty, blood and shit-filled pit. Let me ask you this. Did anyone else besides you and I see that silver broach with the symbol on it?"

"Ah, actually yes, quite a few people did that day," nodded Rae. "After you left the station, a News10Now reporter stopped by and I let her photograph the broach for her story. I was returning a favor for some pressure she put on a murder suspect last month. She helped me close that case successfully. So you know, I scratch the media's back as much as I hate them, they scratch mine."

"Hmm—" hummed Jake, thinking. "With the story out and the broach publicized then the arsonist could have been a local or a juvenile or hell, anyone for that matter. But I think very few people actually know what that broach symbol means or what it leads to anyway, if that is the reason why they acted. I mean, I just found out about the legend with the relic last night when I was on the reservation. I showed the picture you let me take to my uncle and a very old clan mother and they gave me the story I just relayed to you."

"Yeah," Rae replied in a tone that implied she was wrapping up the conversation. "But it's someone who takes Indian symbology seriously though, because of the dog message."

"Yep," Jake said. "One thing is for sure though—"

"What's that?"

"Well, they may be amateurs, Indian or not, but they're also willing to take extreme measures to get their message across right away. Just be very careful what you dig into, Rae."

"Whoever did this is going to be one sorry S.O.B. once I finish with them."

Jake nodded and looked at his watch. "Listen, I've really got to check out and get over to the 98th. I can't miss my appointment. If you have any more questions or want to bounce an idea off of me, feel free. You have my contact info." He shouldered his bags.

Rae moved towards the door. Jake followed her into the hallway. "Will do," she said. "And thanks for cooperating. I can come on pretty strong sometimes." She smiled reluctantly and turned toward the exit. "You have a good day and a safe drive home."

"Okay, see you later," said Jake, edging in the opposite direction toward the lobby, but not before admiring her as she walked away. Then he yelled out, "Hey investigator! There's something I need to ask you."

Rae pulled a 180 and headed back in his direction, looking serious. She walked up to him, her hands on her hips.

"I was actually thinking that, umm, even though we've had a rough start I'm still serious about dinner with you sometime?"

A hesitant smile appeared on Rae's face. She said nothing.

"How about tonight? I was going to head back to Pennsylvania but I can stop in at Kendaia to pick you up or meet you somewhere?"

"You certainly are a persistent and bold man." She paused. "Tell you what. Give me a shout on my cell. I have some more business up here in Rochester first and I don't know how long I'll be held up. That's all I can promise."

"Sounds great. Expect a call."

Rae spun around, and walked off.

Same time. High Point Casino and Resort.

"Couldn't pull the recon off," mumbled Ray *The Mouth* Kantiio on the phone line from his Seneca Sunset Motel room.

"Why wasn't I informed earlier?" demanded Alex Nero of his top field operative. He gritted his teeth. Kantiio had been slacking in his performance as of late and was skating on thin ice, even before taking care of the pit boss the other night. He had let his physique go and had developed a problem with staying awake. Not good signs for the role he played in the organization. "This was very important."

"I know. I know," said Kantiio. "I was tired. I drove nonstop to get there but the place was crawling with cops and fire trucks. They had the road blocked off. Besides, the swamp was on fire."

"What? On fire? Who did this?"

"Got me. Newspaper said it was suspicious and they're investigating.

They always say that shit. I drove by there again this morning but still couldn't get in."

"Unbelievable."

"Whaddya want me to do now?"

"I'm sending you down to Pennsylvania today. I want your sticky fingers on an old Revolutionary War rifle. There's something hidden inside of it somewhere. Do not tamper with it, just get it and bring it back here to me. Do *not* screw this one up," said Nero. "You've been warned."

"I understand. Tell me where it's located."

15

JUST A FIVE-MINUTE drive down Route 104 east from the Holiday Inn Express, Jake veered his Tahoe off the exit ramp and turned south on Goodman Street into a residential area. On his right, not a block away, was the entrance to the U.S. Army Reserve 98th Division Headquarters.

Stopping at the unmanned, wide-open main gate, it was obvious that security threats to this important training facility were on the lower end of the spectrum. He drove into the front parking lot and chose a spot next to a forest camouflaged open-back Humvee. Should the security threat level go up though, Jake noticed there were certainly enough precautionary measures to thwart an attack.

Bordering the front of the property was an eight-foot high, black steel security fence that acted as an obvious barrier to the road. Each of the thick fence posts was topped with three razor-sharp prongs to deter any climbing. It was both to decorate and to deter. He also noticed a row of concrete blocks lining the length of main building — a precaution he had seen many times in Iraq and Afghanistan against potential car bombs. Although the main two-story brick building seemed less than imposing, it was the brain trust of individuals inside that mattered the most.

Barely on time for his appointment and his stomach rumbling, Jake grabbed his gadget-filled briefcase, donned his black beret, and double-stepped it to the front doors. Glancing up at the heavily contrasted blue and orange entrance signage, he smiled when the unit's nickname and logo caught his eye. The words *Iroquois Warriors* sat under the division's logo. It displayed an orange-colored silhouette profile of an Indian head complete with five feathers in a top-knot. The feathers signified the original Five Nations of the Iroquois Confederacy. Jake nodded his approval.

Headquartered in Rochester, but having units located throughout New York, New Jersey and New England, the 3,600 Army Reserve soldiers of the 98th were traditionally tasked to train active-duty and reserve soldiers in war fighting skills and battlefield specialties. The 98th's latest contribution was the training they gave to the Iraqi Regular Army and National Guard, thus expediting the return home of U.S. military units guarding the budding Middle Eastern democracy. It was up to Jake Tununda to capture that unit's moment in history.

As an MHI field historian, he was not only slated to assess historical items for the institute's collection, but he was also responsible for preserving and promoting the Army's history — sometimes one soldier at a time. His assignment today was to orally record the unit's after-action theatre reports as part of the institute's Oral History Program. This material was then made available for public access in MHI's general holdings, an invaluable national asset to educators and researchers. With holdings of 285,000 books, 1,000,000 photographs, and archival items exceeding 6.5 million, MHI was considered one of the most prestigious military educational and historical institutes in the world.

Jake kicked the morning off with three interviews of NCOs who had just rotated back home. He then moved onto the assistant division commander for support, a colonel who had served on a secret task force that hunted down and eliminated terrorist leaders in Iraq. Recording the conversation with his hand-held, voice-activated tape recorder, Jake obtained declassified insight into the operational activities of the most lethal task forces in the military.

Jake then concluded his assignment with a twenty-minute talk of his own experiences when deployed with the 10th. He had a classroom full of personnel eager to hear of his own exploits.

Finishing up his speech he used animated hand gestures and walked back and forth in front of his audience to maintain the attention on himself. He concluded with, "...And to sum things up, whatever your future contribution may be, know that we, as U.S. Army soldiers, have played a major role in American history. In a world that has never known sustainable peace, we have shaped this nation into the most advanced and safest nation on earth. From hand-to-hand combat with the American Indian—" He feigned a cough and got a chuckle. "...to modern-day conventional combined arms warfare. From revolutionary war against a monarchy, to a civil war against our brothers. To world wars, guerrilla wars, hot and cold wars, and now to the war on terrorism, we, the warriors of this nation, have confronted America's enemies abroad so that our citizens may sleep peacefully at home. Thank you all. I appreciate your time today."

The classroom of personnel stood up and applauded Major Tununda. Afterward, his government duties done for the day, he was treated to lunch at a local Chinese restaurant and engaged in some catch-up with several men and women he knew from previous tours of duty.

Returning back to the headquarters in the early afternoon with a full belly, Jake thought about calling Investigator Hart as he prepared to head back home to Pennsylvania. Instead, on a whim, he asked the colonel about using a vacant office to conduct some research on the Internet. His intuition told him he ought to do a little investigative inquiry into some of Thomas Boyd's journal contents before he left. Maybe he would find something to help out Uncle Joe and Lizzie, he thought. But an image of Nero pointing the Glock at him appeared in his mind too. Maybe he would find something to get back at that asshole, despite explicit orders from his own boss not to do so.

The colonel allowed him access to an office of a captain who was out sick. He gave him a password to connect to their WIFI Internet account. Soon Jake was staring at a blank Google Search screen, but the problem was he couldn't decide where to start digging. Boyd's missing officer's sword popped into his mind, or maybe he'd work on the Butler letter to Brant? Maybe the box belonged to Brant, he surmised. But that really had no relation to the White Deer Society and Atotarho's lost crown, from what he could reason.

Instead, he decided to focus on the clues that were most relevant to stopping Nero in his tracks. The Freemason's Cipher intrigued him the most for cracking it would reveal the directions to the Kendaia cave — Nero's presumed goal.

In a Google Search window he typed the phrase *Freemason's Cipher* and hit the search button. Thousands of hits came up. He clicked on the first link for a free encyclopedia site and started reading. He learned the Freemason's Cipher simply substituted letters for symbols based on a grid of how the alphabet was presented. It was first used in the early 1700s for secret correspondence. A decoded example key showed the letters and how they were assigned to the grid.

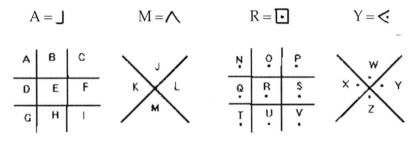

There was the answer staring back at him. It was so easy, too easy. "Utterly ridiculous!" Jake said out loud. One Google Search, one hit, and at his fingertips was the answer to a 230 year-old riddle. He was thrilled but also completely disappointed at the same time. He expected more of a challenge, an investigative research, something. Hell, this was supposed to be a secret code from a secret fraternity. He should have known better, most of the Freemason's inner workings were readily available all over the Internet — information that men once had their lives threatened over if revealed.

And then it occurred to him that if the key to Freemason's Cipher was this easily accessible to the public then surely Nero was already one step ahead of him. With a renewed sense of urgency he opened Adobe Photoshop, the premier image manipulation software on the market, and immediately pulled up Boyd's journal page from September 5, 1779. He scrolled down to the first torn cipher below the reference about Swetland's

Indian cave. It was time Boyd's secret was revealed.

He used the text tool in Photoshop and started cross-referencing the cipher key against Boyd's symbols. He keyed in each letter underneath its corresponding symbol and deciphered the message within minutes.

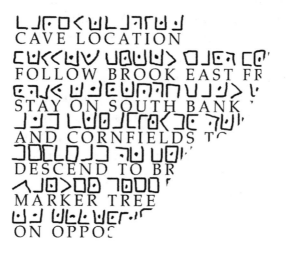

CAVE LOCATION

FOLLOW BROOK EAST FR

STAY ON SOUTH BANK

AND CORNFIELDS T

DESCEND TO BR

MARKER TREE

ON OPPO

He excitedly read the message to himself. He then pulled up Boyd's last journal page and scrolled down to where that page was torn off too — the second fragment. This would be the direction to the buried keg of loot.

KEG LOCATION

EAST FROM KAHAGHSAV

BETWEEN TWO PARALL

UNTIL THEY ALMOST

UNDER THREE L

PLACD EAST W

YOU WILL F

Once decoded, he read this one out loud. "KEG LOCATION... EAST FROM KAHAGHSAW... BETWEEN TWO PARALLE... UNTIL THEY ALMOST... UNDER THREE L... PLACED EAST W... YOU WILL F..." The rest of the message was conveniently referenced by Boyd to be deposited in his most trusted Craft brother's most trusted trade tool. What that tool was, Jake hadn't a clue. But finding it would definitely stop Nero or anyone else from going any further. The White Deer Society's mission would be intact and he could go on with his life.

"Most trusted Craft brother?" Jake asked himself. Easy. The Craft was a short name for Freemasonry and it being a fraternity they referred to themselves as Brothers. Just as he had suspected when he told his boss Ashland, he scrolled back to Boyd's journal and found he had clearly named his Brother in an earlier Thursday, September 2nd excerpt as being *accompanied by my most trusted Sergeant Sean McTavish.* And later at the end of the September 12th excerpt again mentioned *...my most trusted Craft Brother...*

With a clear name of McTavish to go by, Jake entered another Google web search. "18,100 hits! Ah, shit," he said with a sigh. "Wrong approach. Come on, think!"

Refining the search by adding the word sergeant in front of the name, as well as the year 1779, he whittled the hit meter down to 75. Now that's more like it, he told himself.

Sorting through the top web site listings, he found a journal reference from General John Sullivan's land surveyor who accompanied the expedition. Intrigued, Jake read on. The surveyor, Thomas Grant, narrated how on September 14th, a day after the Groveland Ambush where Boyd lost his life, that Sean McTavish had been severely reprimanded by General Sullivan for his and Boyd's direct contradiction of the general's explicit orders. Grant explained how Boyd was specifically told not to take more than four scouts with him, including an Oneida Indian scout, for the September 12th night reconnaissance mission of Little Beard's Town on the Genesee River. Instead, for unknown reasons, Boyd took 26 riflemen.

He was also ordered not to make any contact with the enemy. But he failed in those orders too, ultimately leading to his detachment's demise.

Having noticed four Indians in a deserted village the morning of the 13th, Boyd ordered McTavish to fire on them. McTavish killed one and scalped him, but the others escaped. The detachment gave chase and ran head-on into a 400-man English ambush by Butler's Rangers and Brant's Indians.

Putting up a gallant fight on a high knoll, the outnumbered Americans were eventually overrun, most being slaughtered at close range. McTavish and only three other survivors escaped the massacre after fighting through the enemy lines surrounding them. Boyd was wounded in the side. He and sergeant Michael Parker, along with their Oneida chief Honyost Thaosagwat, were taken prisoner. Honyost was killed instantly. Boyd and Parker were tortured to death the next day. The other survivors, besides McTavish, were listed as a famous Virginian marksman Timothy Murphy, a rifleman from New Hampshire John McDonald, and an unnamed Canadian. Thomas Grant, who had been surveying the swamp area below Conesus Lake at the time, remarked how he had helped the four survivors make it back to the main encampment to raise the general alarm.

Although a colorful battle reference, Jake still hadn't a clue to what exactly McTavish's most trusted trade tool was. Standing up to stretch out, he shed his dress coat and hung it over the chair back. He began his habitual pacing, his bulky arms folded across his chest, his face tense in thought. All thoughts of hooking up with the investigator for dinner were purged from his mind.

The light bulb then went on in his head.

He scolded himself, realizing a wealth of Sullivan-Clinton campaign resources were available to him right through the Military History Institute's main computer database. He bent down and opened a new browser page linking to MHI's web site. After logging onto an authorized staff-use-only section, he tapped into the main database. Sergeant Sean McTavish popped up immediately with two references, one in the 1779 campaign — but an exact match to Grant's description — and the other a Daughters of the American Revolution mention of a McTavish from Upper Exeter, Pennsylvania. The DAR site opened up a short biography of McTavish, written in 1890:

Sean Michael McTavish, of Scottish descent, was from Upper Exeter on the Susquehanna River in the County of Luzerne, Pa., where at the age of 21 he enlisted in January, 1776, as a Private in Captain Stephen Bayard's Company, transferred to Captain Matthew Smith's Company the following November, and January 14, 1778, was made Sergeant in the First Pennsylvania Regiment. Of strong physique, courageous character almost to recklessness, he was endowed with the qualities of a fine marksman which would fit him in the scout detachment he joined under command of Lieutenant Thomas Boyd of nearby Washingtonville, and subsequently under command of Major Parr. He fought under General John Sullivan's brigade at the Battle of Brandywine in September of 1777 where he obtained a new Ferguson style rifle from a British scout he dispatched and scalped. During the Sullivan-Clinton expedition of the summer of 1779, as payback for the Wyoming Valley Massacre the year before, he had been initiated, passed, and raised as a Master Mason under General John Sullivan's traveling Freemason Military Lodge No. 19, thus joining the ranks of gentlemen Patriots of the Craft. McTavish proved a savage warrior during the Battle of Newtown and later up into Iroquois territory. He was known to have taken well over 20 scalps from Indians, Tories and Butler's Rangers. He prayed every night to his most trusted trade tool, widely said to be his Ferguson rifle, as mentioned by the military Freemason brethren who later attended his burial at the Mountain View Cemetery in his hometown.

"The rifle! BINGO!" Jake laughed, his eyes glued to the biography. A grin was now pasted across his face.

After surviving the Groveland Ambush at the end of the campaign, he found the mutilated body of his close friend and commander, Lt. Thomas Boyd, the next day. Grief-stricken with mental illness and demoted in rank for not following orders, McTavish was sent back home to Upper Exeter shortly after the internment of Boyd's body. Having no offspring and never recovering mentally from a state of severe battle distress, he died several years later at the age of 30.

"Damn," Jake whispered, his smile wiped clean, knowing exactly the mental anguish McTavish had experienced on the battlefield.

He looked up and sighed, then deliberately switched his mind back to the trade tool riddle. Finding that one hidden reference jolted him back to exhilaration. It was a military working tool. Shaking his head, he realized he had known the answer all along but just didn't make the connection. After all, he had even referred to the modern assault rifle as a tool of the professional warrior to his own troops in the field.

With that important clue to go on, he now had a jump-start on tracking down where McTavish's rifle might have ended up. It would prove the most challenging part of his investigation, something he now actually looked forward to. He wasted no time.

Knowing that most Continental troops at the time brought their own weapons with them to battle and subsequently returned home with them, Jake figured that's where he'd start searching for the McTavish rifle — his hometown. At about two o'clock in the afternoon, he started making phone inquiries.

The first call he placed was to the Luzerne County Historical Society down in Pennsylvania. He had known them to be an exceptional organization in preserving the history of the Wyoming Valley during colonial times, so he gambled that they might give him a good lead. He explained he was a history researcher with the Army looking into the McTavish Revolutionary War records. An archivist on duty said she too was familiar with the Daughters of the American Revolution reference on McTavish, but could offer no more help other than what Jake had already discovered himself. Just before hanging up though, she mentioned offhand there was a wonderful 97-year-old man named Raymond Gellers who was the Town of Exeter historian and genealogist. He was considered a local expert in matters pertaining to the Revolutionary War. But she said he was very hard to get a hold of. Jake thanked her and wrote his number down.

He immediately tried calling the man but the number rang without any response or follow-up answering service. For the next hour and a half, his attempts proved fruitless. The number just rang and rang. His other research into McTavish's rifle also failed to provide any tangible results. The search for the rifle seemed to hit a hard end before it even got off the ground. Packing up his equipment and feeling a bit dejected, Jake headed out of the building after thanking the commander for his time. Just before starting his truck up, he figured he'd give Gellers one last chance before hitting the road back home. He pulled out his phone and dialed.

"Raymond here," said a crusty old voice on the other end of the line.

Jake sat up. "Mr. Gellers?"

"Yes."

"This is Major R.J. Tununda with the Army Military History Institute out of Carlisle and I'm conducting some research on a Revolutionary War soldier from your hometown."

"Lemme guess, Sean Michael McTavish, right?"

"Yes. How did—?"

"His rifle, right?"

"Yes, but—"

"Can't believe that rifle has generated so much interest lately," said Gellers. "It sat unnoticed for years and all of a sudden, well, have you got something to write with, son?"

"Yep," said Jake, wondering if Nero was already on the same path.

"It's a truly amazing story," Gellers started. "It's a rare custom-made, rapid-fire breech loading rifle designed by a British Major named Patrick Ferguson. Came out in 1776 and was a hit with the British light infantry and marksmen because they were accurate out to 250 yards. You see the rifle could be loaded without a ramrod and then fired. It lessened the chances of blowing their cover. Four to six shots per minute was the rate."

"Sounds like one hell of a breakthrough compared to regular muskets back then," Jake remarked.

"Sure was. McTavish picked up the rifle at Brandywine during a skirmish."

"I'm curious as to what became of his rifle when he came back home," asked Jake, scribbling furiously on his notepad. "Did he bring it back with him?"

"Sure did. It remained in the McTavish family for generations as an heirloom after he died, but during the Great Depression a family member gave it to the bank for partial payment on a debt. It had been stored in a Wilkes-Barre bank vault ever since and was basically all but forgotten, that is until 1996 when the bank's board of trustees bequeathed the rifle to our local library as one of its prized holdings."

"So, can I stop down and inspect it? Say, tomorrow morning? Would you happen to know what time the library opens?"

"Wait a minute there, son. You haven't heard the news?" asked Gellers in a surprised tone of voice.

"No. Heard what?"

"I thought that's what you were calling about. To write an article or something about what just happened. Well, it was stolen today. Matter of fact, just a few hours ago. My son, who's a deputy sheriff, just told me about it."

"What?" Jake stammered. "You're kidding me!"

"Nope. Some young man took it right out from under the nose of the head librarian. He set her up to retrieve a reference item, and then snatched it off the wall mount. It's a very small library you know and she was the only one there. Then he disappeared. She didn't even notice the rifle gone for a full twenty minutes."

"Any idea who took it?" asked Jake in a quiet voice. He thought to himself that everything's lost. That scumbag Nero beat him to it.

"Oh yeah, sure. They got a good description of the suspect and his car. He was driving one of them new sport's cars. Don't know what they're called, but it was on a security camera from the gas station across the street. That's what my son, the sheriff, said. We know his car was from Pennsylvania because the colors on the plates matched. And there's also a partially readable bumper sticker. An A and two Bs, then some other letters we can't make out. He was probably with some antiquities crime ring from Philadelphia, my son thinks. That rifle is worth a lot of money."

"Can I get your son's phone number to get a description of the man and the vehicle?"

"Certainly," said Gellers. "But you know if you wanted to see a picture, he posted it on the police web site already. We don't waste any time down here in dealing with criminals. The web has proven to be a great community crime fighting tool."

"Really? This thief's picture is already posted on web?"

"Yes sir."

After getting the web site address and thanking the historian for all his help, Jake immediately popped open his laptop, fired it up, logged onto the web site and found the crime report. The static security video frame of the car appeared at the top with the suspect getting in.

Jake's jaw dropped open.

"No f-ing way!" The car was a white Mini Cooper with a red stripe down the middle. He knew that car all too well. Behind it, was the suspect, quite visible from the torso up. He was wearing a long overcoat, baseball hat, and sunglasses, but his oversized head and thin mustache gave him away. Jake's heart raced, rage welled deep inside his chest.

The man in the image was undoubtedly his boss, Dr. Steven Ashland.

"That dirty son-of-a-bitch!" And to top off his anger, Jake realized the connection with the bumper sticker of ABB that Gellers had mentioned. It would be a bumper sticker reading ABB2004, short for *Anybody But Bush in 2004*. Jake had questioned him about it not long ago in the parking lot at MHI. It was Ashland's protest against the president way back in the 2004 election, a sticker he had refused to take off even after President George W. Bush had won. And even after Obama's presidential win.

Jake squeezed his fist.

He grabbed his cell phone. Dialing MHI he asked for the director. Luckily, he was in.

"Dr. Jacobson? This is Major Tununda. How are you, sir?"

"Very well Jake. Yourself?" replied the deep commanding voice of the director.

"Fine sir."

A retired Army major general with 30-years of service, Dr. Paul Jacobson was not only the senior executive of the institution, but also an award-winning author of several books on military history. What had turned Jake on to MHI, and what Jacobson was most famous for, was his investigation and discovery of Adolf Hitler's personal gold and diamond studded mahogany cigar humidor.

It was during an MHI oral history interview from a dying U.S. Army WWII vet that Jacobson had learned of the famed humidor. Supposedly looted by an American soldier when his 3rd Infantry unit arrived first at Hitler's Eagles Nest retreat at Berchtesgaden in 1945, the humidor was later smuggled back to the states inside a secret compartment of a Sherman tank.

But it was never recovered.

After several years of intense field research by Jacobson, he finally located the tank outside of a Veterans of Foreign War post in Jonesboro, Georgia. Sure enough, over sixty years later, hidden where the soldier said it was, they found their prize. It was a story that astounded Jake when he first viewed it on the History Channel and caused him to seek out the man responsible for it. Soon a mentorship developed and subsequently a job offer to MHI.

"Jake, I want to tell you how unfortunate it was the way things worked out with the journal they dug up at Fort Niagara. Dr. Ashland told me all about how that sly collector Alex Nero purchased it right after your viewing. That would have been an exquisite acquisition for our collection. In fact, I think it would have topped my discovery of Hitler's humidor a couple of years back."

Jake blinked several times, taken aback. "Sir, I thought MHI would have hit gold had Dr. Ashland listened to me. We had a disagreement and unfortunately had a few choice words exchanged between us."

"Yes, I heard about that. He told you to not pursue this matter."

"But I bet he conveniently left out the rest of the story just before going on sick leave today."

"Oh, really?" asked Jacobson. "There's bitterness in your voice. Please elaborate."

"It looks like our sick Dr. Ashland paid a visit to a local library this afternoon. It's just up the highway from Carlisle — in Upper Exeter along the Susquehanna. Well, he just committed a serious criminal offense. He stole an artifact from the library, a Revolutionary War rifle. And he stole it based on information that I had personally e-mailed to him yesterday afternoon after viewing Boyd's journal. Dr. Ashland has manipulated me, and undermined my trust as well as MHI's trust, and I am asking you for personal advisement on how to proceed with the matter."

"Jake, tell me this isn't true."

"I'm afraid it is. You can see for yourself. Are you at your computer?"

MICHAEL KARPOVAGE

16

Tuesday evening. Route 390 South, near Geneseo, N.Y.

"I EVEN TOLD ASHLAND over the phone that I thought it was Sean McTavish who was Boyd's most trusted brother in the Freemasons," rambled Jake, glaring out the front passenger window of Investigator Rae Hart's sedan. Night had set in as he followed the brightly lit highway reflectors swiftly passing them by.

Rae shook her head, squinted her eyes, and gripped the wheel. When he had finally called her that afternoon she expected to be talking about which restaurant they could meet at back in Seneca County. Instead, the investigator found herself on a completely unexpected twist of events and a new criminal case.

"I gave him the lead to that name," continued Jake. "He has the full September 12th journal page too. I freakin' e-mailed it to him." Jake balled his fist. "It contained the first half of Boyd's directions to his buried war loot. It's where the British paymaster's Guineas are hidden and supposedly another clue leading to a sunken cannon full of gold back in Seneca Lake. That's what he's after." He turned and looked at Rae. She remained silent.

"You see, that torn page fragment has got to be stashed somewhere in McTavish's rifle," Jake pleaded, trying to convince her. "It holds the key to the rest of the directions. I'm sure by now he's already found it and deciphered the rest of the code and is now looking to dig up the loot. He's gonna go for the area between Conesus and Hemlock Lake. Right where Boyd's last encampment was. I know it for sure."

"I tell you what, this whole damn story is getting stranger by the minute," replied Rae, flashing her high beams. A car moved out of the left lane to let her pass. She stepped on the gas, reaching ninety miles an hour. "I wish you told me this buried treasure angle when we met this morning."

"But it had nothing to do with the swamp fire," pleaded Jake. "Besides, Ashland couldn't have pulled that arson off. You've seen his credit card transactions from yesterday and they're all in central Pennsylvania. Hell, he didn't even know I was at that marsh yesterday morning."

Jake noticed a green road sign announcing the upcoming exit of Geneseo a mile ahead. Flicking on the overheard reading light, he pulled his road atlas from his briefcase and laid it across his lap. He opened it to the page they were traveling on. The Geneseo exit off of Interstate 390 south from Rochester told him they still had a good twenty miles to Dansville. A motel called Hogan's Inn in that city, just off the 390, marked Ashland's last credit card transaction. It's where they hoped to corner him and take him into custody.

"This is hard to follow as it is," said Rae. "Any little clue helps piece things together. Gold is certainly a huge motivating factor. I'm just saying don't hold back with any information next time. At least right now he's partially ruled out as a suspect in the swamp fire, that is until I question him."

In explaining to her the Boyd Box assessment story of what led up to Ashland's theft, Jake had deliberately held back the information pertaining to the White Deer Society and Atotarho's supposed crown story. He never lied, he merely didn't offer up those details. He maintained what he told her earlier. It was not relevant, in his opinion, to the theft by his greedy boss. Furthermore, now that Alex Nero and his thugs were clearly not involved in the rifle theft, as he first suspected, he felt the legends should just be kept secret, out of respect to his uncle and Miss Lizzie.

During Jake's call to Dr. Jacobson he presented the same evidence he had given Ashland — even sending the director the same e-mail attachments of the September 12 journal entry and a breakdown of the research he had conducted that afternoon at the 98th's headquarters.

Jacobson immediately questioned why Jake was also trying to find the rifle after he was told that Ashland had ordered him to stand down. He gave the director a clear answer that since Alex Nero did not play by the rules and in fact did not own the content in the journal, that he as a rep of MHI had every right to pursue it. Copyright infringement was bull. He rehashed how Nero and his thugs had tried to manhandle him, pulled weapons on him, and destroyed his digital camera images under threat of death. And now he knew why Ashland had stifled him — he wanted the treasure for himself.

Jacobson expressed shock and anger at what Nero had done to a member of the U.S. Army. After he viewed the police web site of Ashland entering his Mini-Cooper, Jacobson's fury turned into action. He agreed with Jake countermanding Ashland's orders and acknowledged it was what he would have done too and had done on previous occasions when he was a field historian.

Jake had then been given authorization to contact law enforcement and assist them in any way he could in order to apprehend their corrupt employee. Should the cipher fragment evidence turn up in the rifle, Jake was also given the green light to find that keg of war loot and ultimately the sunken cannon of gold. It was now deemed a special MHI mission assigned by the director. Jacobson said its historical significance could not be left buried or, for that matter, sitting at the bottom of a lake. And unlike Ashland, Jacobson wanted to hit Nero back hard. He too was willing to put up a fight, especially since he had his Major in the field as his bulldog.

After their conversation, Jake immediately called Rae Hart but not for dinner plans. Luckily, she was still in the Rochester area. He recruited her to help him pursue Ashland's weapon's theft. Rae was apprehensive at first, stating the theft occurred in the Pennsylvania jurisdiction and the weapon was more of an antiquities theft. Regardless, she did agree to meet him because she could nail Ashland on possession of stolen property. She informed him she was downtown at the City of Rochester Police Headquarters and would await his arrival. She not only wanted to hear his explanation, but also didn't mind seeing him one last time if she could help it.

Rae contacted the Pennsylvania State Police while waiting for Jake to show up, informing them of a solid suspect who matched the theft description. The PSP immediately dispatched a unit with a picture from Ashland's driver's license and confirmed the identity with the librarian. Then, obtaining a search warrant from a local judge, they went to Ashland's residence for the arrest. Nobody was home and no rifle was present. An additional precautionary search warrant was then obtained to put a trace on Ashland's credit card purchases, figuring he was still mobile with the stolen item.

After Jake's arrival and greeting in the front lobby of the Rochester Police Department, Rae escorted him to a conference room for privacy to go over the case. She informed him that she had pulled a national criminal background check on Ashland.

He had a record.

Ashland had been convicted of theft of a rare manuscript in the archives library at a college in Oregon back in 1992, presumably as an undergrad. The material was returned, but he was kicked out of college, and received probation and a fine.

Jake realized the government administrators of MHI, who had presumably conducted the required background check before employing him, either had been lied to or were grossly incompetent. All Jake had known from Ashland's resume was that he had gotten his education at Berkeley in California, where he earned his bachelor and master degrees, and doctorate, if that was even true. The shit was really going to hit the fan at MHI now and it would start with those responsible for vetting Ashland.

Over two cups of coffee, a few stale donuts, and some small talk, Rae filled Jake in on what the authorities were up to. She was awaiting more information as all active leads were being pursued. It wasn't until an early evening phone call from Pennsylvania law enforcement that they scored their major hit.

Ashland's credit card company had faxed his latest transactions to the PA authorities and they in turn called Rae to pick up the trail. About an hour and a half earlier Ashland had purchased a room at a motel in

Dansville, New York, just south of Rochester in the western Finger Lakes region.

According to Rae's estimates, from the initial time of the theft, Ashland had apparently traveled non-stop from the crime scene at Upper Exeter north to his current location. The case then turned into a cross-border weapons theft — a federal crime. Rae said she was in the best position to intercept the suspect and apprehend him before the Federal Bureau of Alcohol, Tobacco, Firearms and Explosives could even get mobilized, let alone take any interest in the antiquities theft. Plus, she didn't want Ashland to slip away. They needed to act fast. Jake decided to leave his SUV at the city police station and would drive with Rae to make the arrest.

"The bastard even took today off as a sick day," grumbled Jake as Rae motored faster to Dansville. "Covered his tracks. His e-mail was sent last night. He had this whole thing planned out. Suckered me good after ordering me to leave it alone. I can't wait until we nail his ass."

Rae glanced at Jake. "Before we do, there are some questions I need to ask you." Jake looked back then shut off the reading light. "Why were you doing this research to find the buried gold? What were you doing looking up McTavish's rifle? And why were you trying to decipher the Freemason's code? Don't bullshit me anymore."

Jake's eyelid twitched. He clammed up, thinking how he could dodge her questioning. She made a good point. He looked to be a part of the theft. Maybe even setting his boss up. "Here we go again. My director asked me the same question right before I contacted you."

"And your answer?"

"After the Boyd journal was purchased by Alex Nero, I immediately called Dr. Ashland to report what had happened."

"Whoa! Hold on there," Rae interrupted. "Alex Nero, the big gambling tycoon here in New York? The Onondaga Indian Nero?"

"Yep, the one and the same."

She slammed the steering wheel. "My daddy was a Trooper you know, killed in the line of duty twelve years ago."

"I'm sorry."

"He pulled over a motorcyclist on Route 81 near Syracuse — the stretch of highway that goes through the Onondaga reservation. As he walked up to the man he was shot once in the head. The bastard was never caught. The investigators said it was a—," she raised both hands off the wheel and made quotation marks in the air, "random act of violence. I happen to think otherwise."

Jake glanced at her. "Otherwise? Meaning Alex Nero had something to do with his death?"

She nodded to Jake. "Yep, I think it was a hit."

"Why order a hit on your father? I don't get it."

"You remember the riots on the Onondaga reservation back in ninety seven?"

"Sure do," said Jake, shaking his head. "Was over the state trying to impose taxes on the tribe. Same crap that's going on now."

"Governor called in the State Police. My daddy busted a lot of heads during the riot. It was chaos he said. And when an elderly woman got in the way he cracked her in the head with his baton too. Well, she turned out to be Nero's mother."

"Oh, I see."

Rae nodded. "She was hospitalized for a long time. Afterward, Nero made some threats against the Troopers while he was still in jail. Needless to say my daddy dies a month later."

"And on Onondaga territory," said Jake.

"Exactly the point. Random act of violence my ass! Then the prick gets out of jail a year later and starts his rise to power. That's when I followed in my daddy's footsteps and became a Trooper myself."

"To put that son-of-a bitch back behind bars, right?" asked Jake.

"Damn right, but never got much of a chance. Did road patrol for three years up in the Adirondacks, then as fate would have it I took down a mutt with an AK-47 at a convenience store and was rewarded with a promotion to the Bureau of Criminal Investigations. That's when I became an investigator. All the while Mr. Nero was building his empire and his criminal network. You know he even had the audacity to donate ten thousand dollars to the State Police one year?"

Jake laughed derisively.

Rae sighed. "We know he's got key politicians and lobbyists in his pocket and some front companies pulling some odd business dealings. We just haven't been able to infiltrate his enterprises to dig up any solid evidence." She then waved a dismissive hand in the air. "Sorry to ramble like that. You already have enough to worry about. Please do go on with your story. This ought to get even more interesting now that Nero's in the picture."

"Wow, okay," said Jake. "Now where did I leave off? Oh, yeah, I proposed to Ashland that since we still had all the clues — we, meaning MHI — we should find the buried loot, which would hopefully lead us to Sullivan's sunken cannon of gold. That it would be a historical bonanza for our institution. Now, just so you know I clearly stated the gold would be the property of the Army. Not me, the Army." He drew a breath.

"Sure."

He looked at her. "No, seriously Rae I am financially secure. It's not my motivation. My passion is to reveal history. Ashland said it was a far-fetched idea and ordered me to *leave it alone.* Said he didn't want to ruffle Nero's feathers. Now I know why. He wants the treasure for himself. That's his MO."

"Yeah, but you went ahead anyway against your own boss's orders and conducted the research, not knowing at that time that he had motivations for it. Why?"

"It's a once in a lifetime opportunity when a historian comes across something like this. It's a hunt for treasure. Plus, I don't like being told no. I wanted to one up both Ashland and Nero at the same time. I felt that whole assessment was shit the way it was pulled out from underneath us. That's why."

"Your ego got bruised, didn't it?" asked Rae, noticing the Exit 4 sign pass them by. "Boys in a sandbox and you got sand in your eye."

"No. A Glock 9 mil is more like it."

Rae glanced at him. "I knew this would get interesting. By who?"

"Your pal and mine — Nero."

"Why'd he pull a piece on you?"

"Because he found out I had digital camera records of all of the journal pages. I was the only one besides him that had seen the entries. He had his thugs track me down right inside Fort Niagara. Blocked my vehicle in, threatened to ruin MHI, threatened to dump me in the river with a concrete block around my neck, and then at gunpoint he erased all of the images from my camera under the pretense of copyright infringement!"

"So Nero is after the treasure too then, is what you're saying?"

"You could say that—"

Rae shifted in her seat. "Dansville exit's coming up. Let's shift gears and focus on apprehending your boss first."

"Yes ma'am."

Late evening. Hogan's Inn, Dansville, N.Y.

"When I take him into custody, we're going to need digital pictures of him and the rifle," explained Rae as she made a left off the exit ramp and headed north on Route 36. "Then once he's held, I can e-mail the pics to the Luzerne County Sheriff and they can contact the librarian for a positive ID confirmation on Ashland and the evidence."

"You act fast," remarked Jake. "Do you need to contact the local cops about this before you move in?"

Rae shook her head. "No, I'm not going to. It's a courtesy if we do but not required. We have jurisdiction over the entire state. This is pretty much open and shut anyway. I don't want to bother them."

The motel was up on her left adjacent to a Citgo service station. She slowly drove her unmarked car past the entrance to size the place up. It was a simple two-story commercial motel structure with rooms on both sides of the building. Exterior concrete stairs led up to outside balconies running the length of the second story. Dimly lit parking lots lined both sides. Several SUVs and sedans sat in the rear lot with a corner exit allowing access to the main road.

Rae proceeded to the front lot where Ashland's Mini-Cooper sat. There were only two other cars present — a Honda Civic and a Nissan Maxima parked outside the office. She pulled in the main entrance and parked next to the Civic, leaving her car idling.

"Stay here," she ordered. "I'll get his room number from the night manager."

Jake nodded and watched her walk inside. She flashed her badge to the middle-aged man at the counter. He nodded and turned to his computer monitor, wrote on a piece of paper, handed it to Rae, then motioned upward. She nodded her thanks and walked back to the car.

Getting back in she said, "Looks like he's on the second floor. Room 21. Faces this parking lot. Been in there for a few hours best the manager can tell. I'm going to swing past his vehicle, verify the plates, then park over there in the dark." She pointed to a spot near the Citgo station's back wall.

Jake nodded.

Sure enough, the ABB2004 bumper sticker was confirmed on Ashland's car. She parked in a non lit area and told Jake to stay put in her vehicle, then exited and popped her trunk. She took off her coat, placed it in the trunk and reached in for her bulletproof vest. Taking just seconds to strap it on, she also scoped out room 21, finding it two doors down from the top of the stairs. She noticed the lights were on and there were shadows moving behind the drawn drapes. She grabbed her coat and threw it on over her vest to conceal it.

Jake appeared at her side just as she finished securing the body armor. Still dressed in uniform, he had pulled on his dress coat and placed his black beret on his head.

"I told you to stay in the vehicle," Rae whispered.

"I insist on being there. I want to see his face when I show up," said Jake.

"No."

"Why the vest?" he asked.

"He's got a rifle doesn't he? It's a precaution."

"Well then, you'll need back up. You be the good cop. I'll put him in his place if he gets out of hand. Come on Rae." He winked at her.

"Alright. But I do all the talking. This isn't a game. Let's go." Momentarily distracted, she shut the trunk harder than she anticipated. Staring up at the room as she led Jake across the lot, she noticed a shadow appear behind the drapes. She whispered to Jake that she had movement in the window. She unsnapped her holster but didn't draw the weapon. She then led the way up the stairs gingerly taking one step at a time, completely calm. Jake shadowed her, following her cue.

Upon reaching the top step, the door to Ashland's room flew open. A hulk of a man jumped out. He had a wide Indian face and demented rolling eyes. He faced them both and waved a tuft of hair dripping with some kind of liquid.

Rae and Jake froze.

The wide-faced man then smiled, revealing two gold front teeth. Rae drew her weapon, a black Glock .45 caliber pistol. The Indian was quicker. He raised his other hand and aimed a long barreled pistol at Rae's chest.

He fired point-blank.

A flash and dull crack came from the man's silenced weapon. Rae took the round in her chest. With a yelp she fell back into Jake, almost knocking him down the stairs. Another blast of air and another round impacted into her, causing her to drop her weapon on the top step.

Jake caught her, grabbed onto the railing, regained his balance, and broke her fall as she slumped unconscious into his arms. With one arm cradling her he looked up at the shooter who had already turned to run down the balcony. A long braided black ponytail with a feather attached to the end swayed from side to side as he sprinted away. On his knees Jake reached for Rae's Glock, leveled it and was just about to pull the trigger when the shooter rounded the corner and disappeared.

"Shit!" He moved to give chase then hesitated and looked down at Rae. Her head was tossed back, mouth wide open. Jake bent down close.

Her breathing had stopped. "Shit. Shit. Shit!"

A check of her pulse. It was good.

He bent over, pinched her nose, and covered her mouth with his. Blowing five quick breaths into her lungs he initiated rescue breathing. "Rae! Rae! Come on. Wake up." He slapped her cheek gently. No response. He wouldn't lose her. He inspected her head. No visible entry holes in the head or neck region. He looked down to her vest. Embedded near the top were two flattened bullet fragments. Good sign. He heard a vehicle start up in the rear parking lot behind the building. It screeched away.

Another pulse check on Rae, still good. But her lungs weren't working. Jake repeated the breathing again, watching her chest rise, filling with air.

Rae flinched. Her lips parted. Her eyes opened and met Jake's. She caught her breath, inhaling. A deep, pain-filled groan followed.

Jake smiled warmly and whispered, "That's it. That's it. You're okay."

With Jake's help, Rae sat up against the railing. She moaned and reached for her chest. "Where is he?"

"Escaped. Just drove away."

She tried rising while fumbling in her vest for something. "Dammit! Portable radio. Forgot it." She then reached for her sidearm but saw it was in Jake's hand. "I'm going in the room," she groaned. "Give me my piece."

"You need help first. You've been shot!"

She winced and rose to her feet. "My piece, now!"

Jake gave up her weapon. She took it and staggered to the open door, arms outstretched with her gun firmly in her grip. The light was still on. She entered the room and gasped, then cursed something a sailor would be proud of. Jake moved in behind her and stood at her side.

The body of a man lay face down near a desk, the head surrounded by a dark stain of blood that had absorbed into the tan carpet.

The entire crown of his head was a bloody mess, his hair missing. A bright red cut line encircled his skull from the top of the forehead to the back of his neck. He had been scalped clean.

Jake blinked. Time seemed frozen. He pictured himself back in Afghanistan in the basement of the prison. He had issued a war whoop when he had finished his deed. He blinked again and snapped himself back to the motel room.

Rae swept the rest of the room, hitting the bathroom, closet, and even under the bed. She announced an *all clear*, holstered her weapon, and bent down to check the man's pulse on his neck.

No beat.

Jake squatted at her side and pointed to the neat hole in the back of the man's skull.

Rae nodded then pulled the shoulder of the body up revealing the victim's face.

"It's Ashland," whispered Jake, blinking several times.

Rae rested the head face down again and inspecting the length of the man's body, finding an item grasped in his hand. "Car keys," she stated, closing her eyes. She then stood up and leaned against the wall in pain. She grunted and rubbed her chest.

Jake was instantly at her side. He took her hand. "You're one tough cop but we need to radio for help."

Her eyes fluttered open and she grimaced. "Thank you Jake, but not just yet."

"But you might have internal wounds."

"No, I'm okay," she said, pulling her hand back from his. "Feels like someone hit me with a sledgehammer, but I can make it." She gave a weak smile, then frowned. "Did you see the shooter? Definitely male. Indian. Big guy. Dark hair. Gold front teeth. Silenced pistol. Wasn't carrying any old rifle as far as I could tell. There's no rifle anywhere in here."

"I didn't see one either," agreed Jake. "That guy was definitely Indian. When he took off I noticed a braided ponytail with a feather. Bet you it was one of Nero's men."

"Probably," said Rae, pulling out a pair of latex evidence-handling gloves from her back pocket. She slipped them on and pried back Ashland's fingers, grabbing the car keys out of his hand. "I'm going back down to get my radio to call this in. And I'm going to search his car for that rifle. You stay up here." She pulled out an extra set of gloves. "Put these on but don't touch a damn thing. I mean it."

"Let me come with you. You need help down those stairs."

"No, stay here. I need you to secure the scene for me. I'll be right back." She went to the door. "Don't touch this door knob either." She walked out, leaving the door open just a crack.

Jake stared at Ashland in disgust. "Glad I wasn't a passenger on your bus ride to excellence you deceptive son-of-a-bitch." He then turned away.

A New York State Atlas & Gazetteer on the desk caught his eye. Several pieces of paper attached to a paper clip stuck out from one of the inside pages. A blue pen sat on top of the large booklet. A roll of clear tape and some loose paper clips lay off to one side.

Jake looked back at the crack in the door, quickly walked over, peered outside and saw Rae leaning inside her vehicle with her car radio transmitter up to her mouth. He turned around and put on the pair of latex gloves she had given him, then hustled back over to the atlas. He opened to the page with the paper-clipped sheets of paper and saw a laser print out of a Ferguson rifle from the Smithsonian Institution — Ashland's apparent research into McTavish's weapon.

He then flipped to the second sheet underneath.

He was not at all surprised to see Boyd's September 12th journal image printed out as a letter sized laser print — obviously from the same e-mail image he had sent Ashland. His lips pressed together. Then he raised his eyebrows. The bottom right ripped corner — where half of the Freemason's cipher code was written — he noticed a small torn piece of aged parchment paper taped in its place. It contained the second half of the lettering in a perfect fit. The buried loot directions were complete! Ashland had found the fragment of the missing paper somewhere in the rifle. This is it. The bastard did it.

Jake flipped to a third sheet of paper and found an MHI letterhead containing the Freemason's cipher code key legend written in black ink. And written under the key in blue ink was the entire deciphered message of where the buried treasure was hidden. The difference in ink color and his institution's letterhead suggested Ashland conducted his research back at the office. The finished message in blue ink, he assumed, was probably done here in his room with the blue pen.

Jake read the deciphered directions and shook his head in astonishment. Sensing he had better hurry up his inspection before Rae came back, he flipped to a fourth and final sheet.

It was another laser duplication, this one of a hand-drawn map showing the area from the south end of Conesus Lake on the right side, to the Genesee River on the left. The title at the top read, *Map Showing the Route of Sullivan's Army and Groveland Ambuscade. September 13th, 1779 With Places of Encampment and Position of Indian Towns in the Vicinity From — Actual Survey By Genl., John S. Clark. Auburn N.Y. 1879.*

Ashland had found an old map re-creation of the day Boyd was ambushed. Circled in blue ink at the south end of Conesus Lake was the Indian village labeled Kanaghsaw. Jake knew this was in reference to the buried loot directions.

There were no more documents. The atlas page that had been bookmarked, page 57, stared back at him. It depicted Livingston County and the area around Conesus Lake. Route 390 stretched from Rochester at the top of the page to Dansville at the bottom. To the east of 390 was Conesus Lake. Ashland had also circled the south end in blue ink. He had found all the clues and was moving in to retrieve the treasure keg.

Jake knew that if he were to stop Nero, he had to confiscate these documents now before Rae took possession of them as evidence, otherwise he'd never see them again. Stepping over to the window, he pulled the drape back and checked where she was. He spotted her inside Ashland's car, a flashlight beam moving about. Good.

He bolted back to the desk and stood looking at the pages. Should he outright steal this evidence? Was it really stealing? Afterall Jake tried to justify, it could be considered MHI research material that I'm merely retrieving. A glance at the murdered Ashland sealed his decision. You only live once. He grabbed all of the pages except the Ferguson Rifle sheet, figuring it would fit Ashland's MO. He folded the sheets carefully and placed them inside his inner coat pocket. He then replaced the atlas as he had found it, even returning the pen to where it sat on top. With a quick exhale, he went back the door and pulled it open, making sure not to grip the knob to contaminate any possible fingerprint evidence the murderer might have left.

Rae stared back at him, expressionless.

Jake jumped back. "Jesus!"

Her head turned to an approaching motel guest. An older lady, dressed in a robe, walked up and asked if everything was all right. She said she had heard a bit of commotion earlier.

"State Police Investigator ma'am." Rae said, flashing her badge. "Everything's okay. Please go back to your room." The lady gave Jake a once over then turned and shuffled back to where she had come from.

Rae motioned Jake inside. He noticed she had taken off her bulletproof vest and unbuttoned her blouse revealing plentiful cleavage. Two purple and red bruises the size of half dollars had spread on her upper chest where the rounds had hit the vest. A few inches higher and she would have taken them in the throat.

Jake stared. "You okay? That doesn't look so hot."

"What do you mean they don't look so hot?" She raised a mischievous eyebrow trying to make light of the situation.

Jake stammered for words.

"Hurts like a son of a bitch," Rae said in a serious tone. "But I'll live — thanks to you."

"Just doing my job ma'am," Jake said with a wink.

"Searched his car," continued Rae. "No sign of the rifle, but he did have lots of digging tools in the trunk. Already called dispatch too and they're rolling emergency back up. This place will be swarming with cops in a minute. Right now I'm going to have to ask you to step outside and hang out in my vehicle. A lot of shit is going down. We're going to be here for hours. I'm giving you a heads up right now that everything has changed now that your boss has been murdered and Alex Nero is potentially involved. This, I believe you say in the army, is called a clusterfuck."

Jake nodded as he left the room. He headed back to her unmarked car, peeled off his latex gloves along the way, and shoved them in his pocket. He sat down inside, his mind spinning at what he had witnessed and how he had confiscated those documents.

Within minutes, a Dansville police cruiser with flashing lights came whipping around the corner and skidded to a stop in the parking lot. A cop jumped out and looked around. Rae waved to him from the second floor walkway. The cop double-stepped it up the stairs. Next came a Livingston County sheriff deputy. He also parked in haste and ran up to the room. Twenty seconds later a volunteer ambulance rig followed by a Dansville Fire and Rescue truck arrived. Shortly after the floodgates of volunteer emergency personnel opened up.

Making sure no one was watching, Jake fingered the three papers inside his coat to make sure they were really there. All was well. He sighed with a mixture of relief and disappointment at his actions.

He realized, when this murder scene wrapped up, he needed to contact Uncle Joe and Lizzie to tell them he had now accepted their mission. But first he needed to check in with someone else. He reached for his cell phone in the briefcase at his feet. He needed to call MHI.

Dialing the director, he shook his head and tried to figure out how this whole affair had unfolded. Was it because he tried doing the right thing in rescuing some guy trapped in a hole — who just happened to have stolen a secret broach. Or was it because some jackass named Nero happened to think he was a long lost all-powerful shaman. Or was it really all because Thomas Boyd's greed led him to an Indian cave in 1779. Coincidence? Not if you ask Miss Lizzie Spiritwalker.

The phone rang several times. A groggy male voice answered. Jacobson.

"Sir? It's Jake."

"How'd you make out?"

"Stephen Ashland has been murdered."

17

Early Wednesday morning. High Point Casino.

RAY KANTIIO'S ARRIVAL at the High Point mountain resort saw him greeted outside in the employee's private parking lot by Kenny Rousseau, the head of Nero's personal Neo-Iroquois bodyguards. Rousseau was dressed in a dark blue suit and wore his black hair as Kantiio did — in a long braid. He had dark eyes with three light blue streaks of tattooed ink under each — face tattoos as in the ancient Iroquois warrior tradition. The brute was intimidating and rightly so, yet he acted in a quiet professional manner, stone-faced about his business. Concealed inside of his coat Kantiio knew Rousseau sported a Browning 9 mm Hi-Power semi-automatic pistol that could appear at any second. The head bodyguard also wore a nondescript earpiece for secure communications.

"You're on time lard ass. That's a first," announced Rousseau.

"Up yours numb nuts," replied Kantiio, chuckling.

Rousseau smiled. "Park over there." He motioned toward the employee entrance.

Kantiio would be headed in to see Nero himself to present what he assumed would be the latest addition to his artifact collection — the antique rifle. But he also brought something special too, a new gift for his boss's private scalp room. After parking his Navigator among other luxury SUVs, and wrapping the McTavish's rifle in a blanket, he followed Rousseau into a side employee entrance leading into the main kitchen area.

Another bodyguard, dressed as Rousseau was, appeared in front of

MICHAEL KARPOVAGE

them and with Rousseau trailing behind they briskly moved Kantiio passed the chefs and prep cooks preparing for breakfast at the five-star restaurant. Pushing through double-swinging kitchen doors, they silently strolled down a service hallway decorated in Native American art. They bypassed the entrance to the main dining area and continued ahead. Several administrative staff offices with closed doors lined each side of the hallway. The end office door, next to Nero's private elevator, was ajar. As they passed, Kantiio glanced in and saw the cute blonde-haired white woman Stanton at her desk. He stopped. She looked up and made eye contact with him. She seemed sad, but gave a weak smile in return. He flashed his gold teeth.

The door closed in his face. Rousseau had reached over and slammed it shut. The occupant's nameplate stared back at him. It read: Anne Stanton, Director of the Haudenosaunee Collection.

"Mouth, she's not your type," said the head of security.

"Bite me Rousseau. At least I'm getting some!"

"I hear you fall asleep before you can even get it up," countered Rousseau. "Now keep moving. You don't want to be late."

Rousseau, an ex-convict, had been caught with Alex Nero in their youth running weapons across the St. Lawrence River. He had been Nero's enforcer during prison and actually recruited Kantiio into their prison gang. After their release and Nero's subsequent rise to power he was rewarded as the head of Nero's security team at High Point. Middle-aged, Rousseau stood at the same six-foot height as Kantiio. Physically, the two looked like replicas of each other — both sporting wide necks and faces — in the mold of a professional football lineman, although Rousseau definitely had kept in much better physical shape.

They proceeded over to the elevator, its mirrored outer doors shimmering in faux-gold. The lead bodyguard, a Mr. Jasper who was fairly new at the company, turned and faced Kantiio.

"You know the routine," said the younger bodyguard.

They would pat him down. Kantiio had been through the drill many times before. As an independent contractor doing Nero's off site dirty work, he often checked in with the boss and was always escorted down to

· 170 ·

his subterranean office. He handed the blanket-wrapped rifle to Rousseau, produced his Beretta 92 silenced pistol, and gave it to the other bodyguard, butt end first.

"Nice piece," said Mr. Jasper, pocketing the pistol. "This new?"

"Yeah, picked it up last month down in the city," said the contractor, knowing he'd receive it back once he left.

Kantiio then held out his arms. Rousseau frisked him up and down. On Kantiio's side coat pocket he felt a lump inside and heard a crinkle of plastic. He pulled out a oversized freezer storage bag with what appeared to be a wig. Upon closer inspection he noticed it was a person's scalp. Rousseau placed the bag back inside Kantiio's pocket and looked up at him with raised eyebrows.

Kantiio's teeth flashed. "A special gift for the Man himself."

Rousseau merely shook his head. "Whatever gets you off." He then checked inside the contractor's white button-down shirt for any electronic recording devices. Kantiio was clean, as always. He handed back the artifact rifle and opened the elevator, allowing the trio to step inside. Rousseau produced a key out of his pocket, inserted it into a slot below the floor numbers then hit the button labeled *HC* for Haudenosaunee Collection. The elevator lurched downward for a three-story ride into the depths of the mountain.

Upon reaching bottom, Rousseau led his guest into a foyer area furnished with a series of Iroquois paintings hung on solid rock walls. Straight ahead sat the main entrance to Nero's famous collection, the façade resembling an Iroquois longhouse. Reconstructed against the stone wall Nero had real logs brought in and secured with genuine corn fiber rope. Several decorative Indian furs adorned the walls adding to the visual authenticity. The log-faceted, reinforced doorway, locked tight as usual, was even flanked by two full-sized bronze Indian statues depicting warriors at the height of the empire.

The three men walked toward the collection's entrance but then turned to their right at a solid oak door displaying a hideous false-face mask. Rousseau knocked twice. An electronic lock sprung and he led the guest in. Mr. Jasper followed, closing the door behind them.

Kantiio looked across the room to an oversized mahogany desk and found his benefactor.

Alex Nero sat hidden behind the desk in a high back leather chair, his back to his guest. Cigar smoke hovered above the chair, trailing into the crack of a partially opened wooden door just to his side. A hoop-shaped branch with a stretched scalp and long brown hair was the decoration of the day on that door. It marked the entrance to Nero's prized Scalp Room, his inner sanctum where high-level security meetings took place. Nero stood up from his chair, his back still to Kantiio, and grabbed a small book off his desktop. He walked through the side door.

Rousseau escorted Kantiio through the same inner entrance. Again, it was locked behind them by the expressionless Mr. Jasper. Standard procedure, thought Kantiio.

Rousseau proceeded ahead into the narrow rock chamber as Kantiio's eyes widened at the sinister collection of victim's scalps hanging on every wall. He was astonished every time he entered the room.

At the far end, Rousseau halted and stepped aside. In front of them was a stone table. On the opposite side of the table, against the back wall of the chamber, sat Nero. Dressed in a stylish contemporary tuxedo, he sat in an elevated high-back wooden chair reading a small leather back book. Kantiio always referred to his chair as the King's chair. A cigar hung out of Nero's mouth, blue-gray smoke floated around his head, blending in with his stone gray colored hair. Bloodshot eyes, from a night of tending to his casino guests, peered out from behind the swirling smoke. He gave Kantiio a grunt and a nod.

His contractor nodded back.

"Please show me the rifle, Ray."

"Certainly," said Kantiio, unwrapping the blanket and exposing McTavish's Ferguson rifle. He laid it gingerly on the table. "The poor bastard who stole this got nasty with me once I got him back up to his room. I think he knew it was coming. Put up a weak fight." He chuckled as he reached into his coat pocket to extract the plastic freezer bag. He turned the bag upside down and let Ashland's bloody scalp fall onto the table.

It hit with a slap.

"Another gift for your collection."

Nero rose from his chair. "Ah, such an unforeseen event." He walked up to the table, placed his cigar on the edge, and fingered the scalp so that it lay flat, hair side up. He then stroked Ashland's blond hair several times. "A nice addition indeed. Many thanks." He winked at his contractor.

Kantiio smiled, his front gold teeth reflecting in the warm light.

"Mr. Rousseau, please prepare this for display," ordered Nero.

Rousseau walked up, opened the bag, and placed the scalp back inside. He handed it to Mr. Jasper who walked it to a side table and stored it in a drawer for later preparation.

"Ah, the famous Sean McTavish rifle," uttered Nero as he picked up the Revolutionary War relic. "Tell me," he continued, as he examined the piece. "How does this rifle end up in Dansville, New York stolen by another thief?"

The gold-toothed contractor shifted his weight and in a rather defensive tone said. "Listen, I was prepared to go into that library and take the rifle myself. I would have taken care of the librarian too. No witnesses. I was waiting right before the library closed to pull the job. But this moron walks up when I was casing it and I knew he was up to something. I have no idea who he was. When he came out, the rifle was sticking out of his trench coat, so I figured he took the piece I was after. I mean most libraries don't have two Revolutionary War muskets now do they?" He chuckled nervously. Nero remained silent.

"Anyways, the dude was a total amateur," Kantiio rambled. "The piece barely fit into his little red sports car. I tailed him from there. He never knew I was onto him. If I didn't make the judgment call to follow him the job would have been compromised for sure. He would have disappeared with it. So, you have to give me credit there."

"I see. Your judgment. Interesting," Nero commented, frowning as he turned the rifle upside down to closely inspect the scuffed wooden stock.

"Yes sir. Listen, he was tipped off. It's obvious."

Nero's eyes found a small symbol on the bottom of the stock. Without looking at Kantiio he asked if the thief had in any way touched or removed any item from the rifle. He was assured he had not. Kantiio said he followed his orders not to tamper with anything either.

"Once I confronted this loser at the motel and got the rifle from his car, I stuck it in my Navigator. Then I walked him back up to his room and finished the job. He never brought that piece up there."

"Never took it out of his car?" asked Nero. "Did he make any long stops on his ride up to New York? Fill up for gas? Take a piss? Pull over to rest? Was he ever out of your sight?"

"Ah, yeah he was," said the contractor. "Just for a moment though. He pulled over once and I had to drive past him. I waited way up ahead so he wouldn't notice me. I thought he made me at that point but he took off after that and I kept up the tail. He made a gas station stop a little later then drove non-stop to Dansville and checked into his room. The rifle never left his car."

"Mr. Rousseau, your knife if you will," ordered Nero.

Kantiio flinched. "Listen boss, I didn't do anything wrong, okay? I got the piece for you. I did the job." He stepped away as Rousseau unleashed a folding lock blade knife from his pocket and walked towards the table.

Nero extended his hand. "Did I say you did anything wrong? Yet?" Rousseau placed the blade, handle first, into his boss's palm. Nero laid the rifle on the table and flipped it over. He ordered Kantiio and Rousseau to each hold one end while he pried at what looked like a tiny round plug the size of a dime.

Kantiio leaned forward for a closer inspection. "Hey, I know that symbol," he said. "It's the Rotary Club."

"No, you idiot," mumbled Nero without looking up. "It's the symbol of the oldest and largest fraternity in the world, the Freemasons. The square, the compasses, and the letter G for Geometry."

The plug popped out rather too easily, rattling on the table. Kantiio caught it before it rolled off. Nero bent closer and looked into the narrow hole it had concealed.

Empty.

He blinked. He looked up into his contractor's eyes. But before he took action his cell phone rang. He snatched it out of his tuxedo's inner breast pocket.

"What!"

"Sir, I have some new information on that murder in Dansville you wanted me to check out," stated his collection's director, Anne Stanton.

"Go on."

"They released the victim's name. It's Doctor Stephen Ashland of the Army's Military History Institute. Same place that Cranberry Marsh rescuer guy was from. You think there's a link?"

Nero's eyes fixed on Kantiio. They pulsated. The large contractor looked down. "Not sure. Continue." Nero then reached for his cigar, placed it at his lips and drew in a deep breath of sweet smoke. It calmed him ever so slightly. He replaced the cigar back on the edge of the table, a thin line of smoke tapering upward in a haze.

"The report said the victim was shot once in the back of the head execution style, in his motel room. The suspect was described as a Native American male, large frame. Driving a dark colored SUV."

"Hmmmm." Nero groaned in fury and bit his lower lip. A drop of blood seeped into his mouth.

"One more thing," continued Stanton. "There are some confusing reports about additional shots fired too — outside of the room. I'm sure they'll release more information later this morning so I'll keep my ears open, okay?"

Nero tuned her out.

"Mr. Nero?" asked the director. "Are you there?"

Nero had heard enough. He pressed what he thought was the *End* button on his cell phone to disconnect the call. He slid the cell phone face up on the table next to his cigar and faced Ray Kantiio.

Stanton heard a click, thinking Nero hung up on her. She almost asked again if he was there, but then heard a loud slap and a man grunt. Then the shouting began.

18

Same time. Strathallan Hotel, downtown Rochester.

AFTER RAE WAS ordered to the local hospital as a precaution, Jake caught a ride back up to Rochester with a state trooper. He then checked into the closest available hotel at four in the morning — the ritzy Strathallan on East Avenue. He was mentally spent. Collapsing in his new hotel room bed, he could not purge the image of Ashland's scalped head out of his mind. Combined with what he had learned of the mind controlling power behind the Crown of Serpents, he knew what memories the scalping would trigger and had fought to keep that dark scene suppressed. But as he lay staring at the ceiling the exhaustion slowly opened the doors of a incident he did not want to relive.

The year was 2001 while deployed under Operation Enduring Freedom in Central Asia. As a young 10th Mountain company commander Jake faced his first combat test in an enemy prisoner revolt at the Qala-i Jangi fortress ten miles west of their Army base in Mazar-i-Sharif in Northern Afghanistan. Eight hundred captured Taliban and al-Qaeda fighters had overpowered their Northern Alliance guards, tortured and killed a CIA operative, and stormed the fort armory seizing weapons. A dozen U.S. and British Special Forces and later an eight-man Quick Reaction Force from Jake's 10th Mountain unit were called in to reinforce the Northern Alliance counterattack. They fought a three-day battle against the prisoners by coordinating air strikes, tank fire, and infantry assaults.

He keenly remembered the adrenaline rush during the battle. It was his first thrilling taste of combat and he reveled in it. He blinked hard as he stared at the hotel room ceiling. He seemed to be floating in his bed, the vivid images playing a movie in his mind.

Just before Jake's column of armored Humvees attacked a Taliban position inside the fort, a stray U.S. Air Force bomb missed its mark and landed almost on top of the U.S. spotters who had called it in. Six Northern Alliance soldiers were killed instantly. Dozens more, including five Special Forces soldiers, were injured. Jake changed the order from an assault to a rescue operation. Leading the way, his Humvee column raced in under heavy enemy fire and evacuated the wounded troops. Jake personally stood in his command Humvee's turret and provided a devastating rain of .50 caliber covering fire. He took down ten enemy combatants himself and was the last vehicle out of the compound. It was a personal high point in the battle.

But the low point, the moment when he lost all self-control, came a day later. With over seven hundred of the prisoners already dead and the enemy reduced to just a handful of hard-nosed Taliban and al-Qaeda hold-outs, Jake found himself spearheading an assault team down into the underground cells of the fortress. Separated from his men after several booby-trapped grenade detonations had collapsed a wall, he was literally blown into the laps of three enemy combatants. They immediately engaged in close quarters hand-to-hand combat. He knocked the first fighter out cold with the butt of his rifle. The second shot at and missed him. Jake returned fire and killed him. The third attacked with a knife. After wrestling the knife away in several quick moves he killed the man with a thrust through his heart.

But then in an adrenaline-filled rage, as if some Seneca warrior spirit from a past life had taken his mind over, Jake ended up scalping the two dead bodies. He had even let loose a war whoop during the act.

As he was about to render the same atrocity on the unconscious fighter the spirit who possessed him exited his body. Jake spared the wounded prisoner and dragged him out with the knife to his throat. He then collapsed in a fellow 10th Mountain soldier's arms not knowing he had sustained a severe cut in his side from the knife fight. That wound would lead to his first Purple Heart.

It was learned later that the prisoner Jake spared was identified as an al-Qaeda American traitor. Ultimately, the turncoat divulged key intelligence before being incarcerated in an American prison. For Jake's actions that day and for leading the previous day's rescue efforts he earned a Silver Star and legendary status within the ranks of the infantry. He was rewarded with a Special Forces assignment on a secret task force in the mountains to continue hunting al-Qaeda. The nicknames soon followed — honorable names associated with his scalping and the war whoops that were overheard by his men.

For Jake though, that dark moment of possession struck fear into him. The loss of reason while watching someone else act inside your body shook him to the core. To have some other soul inside your head, some other voice that took over your actions, was like, well—

"Insanity," he said out loud.

It was a feeling he had wrestled with every day to keep from reliving again. He disciplined himself and had turned into the cold-blooded, calm and collective intellectual killer the Army most desired. Afterward, he killed the enemy often enough in both Afghanistan and Iraq and had not felt that same possession or loss of control again, albeit he killed at a distance and never up close as he did in that basement.

But now, in light of the supposed power behind Atotarho's crown and those who would go to any length to get it, Jake knew if he let that relic fall into the wrong hands there would be much chaos sown in people's minds. He had tasted that feeling of possession and it had left him utterly hopeless. To have a man of Nero's character use it for gain was something he could not let happen.

He looked at the clock. 6:15 A.M. He closed his eyes and let sleep finally overtake him.

MICHAEL KARPOVAGE

19

Same time. The Scalp Room.

IN A BLUR, Nero reached across the table and backhand smacked his trusted contractor across the face. The sound of flesh being whacked reverberated inside of the stone chamber.

Kantiio touched his lip, exposing blood on his finger. "Goddamn Alex, what the hell was that for? You losing your mind or something?"

"For failing me you lazy fat piece of shit! For allowing this thief to steal the rifle first and finding what was inside of this plug." He pointed to the concealed shaft in the rifle. "Now you tell me everything that happened and then I'll decide what to do with you. I want to know about the shots fired outside the room."

Kantiio had to let the entire story out now and hope for the best. He knew firsthand of Nero's ruthlessness if crossed. "They surprised me," he said in a shaking voice. "I just popped the thief in the head and scalped him and then was searching his room for other shit that might benefit you when I heard a car door slam. I looked in the parking lot and saw an undercover cop drawing her weapon, and some Army dude coming up with her. I knew they had to be after that rifle. Hell, the thief was like the only person in the damn motel—"

"Wait a second," Nero interjected. "An Army dude?"

"Yeah, I guess so. Listen, this was a botched op from the beginning. They had to be after the thief is all I can figure. So I ran out of the room and popped the bitch cop twice. She went down. Couldn't get a shot off at the soldier. Then I got the hell out of there. I drove nonstop to get here. That's it. That's the whole truth."

Nero dipped his chin and leaned both arms on the table. He shook his head slowly.

"So, you killed a cop?"

"Wouldn't be the first time, right? Listen, nothing will come back to you, sir." Kantiio tried to keep his voice steady. "I did as you ordered. I retrieved the rifle as asked. I didn't know anything about that secret plug or anything inside of it. You also said if anyone gets in my way take care of 'em. So I did."

Nero extracted a gold butane lighter from his breast pocket and nonchalantly reached for his cigar. He relit it and coughed. He inhaled then blew a patch of smoke into his contractor's face. Kantiio's eyes fluttered. Nero coughed again then said, "You broke procedure by not communicating with me when the thief initially interfered at the library. Your actions thereafter botched the job."

"But I got the rifle like you asked didn't I?"

"Why did you wait until what, fours hours later, to dispatch him?"

"He was on the road the whole time," pleaded the contractor. "Stopped once and pulled over on the shoulder like I said. I couldn't do the mark since we were in public. I couldn't risk being seen. So, I waited until dark. Pulled a recon on his motel room for a few hours and then faked him at his room door, told him that I was the night shift manager and his car had been broken into."

Nero let out a disdainful laugh. "Wait a minute. You pulled recon for a few hours?"

"Sir, I have to be thorough."

Rousseau interrupted. "Ask him if he fell asleep."

"Is that true?" Nero demanded. "Is it?"

"Ah, yes, sir. It is. I did sleep a little bit." Kantiio glanced at the thug who just signed his death warrant. Rousseau smirked back.

Nero cut in, his deep voice like a rough saw. "We all know you have problems staying awake. That is why you allowed the thief to steal the rifle first. That is why you took a few hours to recon the motel. I bet you literally fell asleep at the wheel and botched everything up. You have twisted the path of my destiny because of your incompetence. There was a note hidden inside that plug which held a key to a great legacy from my ancestor." Nero sucked hard on his expensive cigar and blew more smoke on his contractor.

Kantiio tried to speak. Nero raised his hand. "Silence! I put my trust in you to pull off a simple job. I compensate you well. Have for many years. You are allowed any pleasure you desire. I don't pay you to take a nap while performing a mission. This is unacceptable. And this," Nero pulled out a pistol from his side pocket and pointed it at the contractor's forehead. "This is my judgment."

Kantiio flinched. Sweat trickled down his neck and he couldn't catch his breath. He closed his eyes. But Nero didn't pull the trigger.

"For failing me, here's your choice," Nero rasped. "You may run the gauntlet and have a chance at redemption should you survive. Or take the easy way out by telling me to pull this trigger right now. What'll it be Ray? What'll it be?"

Kantiio's lips parted, but no words formed.

"Make a decision or I will!" The pistol inched closer.

"The gauntlet," whispered Kantiio. "The gauntlet. I'll run the gauntlet."

Nero smiled, lowering his weapon. "Ahh, this will be fun." He snapped his fingers and his two bodyguards pointed pistols at the back of Kantiio's head in case he tried to escape. "Rousseau, call in all the men, pick four who you want to fight, then I want you to face him in the end. Five running the gauntlet total. We'll do this right here, nice and private so no one hears a thing."

Nero grabbed his cigar and retook his seat at his throne. He left his cell phone on the table. On the other end, Stanton was bent over her own cell phone with a mini-tape recorder.

Within minutes, several more Neo-Iroquois thugs arrived at the Scalp Room. Totaling eight of Nero's security detail, they stood at attention awaiting orders. Rousseau picked his four toughest and had them shed their coats and shirts. They gave their weapons to the remaining guards who stationed themselves at various points in the room. Rousseau too stripped off his shirt, revealing a wide array of prison tattoos across his broad chest and arms. He took a position in front of the table where the rifle and cell phone lay. He faced the other end of the room and Kantiio.

The condemned man had stripped to the waist, his back to the guarded entrance. He knelt with closed eyes, mumbling a prayer.

Nero stood up from his throne, plucked an eagle's feather from the highest point of his chair back, and bellowed to his failed contractor. "Should you make it through the gauntlet and grab this feather, you will then face final judgment by me. I will decide to keep you on or put you down. There will be five one-on-one fights to the death, lasting no longer than one-minute each. I keep the time. I will add time if I feel you are stalling. If you last the entire minute, knock out, or kill each opponent, you may advance to the next round when you are ready. Understood?"

"Yes," yelled Kantiio. He stood up and took a step forward. He became a raging bull.

Nero held up the feather, checked his diamond and gold wrist-watch, then lowered the feather. "Begin!"

Kantiio's first opponent was Nero's top driver, a former New York City steel worker, a Mohawk named Mr. Kay. He had large Popeye-like forearms and a barrel chest. After a quick stare down they locked arms and grappled each other to the ground. Kantiio bit him on the bicep. Kay screamed, losing his grip. Kantiio then executed a close quarter pummeling with several elbow smashes upon the Mohawk's nose and cheeks until he was unconscious. He then stood up, glistening with sweat.

"Shit. That was easy." Breathing hard but still full of fury, he motioned for the next opponent. "Come on Jasper. Let's see what you've got."

Mr. Jasper, an Oneida, had been a former pit boss at the Turning Stone Casino near Syracuse. Kantiio cursed at him and lunged forward. The younger man stepped aside planting a fist in his opponent's ribcage. Jasper then kicked the back of the Kantiio's knee out, dropping him. Another kick was aimed at the ribs but Kantiio caught it and pulled him down.

Pouncing on his prey, Kantiio choked his opponent, almost crushing his throat. The move didn't last long as he was jabbed in the eyes. Kantiio threw an elbow but missed, smashing it on the floor. He grimaced in pain and collapsed onto his opponent. Jasper couldn't get out from underneath the larger man. He threw several weak fists catching Kantiio in the side of the head. He then kneed the larger man in the groin with better effect.

Kantiio rolled off in dire pain. Bolting upright, Jasper finally landed his kick to the ribs, same spot as the earlier punch. Kantiio issued a guttural scream.

Nero whistled that time was up.

Jasper moped away, hands to his throat.

Kantiio lay on his side, panting hard. He took a full minute to recuperate and managed to get to his hands and knees. He looked up at the next guy, an Indian from the Seneca Allegheny reservation.

Mr. George was wiry-muscled and fast. Kantiio faked injury and waited until the Seneca moved in first. Springing into action, Kantiio drove his head into the guy's face, knocking him backward. Blood ran down George's nose. Surprised at the blow and wiping the red smear from his face, George curled his lips and faced his foe. Both took a boxer's stance holding fists high, waiting for the other to bring it on.

The bloody Seneca yelled a war whoop and swung first with an uppercut. He missed. Kantiio kneed him hard in the groin, dropping him. He stomped the guy's face five times until Nero whistled again. The Seneca was motionless. He looked dead, his face crushed in. Bright red blood oozed from his nose and mouth. He slowly groaned back to life and was helped away by the other security guards.

Kantiio's fourth opponent was a former Cayuga Nation drug dealer, Mr. Makowa. He took a breath and stared Makowa down as they circled each other. He needed to buy time to regain his strength. He spit blood and taunted his new opponent until Nero shouted, "Fight or get the bullet."

Makowa went in first and slammed the contractor in the gut like a bat against a slab of meat. Kantiio doubled over. Makowa then kneed him in the face catching him high on the brow. A cut formed and sprang a leak. Kantiio dropped to his knees with a grunt. Another kick was blocked. Makowa then landed a punch to Kantiio's skull, breaking his knuckle in the process.

Kantiio collapsed on his back. Makowa held his hand in pain but shook it off as he saw his opponent start to rise. A stomp on his stomach took what little breath Kantiio had left.

Nero whistled.

Kantiio rolled back and forth holding his stomach. He mouthed the air like a fish out of water, not making a sound. Then finally a large inhalation of air gave way followed by coughing and groaning. Makowa spit on him.

"Get up," Nero barked.

One man left. It was Nero's top thug, the half Mohawk, half Quebecker Mr. Kenny Rousseau. He walked up to Kantiio. "Whenever you're ready you gold-toothed mother fucking Mouth."

"Fuck. You. Frenchy," spat Kantiio between breaths.

Rousseau flipped his long black braided ponytail from his shoulder and held up stiff extended hands in a martial arts pose. "Get up," ordered Rousseau again. "I've been wanting to do this to you for years."

"Ray Kantiio," interjected Nero. "One more opponent left. Get through him you get the eagle feather and my final judgment."

Kantiio managed to stand, although swaying like a drunk. His inflamed skin was bright red. Blood smeared his body and dripped from his brow, nose, and mouth. His elbow was fractured at the tip and several broken ribs stifled his breathing. His fists were bloody and disfigured.

Rousseau knew he had him. He wound his arm all the way back for a full force roundhouse to finish the contractor off. Kantiio just stood, watching it come. At the point of facial impact, Kantiio blocked the blow with his forearm in a bone-jarring crunch. With his other hand he plunged two fingers into Rousseau's eyes.

A scream announced he had hit his mark.

He grabbed Rousseau's ponytail and pulled as hard as he could, swinging the enforcer around and slamming him into the corner of the stone viewing table. Rousseau dropped at Nero's polished dress shoes.

Nero's mouth was agape.

Kantiio reached for the eagle feather and was just about to snatch it out of Nero's hand when his body fell out from under him. Rousseau had kicked out his legs. Kantiio hit the tile floor hard on his back. Rousseau sprang to his feet, blood pouring from an open cut on his forehead.

Rousseau stomped Kantiio's gut, blowing air out of his lungs for the second time. The contractor's eyes rolled toward the back of his head. Rousseau watched Kantiio squirm but an upward fist slammed Rousseau directly in the testicles. His knees buckled and he joined Kantiio on the floor, both men moaning and gasping for air.

Finally the doomed contractor inhaled. "Mercy Alex. Show me mercy," he grunted as he rose to a seated position. Rousseau was already on his hands and knees and snatched Kantiio by his hair, bending his head backward. He collapsed back against the floor. His head bounced. He saw stars. "Mercy. Please Alex," Kantiio pleaded again in a pain-filled whisper.

Nero approached and towered over him. He looked at his watch. "Ten seconds." He held his thumb out horizontally in anticipated judgment — the man's fate in his hands — just as the brutal Emperor Nero had done centuries ago. He let the clock run out.

"Please," Kantiio moaned. "I beg you."

Rousseau stood up.

"You have shown great bravery, Ray Kantiio," announced Nero. "For this I will have mercy on your *soul*. Your scalp shall not grace my wall. But for failing me in my ultimate quest your body will pay the price!"

Thumbs down.

Kantiio couldn't react in time. Rousseau dropped his whole body, his weight positioned into three stiffly extended fingers aimed at the contractor's throat. The aim was true. He drove his fingers through flesh, crushing the larynx. Kantiio's eyes bulged. He squirmed on the ground and clutched at his throat with a gurgling sound.

"Time's up," quipped Nero.

Thirty more excruciating seconds of grotesque spasms and Ray *The Mouth* Kantiio's body froze. Nero walked up with the eagle's feather and released it over his head as his contractor's eyes glazed over.

"He's gone," Rousseau noted.

"Put him in his Lincoln and send it to the bottom of the reservoir," ordered Nero.

His cell phone disconnected.

Wednesday morning. Strathallan Hotel.

A KNOCK AT his hotel door, a glance through the guest spy hole, and Jake allowed his uncle to enter. He gave him a nod, held up a finger to keep quiet, and resumed his cell phone conversation with MHI.

"Sir, listen, all I'm saying is we still stick with the original mission. We don't falter because of what happened to Ashland. Finding that keg before Nero does will be a coup for MHI. It'll expose that he was behind Ashland's murder. I know it."

Joe perked up. He moved closer to Jake to eavesdrop on the conversation.

"Do you have any hard evidence to back up your theory that Nero is behind all of this?" asked Dr. Paul Jacobson in a raised voice on the other end of the line.

His voice was so loud Jake had to pull his cell phone away from his ear. Joe raised his eyebrows wondering what was going on.

Jacobson wouldn't let up. "Other than what the state police told you about this Kantiio guy serving time with Nero many years back, you've just got speculation to go on, don't you?"

"True, I don't have anything concrete," acknowledged Jake. "But everything adds up to Nero pulling the strings. He thinks that keg of loot and gold belongs to him. He wants it to finish his collection on Thomas Boyd. Look how fast he acted on researching and stealing that rifle. It wasn't but a day after buying the Boyd Box at Fort Niagara. I'll even wager he's going for Sullivan's sunken cannon of gold too as his ultimate prize. Its location is on a clue supposedly inside of that buried keg." Jake winked at his uncle.

"Not good enough Jake!" retorted Jacobson. "I've got a public relations fiasco down here. The media is camped at our front doors. On top of that I've got the Secretary of the Army breathing down my neck wondering what the hell kind of ship I'm running. I'm supposed to report back to him later this morning and it ain't gonna be pretty—"

Jake cut him off to plead his case. "Give me some time and I'll get you answers. I'm here. I'm in the field. I'm still working with the police. I've got tons of experience in tracking down killers—"

"That was in the battle zone. The rules of engagement are different in civilian life. You can't just go out and call in an air strike on a target to bring him to justice."

"I understand there are limitations. I understand I need hard evidence. But the means to accomplish the mission remains the same. It's down and dirty leg work that's — that's *up my alley.*" Jake closed his eyes, cringing at using Ashland's line.

There was a pause on Jacobson's end.

Jake took advantage, sensing he had Jacobson moving to his side. "We get that keg and its contents then we start calling the shots."

Jacobson sighed. "I want it just as much as you do. Hell, if I were any younger I'd be right by your side. But I can't ask you to go this alone and risk losing another employee."

"Well, that's just the thing, sir. When you hired me I told you straight up you'd never have to ask me if I wanted to take these kinds of risks. You knew you could count on me that I would."

"You better know what the hell you're getting into. Don't mess this up, for your own sake."

"Thank you sir." Jake looked at his uncle and nodded with a smile. Joe frowned back.

"Call me as soon as you've got something. And listen, good hunting out there." Jacobson hung up.

Joe took off his coat and threw it on the bed. He shrugged angrily.

"What's going on? I got in the truck and drove over as soon as Billy told me you called. Said you couldn't let on. And then I hear you talking about Nero and the keg and a murder?"

Jake sat down hard on a lounge chair. He was still in his sleeping clothes of gray sweat pants and t-shirt, both with silk-screened Army logos. He pointed to a white pocket folder on an end table. "Open that up. You need to see for yourself."

Joe picked up the folder, sat on the edge of the bed, and opened it. He pulled out the first of several documents — a laser print of the September 12th Boyd journal page. Jake pointed to the lower corner. Expecting to see the partially ripped Freemason Cipher at the corner, Joe instead noticed that an old fragment had been taped next to it, fitting perfectly to complete the code. Joe looked up. "You found the rest of the code?"

Jake nodded. "Let's just say I acquired it — if you will. Look at the next page."

Joe pulled out the next sheet and saw the Freemason Cipher legend key in its decoded form. And right below that was Boyd's buried keg directions – fully deciphered. It read:

KEG LOCATION

EAST FROM KAHAGHSAWS

BETWEEN TWO PARALLEL CREEKS

UNTIL THEY ALMOST MEET

UNDER THREE LARGE BOULDERS

PLACD EAST WEST SOUTH

YOU WILL FIND WHAT YOU SEEK

"You're kidding me?" whistled Joe. "Where did you find this?"

"I didn't. It was my boss who found it." Jake mumbled while rubbing his temples.

"The one on the phone?"

"No, he's the director of MHI. My immediate boss, Stephen Ashland. He took it upon himself to research some of Boyd's items. And then he was murdered last night — a bullet in the head. Oh, then promptly scalped."

Joe's eyes widened. "What the hell?"

"We saw the killer face to face. An Indian named Ray Kantiio. Goes by the nickname of *The Mouth* because of some gold teeth he has. We picked him out of a criminal database. Most likely he's one of Nero's guys. The bastard shot a cop too. Then got away. The cop is all right. She had her vest on."

"What were you doing with a cop?"

"Listen, there's no time to rehash all the events that led up to his murder," said Jake, rubbing his bleary eyes. "The thing is the cops don't know I have this stuff. So, I've made a decision that we need to jump on this today before they or Nero move in."

"You're with us then? You're convinced of the threat. You'll help us?"

"Yes, Uncle Joe. Yes, I am. You heard me on the phone. After what happened last night, this changes everything."

Joe crossed his arms. "Does your director know about Nero seeking the crown?"

"I kept that part secret."

"Thank you."

"He only knows of Nero's role in wanting to find the keg to add to his collection, not his ultimate goal of gaining the crown. You heard me."

Joe nodded.

Jake went on. "He has no idea about the Kendaia cave directions or even what it means. So, let's make a deal. If that particular fragment of paper is still in the keg, then it will go to you and Lizzie to do with it what you want. Everything else goes to MHI. Agreed?"

"I do want the silver broach though — Swetland's broach. That's supposed to be in there too."

"Agreed," nodded Jake. "I am on call right now with the state police. They want me around for more consultations, as they're calling it. So, I need you to do some recon and shopping for me today. We are going in to find the buried keg at dusk."

Joe ran his fingers through his long hair. He peered at the other documents in the folder.

"The Groveland Ambush map in there will help you," directed Jake, standing up. "It shows the village of Kanaghsaws and the two parallel creeks." Joe pulled it out. "I've already compared that ambush map to a terrain contour map online," Jake continued. "Plus, Google Earth gave me satellite imagery. Go to the next page."

Joe shuffled the papers. "This one?"

"Yep. I found that the old Indian paths are in perfect alignment with the present day paved roads. So, we know the route going in. But I'm concerned because there is a house right near the north creek. Which means private property—"

"—and people interfering," finished Joe.

"Which is why I need you to shoot down there and scope things out, a fact finding mission. Make contact with any landowners. Be honest. Explain you're doing some historical research of the old Indian village that was once part of your tribe. Ask for permission to walk their lands. Be sincere. See if you can locate three large rocks at the closest point of the convergence of the parallel creeks. That is the key."

"Got it. But say I find the boulders. I can't just start digging. And what if I can't even get on the property?"

"That's Plan B. We go in as soon as it gets dark. So, I need you to do some equipment allocation beforehand. I have a list in the folder of what we need."

Joe took the paper out and went down the list. "Shovel. Got one. Cold weather clothing, dark colored. I'll find some. A backpack to carry the keg. Got one. Two-way radio phones. Just got a pair for my birthday. Extra flashlight and batteries. Okay. And a metal detector. No problem, I'll dig my old one out."

"We can't waste any time on this," pressed Jake. "We can assume Nero is racing to get there too. He's already killed for it. So, tonight is it. This has already gotten way out of hand as it is."

"Okay. I'll make it happen. Hey listen, can I borrow your digital camera?"

"Good thinking. Let me get it for you." Jake fished it out of his briefcase and handed it to his uncle. "I'm thinking we should meet up at the junction of Routes 390 and 5 and 20 at the Avon exit. That's a good halfway point. What's a good landmark to meet at?"

"There's a McDonalds at that exit."

"Fine. Then we can transfer all the equipment to my truck. We'll make it official government business if we get into a jam. My director will back me. Okay? We all set?" He grabbed Joe's coat off the bed and handed it to him.

"What about weapons? I mean just in case," asked Joe, with a concerned look.

"It is deer season, right?" pointed out Jake.

"As of yesterday. I've got a couple of shotguns we could use."

"A shotgun is fine for you but I want my Colt M4 semi-automatic rifle I left at your house for target practice," ordered Jake. "Make sure my night vision scope is on it too."

"But it's shotgun season."

Leading his uncle to the door Jake said, "I don't play by the rules."

Later that morning. Strathallan Hotel.

Just after pulling on blue jeans and a button down shirt, Jake received another knock at his hotel room door. Rae Hart stood before him again.

"Hey there!" greeted Jake with a mixture of surprise and relief to see that Rae was doing well. "You holding up alright?" he asked. He let her in and took her coat, hanging it in the closet.

"Sore as hell but overall pretty good," she said, sensing his excitement at seeing her. She was still dressed in her suit pants and blouse from the night before — a bit wrinkled but still accentuating her lean, fit body.

"Come in. Sit down," offered Jake. "You've got to be exhausted."

Rae walked by Jake, her long auburn hair swaying at her shoulders, several strands falling across her face. She flipped her hair back and Jake caught her stirring natural scent. She stopped at the window and a set of facing chairs and stood with her hands on her hips. "You know Jake, I'm just glad the bastard already served time in jail or we would never have identified him so quickly on the database."

Jake chuckled. He stood right behind her, a little too close. "His gold teeth did him in."

Rae turned and smiled. "Yep. Ray *The Mouth* Kantiio. I still can't believe that's his nickname." She sat down.

Jake took the other chair. "When you pulled that cross reference of distinguishing body features on top of his Native American background it gave us all we needed for the ID."

Rae nodded. "And check this out. After you left we contacted the prison where he and Nero served together. They said he gained that name not so much from his teeth, but the fact that he talks too much and always had an excuse for everything."

Jake caught himself staring at her. Rae caught it too and met his eyes briefly. Jake then blinked and said softly, "Well, once you catch him, he'll sing like a bird."

Rae tucked a loose strand of hair behind her ear. "Not gonna be me who bags him," she replied with angry eyes. "My captain slapped me on administrative leave because of my injuries. Oh, and get this — due to the fact that I have a biased conflict of interest, as he put it, because of the potential Nero factor." She then slouched in her chair. "Told me to take a week off, that the case had been turned over to another BCI investigator out of Albany."

"That's bullshit," said Jake.

"The real reason is top brass wants Nero handled very delicately because he is a well-connected political figure and a heavy contributor to the key players in the state." She couldn't help but let her eyes meander across his body. She partially did it on purpose.

Jake caught her looking him over. He felt a surge of excitement wash over him. "Isn't it really a matter of bringing him in alive?" he asked. "I mean cop shooters usually come in with about fifty bullet holes in their bodies."

"It does save the taxpayers a whole lotta money," laughed Rae. "But you didn't hear me say that!"

"Say what?" He winked.

"So listen," Rae said softly. "I've got some good news. We performed Ashland's autopsy this morning and the slug he took matched the two that Kantiio fired at me. With you and I giving positive identification that he was in that room, we've got our suspect nailed on the evidence."

"Nice," replied Jake.

"And also," continued Rae, leaning forward and looking into Jake's eyes. "They cleared you too. That's the real reason I'm here."

"Why thank you investigator," Jake said, smiling.

Rae smiled back. "Your story was still crazy to consume, but by you being very candid in the interviews and when your director at MHI confirmed what he knew about Ashland and the Boyd journal it all came together. So thank you. You've been an incredible help."

"You're welcome Rae."

Rae leaned back in the chair and shook her head with a muffled snicker. "I tell ya Jake, this Mouth guy was sloppy, very sloppy. He is nailed on so many fronts. That parking lot security tape we confiscated—"

Jake nodded, his interest stoked. "Yeah?"

"We just finished piecing it together before I got here. We've got him on video with the rifle."

Jake's eyebrows rose.

"Yep. Plus," she continued, "earlier on the tape a black Lincoln Navigator pulled up next to Ashland's Mini-Cooper. It had New York plates that match his registration. This was just after Ashland checked in around eight o'clock. Kantiio then got out and looked inside of Ashland's car. He checked all of the doors to see if they were unlocked."

"So, he must have been trailing Ashland then if he pulled up that quick," suggested Jake.

"We're unsure of that because he never reappeared until later that night," Rae countered. "Where he was from eight until eleven, who knows? We thought maybe Ashland contacted him for a meeting, but his cell phone and room phone records don't back that up. We aren't ruling it out though. He could have used a pay phone."

"So you're suggesting Ashland was playing Nero too? Damn, I never thought of that." Jake rose up and started pacing. "Steal the rifle, sell it to Nero — it would round out Nero's collection on Boyd." He stopped and looked down at Rae. "Those rifles go for a cool sixty to ninety thousand dollars each. Add in an extra mark up for Nero to purchase and you up the ante."

"But why did Kantiio try to break into the car as soon as he pulls up? His actions don't make sense if they were to have a meeting later. He seemed to know the rifle was in the car and he wanted it right away."

"And once he found it, he killed the only witness — the original thief Ashland," Jake summarized, sitting back down.

"We do know for a fact that Ashland was planning on digging up that keg of war loot just as you speculated." Rae unbuttoned the top of her blouse and rubbed her upper chest and throat. "He made the trip all the way up here, had digging tools in his car, and did have the Conesus Lake inlet area circled on the road atlas we found in his room. So, if he was going to cut a deal with Nero, then why drive all the way up to the Dansville area? Why not go directly to Nero's casino in the Catskills?" She inhaled slowly and grimaced.

"You okay?" Jake asked with sincerity in his voice. He glanced at her chest where the rounds had hit.

"To be honest Jake, it freakin' hurts."

"Can I get you anything?"

"No thanks, let's stick with our train of thought here. We're on to something."

"I know, investigator, but you're not supposed to be on duty anymore, right?" Jake smiled.

"I know what you mean by having a bruised ego."

Jake laughed then nodded his head at her partially exposed chest. He swallowed hard.

"Will these bruises get me a Purple Heart?" She gestured to where he was looking.

Jake laughed, shifting in his chair. "I'll let you borrow mine."

Rae leaned forward reaching for his hand. "Hey listen, there's something I really need to tell you." She held his hand in hers. "Jake, I want to thank you for bringing me back, for saving my life."

Jake felt the warmth of her hand. He had trouble concentrating. He shrugged. "Your decision to wear your vest saved your life. All I did was blow some hot air into you, not that I minded doing it." He grinned.

She laughed and sat back, slightly blushing. She buttoned up her shirt and returned her demeanor back to business. "Have you heard the murder on the news yet?" she asked.

Jake cleared his throat. "Just that short paragraph in the paper this morning when they released Ashland's name. No details though. I haven't even turned on the TV. Been trying to catch up on sleep."

She checked her watch, then grabbed the remote control on the end table to turn on the TV. "It's just before noon. They'll have it at the top of the hour."

Within a few minutes a local news station aired the murder as a top story to start the segment. A yellow crime scene tape graphic appeared over the male anchor's shoulder. Rae and Jake both stood in front of the television set. She placed her hand inside of his arm as they listened in. Jake liked it. He felt comfortable.

"Breaking news from the murder in Dansville of Doctor Stephen Ashland of the Army's Military History Institute. We've just been told that there was actually a State Police Investigator who was *shot* when trying to apprehend the suspect last night. A fifty thousand dollar reward has been issued for his capture. Let's go live to Amanda Linder who is on the scene where the murder and cop shooting took place. Amanda?"

"Wow!" exclaimed Jake. "Fifty grand. They must really like you."

"Shut up you," replied Rae in a playful way. "And watch the news. Let's see if they get everything right."

A younger female reporter dressed in a purple hat, matching coat, and scarf stood stern-faced with her microphone in hand. The second floor balcony of Hogan's Inn was plainly seen just over her shoulder. Yellow and black crime scene tape fluttered around the perimeter.

"That's *right* Chuck. I'm here live at Hogan's Inn in Dansville, just off of Route 390 and we have some more details from the brutal murder that took place around eleven last night. A high-ranking law enforcement official told me that State Police Investigator Rae Hart was *shot twice* in the chest as she approached the room where the murder had taken place, not minutes before. She *was* wearing her bulletproof vest and survived without serious injury. She is currently on administrative leave as is the policy when a shooting occurs." The reporter paused for effect, nodded, and sighed heavily with rising shoulders to accentuate her act of genuine concern.

"What a joke," replied Rae.

"Now to the murder suspect," said the reporter. "He was caught on a security camera casing the victim — Stephen Ashland's — car in search of something. Let's roll that video if you could."

Videotape of the large Indian looking into the small sports car appeared on the screen. Then Kantiio's mug shot from his first arrest many years back filled the set. A wide smile exposed his gold front teeth.

"The suspect has been positively identified as Ray *The Mouth* Kantiio, an ex-convict who lives in the Catskills. The Mouth nickname obviously comes from his gold front teeth. The picture on screen has been photo enhanced to reflect a gain in weight and age. He is a Native American from the Mohawk tribe. Has black hair he wears in a pony tail. Stands six foot tall and weighs approximately two hundred and fifty pounds. He was dressed all in black and drove a dark colored Lincoln Navigator with New York plates M-T-H-4-3-7-8. He is considered armed and dangerous. Anyone with information leading to his capture can collect the fifty thousand dollar reward."

An illustration of a Revolutionary War era rifle appeared next on screen.

"And *this* is what the victim was apparently murdered over. A *musket* from the Revolutionary War. This musket was…"

"It's a rifle. Not a musket," said an irritated Jake.

"Sshh!" interrupted Rae, smacking him on the arm.

"...stolen earlier in the day from a library in Upper Exeter, Pennsylvania by none other than Ashland himself. It is said this particular musket could fetch almost *one hundred thousand dollars* on the antiquities black market."

The television screen cut back to the security video as the reporter continued to narrate. "Later that night, the security video showed the suspect holding Ashland at gunpoint, going to his car, taking out this musket, then walking away behind the hotel." The screen cut back to the reporter who was now reading from her notes. "It is assumed that the suspect put the musket in his SUV at that point, then brought Ashland back to his room and *murdered* him with a bullet to the head. This looks like a theft and buyoff deal gone bad."

She looked up at the camera. "And it's at that point when the state police walked up to the room. They had been tracking Ashland since the theft occurred and were closing in to make the arrest, but were literally *surprised* by the presence of Kantiio. That's when the shooting of Investigator Hart took place. The suspect then fled the scene. Chuck, that's everything we have at this point. The investigation continues. Back to you."

The screen cut back to the news anchor in the studio.

"Nice work Amanda. It sounds like quite a mystery indeed. Now to our next top story. Buffalo Bills quarterback P.J. Cain has—" The screen went black. Rae had shut off the television set and tossed the remote onto the bed.

"No mention of the scalping, no mention of me being there," said Jake. "Looks like your brass leaked exactly what they wanted. Not a bad move actually."

"We have top-notch investigators on the case, even though it burns my ass not being involved," replied Rae, her brows furrowed. "I've got to get back on this case somehow."

Jake held up his hands. "Take it easy there. Don't go cowboy on me just yet. Let's at least go downstairs for some lunch and think this over. I'm starving and could use some company."

Rae nodded her immediate approval, grateful for the distraction. "Actually, I need an ice cold beer." She stood up and retrieved her coat from the closet, throwing it over her arm.

Jake grabbed his black leather jacket out of the closet and put it on. Rae was already in the hallway. On the desk next to his laptop he gathered his phone and room key. He picked up his wallet and with his back to Rae, opened it to check on a mini-DVD. This would be with him at all times until he got home, he decided — a precaution in case Nero's boys came looking for his laptop. The DVD held all of the Boyd digital photos he had transferred off the laptop. This disc was his only back up copy, made as soon as he had checked in after the interviews this morning. He placed the wallet in the rear pocket of his jeans, then followed Rae down the hall to the lobby restaurant.

Seating themselves at a corner booth in the bar area, Rae looked troubled. After they each ordered a beer she started out with, "I've got to apologize for the way I treated you in the interview last night. I had to appear to be on the state's side, just so you know. It's just that with the discovery of the Indian grave, the accidental death of the trapper, the arson, the rifle theft, and now the murder of your boss, well, we couldn't help finger you as a key suspect in all of this."

"Material witness, not suspect. Besides you said I'm clear," Jake looked up with questioning eyes. "Right?"

"Yes. Yes. But—"

"But what? The grave accident has nothing to do with Ashland's murder. That's just sheer coincidence. Like I told you and the other investigators, I think Ashland was simply going after the gold once I planted that seed in his head from Fort Niagara."

"But all this Indian stuff is linked somehow to Nero."

Jake went silent, looking away. As he pondered whether he should tell her the whole truth about the Crown of Serpents he didn't notice a Native American man that entered the restaurant and sauntered up to the bar for a drink. The man wore sunglasses and had several fresh bruises on his cheeks.

"Look, at MHI we are researchers and historians," Jake retorted, somewhat fired up. "We gather information and expose history. It's what we do for a living. Ashland had the same clues from Boyd's journal entry of September 12th that Alex Nero and I had. That's the link you're after. Ashland simply deciphered it first and took off down the path. It was rather easy with the help of the Internet. He had a one day head start before I even thought about pursuing it."

"So, as soon as Nero saw the journal, he too could have acted on it," asked Rae.

"Right. That's what I explained to your brass."

"I'm really sorry," Rae's eyes softened. "I mean it Jake. We just have to analyze ever little nuance."

"I know and you hung by my side, which I do appreciate. All I'm saying is Nero found out about the journal's contents the same day Ashland found out. And Nero is an avid collector too, so he knew what he was doing. So, either they were in on the rifle theft together or acting alone and happened to cross paths. That I don't know."

Rae looked down. She nodded to herself.

"Hey, our drinks are here." Jake glanced at the waitress holding two beers. Just beyond her the man at the bar walked out, catching Jake's eye for a fraction of a second.

"Sir, your drink," said the waitress, recapturing his attention.

"Oh, sorry. Thanks."

Rae also thanked the waitress and grabbed her frosty mug by the handle. Jake raised his glass and clinked it against Rae's. She went to sip her beer when Jake announced, "Here's to bulletproof breasts. I mean vests! Vests! Oh jeeze!"

In a snorting chuckle, Rae blew the foamy head out of her mug, spraying Jake in the face.

"That came out all wrong. I'm sorry, still got a couple of things on my mind," Jake embarrassedly said, as he wiped foam from his cheek.

Rae kept on laughing, a loud, true natural laugh. She shook her head and rolled her eyes, now much more relaxed. "You are something else, Major," she said with a wide grin, holding up her beer. "Alright, here's to bulletproof breasts."

"I'll drink to that!"

They clinked glasses once more and sipped their beers. Another round and some bar food later, Rae sighed. "I have to get back home to Seneca Falls, I really need some sleep." She confided in him that even though she was on leave she was still going to follow up on the arson case and anything else that led to Nero. Jake paid the bill and held up her coat. She turned around and put her arms through the sleeves.

She faced him. "What are your plans?"

"Going to check out, then head over to my uncle's house on the reservation. Spend the night there with family. Then tomorrow afternoon I'll head back home to Carlisle."

"I see," she said, disappointed.

"But if I'm traveling through Seneca County I'll stop by your station, if you don't mind."

Rae lit up. "You sly dog. Of course I don't mind. Give me a shout tomorrow, about an hour's notice if you could."

"Absolutely."

He took her hand in his arm and walked her out to the front lobby.

"You have a safe trip home now," said Jake.

Rae stopped, leaned into him, and gave him a quick kiss on his lips as a goodbye.

21

Route 390 South. Near Avon Exit #10.

"GOOD NEWS MR. NERO," said Rousseau in his cell phone headset. He sat in the back seat of a black Hummer, a bandage across his forehead protecting the deep cut suffered from the gauntlet. An open laptop computer sat on a tray across his lap, the battery recharge cord plugged into a traveling office console socket. He followed a green dot over a roadmap displayed on the laptop's monitor. "He's on the road. We've been tracking him from his hotel in Rochester for about twenty minutes now."

Sitting in the front seats were his other two security agents. The man driving the Hummer, Mr. Kay, the Mohawk, nodded his head. He had observed Jake at Fort Niagara and had just placed him in the Strathallan restaurant. Sunglasses now off, two black eyes were revealed where the late Kantiio had elbowed and broken his nose. He tried to steady the Hummer as wind gusts whipped the vehicle.

"Very good. Where is he headed?" asked Nero, on the other end of Rousseau's line.

"We've got him pulled over right now on Routes 5 and 20 off the Avon exit of 390 south. He's been heading in the direction of where you said he'd be going. Maybe he had to take a piss or something."

The agent in the front passenger seat chuckled and smiled back at Rousseau. It was Mr. Jasper, the Oneida. He sucked on a cigarette and exhaled the smoke through the crack in his window. Every time he gulped though, his throat ached from where Kantiio had choked him.

"Do you have a visual on him?" asked Nero.

"Negative sir," answered Rousseau. "We don't want to spook him. We're tracking him about three miles back. He has no idea."

"Get a visual of what he is up to then back off again. I want another report in twenty minutes. I'll check back as soon as I get out of this lawyer's office and close the deal on the Depot." The phone call disconnected.

Between Conesus and Hemlock Lakes.

Having met at McDonalds where his uncle transferred two long duffel bags of equipment into his parked SUV, Jake asked, "How did you make out with the recon?"

Joe grinned from ear to ear. "The land where the old village sat was just purchased by a white woman. She bought the house and surrounding property. She was very cooperative to say the least. Even made me coffee."

"Made you coffee?"

"Let's put it this way. She was about as big as me, alone, and simply needed someone to talk to."

"You charmed her you old goat," Jake smiled.

"Runs in the family," Joe chuckled, taking out the digital camera. "Here let me show you what I found out." The first photo showed the creek. It was no more than eight to ten feet wide and probably a foot deep at the most. On the bank of the shallow creek sat a two-story country style home and a brown barn. "She also has a barn and horses out back." The next photo showed three horses within a wooden fenced-in pasture. Beyond the horses was the start of a ridge on the eastern slope. "Her horse field is fenced in and basically takes up most of the land in the flats, between the two creeks. It's to the east of the main road."

"Good work."

"Check out this next photo. Surprise!" Joe switched to an image of three beach ball-sized rocks, covered in moss. "The three boulders placed east, west, and south. Just as Boyd said they'd be."

"No way!" Jake stared with a grin. "Are you shitting me?"

"Nope. All I had to do was ask about three large boulders that had supposedly been near the original Indian village and she showed me exactly where they were. Said the only reason she knew about them was that her real estate agent mentioned they were part of a central fire pit or gathering area of the old village. Apparently it was a landmark that had survived all these years. Go figure."

Jake punched his uncle in the arm. "I can't believe you found them."

Joe rubbed his shoulder. "Sometimes a bit of honesty combined with the famous Tununda wit goes a long way."

Jake rolled his eyes. "Let's get moving."

"Oh, and one more thing. She's out of town until tomorrow afternoon. She said if we wanted to, we could park in her driveway if we needed to walk her property some more."

"Too good to be true. Too good. I'll take it!"

Making the run to the target area, Jake wanted to approach from the same direction that General Sullivan did in 1779 — from the foot or north end of Hemlock Lake down through the rolling hills to the head or south end of Conesus Lake — on present day Route 15 South. The traffic on the roads posed no problem, but the weather was another story. It had been in transition all day, the winds of change in November at full force.

Experiencing a warm front of 60-degrees earlier in the day, but marred by rain, high winds, and low cloud cover, a cold front had moved in. Temperatures were expected to drop by almost 30 degrees with possible snow showers. As they drove south, Jake glimpsed leaf covered green grass, and harvested farm fields of cut corn stalks. It wasn't long before thick snowflakes blew in from the west to cut down on visibility. To his uncle, the weather was a hindrance. To Jake, it was a blessing. The worse the weather, the more people would stay indoors allowing those who ruled the night to exact their stealthy business. It was exactly what a 10th Mountaineer had hoped for.

As he approached the south end of Conesus Lake, he pulled off onto the right shoulder of Route 15 and consulted his maps. The Groveland Ambuscade map came out first, followed by the NYS Gazetteer of topo maps. Jake studied both and said they would be swinging a right onto Foots Corners Road, which would turn into Henderson Hill Road, and

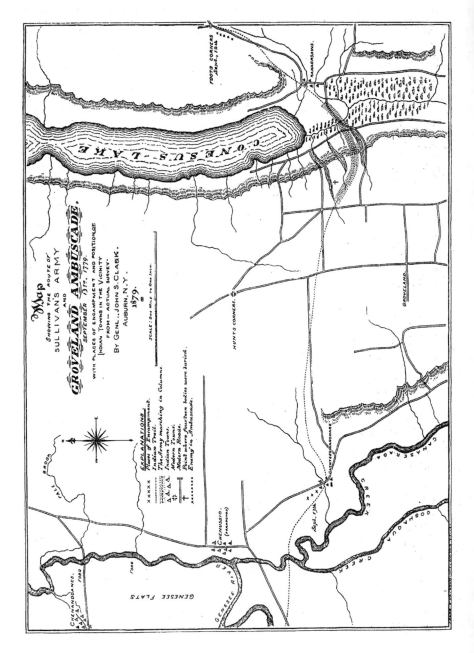

their descent down into the lake valley.

Yielding back onto the main road, they proceeded closer. A few minutes later they made the right turn and slowly drove past flat open farmland on both sides of the road — Foots Corners. Jake mentioned, "This was where the Continental Army encamped on September 12, 1779. They set up on this hill overlooking the lake." Jake pointed to the far right side of Groveland map.

Joe glanced at the modern day topo map to read the name of the hill — Turkey Hill. "I'll be damned." Joe peered over to open meadows darkened by a dying sunset. "Like driving right into history."

Jake pointed ahead. "And down there is Conesus Lake on the right. To the left are the inlet creeks and swamp they had to reconstruct a bridge across. Butler and Brant had destroyed the old one upon their retreat."

"Sullivan picked a good strategic high ground by encamping up here," Joe noted.

"And look, on the far side, there's the steep hill Boyd climbed that same night and then reconned further west about seven miles to the Genesee River. The next day, as he headed back to the camp, he was ambushed just at the top of the hill."

"That's the route I came down from earlier today. The Geneseo side."

Jake drove another mile and descended further into the valley, passing an open gravel pit on their left. At the end or bottom of Henderson Hill Road, Jake stopped at the junction of East Lake Road, looked in the rearview mirror to make sure no one was behind him, and turned on the overhead map light.

"We need to take a left," he said. They entered the flats of the valley where the village of Kanaghsaws once stood. He pointed to the old ambush map tracing their route.

"It's like we're shadowing Thomas Boyd's footsteps." Joe remarked.

Jake nodded. He then opened the folder of documents and pulled out Boyd's September 12, 1779 journal entry with the original parchment cipher fragment reattached to the corner. Following his index finger down, he stopped in the middle of the entry and read. "He was summoned to General Sullivan's tent that night and given the order for the early morning reconnaissance mission. Sullivan said to Boyd as a Brother of the craft he knew he could be trusted and that he had proven his worth in courage, service, and duty."

Jake perused further down the passage. "Here, this is what we want." He read the passage verbatim. "Upon refilling our water pouches at the parallel streams near the village, McTavish and me slipped away to have our fortunes buried for it proved too heavy a burden for the mission. We will come back for it on our return journey after reaching objective point." Jake switched off the light, gunned the engine, and turned left.

Jake continued. "For them to bury their loot was not uncommon at this stage in the campaign. Most soldiers, from what I've read in other journals, mentioned they were heavily weighed down. And these were scouts who had to travel light."

"And since Boyd and McTavish basically had a pot of gold, they surely wouldn't leave it behind at the main camp for others to plunder," said Joe.

"There, on the left," announced Jake. "The sign for the first creek." He read it out loud. "North McMillan Creek."

The SUV passed over the creek culvert. Joe pointed left to the woman's house just beyond a row of pine trees lining the main road. "Pull up behind her house back by the barn. We'll be better concealed from the main road."

Jake turned into the vacant driveway and parked at the rear. Even though the SUV was concealed from the main road it sat under a spotlight shining down from the roof.

Grabbing the September 12 journal excerpt, he read down to the keg inventory for one last reminder of what they were going after. "Plunder in keg is inventoried as: Butler's 200 Guineas and a bear claw necklace taken from the spy; location of sunken cannon near Catherine's Town; Swetland's silver broach, cipher directions to his cave and case containing his cave map drawing; 3 silver rings, 7 pipes, 5 knives, 2 wampum belts from Savages; a British Ranger Officer's corset, compass and gold match case."

"I just hope it's all there," said Joe, exiting the vehicle.

Jake placed the paper back in the folder and left the packet on Joe's seat. He too exited the vehicle and proceeded around to the rear, where Joe already had the back hatch open and equipment duffel bags unzipped.

South end of Conesus Lake.

"Mr. Nero, he's stopped about a half mile away in the vicinity of the old Indian village," said Rousseau, over his headset. "Off East Lake Road. I think this is it. He may be heading out on foot now. How do we proceed?"

"Where are you now? Can he see you?" asked Nero, on the other end of the cell phone connection.

"Negative. We are blacked out. Parked at a gravel pit. We cannot be seen from the main road."

"Good. Keep Kay with the Hummer there. I want you and Jasper to approach his location on foot. See if he's there. If so, let him conduct his business. He'll do our dirty work for us. He should be trying to dig something up in the area. But when he gets back you're going to ambush him."

"My pleasure," Rousseau said, his lip turned up.

"Confiscate whatever he digs up," ordered Nero. "It should be a small wooden keg loaded with Revolutionary War loot. I want everything that's in it but make sure you get three items in particular — a small fragment of paper with a code on it, a wooden cylindrical case with a map drawing inside, and a silver broach with an engraving of a deer on it. Got it?"

"Yes sir," Rousseau replied, nodding his head. "Then what do you want me to do with him?"

"The business deal will be concluded. Terminate the subject. Make it hurt. And don't forget to take the locator off his truck. Search it for anything of value too. Leave the body in the truck. Then burn it."

"Yes sir." Rousseau smiled.

"Report back to me when you've accomplished the mission." The phone connection ended.

MICHAEL KARPOVAGE

Former site of Kanaghsaws.

"**D**O WE REALLY need these weapons and the radios?" asked Joe, pulling on his gloves. "The boulders aren't but a hundred yards away. Just back at the base of that ridge." He pointed, but the ridge had already faded into darkness.

"Somalia 1993. Rangers," answered Jake. He clipped a two-way Motorola radio onto his belt. "Was supposed to be an easy daytime raid to grab some prisoners. The Rangers decided to go in light. They got complacent with using their proper equipment. They left behind their night vision gear, extra ammo, and extra water." He pulled on his head cover. "Little did they know they would be engaged in one of the deadliest urban battles since Nam. It didn't end until the 10th rescued them the next morning. We go in prepared no matter how inconvenient or how short the mission may be."

"Lesson learned, Major. Go to channel three," sighed Joe.

"Roger Big Bear. Get your earpiece in too. Make sure that your microphone is clipped on your collar. You need any help?"

"No, I got it," Joe struggled with wire around his large belly.

"Good. Is your radio on vibration ring?"

"Yep, good to go. I'm all set. All loaded up. Freakin' cold out here."

"Keep your focus on the mission," Jake directed. "Got your shotgun loaded?"

"Yeppers. Deer slugs. On safety too, Major."

"Okay, let's do this thing," commanded Jake.

His uncle gave him a nod. Jake then shut the rear hatch of his SUV and led the way back behind the barn. Three horses inside snorted as they passed by. Slung on a 3-point harness across his chest was his black matte Colt M4 semi-automatic assault rifle mounted with a powerful Generation Five 4x14 night vision scope. He had kept it at Joe's house when visiting where he would often go out for target practice on the wide-open reservation. Jake's M4 had a shorter 11" barrel on a rail interface system with an expandable polymer stock — a true close quarters killing tool. Twenty eight rounds of .223 caliber Hordany plastic tip bullets were loaded in the magazine, with one round now in the chamber. Another three spare magazines were hidden in his pants' pockets. Over his shoulder, rested a speared edge shovel on top of an empty backpack. He wore, as Joe did, a one-piece, close-fitting, dark Goretex coverall suit to protect against the elements. Around his waist, a web belt held his flashlight, multi-purpose tool, and his two-way radio. An earpiece and microphone clipped at his collar led down to the radio. Covering his head and face, except for the eyes, he wore a black balaclava — the bottom tucked under his collar.

"You're one scary SOB, Jake," quipped his uncle.

Jake waved his hand forward. "After you Big Bear. Show me them boulders."

Joe led on. Slowly. Even though the terrain was flat and grassy, his large body was weighed down with a metal detector and a Remington 870 pump action shotgun mounted with a Tasco 2x15 scope. Every so often he sent a flashlight beam of light ahead to keep his bearings. Behind him Jake panned his eyes back and forth.

"Use the flashlight as little as possible," ordered Jake, as he almost stepped on his uncle's heels.

Joe walked along the wooden fencing that enclosed the horse pasture. Several barrels and hay bales obstructed their path. About seventy yards back they ducked underneath another line of fencing and entered the equestrian exercise area. Joe's large frame and the extra weight caused him to nearly topple over after the barrel of his shotgun caught on a fence beam. Another twenty-five yards of bypassing several jumping stations and they arrived at the rear of the property. It backed up to a tree-filled ridge, which bisected the parallel running creeks.

Joe stopped. He pointed down at three boulders. "And here we are," he whispered.

Jake shot a quick blast of flashlight to illuminate three knee-high, moss-covered rocks aligned south, east, and west. He noted that the arrangement was consistent with the way a Mason's Lodge was laid out inside. Clever of Boyd and McTavish, he thought. Between the three rocks was a grassy circular area five feet in diameter. The light beam went out. "Get that metal detector sweeping and I'll pull perimeter security."

"Yep," acknowledged Joe. He rested his shotgun against a boulder. He pulled his detector's headphones from a pocket and placed them over his head and ears. After attaching the cord to the handle of the device, he powered it on and started sweeping.

Jake busily scanned through his night vision riflescope. Several times, a car would pass at the main road sending a quick green streak across his black and green field of vision. He detected movement behind him up the wooded slope — a rabbit. Back near the farmhouse, all looked quiet. He couldn't see well due to the spotlight illuminating the rear parking area. The white light burned like the sun inside his scope.

The barn, to the right, was another matter. The three horses generated a large heat signature. They could plainly be seen through a side window. They were agitated, knowing intruders had trod on their turf.

Within minutes, Joe hit pay dirt as a loud beep screeched in his ears. He lowered his headphones and whispered, "Jake, I've got something!"

"Okay," acknowledged Jake. "I'll start digging. You keep on the look out." Jake unslung his rifle and set it on the ground next to him. He grabbed his shovel and slammed it into the soft earth, scooping out his first load.

Jake continued digging for several minutes, breaking a sweat under his balaclava. He paused to catch his breath and also to make a quick security scan with his rifle. A red fox bounded down to the northern creek's edge. A truck whistled by up at the main road. The horses still danced in the barn and the main house was lit like a bonfire. And Uncle Joe sat on one of the boulders eating a candy bar. Jake gave a chuckle under his breath and went back to work.

Three feet down his shovel hit something hard. He pulled out his flashlight, dropped the shovel, and bent down into the hole before flicking the light on. He also pulled out his multi-purpose tool and locked in place a four-inch knife. Joe was already at his side.

"Whatcha got?"

"Let's see," whispered Jake. "Hold the flashlight inside the hole so no one sees it." He handed it off, then started scraping around the hard item the shovel had struck. It was a curved metal band attached to rotten wood. Scraping quicker, his heart raced. He scooped out the excess dirt with his free glove. Slowly a circular shape emerged. Sure enough, the metal ring framed the top of a small wooden barrel sealed with a plug. Jake stopped and looked up at Joe with a glimmering smile. Joe smacked his nephew on the back.

"I don't believe it." Jake shook his head as he scooped more dirt out around the barrel.

"I thought it would be bigger than this," whispered Joe, as he too helped dig around the edges.

"Well, it's a gun powder keg for foot soldiers. They strapped them to horses and mules. They needed to be small to transport. This is about what I figured. Ten inches in diameter and probably about a foot long."

A frantic few more minutes of digging and finally they plucked the fragile keg out of the ground. It was heavy. Jake estimated about thirty pounds. No wonder Boyd and McTavish were sick of lugging it around with the rest of their equipment, he thought. He checked the bottom of the keg to see if it was rotted and any of the contents had spilled out. It remained intact. He sat back, the keg on-end between his legs. Joe moved the light beam on it as Jake brushed away more dirt. The rotted barrel was bursting at the seams. If not for the two rusted metal end caps and thick metal belt holding the middle together, the keg would have long since lost its structural integrity. Jake fingered the plug on top and searched for a way to open it. Simply prying it off would probably work, he thought. But as he reached for his multi-purpose tool a loud neigh arose from the horse barn.

"Kill the light," forcefully whispered Jake. Joe fumbled with the switch and the flashlight beam died. Darkness again enveloped the pair. Jake immediately sprung to his feet, grabbed his rifle, and scanned the barn area through his riflescope. The horses snorted louder, echoing their displeasure across the pasture. He could clearly see one of them through the window, bobbing its head up and down. Then, for an instant, he thought there was a flash of bright green near the house, back behind his Tahoe. He wasn't positive though, because the damn spotlight hindered his vision. "Joe, do not move," he ordered in a whisper. "Stay still. I thought I saw something."

"Them horses are spooked," replied Joe. "The path to Atotarho's crown has been unearthed. They can sense it."

"What?" Jake took his eye off the scope and looked back at his uncle for just a split second. The distraction caused him to miss a bright green-silhouetted figure run from the barn and disappear behind the house.

"The evil has awakened."

"Stop talking, dammit!" demanded Jake, looking back through his scope. The miserable conditions hampered his view. He held his position for a full two minutes until he was satisfied nothing was there. Maybe Joe was right. He placed the rifle back on the ground.

"Let's get the keg inside the backpack in case it breaks open," ordered Jake.

Joe held the backpack open. Jake gingerly lifted and set the keg inside, still on its end. Joe switched the flashlight on, inside the backpack. Back on his knees, Jake used his multi-purpose tool and started prying at the plug with a knife. With a crunch, a piece broke off and fell into the backpack. A few more chips and the plug disintegrated.

Both men peered inside.

Same time. Same place.

"Jasper, you move again I'll skull cap you myself. You understand?" whispered Rousseau to his young minion. His binoculars were up to his eyes as he tried to pinpoint the flash of light he had just spotted at the back of the horse fields.

Nothing. The snow flurries marred his vision. His ears were freezing because of the biting cold wind. They had come unprepared.

He pulled back from the corner and bent down. "You blow our cover and we're going to have more than this Tununda guy to deal with. Look what happened to Kantiio."

"Jesus Christ, I'm sorry," apologized Mr. Jasper. "I didn't know there were horses in that barn." Breathing heavily, he sat at Rousseau's feet, at the side of the house. "I need a smoke. Those horses scared the shit out of me."

"When he comes back I'll confront him first," stated Rousseau. "I want you to circle around the front of the house and sneak up on him from the rear in case he bolts. If he runs, we take him out then and there. Otherwise, I want to make sure he's got the buried shit Nero is looking for. Then I'm going to beat the fucker to death."

Jasper lit up a cigarette and offered one to Rousseau. Rousseau gladly accepted. After all, he had been hooked on nicotine since he was twelve years old. Exhaling and shivering in the cold, they waited for their prey to return to its nest.

Same time.

Headlights from a vehicle swept across the field as it pulled a U-turn in front of the house. Jake looked up toward the main road. He noticed the car had a silhouette of a police patrol as it pulled off the shoulder of the road. He grabbed Joe's flashlight and clicked it off. "Get behind the rocks and lay flat!" Jake ordered.

Suddenly, a large spotlight appeared from the patrol car. The white beam hit the house and barn then swept across the fenced-in pasture coming toward Jake and Joe.

Both men pressed their faces to the ground just as the spotlight moved over them. It crossed the entire field. Then it turned off. The police car's emergency red lights then turned on and it sped off north. The two men watched the revolving lights as they climbed Henderson Hill Road and disappeared.

"Do you think he saw our truck?" asked Joe, standing up with a huff.

"Don't think so. I parked well behind the house. But they're on patrol. They're anticipating something happening out this way. We've got to blow out of here now. That was too close a call."

"Where do you think he went?"

"Maybe got another call, the way he hauled ass out of here," replied Jake, as he grabbed the shovel. "Come on, help me fill in this hole."

"What about the keg?"

Jake bent over and stuck his hand inside the keg. He fumbled around then pulled it back out. Whispering for his uncle to come closer, he told him to get down low. Turning on his flashlight, Jake opened his palm to reveal a single shining British gold Guinea coin displaying the royal crowned shield. Flipping it over revealed the side profile of a chubby King George III along with the wording: GEORGIVS III DEI GRATIA.

Joe smiled. Jake placed the coin back inside the keg and zipped up the backpack. He killed the light. "We wait until we get to a safe spot, then we check the contents." He stood and shoveled dirt back into the hole. Joe remained on his knees and scooped with his hands.

After replacing the patches of grass on top of the filled hole, they grabbed their equipment and headed back to the truck. Jake took the lead — backpack with keg, rifle across his chest, and shovel in hand. As he neared the fenced-in pasture, he gave a quick night vision scan. Illuminated ahead near the base of the ridge and creek, about fifty yards away, were two grazing deer. Their bright green silhouettes clearly stood out as sources of heat against the cold dark shapes of trees and black ridge beyond. Both were doe, one head down and eating, the other looking his way with bright white eyes. He turned back and checked on his uncle.

Joe lagged behind, weighed down with the metal detector and his shotgun. He was clearly winded after the labor of filing in the hole and being so out of shape. Jake turned and marched on, smiling. He picked up his pace, then keyed his microphone to speak into the two-way radio. "Come on soldier, pick up the damn pace," he said with a chuckle.

"Screw you Major," Joe radioed back. His breathing was heavy. "The most exercise I get is moving on and off that stool back at the shop."

Jake grinned. "You know, an ass is a terrible thing to waste." He glanced back as he increased the distance between them.

"If I wanted to hear from one I would have farted myself," said Joe, through slight static. "I'll meet you back at the truck. Make sure you heat it up too. I gotta take a quick break. Catch my breath."

"Well, hurry up twinkle toes. I want out of here ASAP." A minute later Jake entered the circle of bright light at the rear of the house. As he approached his SUV, he smelled something peculiar. He couldn't place the aroma at first but then instantly realized it was cigarette smoke. Dropping the shovel and backpack, he lifted his rifle.

Too late.

A hard piece of metal cracked him on the back of his head. He saw stars. Shooting pain bounced inside of his brain.

"Take that muthafucka!" said a male voice.

Jake crumbled to the gravel driveway — face up. He lay just underneath the rear bumper of his truck. He blinked several times, barely conscious. The pain sliced through him like a nail had been driven through his skull. Strange, he thought, a blurry red light blinked above him. He frowned.

"Get his rifle," ordered a second male voice.

The voice sounded somewhat familiar to Jake.

"I'm on it," said the first man.

Jake's vision faded in and out. The red light confused him even more. He wasn't sure where he was. He heard footsteps crunch up near his head and the metal scrape of his rifle being unsnapped from his 3-point chest harness.

"Now, let's see what's inside of his backpack here," said the familiar voice.

Jake heard the pack unzip. He tried to move his head to look over. He let out a moan.

"He's coming to," said the first man.

"Well, well, well," said the known voice. "Look what we have here — an old keg. Freshly dug up. Good work Major Tununda. Saved us from getting our boots dirty. But then again, I like getting my boots dirty."

Jake turned his head just as a black booted foot swung back for a kick to his face. He rolled over. The boot glanced off his cheek and cut it open. Jake sprung up like a cat and faced his attacker.

It was Clown Face, as Jake knew him. A glowing cigarette butt protruded from the ugly man's smiling lips. He wore a bandage on his forehead and grasped Jake's backpack in one hand. Out of the corner of Jake's eye another behind-the-back blow came at him from the other man. This time Jake stepped aside. The man missed and was thrown off balance. Instantly reacting, Jake cocked his elbow and drove it into the guy's jaw, followed by a hard punch to his temple. The thug was knocked out cold and dropped like a sack of horseshit. A silenced pistol tumbled out of his grip next to Jake's M4 rifle.

Jake moved for the weapons.

Not in time.

Clown Face punched him below the sternum. The blow felt like a metal giant had hit him. The wind blew out of Jake's lungs and he dropped to his knees. Clown Face gloated with satisfaction, then pulled his hand back to reveal brass knuckles. The next blow cracked Jake in the side of the head. He sprawled face first on the gravel driveway.

"That's for disrespecting Nero." The thug lifted his boot and prepared to stomp Jake's head. "And this is for screwing with me."

Jake rolled away, narrowly eluding his adversary's stomp. An explosive shotgun blast boomed. Rousseau flinched. The spotlight on the house blew out. Darkness enveloped the area. Shattered glass fell to the driveway.

About time Uncle Joe joined the action, Jake thought grimly. He wobbled to his feet and painfully sucked in a breath of air. A dark figure loomed large. Jake charged forward and tackled Clown Face. He drove with his legs and lifted the larger man off the ground and then body slammed him against the back of his SUV. Clown Face's head spider-webbed the rear window.

Like a hockey goon, Jake pumped a series of right fists into Clown Face. He connected multiple times and it felt good. Then all of a sudden, something overcame him — the same feeling he had in Afghanistan, as if someone else had taken over his thinking. His fists kept working, charged with a new sensation, pummeling his foe — seeking to end the man's life. Then a flash of light appeared from behind, illuminating the thug's face. It gave Jake a clearer target for the final blows.

But his fist stopped in mid air.

"Enough!" shouted Joe. He held Jake's wrist tight. "You're going to kill him."

Jake shook his head, dazed, not sure where he was. He looked back at his uncle — shotgun in one hand and sweat streaming down his face.

"What's wrong with you?" Joe huffed.

Jake's eyes glazed over. His head pounded from the blows he had taken. He looked down at the man he was beating to a pulp. Clown Face was out like the shattered light, his nose, mouth, and cheeks spouting bloody cuts and hideous swelling.

"We need to get out of here now!" said Joe. He gave Jake a shake.

Finally Jake came to. He pulled out his vehicle key ring and tweaked the remote unlock button toward the Tahoe. Joe raised the back hatch and threw his equipment inside as Jake gathered the backpack with the keg along with his rifle. Joe grabbed the two unconscious men by their ankles and dragged them off the driveway to avoid being run over. Jake confiscated the silenced pistol, noting it was a Beretta 92. Finally, he also stole the brass knuckles off of Clown Face's hand. He then promptly jumped in the driver's seat. Joe hopped in the passenger seat.

Jake slammed the truck into reverse, backed out, shifted to drive and accelerated out of the driveway. As they turned onto East Lake Road they noticed several nearby residential houselights turn on. The shotgun boom obviously awakened the neighborhood. As he sped back up Henderson Hill Road to escape probing eyes, Jake glanced over to his uncle. "Nice shot, by the way." Joe simply nodded, still breathing heavily.

Jake needed a safe resting spot. His injuries hurt like hell. But he also wanted to see what was inside the powder keg that he risked their lives for. They decided their best bet was to get his uncle's truck back at the fast food restaurant then both head over to the reservation and Miss Lizzie's house. There they would hunker down in safety.

23

South of Conesus Lake.

"SIR, IT'S KAY. We, ahh, ran into, ahh, some complications." Mr. Kay pulled the Hummer to the shoulder of the road and stopped. He looked over at Rousseau in the front passenger seat. His head was thrown back on the headrest. Cuts, blood, and nasty bruises covered his face. His jaw was swollen and misshapen. Kay then looked in the rear view mirror. Mr. Jasper rubbed his temple, but was essentially back in business. He had the laptop out and was tuned into the GPS tracking software.

"Put Rousseau on," demanded Nero, over the cell phone connection.

"He's not doing so good," murmured Kay. "Can't talk. I think his jaw is broken. I just picked him and Jasper up."

"Then you explain."

"Bottom line, sir, we messed up. Tununda beat the shit out of both of them. Took Mr. Rousseau's brass knuckles too. And he got off with The Mouth's silenced pistol—"

"The one Ray used in the Ashland hit?"

"Yes sir. Jasper had it."

"Duly noted," Nero angrily spouted. "Continue."

"He had help. There were two of them out there. Someone with a shotgun."

"So basically, you fucking idiots got ambushed yourselves!" Nero growled. He then calmly demanded, "tell me about the keg."

"Tununda dug it up. But then he escaped with it."

Nero roared. "Imbeciles! Put me on speaker phone *now!*"

Kay pressed the speaker button. "You're on, sir."

"Are you tracking him now?"

"Yes sir," Jasper loudly said from the back seat. "He's headed north on Route 15. Same way he came in."

"Are all three of you listening?" asked Nero in a calmer voice. He received two replies and a grunt back.

"I'm going to tell you the story of how Thomas Boyd, the owner of that keg, died back in 1779. Listen very carefully and learn from your mistakes."

The three men sat up.

"After the Iroquois captured Boyd they stripped him bare and found he had been shot in the side. So they whipped him with thorns, right on that wound. Then they tied him to a tree and practiced throwing tomahawks around his head to get him in the right frame of mind. After that, they pulled out his nails, cut off his nose, plucked out one of his eyeballs, cut out his tongue, stabbed him with spears, and sliced off his shoulder. They even cut off his cock and balls. All the while they deliberately kept him conscious as they enacted their revenge. Finally, they opened his gut and pulled out his small intestine. They nailed it to a tree and forced him to walk around the tree until all of his guts unwound around the trunk. Then they scalped him. And then cut off his head for good measure. I swear, on my mother's grave, if you three fucking idiots don't get that keg back, I promise to use every technique our forefathers used on Boyd. There is a great secret in that keg that belongs to me. Do not come back without it."

The phone clicked dead.

Rousseau and Kay looked at each other with wide eyes.

Jasper shook in the back seat. "He's insane, he'll do it. Let's go!"

McDonald's restaurant. Avon, N.Y.

Back at the McDonalds parking lot Jake transferred all of the equipment to Joe's pick up truck, with the exception of the keg backpack and M4 rifle. Those, he kept in his Tahoe. He then paced outside of his SUV while Joe ran into the restaurant to grab a couple of chocolate milkshakes.

A nagging question persisted in Jake's throbbing head — the red light he saw after he was hit in the back of the head. Where did he see it? What was it? He retraced his steps during the fist-fight. Then suddenly it came to him. He walked the rear of his truck, bent low, and looked underneath the bumper where he had been knocked down. There it was, the blinking red light attached to a metal chip. He grasped it between his fingers and pulled it off. It had been kept secure with a magnet. Joe returned just as Jake rose up with the quarter-sized device in his hand.

"Whatcha got there?" asked Joe. He sucked hard from a straw dipped into a milkshake.

Jake flipped the chip in his hand. "A GPS tracking device. It's how they ambushed us. And how they're tracking us right now." He stood up and showed his uncle. "I think they attached it up in Rochester while I was having lunch at the Strathallan. I barely remembered some guy walking in that looked like one of Nero's boys.

"Ditch the thing."

Jake grabbed the other milkshake out of Joe's hand and dropped the device in. "I'm going to buy us a few minutes head start. Be right back. Get in your truck and start it up." Jake ran into the side entrance of the restaurant, entered the men's room, and placed the milkshake on top of a urinal.

Now back out in the parking lot he nodded for Joe to leave. Jake jumped into his vehicle and sped off on Joe's tail. Two miles down the road they noticed a black Hummer barrel past them in the opposite direction. It turned into McDonalds.

Minutes later. McDonald's.

"Mr. Nero, ah, they found the tracking device. We lost him," said a hesitant Kay, in his cell phone. "But we think we have an idea of where he's headed." As he spoke he watched Rousseau in the passenger side with the blinking GPS tracking chip in his hand. It dripped with milkshake sludge.

Silence marked the other end of the phone connection.

"Mr. Nero?"

"Go ahead," whispered Nero in a hoarse voice.

"Our tracking records show it's either back to Rochester or back to the Tonawanda Reservation. Jasper just ran a summary of his travels since day one," noted Kay. "We found that when he left Fort Niagara he went directly to the reservation. He made a quick stop at a gas station, probably to fill up, then continued on to a remote location where he spent a couple of hours."

"Go on," urged Nero.

"We pulled up that address and it belongs to an Elizabeth Canohocton—"

"Ahhhh," rasped Nero. "Dear old Miss Lizzie Spiritwalker. I should have known that dirty old wench was behind all of this. I'm surprised she's still breathing."

"Sir?"

"Get to her house now," Nero ordered. "Search the place for my treasure. If she's alone take her hostage. I've got some questions for her. If Tununda is already there, take them all out. Bring me their scalps as proof. And then bring me my keg!"

"Will do."

"And burn the place down."

24

Late Wednesday night. Troop E Romulus Station.

"STATE POLICE, Hart speaking," answered Rae on a late night telephone call. She had just finished packing her briefcase with some paperwork and was headed out the door. No one else was in the sub station. She took the call even though she was technically on leave. Having been bored out of her mind and freshly caught up on a full day of sleep, she thought she would pop into the station, grab some notes on the Indian grave arson, and then head back home to Seneca Falls. "How may I help you?"

"Hello? Yes," started a female voice on the other end.

Rae seemed to recognize the voice.

"Umm, I... umm, I have some information regarding the murder of Stephen Ashland."

"Yes, ma'am, go right ahead," Rae quickly replied. She switched the phone receiver to her other ear and grabbed a pencil. She sat down at her desk, all the while thinking of where she had heard this woman before.

"Is the fifty grand still available?"

"Sure is. For information that leads to the arrest of our murder suspect Ray Kantiio."

"Listen, I want to remain anonymous."

"Absolutely," assured Rae. Then it came to her — the voice. It was the woman who called just after the Cranberry Marsh incident. She had said then she represented the head of the Iroquois Confederacy Burial Rules

Committee and wanted to arrange a meeting to view the old broach from the Indian corpse. Rae now realized this woman worked for Alex Nero. Her hands started to shake, but she kept her own voice solid. "We'll protect your identity from the public. No one will ever know you gave us any information. But we're going to need to know who you are so we can give you the reward. Is that going to be a problem?"

There was a pause.

"Ma'am?"

"I don't know. I don't know. I'm scared," the woman replied, her voice cracking. "I can't let my name out. It's too risky."

"That's fine ma'am. Just take your time. We'll work with you. What information would you like to pass on?"

"I know where The Mouth is?"

Rae tried to suppress her excitement. "Very good. Very good," she said, scribbling furiously on her note pad. "Can you tell me where exactly? Time is of the essence, in case he moves."

"Not now. I need to meet with you in person. I have some evidence to give you. Besides, he's not going anywhere, believe me."

Rae scratched her temple with the eraser of her pencil. "Alright, I'm on board. When and where can we meet?"

"I'll be in your area tomorrow morning at eleven. I reserved the research room in the largest of the Three Bears Courthouses in Ovid. Just down the road from your station."

"I know where it is. But can't we meet any sooner? I don't want the suspect to get away."

"Trust me, he's not going anywhere."

"Okay, I trust you," Rae acquiesced. "And how will I know who you are when we meet? What do you look like?"

"Umm. I'll put on a New York Yankees baseball cap. How's that? Listen, this is just going to be a drop, then you're gone."

"That's fine," replied Rae. "Would you tell me the nature of the evidence I'll be receiving from you?"

"I've got his death recorded on tape."

Rae's eyes grew wide. She squinted. She stopped writing. "Whose death? Stephen Ashland's?"

"No, Ray Kantiio's. See you tomorrow."

The phone connection ended.

The tip of Rae's pencil broke off.

MICHAEL KARPOVAGE

25

CAREFULLY EXTRACTING HIS hand from the old wooden keg sitting on Miss Lizzie's long coffee table, Joe placed the last of the British gold coins on one of several stacks he had made. "One hundred ninety-eight, one hundred ninety-nine, two hundred. They're all here, all two hundred Guineas. Damn, this gold sure does look nice," he remarked. Placed next to the glimmering stacks of coinage was a scattering of the rest of the war loot, including hand-carved smoking pipes, rings, wampum belts, and various hunting knives.

Miss Lizzie, sitting in her rocking chair petting her wide-eyed pet Chihuahua, named Choo-Choo, merely shook her head. She wore a toothless puss on her face.

Jake leaned over from his sofa seat next to Joe and meant to say something but his head pulsed with pain, even after the five aspirin he had already downed. He closed his eyes to fight off the throbbing. "Thomas Boyd wasn't really *that* accurate now was he?" Jake managed to say with a smile.

"Whaddya mean?"

Jake pulled a gold coin off the top of a stack and flipped it to his uncle. He took another one and handed it to Lizzie. "Keep 'em as a souvenirs."

Lizzie held her coin up to the light and gazed at it. Her long white hair fluttered with a cock of her head. She gave a disapproving grunt and handed the coin back to Jake. "This is symbolic of everything that is wrong in this world," she replied. "Royalty. They blind your vision and take away your dreams. I have no use for this crap."

"Well, I don't mind being king for a day." Joe placed his coin in his pocket. He then leaned over and stuck his hand back in the keg to extract more loot. He pulled out a silver corset, then a compass, and finally a gold match case.

Jake's eye lit up. "According to Boyd's journal entries, those items were apparently from a dead officer in Butler's British Rangers. A Virginian marksman looted them from the officer he killed and traded them with Boyd."

While Joe was preoccupied with the British officer's items, Lizzie picked up from the table one of the two wampum belts from the keg. Jake meanwhile, went back to his work creating a digital photographic record of each item. In front of him, on the table, was the silenced Beretta 92 he had grabbed from the man who pistol-whipped him. Next to the gun was Clown Face's brass knuckles. And next to that was the torn fragment of paper containing the other half of the Kendaia cave directions. With his camera, Jake snapped a close up photo of that little piece of paper. As soon as he finished cataloging the rest of the items he was going to decipher the cave directions in full. He then carefully moved the paper artifact aside to view his next item.

Luke Swetland's silver broach.

Jake lifted the small jewel off the table. It looked identical to the one he remembered at the Cranberry Marsh site. "It all started because of this," he remarked, holding the disc between his index finger and thumb. Joe looked up, his eyes fixed on the broach. Lizzie joined his gaze and for a long moment they just stared as Jake rolled the silver piece of jewelry between his fingers.

A reflection off the silver caused Lizzie to blink. She nodded her head as if deciding something. "Jake Tununda, you keep that broach. You are the worthy guardian now. Keep it on you at all times. It will protect you."

Jake shot her a glance, held the seriousness in her old fragile eyes and replied, "I will Lizzie Spiritwalker. I will."

"The crown has sought you out," added Joe. "It wants you to protect it."

Jake nodded. He was beginning to believe them. He placed the broach back on the table, photographed each side then dropped it in his shirt pocket and buttoned it up.

Next on tap was the cave map drawing. Jake gingerly popped off the top of a tubular hand-carved maple case and turned it upside down. Sliding into his hand was a small antique glass bottle of black ink along with a goose-quill scribing pen. He then extracted a rolled up, very fragile long piece of parchment paper. Unfurling it slowly, he laid the paper flat on the table and weighed each corner down with a stack of gold coins. Shaking his head with an accomplished grin, he photographed the simple line drawing with his camera.

Jake wasted no time in rolling the map back up and returning the items to their protective case. "Now, where's that little note about the location of Sullivan's sunken cannon?" he asked.

"Right here," said Joe, handing him what looked like a page out of Boyd's journal.

Jake recognized the handwriting as that of Boyd's. He laid the page flat and took a picture of it. He then read the contents out loud. "September 2.

Northeast of Catherine's Town, site of Butler's escape to lake below where we ambushed the old savage spy. By orders of Worshipful Master John Sullivan of Traveling Military Lodge No. 19, the Craft symbol was carved by Senior Deacon Lieutenant Bennett Smith on the cliff face directly above the sinking site of the Cannon of Fortune."

Joe spoke up. "I'll be damned. That's gotta be the same location of the Painted Rocks — the same spot where the Seneca commemorated the fallen chief from that ambush."

"And the Craft symbol is carved there too, apparently," added Jake. "Right where that cannon of gold got loose and tumbled in the lake."

"Most likely it would be the Mason's square and compasses," offered Lizzie. Her dog Choo-Choo perked up, sensing something outside.

Jake rubbed his chin. "An underwater adventure in the waiting. Wow, this keg just keeps on giving."

"I can't believe we pulled it off Jake," congratulated his uncle. "We couldn't have done this without you."

"Indeed Jake, very nice work," added Lizzie with a warm smile. "The White Deer Society thanks you very much for your help. We are forever grateful for what you've done."

"Huh?" Jake replied. He looked at Lizzie then to Joe then back at Lizzie again. "I thought— Hey, wait, you guys are guardians of the White Deer Society?"

"We are," confirmed Lizzie.

Jake looked at his uncle who nodded his agreement.

"I am a direct descendant of the same medicine woman who adopted Luke Swetland in Kendaia," Lizzie explained, her voice cracking. "Her name was She Who Heals."

"Oh, my God," said Jake. "You two lied to me. You said the society was dead."

"I said the society withered away," retorted Lizzie. "I never ever claimed it was dead."

"Neither did I Jake," added Joe. "You just never came right out and asked if we were guardians until now. Plus we are sworn to never divulge that information until someone is deserving of the right. And now, you more than deserve this right."

Joe went on. "She Who Heals was the last remaining clan mother of Kendaia. She watched the black smoke rise from a distance as Sullivan's troops burned the village to the ground. She died of starvation that winter at Fort Niagara, but not before passing on the mantle of the guardianship to one of her daughters. The problem was the true location of the cave entrance also died with She Who Heals because her daughter was never able to go back and find it. And then white settlers took the land over."

Jake's eyes lit up. "I see."

"Luke Swetland, it turns out," started Lizzie, "was a trusted guardian under She Who Heals. He came the closest to disclosing the location of the cave when he mentioned it years later in his memoirs. He wrote that he found a cave not too far from Kendaia where he took refuge for prayers."

"But Boyd and McTavish," added Jake, "knew the real location because Swetland showed them. They had the cave map and they took his guardian broach too. The one in my pocket." He patted his shirt pocket.

Lizzie cleared her throat. "Fortunately for all, the secret location slumbered. Over the next two centuries guardians of our society returned to the area from time to time just to make sure nothing was out of the ordinary. They established good relationships with the local farmers in Kendaia and Romulus. They explained to them that any white deer that were spotted were sacred to the Seneca and Cayuga tribes and should be protected — that they should not be taken as trophies. The settlers allowed the guardians access to their property where they performed secret ceremonies to the white deer protectors. It was said that when the deer appeared they were letting us know that all was well."

"Then in 1940," said Joe. "The federal government enacted eminent domain and seized the land around Kendaia and started building the Army depot and naval base. Our sacred lands were off-limits completely within a matter of days. Everything was fenced-in."

Lizzie bowed her head, long white hair falling over her face. "My own mother, who was head of the society at the time, was distraught," she said. "The white deer disappeared. My mother died that same year. I then became the matriarchal head."

Jake rose up off the couch and paced. He couldn't believe what he was hearing.

"It wasn't until many years later that the Army announced that the white herd had actually re-emerged and had expanded because of their fenced-in isolation," Lizzie continued. "And the Army then made a policy to protect them."

"A bit ironic," said Joe.

"To say the least," followed Jake, his arms folded across his chest.

Lizzie coughed. "If the herd flourished then I knew that all was well — that the Army hadn't found the cave, literally hidden underneath them. This remained the case for over fifty years. I became complacent thinking the secret was safe. I raised a family, outlived my husband, my daughter moved off the reservation and entered the white man's world. She settled in Atlanta. We became estranged. I grew old. I was alone, the last remaining guardian and no daughter to hand the society to. I was miserable. I became a witch in people's eyes."

"Yeah, you certainly scared the crap out of me as a kid," Jake said, straight-faced.

"But Alex Nero had been rising in power, his mother making claims of direct ancestral lineage to the great Atotarho," explained Joe. "On top of that there was talk that the Depot would be closing."

"Prophecies of an evil walking the surface were beginning to come true. And so I approached Big Bear for help," said Lizzie, now petting her dog Choo-Choo as she looked at Joe. "He was the only one who really cared for me in the clan. The only one who showed me respect as an elder. When he took you in after your parents died, Jake, I knew he was a good man at heart. I explained the true oral history to him. I then asked him to be a guardian and he has served the society ever since."

Jake shook his head. "This just boggles my mind." He stopped pacing and plopped back down on the sofa and sighed heavily.

Lizzie said, "And I suppose we should talk about making you an official guardian of the White Deer Society too, Jake Tununda."

"Whoa!" Jake blurted.

"But first I'm going to make some tea," stated Lizzie, pushing her dog off her lap. Choo-Choo jumped down and made a movement toward the front door, its ears still straight up. Lizzie rose up off her rocking chair, leaving it to sway back and forth several more times. She sauntered into her kitchen and called her dog after her. Instead, the dog sat at the front door and cocked its head.

Jake caught the animal's movement, but before he could register the warning, the front door crashed open and slammed against the wall. In charged Clown Face and his two thugs, weapons drawn. Choo-Choo yiped and ran behind the couch to hide.

Rousseau was on Jake in an instant, a Browning 9 mm pistol aimed at his head as he remained seated behind the coffee table. The other two men covered Joe. "Move one inch and you're fucking dead," barked Rousseau, his voice muffled due to the pummeling Jake had given him back at the keg site.

"No problem," Jake said. He raised his hands in the air.

Rousseau's eyes darted over to the rocking chair, still slowly swinging. "Who was in that chair? Where's the old bitch?"

"She's dead," answered Joe. "The dog was sitting in the chair."

Rousseau turned and glared at the older Indian.

"She passed away a few days ago," Joe lamented. "She was something like 105 or 106 anyway. I'm the caretaker of her home."

Rousseau glanced down to the table, quickly scanning for weapons. Noticing Ray Kantiio's silenced pistol and his own brass knuckles, he snatched the items up and dropped them in his inner coat pocket.

"Where's your guns?"

"Out in the pickup truck," answered Joe.

"Yo Clown Face," goaded Jake, drawing the attention back to him. "Your face tattoos really look awful with all that swelling. And man, my hand really hurts too." He opened and closed his fist for added effect.

The veins in Rousseau's neck almost burst. "Why you ballsy little punk—" He moved around the table, grabbed Jake by the crown of his hair, snapped his head back, and positioned the barrel of his pistol right between Jake's eyes. Rousseau's mouth then widened into a sinister, distorted grin. "My name is Kenny Rousseau. Remember it because tonight I'm sending you to hell."

It worked. Jake gulped, worked too well. He wanted Rousseau to get as close to him as possible. It would be his only chance at survival. He knew from close-quarters combat that if a gun or knife was already in play, the weapon must be the focus of the attack, not the individual. Now that the weapon was on him all he needed was a distraction to take action. And a bit of luck.

"Before I have my fun with you, my employer requires three items that came out of this keg." Rousseau let go of Jake's hair, but kept the gun next to his head. "Give 'em to me right now and I'll make your deaths quick with a bullet to the brain. If you don't cooperate I'll have grandpa over here scalped in front of you — while he's still alive. And that's just for starters. Nero gave me some good tips of what happened to Thomas Boyd and I have no problem repeating history on another U.S. Army soldier."

Jake closed his eyes. "Point made Rousseau. What do you want?"

"A silver broach, a ripped piece a paper with a code, and a cave map."

Jake turned his eyes downward. "I've got everything. The broach is in my shirt pocket. I'm going to reach for it. Slowly, okay?"

"Slowly," instructed Rousseau.

Jake fumbled with the button and fished out the broach. He dropped it in Rousseau's outstretched hand. The head thug pocketed the item in his coat. He kept his stare steady on Jake.

"Don't do it Jake!" yelled Joe. "Don't give him any more—"

Whack!

Joe was struck hard in the forehead with the butt of Mr. Kay's pistol. A gash opened above his brow. A thin stream of blood trailed down.

Jake raged inside. He couldn't watch his uncle be beaten in front of him. Rousseau could sense Jake's fury and pressed his Browning tight against Jake's temple.

"Go ahead. Make your move. I'll splatter your brains."

Jake sat still, turning red, jaw muscles throbbing. Rousseau ordered him to give up the next item. He also ordered his minion, Mr. Jasper, to go outside and fetch the gas can. Jake watched the man walk out the front door. He stole a glance at his uncle who was stemming the flow of blood in the palms of his hands. Joe caught his glance.

"The paper. Now!" shouted Rousseau.

Jake moved slowly, trying to buy time — thinking of how best to turn the table on his enemy. He needed that distraction. Where's Lizzie? "Why is your boy getting a gas can?" asked Jake.

"I ask the questions!" barked Rousseau, taking a line from Nero's playbook. "Because when we're done with you we're gonna burn your asses to a crisp! Now give me the paper with the code on it."

"Was it you that pulled the arson at Cranberry Marsh?" asked Jake as he handed Rousseau the paper fragment containing the Kendaia cave directions. Rousseau briefly shifted his eyes to the paper to check it out. Jake almost jumped into action but stalled. Rousseau pocketed the fragment.

"What arson? Quit talking and give me the map," ordered Rousseau. He moved the pistol away from Jake's temple but still kept it trained on his head.

Jake picked up the wooden map case on the table. Time was running out.

"This contains the map," said Jake.

"No shit. Open it and show me," grunted Rousseau.

Jake did as he was ordered, but asked, "Answer me this at least — how'd you find us here? I got rid of your tracking chip back at McDonalds."

"We've been tracking your whereabouts since Fort Niagara, when we first met," answered Rousseau, with a deformed smile. "It was a hunch you'd be here."

Jake shook his head, remembering the limo driver in the parking lot bending down out of sight near his SUV. He had thought they were just taking his plate number at the time. And that night he went directly to the reservation, to Joe's gas mart and then on to this house. They had his travels recorded. He swore to himself, then popped the cap off the map case and turned the tube upside down allowing the old pen and bottle of ink to slide out on the table.

"Speed it up!" barked Rousseau.

Jake reached inside the case and slowly extracted the rolled up map drawing. Unfurling the document, he showed Rousseau, whose eyes lit up.

"Give it to me."

Jake rolled the map back up, stuffed it in the case, added the pen and ink, and capped it. He then heard a floor board creak in the kitchen. Finally. He kept his eyes glued on Rousseau. In a moment, he heard Jasper re-enter the house closing the front door, announcing he had the gas can.

Rousseau snatched the map case out of Jake's hands. He stuffed the case inside his jacket. "And I want your camera too."

Another creak and Rousseau's head turned and his eyes darted over to the kitchen, taking his aim off Jake's head for a fraction of a second.

That's all Jake needed.

His arm went up in a flash and connected with Rousseau's shooting hand. He knocked the Browning to the side just as a round fired off. The bullet whizzed past Jake's ear and plunked into the sofa. Jake slammed Rousseau with a hard upper cut in his already-injured jaw. Rousseau lost the grip on his weapon. It clattered to the floor as he staggered backward from the force of Jake's blow.

Joe sprung into action too. He slammed a fist into Mr. Kay's nose. Kay grimaced and slammed back against his cohort — the two thugs sandwiched up against the front door, back to chest. The gas can hit the floor with a loud clang. Kay managed to get a wild shot off from his pistol too. The bullet missed Joe and lodged into the wall.

Joe ducked.

Jake dove for the Browning pistol as Rousseau's big body careened across the room. Rousseau tripped on an Indian drum and smashed heavily into a tall window. It shattered completely. He tumbled backward through the jagged opening and hit the ground outside in a shower of glass shards.

Crouched on one knee with the Browning pistol in hand, Jake swung the weapon toward the other two thugs near his uncle.

A slice of air zipped over Jake's head.

Boom!

The cannon blast shook the house.

A large hole opened up in Mr. Kay's chest. Directly behind him, Jasper's eyes went wide and he screamed. Both men's legs gave out. The two bodies crumpled to the floor in a heap — pistols still clutched in their hands. Blood and guts smeared down the door. The round that took their lives not only penetrated two bodies, but also blew a large hole through the solid wood front door.

Jake looked back toward the kitchen where the blast originated. Joe followed his gaze. It was a sight they would never forget.

In a shooters pose stood the frail Miss Lizzie. She lowered her smoking, long-barreled .357 Magnum pistol. "Nobody enters my house without knocking first."

Choo-Choo ran out of hiding and stood by Lizzie's side. Jake and Joe looked at each other with raised eyebrows.

"Rousseau!" shouted Jake. "He's got the Beretta. Joe, cover me from the window."

Joe grabbed Kay's pistol and made for the window where Rousseau fell out. Jake moved the two bodies and ripped the front door open. He moved quickly outside and crouched over to the corner of the porch, then stopped and gave a quick glance around.

Rousseau had disappeared.

Jake re-emerged inside. "Kill the lights. Check the back door." He jumped back outside just as the lights went dark inside. He heard footsteps running away. He went to the rear of his truck and opened the back hatch. He stored the Browning pistol in the waistband at the small of his back and grabbed his M4 rifle, flicked on the rifle's night scope, and placed the lens to his eye. His vision turned to a glowing green and black field. Scanning left and right across Lizzie's front yard, he caught sight of a bright green silhouetted figure running down the dirt road. The range was about 300 meters away.

Jake popped off a three-round burst and saw Rousseau stumble to his knees. Rousseau clutched his arm. But his target immediately got up and zigzagged off. Another three round burst kicked up the dirt at Rousseau's feet. The man gained more distance.

"Damn!" Jake lowered his weapon. In an all out sprint, he gave chase.

The footing proved difficult on the dark, uneven surface of the road. Before he knew it, Jake's ankle twisted in a pothole and he went down hard. He slammed his knee on gravel and crunched both elbows, still clutching the rifle. He scrambled back up and heard a vehicle start up a ways away. He dropped to one knee in a shooters stance, raised his rifle, and peered through the scope. He found what looked like a civilian Hummer from its silhouette. It sped away at a high rate of speed. Jake fired off six rounds and saw a few sparks indicating impact on the back of the Hummer. No effect. He watched the Hummer disappear around a bend.

"Son of a bitch!"

26

Early Thursday morning. East Lake Road.
Town of Varick. Seneca County, N.Y.

YANKING HIS HAND back in excruciating pain, the large man clenched his smoke-stained yellow teeth. A muffled obscenity spilled from his mouth. The fresh steak he used as a lure dropped on the grass. He also lost the grip on his mini-flashlight. It too fumbled to the ground. Stumbling backward against the dog pound fence, the man clutched his latex-gloved hand. Blood streamed out of the missing tip of his middle finger.

A white-haired West Highland terrier entered the dropped flashlight beam, showed its bloody teeth, and emitted a low growl from its muzzle. It then spit out the man's fleshy extreme fingertip, latex still wrapped tightly around it. In a fit of rage, the heavy-set man kicked the dog hard in the mouth. The dog flipped upside down, but immediately got up whimpering and moped back into the flashlight beam, refusing to give ground. It growled again and showed its teeth, taunting the larger man for more. As the man drew back for another kick, the dog emitted a terrifying high-pitched bark.

A light immediately turned on in the main house, not twenty feet away. Several more dogs, roused from their sleep inside, joined in with responsive barks of their own. They soon exited the dog doors from the house and entered the run to back up their pack leader.

The wounded man took a last look at the lead terrier knowing his second dognapping of the place had failed. He should have known better than to return to the scene of his first crime. As he scrambled out of the gate to make his escape, the small dog, still standing in the beam of light, began to howl in victory.

Same time. Tonawanda Reservation.

Jake gave one last sweep of the clan mother's property with his night scope and rifle. He figured either Kenny Rousseau would return to finish the hit or a cop car would show up from all the gunshots fired. But nothing had stirred for the last ten minutes. The night remained black, quiet and depressing.

Satisfied, he re-entered the house to discuss their next moves. Joe swept glass shards near the window while Miss Lizzie paced back and forth across the living room. She spoke out loud in an ancient Iroquois tongue. She bowed her head and mumbled her emotions, but at times she threw her hands in the air and shook her fists violently at the unseen Great Spirit.

Jake approached his uncle and whispered in his ear. "We need to do something with these bodies. We can't go to the police. They won't see this as an act of self-defense from a home invasion. They'll see my connection with Nero and that the keg was dug up. We are in this as deep as Ashland was. They'll put us all away for murder."

Joe's voice cracked with fear. "And if anyone on the reservation finds out, well, loose lips sink ships."

"Right."

"Do you think Rousseau will come back?"

"I'm not sure," Jake whispered. "He retrieved what Nero wanted him to, but he knows we have firepower and we shoot back to kill. I think I wounded him but not sure. He's outnumbered as far as I know. So, my bet is he won't, but still I'm not going to chance it. We've got to get Lizzie out of here and into a safe house and we've got to get rid of those bodies."

"I know. I know," said Joe, his hands shaking. "I'm just trying to think where we can take them. Hell, I've never done this before. What are we going to do with them? Bury them, sink them, hide them, burn them?"

Lizzie's pacing stopped. Both men looked over to the clan elder. On the rocking chair, Choo-Choo even perked up. Lizzie parted her fine white hair and exposed her red face. She scowled at the men with fiery eyes.

"Robert Jake Tununda," she rasped and pointed. "You are now a guardian of the White Deer Society whether you like it or not! Nero will soon be in possession of the last clues to the cave entrance. We are now in the final race to find the almighty Crown of Serpents. You must go to Kendaia tonight and head him off. If he finds the crown, he will unleash the powers of darkness and slavery and we will suffer beneath his boot."

"But the bodies—"

"Shush!" Lizzie scolded. "I took their lives. I own their souls. This is my house, my responsibility. Big Bear and I will handle the bodies. You are much more valuable to us by finding the crown and securing it so Nero cannot possess it."

Jake looked at his uncle. He received a reassuring nod.

"As you wish," Jake promised. "Let me grab my stuff and I'll hit the road to Kendaia. And remember, I was *never* here."

27

Thursday morning. Varick Fire Station.

STATE POLICE INVESTIGATOR Rae Hart thought she'd kill three birds with one stone before meeting her so-called anonymous tipster in Ovid. The first, fix the hunger pains in her stomach. The second, check on the status of the emergency coordinator injured in the gravesite arson. The third, find an outstanding material witness related to that arson. And the perfect place to try and nail all three birds was this morning's fundraising pancake breakfast just north of the Army Depot on Route 96A at the Varick Fire Station.

She pulled into the busy parking lot and stepped from her vehicle. She wore a black trench coat over a dark blue turtleneck sweater, jeans, and black leather boots. In the meeting hall, where breakfast was being served, she was greeted warmly by several of the firefighters in the serving line. She thanked them for their inquiries on how she was feeling after being shot, and was treated to a plate of pancakes and home fries, plus a cup of coffee. As she ate and chit-chatted with some local residents curious about her ordeal, her stomach responded kindly.

First bird stoned.

Afterward, she wandered down the hall, coffee cup in hand, and found the handlebar-mustached fire chief Chet Bailey sitting in his office. She immediately voiced her concern and inquired about the county emergency coordinator's condition.

"I just heard from the doc this morning," answered the chief, rising up to greet her. He motioned for her to sit down while he slipped on his reading glasses. She placed her coffee on the desk while he read from a notepad near his phone.

"Ed is actually going to pull out of this just fine. Let me see here, Doc said he's got a busted shoulder, broken ribs, severe burns on his arm, and a bad knot on his head, but nothing life-threatening." He looked up at Rae.

She breathed a sigh of relief. "I'm glad to hear that. I'm going up to Geneva today to pay him a visit."

Bird number two stoned.

The chief asked how she was feeling. She gave him an explanation of the shooting, with credit to Major Tununda for helping her, and a comment that they were making good progress on finding the killer/cop shooter. He then asked if she had any suspects on the Indian grave arson.

"All kinds of good evidence, but no clear suspects yet and no motivation other than maybe an anti-Native American resentment." Rae pursed her lips.

"Yeah, tensions are sky high about the sale of the Depot," noted the Chief. "I hope people around here behave today. Word leaked out that it's that casino guy Alex Nero who's gonna be buying up the land."

"Yep, heard the same," said Rae. "It just chaffs my ass that he'll literally be in our own backyard. We put all our patrols on alert. Sheriff's department is helping us out too." She pulled a note pad out of her trench coat pocket. Thumbing through her notes she found the name she was looking for.

"But listen, I want to ask you about one firefighter in particular who was on scene that morning—"

"Oh, lemme taking a wild guess — Tommy friggin' Owens, right?"

The chief killed bird number three for her. "That would be the one," she nodded.

"He treated our good Samaritan pretty goddamn crummy," replied the chief, pushing his spectacles back up his nose. "I can see how you made the connection, but he better hope to high hell he's got nothing to do with that arson or I'll roast his ignorant, uneducated ass myself."

"I stopped by his house twice and he hasn't been home. Was wondering if you might know where I could find him."

"Last I heard that boy lost his job when his daddy shut down their convenience store up in Seneca Falls. Now he's delivering for Mark's Pizzeria out of Ovid."

"Well, I'll just go ahead and get a pizza delivered to our Romulus station then," Rae laughed. "See who shows up."

"Better yet, I saw his daddy eating pancakes earlier, maybe he's still out there. Can't miss him. He's bigger than me with gray hair and shitty teeth. I think he's got a dark blue coat on if I'm not mistaken. Name is Tom Owens Senior."

"Thanks Chief."

"Listen," Bailey continued, lowering his voice. "Tommy Junior specifically mentioned last week that his pop's business shut down because all their customers started going to the Indian-owned gas stations for tax-free sales. His whole family has hated the Indian tribes for years. Blames the state for not enforcing the laws. So, watch your ass Rae. I mean it. There's a number of people out here that do very, very stupid things out of unfounded fear and resentment."

Rae stood up and grabbed her coffee. "I hear ya Chief. Thanks for the tip. I'll go see if Senior's still out there. You take care."

"Alright now, you have a good one."

Rae re-entered the meeting hall and gave a quick look around. She couldn't help but miss the man fitting the chief's description. He sat in the corner. She put on her friendly smile and walked over.

"Good morning. Tom Owens Senior?"

The man's beady little eyes, barely visible behind overstuffed cheeks, looked Rae up and down. He set his fork down and spoke through a mouthful of pancakes. "Who's asking?"

"I'm investigator Hart with the State Police." She then paused to judge his reaction. He turned his eyes slightly downward and chewed his pancakes with a wet smacking sound. Definitely hiding something, she concluded. "I'm just wondering where your son Tommy is. I need to ask him a few questions." She then observed his dark blue coat sleeve ripped at the elbow. The fabric seemed to match the patch taken from the swamp. Her heart jumped.

"Bout what?" asked Senior, belching defiantly.

Rae leaned down and came face to face with the grotesque man. She held his gaze. "About the arson and attempted murder of Ed McMann. That's what?"

"You think my boy did that?" he asked loudly, spitting a little piece of food across the table.

Rae stood back up and crossed her arms. She noticed a hush fell over the meeting hall. "Tell me something Tom, how did you rip your coat sleeve?"

"Shoveling shit on the farm. It's what I do for a living now that the fucking Indians put me out of business. Here, you wanna smell?" He stood up and extended his arm in provocation.

Rae didn't bite. She just stood there and stared angrily at him.

"How dare you accuse my son. I'm done with this shit." Senior slammed his chair aside and immediately made for the side exit door.

Rae realized she came on too strong — again. She pursued Tom outside to his vehicle and observed him entering a beat up, blue Chevy pick up truck. He drove passed her, leaned out his window, and shouted for her to leave his son alone. She wrote his plate number down and watched him speed off north on 96A. She jumped into her unmarked sedan and followed.

Allowing him plenty of distance during the tail, Rae placed a call to the E-911 dispatch for a background record check on both Tom Senior and Junior. A minute later, to her detriment, she found out both the father and son had clean records. She smacked the steering wheel. The torn coat and the hearsay anti-Indian rhetoric would be flimsy evidence anyway, she realized. Nothing a judge would base a search warrant of their house on.

Rae's cell phone rang on her seat. She pulled over to take the call, letting Tom Senior disappear down the road.

"State Police. Hart."

"Miss Hart? This is Alan Payton, the West Highland Terrier breeder over in Varick—"

"Yes, sir. What can I do for you?"

"Well, I think that son of a bitch who killed my dog in that arson was trying to take another one last night."

"Is that right?"

"Yep, they got all riled up early this morning, barking and howling," said Payton. "I thought maybe they just saw some deer or something. All were accounted for so we went back to bed."

"Uh huh," pondered Rae.

"But then after feeding this morning, my wife noticed blood on Horatio's muzzle. He's the pack leader. He did not have any cuts on him so we started looking around out in the run."

"And?"

"And well my Horatio got the better of that bastard. Bit the tip of his finger off! I've got it sitting under the water bowl. Didn't want to move it or anything. I also found a flashlight too. Left it alone as well."

"Mr. Payton, I'll be right over," Rae said, realizing Tom Owens Senior could be ruled out. He had all of his fingers back at the pancake breakfast. "I'm going to call ahead for some deputies to secure the scene. You did good."

"Thank you ma'am. See ya in a bit."

In front of Alan Payton's house Rae noticed a black Seneca County sheriff's deputy patrol car had already responded. She recognized the patrol car's ID number as that of the rookie and vet combo. Putting on the latex, she met the owner, who took her around back where the young rookie sheriff was standing in the dog run. She nodded to the thin mustached, small-framed deputy who stood next to an overturned stainless steel dog bowl. A short black flashlight, its beam long since faded, sat nearby.

The rookie nodded a greeting. "Investigator, I've secured the evidence just as you requested," he smiled, pointing to the bowl and flashlight.

"Thanks deputy," acknowledged Rae, noticing some unusual discoloration on the grass near his feet. "Just do me a favor and don't move. I think there's blood evidence near your shoe."

The deputy looked down, realizing he had potentially compromised key evidence on the crime scene. Angered and embarrassed, he apologized to Rae.

Emphasizing the point, she asked where his partner Wyzinski was, knowing full well the vet wouldn't have sent a rookie alone out on an important scene like this.

"Wyz called in sick with a bad case of the flu. Couldn't get his big butt out of bed." He smiled nervously.

"Heard there's a strain going around," agreed Rae. She picked up the dog bowl and inspected the fingertip. At first glance she noticed white discoloration, due to the death of the skin cells, but upon closer examination she realized the fingertip was wrapped in latex. The Cranberry Marsh arsonist also used latex — remnants of which were found burned at the scene. The tip seemed to be the first segment of the middle or even ring finger. It was just the pad of the finger behind the nail, but gave her enough of a fingerprint for the crime lab to hopefully make a match. She left it alone and placed the bowl back over for protection.

"Tell you what," she suggested to the rookie. "How about you ease back slowly, get to your patrol car and start making some calls for me? Call doctor's offices and hospitals, see if anyone came in with a finger injury as of last night."

"Yes ma'am," replied the deputy, looking down as he backed away from the run.

"And get Mr. Payton's statement too," she ordered.

"Sure."

"And one more thing," added Rae. The rookie stopped and looked up. "Have a patrol sent to Mark's Pizzeria. See if the deliveryman, Tommy Owens Junior, is working. Find out if he lost a fingertip."

"Will do."

"If he did, arrest his ass."

Rae then placed a call on her cell phone to activate the crime scene van. She slowly and methodically searched the dog run, finding more blood on the grass trailing away. She tracked the blood across the owner's side yard over to the shoulder of the road where the blood ended at a set of wide truck tire tracks in the mud.

Same time. Three Bears Courthouses. Ovid, Seneca County, N.Y.

On the day she intended to initiate the downfall of her boss, Anne Stanton left her Kingston home at six in the morning to begin her road trip west into central New York. She had convinced Alex Nero the night before that advance research and scouting on terrain features in the Kendaia area would better substantiate the cave location before they began their primary ground search, rather than waste time by going at the search willy-nilly, as she put it. She agreed to meet him later in the day for his big real estate announcement over at the Seneca Army Depot. There she would present any findings she had come across. In the meantime, Nero would be coordinating the manpower and equipment needed for the search and for the spelunking expedition sure to follow — all the while waiting for Rousseau and his team to recover the last of the Boyd journal clues. Nero told her he would send her a text message with the final cave directions once the code had been deciphered in its entirety.

Arriving just south of the Depot in Ovid, a sleepy rural village once the original county seat before being moved north to Waterloo, Stanton drove up to the village's main tourist attraction. On a small knoll sat three red brick, white-framed buildings built in similar architectural style, but varying dramatically in overall size. The largest building was on the left, the next one in the middle a bit smaller, while the tiniest sat on the right. Named the Three Bears Courthouses these buildings took on various functions and housed many organizations over the years. Today, the smallest courthouse housed a local Veterans of Foreign War branch, the middle courthouse a Rotary International and Lions Club, and the largest structure — freshly renovated — hosted the Seneca County Historical Society, which had just moved from Seneca Falls.

With briefcase in hand, a faded New York Yankees baseball cap over blonde upturned hair, Stanton quickly ascended the main steps of the Papa Bear courthouse and entered the historical society. The president of the organization, an overly zealous man in his late thirties, introduced himself as Danny Wood. He led her up to the private research room on the second floor.

Already laid out on an old cherry table was a copy of the post-Revolutionary War Military Tract land map for the Finger Lakes region. This was land confiscated by the Continental Congress and given to the veterans of the war for their service in hopes they might settle the lands once owned by the Iroquois Confederacy. Many vets had taken the opportunity to resettle, but most simply sold their awarded lands to farmers or prospectors.

Stanton smiled, already perusing the map. It would be very helpful. She was about to compliment the president for being so prepared for her visit when her cell phone vibrated in her pant's pocket. A quick glance at the display announced the expected text message from Nero.

It was the deciphered Freemason cave directions.

She read the code: CAVE LOCATION. FOLLOW BROOK EAST FROM APPLETOWN. STAY ON SOUTH BANK PAST ORCHARDS. AND CORNFIELDS TO BURIAL GROUNDS. DESCEND TO BROOK AND SEE OAK. MARKER TREE FACE LOOKS AT ENTRANCE. ON OPPOSITE SIDE HALFWAY UP SLOPE.

Huh? Marker tree face? What does that mean, she wondered.

At the bottom of the text message was another sentence: *you are in this too deep, your life now depends on the success of your research.*

After slipping her phone back in her pocket and donning white cotton handling gloves over shaking hands, she leaned close to the map, nose almost touching. She searched the east side of Seneca Lake. "This is an amazing replica Mr. Wood," she noted to the society president, in a voice veiling her fear of Nero.

With a lisp in his western New York whine, the man replied, "Oh my God, call me Danny. I'm so glad you like it. It's an honor to work with the Haudenosaunee Collection. Mr. Nero is a big fan of mine."

Stanton thought, if only he knew. She smiled weakly and put on her eyeglasses.

"I tried to get as much material as possible ready for you after your call yesterday," continued the talkative Danny. "And there's more. Just wait!" With a double clap of his hands, he skipped off into the library room.

Stanton turned back to the map and in Military Tract Lot 66 she found Kendaia Creek. She then opened her briefcase and removed a notepad and pencil, but her eyes wandered to a manila envelope containing a mini-cassette tape recording and a topo map of the Ashokan Reservoir. In just an hour's time she would turn the package over to the authorities to play her final ace in the hole. She wanted Alex Nero to die in prison where he belonged.

Danny bounded back into the research room. He carefully placed on the table beside her an oversized, scuffed and stained thick black leather bound book with threads hanging from its linen cover. "You won't believe what I have here," he announced with oozing enthusiasm. "It's a rare, limited edition, one of only ten surviving history books of Seneca County. It covers the years 1786 to 1876, complete with illustration plates and personal accounts of the early settlers." He drew a breath.

Stanton whistled softly.

"And I already bookmarked for you several excerpts on the early Indians, the Sullivan's Trail, and the village of Kendaia. So, feel free to dig right in. I'll be downstairs putting some Chamomile tea on. Would you care for some?"

"Certainly Danny and thank you so much for your hard work already. You're very thorough. Oh and by the way, I just love your shirt."

Danny blushed, thanked Stanton, and told her he'd be back in a jiffy with their tea. With a pirouette he was off.

Stanton shook her head with a smile, but then delved into the large volume and hit the first bookmark Danny had noted. It was a skewed history on the birth of the Iroquois Confederacy, obviously written from a white man's perspective. The next bookmark gave a short overview of the Sullivan-Clinton campaign and how it broke the backs of the Iroquois when they aligned with the British. Nothing she didn't already know. And then Kendaia popped up, also referred to as Appletown. A mere sentence described how it was destroyed in 1779, but that some old apple trees had gone untouched. Finally she hit a bookmarked reference on an excerpt called the *Trophy of Indian War*, listed on page 143 of the book.

The following paragraph she read caused a chill to creep up her spine.

Let the record show that in the year 1801 settler Wilhem Van Vleet, in the northern part of his Lot 79 bordering Lot 73, found a souvenir of Sullivan's invasion in a large oak tree felled at the rear of his farmhouse plot. The tree measured about three feet in diameter and straddled the brook flowing west to Appletown on the lake. In the crotch about eight feet up, thoroughly embedded in the growths of the tree, a horseshoe of very fine workmanship was discovered. Upon strict examination, a Freemason symbol was found engraved along with a date marked Sept. 5th, 1779, that fateful day 22 years hence when Sullivan's soldiers torched the Indian village once standing near Van Vleet's acreage. Wilhelm kept the horseshoe on his fireplace mantle as a Trophy of the Indian War. In 1845, after he passed away, his son J.W. Van Vleet donated the souvenir to the Grand Lodge of Free and Accepted Masons of the State of New York.

Stanton wasted no time. Calling the ever-helpful Danny back upstairs, she showed him the excerpt and explained that she needed to find the present day location of the Van Vleet homestead near the spring and brook where that horseshoe had been found in the tree. Danny jumped at the chance.

"I need all the maps you've got around the Seneca Army Depot area. We're going to resurrect the lay of the land at Kendaia. Those orchards, brooks, and old homes may not exist anymore today, but they did once on paper as recorded landmarks."

In an instant, Danny produced a modern Seneca Army Depot map from a flat file. "We can start with this and work our way back in time. It was rendered by the elite cartographic illustration firm Mapformation. Best big picture 3D view of the Depot there is to date."

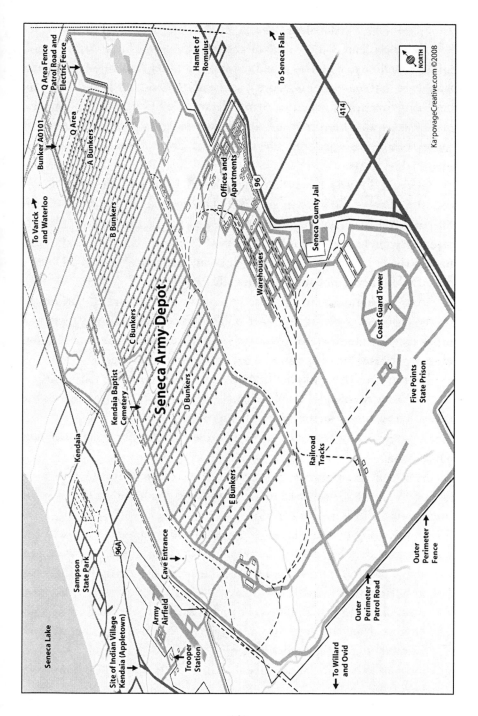

Stanton observed Seneca Lake, colored in bright blue on the far upper left. Sampson State Park — site of the old Sampson Naval Base — took up the shoreline in a myriad of old roads until it met Route 96A. Running parallel to that main thoroughfare was the north-south abandoned railway bordering the expansive Seneca Army Depot. The Depot's inner perimeter, east–west parallel bunker roads clearly delineated its sprawl. Centered at the top of the map was the hamlet of Kendaia. She pointed to the label and mouthed its name.

"That really isn't the site of the original Indian village you know," remarked Danny. "It's just named Kendaia because an old train station for the naval base used to sit there. The real site of the Indian village is actually a couple of miles south on 96A—" His finger drew down the road toward the left. "At this little rest area bend, just across from the Depot's old airfield. There's a commemorative site marker there."

"Yes," said Stanton, with a raised eyebrow. "I was aware of that. But in reality, that spot is wrong too. That marker was deliberately put there as a decoy by the state so artifact hunters wouldn't desecrate the true location of where the Indian village and burial grounds really stood."

"Hmmm… That I did not know. Where is the real location then?"

"Well my friend, all I'll say is that the true location is a bit closer to the lake. I have a vested interest to reveal no more."

"I see," Danny conceded as he returned to the flat file to conduct another map search.

This time he produced not one, but three maps of the area — from 1850 down to 1839 and 1812. He carefully laid them out on the table for inspection. "This is all I've got."

It was easily determined that the 1850 topographical map held the most terrain detail and local landmarks. The earlier versions were just too vague. Stanton leaned in and found the general vicinity of where the Indian village would have stood. It was labeled as Appletown, written on a vertical, bisecting a small brook. From her briefcase, she produced hand-written notes from the Boyd journal entries Nero had allowed her to copy. She thumbed to the September 5th entry.

She read to herself. "Sunday, Sept. 5th … Came upon old Indian town call'd Kendaia or Apple Town."

"Appletown." Stanton touched the 1850 map on the shoreline.

WM. T. Gibson, 1850.

Looking closer, she noticed a faded dotted line running parallel to the lake a short distance inland from the village name. It too bisected a brook.

"Check this out," she said, pointing to the dotted line.

Danny squinted at the map. Then from a pocket he extracted a magnifying loop. At close magnification he could make out the words, *Sullivan's Tr.*, clearly in reference to General Sullivan's line of march up that shoreline in the summer of 1779.

Stanton clenched her fist in satisfaction. "You see what I'm talking about now."

Danny nodded. "And here is a reference to Wilhelm's son J.W. Van Vleet, right here in Lot 79. You can see how that brook cuts right through his land and ends at the northern boundary with Lot 73, just as it's explained in the book."

"Danny listen, no offense, but I need some privacy now."

"Absolutely," Danny responded. "Stop downstairs for some tea when you need a break."

Alan Payton residence. Varick.

WHILE SEVERAL WEST Highland terriers milled about sniffing her pant legs, Rae informed Mr. Payton that her crew was finished with evidence collection. She also told the dog breeder that none of the hospitals had reported any finger injuries, and that he should set up a video surveillance camera should the dog killer return again.

She continued. "And what we're going to do is get that severed tip to our lab and run a fingerprint and pull DNA to see if we can make a match in our database. But it may take a few days."

"Can I shoot the bastard if he comes on my property again?" asked the breeder.

"Mr. Payton, you're not going to shoot anyone," admonished Rae. "Just set up the camera and call us if you see or hear anything unusual. I hope your day goes better, sir."

Back inside her sedan, Rae watched as the state crime scene van rolled away. After gathering her thoughts, she placed a call to the sheriff's deputy. He had just located Tommy Owens Junior at the pizzeria. She was informed he had all of his fingers and furthermore, refused to speak to any law enforcement officials because of the public harassment his father received earlier that morning.

Rae ended the call and squeezed the steering wheel in frustration. "Dammit! I'm out of leads."

She checked her watch and realized she'd be five minutes late to her appointment at the Papa Bear. Hopefully she would find out where the man who had shot at her was located. And if it was true that The Mouth was dead, then she had to find out who killed him and why.

So many questions — and all intricately related somehow to Army Major Robert Jake Tununda's meddling. She couldn't help but speculate what kind of trouble that fine specimen of a man was causing right now. She would call him back in due time to try and arrange their delayed dinner date. Heck, she even wondered if he was missing a digit. There was something he wasn't revealing regarding this whole mess. She just hoped she hadn't judged him wrong or even cleared him too quickly.

Same time. Three Bears Courthouses.

Stanton referred back to Boyd's September 5th entry and read out loud. "The finest Indian village yet with about 20 well-finished houses. They have an extensive apple and peach orchard within a half mile of Seneca Lake situated on a level ground with a brook running through it. Some apple trees look ancient in growth. We counted over 100 trees." She peered at the 1850 map again, her eyes following the brook across open land.

"We find 2 Indian Chiefs' vaults in their burying grounds. One of these was some great man and was buried in this manner..." She skimmed ahead. "We later burned these vaults to the ground. We burned it all down, the orchards, the cornfields, the village. This was for Wyoming."

She blinked. Revenge was never pleasant, but it is necessary.

"We rescued a captive, Luke Swetland, taken prisoner by the Savages near Nanticoke in the Wyoming Valley in the summer last. He was most overjoyed at making our acquaintance. He was brought to this town and given to an old witch who kept him as her adopted son. He said she cursed him from leaving. He showed us her sacred location in a nearby ravine, a ten minute walk east. Much to explore here. We also see a site never encountered before. A pure White-furred deer. Swetland warns that evils await those who kill a white deer. McTavish shoots and misses the trophy much to Swetland's relief. Swetland says much about Butler and Brant and disposition of the enemy's men."

"Okay, the sacred location in a nearby ravine. A ten minute walk east. White deer seen. Now we're getting somewhere."

Stanton flicked open her cell phone and produced the completed cipher code directions in Nero's text message. CAVE LOCATION. FOLLOW BROOK EAST FROM APPLETOWN. STAY ON SOUTH BANK PAST ORCHARDS. AND CORNFIELDS TO BURIAL GROUNDS. DESCEND TO BROOK AND SEE OAK. MARKER TREE FACE LOOKS AT ENTRANCE. ON OPPOSITE SIDE HALFWAY UP SLOPE.

"If I follow the brook east along the south bank — that's where the apple and peach orchards and cornfields must have been," she mumbled, tracing her route with a finger. "So, ten minutes at a walking pace—" She estimated another half mile or so and found where the brook ended, or rather began. It was right where a tiny asterisk marked a location of a spring at the northern sector of Lot 79. Sure enough, next to the spring symbol was a small black box labeled, *W. Van Vleet* in almost unintelligible lettering.

Wilhelm's farm. It's where the Boyd marker tree once stood — the marker being the old horseshoe with the Freemason's symbol.

And where the cave entrance to the Crown of Serpents awaits.

Same time outside. Three Bears Courthouses.

Rae donned her bulletproof vest, patted the service weapon hidden under her coat, and walked up to the largest of the Three Bears Courthouses — the Papa Bear. After greeting the flamboyant president of the historical society, she informed him that she was simply there on a mental break to browse around the new facilities. Danny offered to take her coat, but Rae refused, saying she wasn't staying long. He said feel free to roam about through the library on the first floor and the research room and mapping archives on the second level — that there was only one other guest upstairs conducting research. He even offered her tea.

After posing her way through various rare books and asking general questions, Rae made her way upstairs when the clock hit 11:10 AM.

The New York Yankee baseball cap was the first thing she noticed as the woman wearing it was hunched over several maps. Her next reaction was surprise at the woman's age. She had expected an older academic to be heading Nero's Iroquois artifact collection, not a good-looking woman in her mid-to-late twenties.

"I'm here about Kantiio," Rae whispered to her from across the table. She flashed a state police badge.

The woman stood up, eyes bright. "Does the man downstairs know who you are?"

Rae confirmed that her voice matched the one on the phone. "He does not. I told him I was just browsing about."

The woman extracted an envelope from her briefcase. "Everything you'll need is in this package. Take it and leave please," she pleaded. "Time is running out."

"Certainly," said Rae, stepping around the table to receive the envelope. She quickly hid it in her coat. Her eyes then darted down to several scattered documents on the table. She noticed a map of the Seneca Army Depot, as well as a blown up drawing of the same deer and snake engraving found on the Cranberry Marsh Indian corpse broach. The woman stepped in front of her and blocked Rae's view.

Rae spoke. "Anne Stanton, I presume? The head of the Haudenosaunee Collection? I recognized your voice. Remember the day you called after that broach, with that same deer engraving, was found in Cranberry Marsh." She pointed to the drawing on the table.

Stanton blinked. The blood drained from her face. She looked away.

"I take it this all has to do with the white deer and some guardian cult they represent, right?"

Stanton issued not a word.

Rae pressed further. "This cult protects some ancient Iroquois relic hidden in Seneca County — wait let me guess, on the Depot lands. Am I getting hot?"

Stanton glanced back, anger in her eyes.

Rae took a step closer and whispered to her, face-to-face. "And I bet this all-powerful relic is what you and your boss Alex Nero are after? And that he would kill for?"

Stanton flinched, then finally gave in, whispering back, her eyes locked with Rae's. "Listen, I detest the bastard. I'm on *your* side. That's why I gave you evidence of Ray's murder. And yes, we are looking for a legendary Indian treasure. I just — well, I just have other motivations for helping him find it, okay?"

"Is everything alright up there?" shouted Danny, from the first floor.

"Doing just fine, Mr. Wood," Stanton answered. "I'll be down for tea in a minute."

Rae shook her head. "There have been three people killed, and a dog. And another person badly burned, and yours truly shot at—" she said, tapping her chest. "All because of this treasure hunt you're on. I appreciate the package you gave me, but I'm also very aware you're using us too. For what, I don't know. But I will find out very soon. So, you keep in mind that if this information doesn't pan out I'll be breathing down your neck as an accessory to murder. Good day."

Ten minutes later, as Rae turned into the entrance to her Trooper station, she couldn't help but notice all the commotion up near the old Army airfield control tower. Four news reporter vans and a slew of media types with flashing cameras indicated Nero's press conference was already under way. She then noticed a crew of contractors erecting a new chained-linked fence separating the road to the control tower from the law enforcement and fire training structures. One of the contractors was tossing a lock in the air as he leaned against the fence.

It all made sense to her now.

Nero would lock the public out of his private property in order to search for the artifact alone. He wanted no distractions. Rae needed to talk to Jake Tununda. She needed him to open up once and for all about why this Indian relic was so damn important and worth dying over.

29

Noon. Seneca Army Depot airfield control tower.

BEHIND A MAKESHIFT podium of microphones, set up for the media-only press conference, the balding Seneca County Industrial Development Agency executive director gave his nod that he was ready to begin. The podium stood on the cracked runway of the Seneca Army Depot's old airfield. Behind the speaker stood two buildings in a state of disrepair — the old control tower and a two-bay fire station. They presented a perfect photo op background to the morning's affair. Several hand held still cameras in the media pool flashed to the front of director. Larger video cameras whirred to life.

The director grinned. "Thank you all for coming. I'll get right to the heart of the matter. I am happy to announce that the esteemed Tadodaho of the Grand Council of the Haudenosaunee Confederacy, Alex Nero, is now the proud owner of the 8,000-acre inner perimeter and airfield of the former Seneca Army Depot." He smiled widely as several other IDA officials standing off to the side applauded.

"As one of New York State's greatest entrepreneurs I can't stress enough what a landmark deal Mr. Nero has given the taxpayers of Seneca County. Mr. Nero's proven success in job generation will only add to the continued success we've already experienced in the Depot's transformation." The director posed for the cameras again amid more applause.

"To alleviate any taxpayer fears up front I wanted to say that Mr. Nero has agreed to pay property taxes, just like every other entity in the development zone. So, only his creative business imagination awaits on how best to develop this land for the benefit of this county. He now wishes to make a few comments regarding this milestone return of government property back to the Haudenosaunee Confederacy. Without further ado, I present to you Alex Nero." As Nero walked up, the director and his cohorts applauded.

Troop E Romulus Station.

Rae entered the station and headed to her office. She immediately pulled out a pair of binoculars to get an up close view of the press conference two hundred yards away outside her window. A quizzical look came across her face. She spotted three men dressed in black heading down the runway lugging a strange piece of equipment on a cart. She panned back to the control tower. Five more men, dressed the same, and all obviously Indian, presented themselves in a stiff line in front of the media pool. A security detail for the VIP.

And then the man of the hour came into view, stepping behind the podium. Rae's heart pumped faster. She adjusted the focus rings on the binoculars. Long gray hair on a perfectly dressed lanky frame. And a face that had been burned in her mind since her father was gunned down years ago.

Alex Nero.

Fire raced through her veins. She placed the binoculars on the desk, hung up her coat, pulled off her protective vest, and sat down with a deep sigh. Now he's officially a Seneca County resident. Well, let's hear what he's got to say. She turned on a nearby television set.

Airfield control tower.

Nero gripped the sides of the podium and leaned forward. His eyes were bloodshot with heavy bags underneath. Five of his thug bodyguards moved in front forming a physical barrier. Mr. Makowa and Mr. George, from the gauntlet fight, took up both ends. Rousseau was noticeably absent. They all wore dark suits, sunglasses, and their typical expressionless intimidating faces. The press pool gave them a wide berth.

Nero cleared his throat. In a deep rasp, he began.

"As Tadodaho of the Grand Council of the Haudenosaunee Confederacy, I wish to extend to you greetings from our great people. We, people of the longhouse, do not love any land more than the land of the Haudenosaunee Confederacy. Many thanks go to the Seneca County IDA for offering this property to their rightful owners first and foremost over any outsiders. And many thanks to closing the deal in such an expedited manner." Nero gave a nod to the director. The director nodded in return, his colleagues patting him on the back.

A cloud passed over Nero's eyes. He jutted an index finger in the air.

"But," he barked angrily. "Not since 1779, when the Town Destroyer George Washington expelled us with his burning army and his brutal atrocities, have we ever been treated just and fair."

The director shook his head in confusion and insult.

Nero pressed on. "It has been almost a 230 year hiatus of watching our heartland split to the core. This will not happen again. Not under my watch. The lands at the Depot, owned again by our confederacy, mark the first step in the rejuvenation of the mighty sovereign empire we once were and will become again.

"Following in the words of my great forefather, my blood kin, the great shaman Atotarho, the very first Tadodaho of the Grand Council, I, Alex Nero, shall return to you, by the Great Spirit's will, every grain of earth that was quenched by the blood of our warriors and the sweat of our clan mothers and fathers."

He stared directly into the cameras. "The people of the Haudenosaunee, the true owners of these sacred lands that surround you—" He waved his hands in the air. "These lands raped by the irresponsible, these lands whose graves have been robbed and desecrated by the ignorant and arrogant, I shall return it all, I shall return and conquer those who stand in our path." He paused to catch his breath.

The press pool and IDA personnel shifted uneasily.

"Our willingness to develop casinos and gas and tobacco businesses as a source of income for our people has proven successful." Nero flashed a smile. "After all, it is a form of reparations by you, the American people. It's your money you gamble away every day in our casinos. We simply rake it in and then invest it." He shook his head in mock insult and laughed.

"What your money does is it gives us the means to bypass the long injustice of your state and federal court system, the broken treaties of history, and the deceit of those who would see us fail in our sovereignty rights. This new source of income has turned us into true players in your game of capitalistic racism. We are now players to pursue our own interests in buying back our rightful lands." He chuckled. "And to buy them back with your own cash.

"You see, you Americans only believe in one thing. Money. And more money. That is the only language you speak. Yours is a consumer nation. You celebrate your religions by shopping. You measure your success with who has the most toys or the biggest house. So, in keeping harmony with your culture I'll keep giving you back your own wasted money from my casinos and you can keep giving us back our rightful sacred lands. It's a win-win situation all around."

He placed his hands on the sides of the podium to steady himself. "Why do we do this, you may ask? Because the blood of our forefathers demand it for the wrongs beset upon us!" He slammed a fist down, his face twisted in rage. "The people of the Haudenosaunee, the rightful citizens, are a separate people — distinct from the U.S. citizenry, above the U.S. citizenry. This is simply the right thing to do in the name of my people." He paused for effect.

"And really that is the bottom line and all I have to say on the matter. Thank you very much. I'll take your questions now."

A cold silence hovered over the media pool for a few moments. A male reporter finally broke the ice.

"Mr. Nero, does this mean you will be building a casino here at the Seneca Army Depot?"

"Almost certainly. Why not? I will also build a new tobacco factory and a storage and distribution center in all of those empty igloo bunkers too. Plus, several gas stations on the base. My prices on both gas and tobacco will be unbeatable. But aw heck, I've got even bigger plans."

"Such as?" asked the reporter.

"As many of you know I collect and preserve Iroquois artifacts. My collection is the greatest in the world. At one time, on this very ground, stood one of the most spiritually important villages of the confederacy — the Seneca-Cayuga tribal village of Kendaia. They worshipped the mystical white deer that populate these lands. Starting today, I will give rebirth to this ancient village and to the sacred white deer herd. My people from the Haudenosaunee Collection are already searching the fields at the end of the runway." He pointed north to three of his suited security detail rolling a cart trailing wiring across the end of the runway. The cameramen panned their equipment to film the workers so the TV audience to see. "They have directions to scour the area in search of remnants of the lost village, so that one day I may rebuild what your famed General John Sullivan destroyed in 1779."

"Mr. Nero?" asked a female reporter from News10Now. "My sources tell me that's just your cover story. They say you will turn the white deer herd into an elite hunter's trophy showcase, charging tens of thousands of dollars for a kill."

Nero glared at the reporter. And for a moment she felt a pang of fear shudder through her.

"Sweety," Nero said, kindly. "Do not provoke me. Next question."

"Then explain this—," said the same persistent reporter. "My sources also tell me you have been diagnosed with throat cancer and have just six months to live. Care to comment?"

Nero's nostrils flared and his lips curled. "And I suppose you'll be the first vulture to pick from my carcass. Honey, this circus is over. All of you get off these sovereign lands. Now!" He spun around and strode toward a group of black SUVs. With several bodyguards converging around him, he approached the lead Hummer. A beat up, and visible exhausted Kenny Rousseau had the rear door already open.

"Take me to the search party! Where's Stanton? God dammit! Where is she?"

Troop E Romulus Station.

Since he's already dying, Rae thought, hopefully this will make sure he dies in jail. With a sure and steady hand she opened Stanton's envelope.

Several minutes later she hit the stop button on her cassette player. Chilling.

But she smiled. This recording of The Mouth's death was all Rae needed. Stanton had kept her word. She *was* on their side. She had also conveniently marked the location of Ray Kantiio's body on a map of the reservoir, near Nero's High Point Casino and Resort. Along with a note that the body would be inside his SUV Navigator, Stanton said she had witnessed the whole dumping of the vehicle with the body in it from afar.

Rae placed a call to her captain up at the Troop E Headquarters in Canandaigua to inform him of the situation. Minutes later, after faxing the map information, her captain informed her a state police dive team out of Kingston was activated for recovery. He ordered her to stay put and await further orders once he contacted BCI in Albany — that she should not, under any circumstances, make contact with Nero. Top brass would have to develop an action plan for arrest warrants and a raid on his enterprise at the crime scene of his resort. The captain informed her that the political nightmare was just beginning and lawyers would have to be called in to tackle the sovereignty and immunity issues sure to rise because technically Nero's properties are a nation within a nation. He left Rae with one final order — that she should protect Anne Stanton, their star witness, at all costs. That woman would make or break their case.

Thursday afternoon. Yale Manor Inn Bed and Breakfast.
Northwest of Seneca Army Depot.

A S THE ONLY off-season guest of Yale Manor Inn, a secluded farmstead mansion turned bed and breakfast retreat, Jake was assured complete privacy by the accommodating, friendly owner. Arriving early that morning, Jake stepped into his posh room and collapsed on the king sized bed for a dreamless six-hour slumber. He awoke just in time for a delicious breakfast spread while the owner listened to an important news conference on local television. Soon Jake was standing in front of the TV himself. The man speaking was Alex Nero.

After the news conference Jake returned to his room, the pain in his head growing. He called Joe to see if he too had caught Nero's speech.

"That bastard," Jake blurted, pacing across his room.

"He's desperate," replied Joe, on speakerphone. "And why not? He's dying of cancer."

"I know. Did you see he's using ground-penetrating radar in his search for the so-called *remnants* of the village? He's got barbed wire fencing to keep everyone out and carte blanche to do whatever the hell he wants within."

"He's also got complete control of the sacred white deer and the lands of our forefathers," added Joe. "He'll turn the Depot back into a shoot to kill, free-fire zone like it was when it was active. And all he needs now is Atotarho's crown to complete the prophecy. It's just a matter of time before he finds a way under the Depot."

Jake nodded to his phone. His pacing stopped, his arms now folded across his chest. "Did you hear that speech — he thinks he's like some lost king or something coming to save his minions."

"Yeah, just as twisted as the real emperor Nero," agreed Joe. "But his mind is clearer than ever. He's not mincing words. He laid out his ultimate goal for all the public to hear. The Haudenosaunee people will be behind him full force. They like this tough talk from a demagogue. They're tired of being trampled on by the white man. But we know what he really wants. Once he gets a hold of that crown, he's going to infiltrate people's minds and wreak havoc. Who knows the mental chaos he would inflict. His life and his immortality in history now depend on it."

"And once he gets inside the cave he's got the original map to guide him to his prize."

"Looks like we may have lost."

Jake paused before commenting. "I didn't expect him to act so fast." He rubbed his arm.

"I know. Me either," agreed Joe. "But he is dying so he has nothing to lose."

What followed was a long uncomfortable silence breaching their conversation. But something his uncle had said earlier suddenly resonated in Jake's mind.

Under the Depot.

"Wait, not so fast." Jake's eyes lit up. "I think we may have a chance to head him off. It's a long shot but here's my thinking."

"Fire away."

Jake paced again. "We're going to do a little digging ourselves. The Seneca Army Depot contains hundreds of storage bunkers for the Army's most lethal weapons. It was said that it could even survive a nuclear attack, which means—"

"Huh?"

"The government never admitted this, but I know for a fact from an old Army vet who was an MP there, that they built underground bunkers for the storage of secret weapon systems and also for the survival of base personnel in case of an attack. The official version was that everything was above ground. But the Army holds many secrets. I know."

Joe piped up. "So, if they dug down deep enough when they were constructing these bunkers then surely they must have hit something below the surface, right? Like a cave?"

"Yes, that's the straw I'm grasping at. And here's the kicker. Any anomaly in construction would have been documented. And if I remember correctly, the entire documented history of the base was handed over to the Town of Romulus Historical Society a few years back when the base transferred to civilian control. So, it's just a matter of me gaining access to those materials and the tried and true method of sifting through the chaff to find the proverbial needle in the haystack."

Joe laughed. "Right up your alley."

"It certainly is."

"Listen, while you do that I'm going to call on an Ithaca College geology professor I know to see if a cave network could really exist in this location."

"Are you now questioning the legend?" asked Jake.

"No. I'm confirming the legend. I want to know what perils we'll face if we go underground. You know, the terrain features or obstacles. I just, I just don't want to see anyone else get hurt if I can help it. If we are going in then we have to be prepared with the right equipment."

Jake moved closer to the phone. "Sounds good. I'll hit the historical society as soon as possible. It's just down the road. But first I have to place the dreaded call to my director at MHI to see how much havoc I've caused, let alone see if I still have a job."

Afternoon. Airfield. Seneca Army Depot.

Spread out in the rear leather bench seat of his Hummer, smoking a fat glowing cigar that he tapped out of an open window, sat Alex Nero. He watched impatiently as his crew of security personnel walked the fields at the end of his newly acquired military airfield runway. He told his men they were searching for a cave belonging to the their forefathers and he wanted them to be thorough in moving logs and brush in case it might be concealed. The snail's pace process was painfully slow to observe. Additionally, Nero had been informed that nothing significant had been revealed on the ground penetrating radar and still there were hundreds of acres to be covered in their target area.

At this rate, finding the entrance, should it even exist would take months, Nero thought. He would be dead before his plans could be fulfilled. Stanton was right in convincing him she should go looking for other clues to help their cause. Shaking his head, he placed the cigar to his lips and sucked in sweet smoke to calm his nerves. He exhaled then glanced down, the swirl of white gray smoke trailing out the window. On his lap he balanced the old map of the White Deer Society cave. It was now contained in a stiff plastic protective sheet. He was still amazed at its simplistic detail and its length. The cave looked to go on for miles.

Studying the map, he moved his free hand inside his shirt and pulled out his newly acquired piece of jewelry. It was attached to a chain around his neck. The old Kendaia guardian clan mother's silver broach felt good on his chest. It had been bequeathed to Luke Swetland, stolen by Thomas Boyd, and rediscovered by that thorn in his side, Jake Tununda. But now, it was finally in his possession.

He noticed movement out of the corner of his eye. His dozing driver, the banged up Kenny Rousseau, also caught the approach of a visitor and jumped up before realizing who it was. A face appeared in the cloud of smoke outside the window. Nero looked up at the intrusion then relaxed. It was Miss Stanton. He unlocked the door and let her slide in next to him.

Nero pointed at her with his cigar. "You missed the press conference," he stated in a demeaning tone.

Stanton ignored him, getting right to the point. "I was studying a history of Seneca County and I've concluded that we're searching in the wrong place. We need to go further inside the Depot." Although it was coveted information, she gave it up with a deep sense of inward gratification, knowing she had already set his downfall in motion. In fact, it was she who leaked to the press that he was dying of throat cancer. "I found some clues of the cave location when these lands were first settled, after it was turned into the Military Tract."

"Go on," Nero grumbled.

"In the Boyd's cave cipher you text messaged me, he refers to a marker tree, right? Well, that marker, I'm pretty confident, was actually a horseshoe with a Freemason symbol on it and a date of September fifth, seventeen seventy nine. He placed the horseshoe in a tree — the marker tree. I think I know where that tree once stood. It will take some time to find where it was of course."

Nero's eyes widened. He studied her face. A glimmer of hope sparkled in his eyes. "And my cave is supposed to be directly across from this tree."

"Yeah, but first it involves us finding the foundation of an old farmhouse once belonging to a Wilhelm Van Vleet, *if* that even still exists. The tree fell down in the back of his lot, across the brook near a spring. And from a modern-day contour map cross-referencing on top of an old 1850s map the supposed location is just past the railroad tracks over there, deeper into the base."

"Let's get there, now."

"Rousseau!" yelled Stanton. She jolted the man from his drowsiness. The head thug turned slowly, his battered face giving her a nod. "Follow that little brook past the main rail lines and into those woods," she ordered.

"Yes ma'am," replied Rousseau, in a barely audible voice.

As the Hummer lurched forward, Stanton glanced at the necklace around Nero's neck. It held the White Deer Society broach. Her heart skipped a beat. Her mouth opened. Then she couldn't help but notice the old map with strange markings on his lap. "What have you there?"

Nero smiled. He flipped the map over, hiding it. He also hid the necklace back inside his shirt and then patted her thigh. "In due time my dear, in due time. Just find me that cave."

MICHAEL KARPOVAGE

31

Town of Romulus. Seneca County, N.Y.

R EFRESHED AND ONCE again dressed in his Class A uniform, Jake felt a bit back on track after the emotional and physical beat down of last night. He looked in his rearview mirror at his bruised face knowing that in his current condition he would have to bypass Rae Hart's police station and any chance meeting with her. There would be too many questions.

Heading down 96A, Jake noted that the weather had been cooperative for this time of year. Clear blue skies and mild temperatures were forecast for the day, although he did hear scattered reports of another cold front moving in later in the evening. Rolling farm fields and a glimpse of Seneca Lake on his right kept his spirits up. Several old farmsteads dotted the landscape next to upscale country homes. He passed a new start-up winery and rows upon rows of harvested grape vines. The beauty of the region always astounded him.

Up the road ahead a triangular-shaped, blaze orange hazard sign on the right shoulder of the road caused him to ease up on the gas pedal. As he approached, he saw that the sign was attached to the back of a black horse-drawn carriage. Slowly and cautiously Jake passed, noticing an older couple sitting under the carriage canopy. The old man wore a wide-brimmed black hat, a Lincoln-like beard on his face, and the plaid shirt of a Mennonite. His wife was dressed in a floral country frock and white scarf about her head. A fine black horse pulled their carriage. Jake produced a wave out of his window and received the same in return. He pressed the gas pedal.

It wasn't long before he slowed down again. This time a large eight-wheeled John Deere farming tractor, pulling a 5,000-pound tank of liquid cow manure, took up three quarters of the road. Jake followed behind for a short distance, unable to pass. Finally, it veered off, entering a freshly turned farm field. A brown spray immediately emitted from the back of the tank as it fertilized the earth. Jake motored on.

Soon the Depot lands appeared on his left. With a furrow in his brow, Jake observed several individuals milling about with signs along the base perimeter fencing. The same anti-Indian sticker that adorned the volunteer firefighter's helmet he saw a few days ago had been duplicated on their signage. Further down the road, near a trailer park, more placards and banners had been erected along the fence, announcing the opposition to the sale of the lands to the Indian Alex Nero. The belligerent press conference earlier in the day had apparently galvanized some of the locals to voice their opinion. And quickly they responded.

The crowds thickened as Jake approached the hamlet of Kendaia. With vehicles now parked along both shoulders of the road and people waving their homemade signs toward the drivers, Jake had to slow down for fear of running one of them over. Then an odd sight caught his eye. Sitting on a boat trailer in front of a home strewn with old lawnmowers and rusty cars sat an old pontoon boat. Three grungy looking young men sat under the pontoon canopy with scoped hunting rifles at their side. One of them waved a large red, white, and blue sign. Their message was filled with simple ironic humor to Jake. It read *Save Our White Deer*.

Fifty feet away were two black Seneca County Sheriff's vans parked on the shoulder of the road near a collision shop. Several deputies kept watch over a larger gathering of protesters converged there. Then Jake noticed a black luxury SUV, its windows tinted black, parked near a small junkyard. As he passed, he slouched low in his seat, angling his black beret down over his face just in case it was a security detail for Nero.

Peering at the road ahead, he tapped his brakes as two men dashed across his path with a flowing bed sheet scrawled with red lettering. Their clever slogan read, *No Reparations, Tax the Indian Nations*. Cute, Jake thought. He continued on.

Driving by the Sampson State Park entrance on his right, he suddenly slammed on his brakes. A rusted, blue, Dodge Ram pickup truck cut him off from a copse of woods on his left. Jake noticed a heavy-set man with a baseball cap behind the wheel, completely oblivious to the boneheaded move. Jake sped up and maneuvered his SUV right up on the pickup's rear bumper to make his presence known. A quick scan of the cab's sticker covered rear window gave a glimpse of what the driver apparently valued most in life. A 9-11 memorial sticker sat next to a NYPD logo and an American flag followed by a cartoon boy urinating on a Chevy logo. Several more stickers showed his hatred against Native Americans, Muslims, and immigrants but his support of U.S. troops. Go figure, Jake thought.

Jake tried to make eye contact with the driver by flashing his high beams. Still the man made no visible response. He then laid on his horn. The driver jumped in his seat, fishtailed, and finally glanced back in his mirror. Jake slowly eased off, giving the pick up some distance had the driver decided to slam on his brakes as payback. Instead, the driver flicked a cigarette butt out his window, followed by a bandage-wrapped middle finger for extra emphasis. The cigarette hit Jake's SUV hood in a shower of sparks. The man then accelerated away in a cloud of black exhaust. Jake returned the salute, counted to ten, then drew a deep breath. He'd let the prick go.

A little further on, after passing several farm fields, the Depot's airfield runway appeared on Jake's left. He knew Rae's state police station turn off was just up ahead, but he couldn't help but wonder at that time and place the farmland he was driving past once held the true location of the Seneca Indian village of Kendaia. He had come full circle in just a few days time.

And that precious time was slowly ticking away.

As if to validate his arrival in history, a granite block appeared on his right at a pull off rest area. Jake slowed down as he passed. The stone block was a tribute to the Sullivan campaign, advertising that key moment in history when the Americans rolled through. Jake pulled over on the shoulder of the road and backed up in front of the monument. A weathered brass plaque gave some verbiage about the importance of the military mission and also showed a map of the route the army took through the Finger Lakes. Next to the granite marker was a dark blue state historical sign proclaiming the supposed location of the Indian village at the ground he stood on.

He looked around to take in the moment, glancing out of his driver's side window back across the farm field toward the Depot's airfield control tower. Jake's thick eyebrows then pressed together. In the distance, off to his left, he could make out several black SUVs and a dozen or so black-clad men walking about.

Nero's boys. Searching for the cave. His enemy was in sight.

Spurred back to action, Jake eased out into the roadway and speculated if his visit to the Town of Romulus Historical Society would help him find an alternative way into the cave first. Or would it be a dead end? It was just a few more miles down the road. As he drove on, he thought of his whisper with death the night before. It shook him to the core. Never, in all of his years in the hottest combat zones, had an enemy ever gotten close enough to press a gun against his temple. Kenny Rousseau's problem was that he hesitated. A professional soldier never did. And because of that simple delay, Jake had a chance to fight back and survive. His life could have been snuffed out like a light. Surviving that moment reinforced his personal philosophy even more — that life needed to be lived on the playing field, not wasted as a detached observer in the audience.

Between a News10Now reporter's van and a state police patrol car, Jake spotted the road leading to Rae's Trooper station and airfield facilities. He drove right by. A jaunt further down 96A and he entered Willard, a small hamlet overlooking the bright blue waters of Seneca Lake's eastern shore.

The town historical society was housed in the old railroad depot dating back to 1878 just outside an abandoned state agricultural college now converted into a probation violator's boot camp and mental hospital. Instead of pulling in however, Jake drove to the end of the lane waiting to see if any black vehicles had tailed him. Feeling comfortable after a few minutes, he swung back around and parked in the society's lot. He then gathered up his research materials, patted Rousseau's confiscated Browning pistol hidden in his coat, and walked under the covered front porch. He took off his black beret and entered.

Several hours later as dusk crept over the area, Jake enthusiastically exited the front door. He shook the head historian's hand and thanked the gentleman profusely for his time and the documents he was allowed to photocopy. The man told Jake to drive safe — that it was his pleasure to serve the Army and a fellow Brother.

Jake strode to his vehicle with a distinct feeling of confidence. The afternoon's research was a complete success, allowing him to hopefully gain ground on Nero. If not for the historian's due diligence in cataloging and organizing the Seneca Army Depot materials, he would have needed a whole week to sift through the information. He lucked out again. But in the same thought, he wondered how long his streak would last.

Settling in behind the wheel of his truck, Jake placed his cell phone in its dashboard cradle and dialed his uncle on headset. As he waited, he scrutinized the area around the parking lot making sure no one was staking him out.

"Joe? Yeah, Jake here. How's Lizzie doing?"

"She doing okay," answered Joe. He sounded tired. "She picked up a bit of a head cold last night from the weather while we were, ahh, you know, taking care of our two guests. But she's strong. She'll be alright. She's safe."

"Well, I guess I don't want to know where our guests ended up."

"We gave them a proper send off six feet under. Truly. Lizzie showed mercy and blessed them. She says they will accompany her on her journey beyond the sunset."

"I see." Jake didn't want to know any more details. He quickly changed the subject. "Listen, how did you make out with the local intelligentsia on your end?"

Joe cleared his throat. "Well, I spoke with professors at Hobart and William Smith, Ithaca College, and Cornell University. Here it all is in a nutshell. Here's what's under Seneca County." Joe went on to describe how after the one mile thick retreating glaciers of the last Ice Age — twelve thousand years ago — had cut deep steep-sided trenches in the existing river valleys, what was left were ten long parallel lakes oriented north-south as fingers in a pair of hands.

He added, "Indian legend has it that the Great Spirit placed his hands over this beautiful area as a blessing."

"Indeed, it is God's country," said Jake, nodding to his cell phone. "The Finger Lakes are called the Switzerland of America for good reason."

"Anyway," continued Joe. "Seneca Lake is one of the deepest in North America at over six hundred feet deep, while Cayuga Lake is the longest of the ten lakes at over thirty eight miles. But legend has it that both of these large lakes have bottomless, spring-fed holes or cavities that are receptacles for the dead who drown in their waters."

"I've heard that theory before too," commented Jake. "That these two lakes rarely give up its dead. But they can't be bottomless. I do know that the bottom bedrock of both lakes is well over a thousand feet below sea level, which is rather a mystery in itself. But on top of all that bedrock are hundreds of feet of sediment. Mud."

Joe confirmed that. "And it's also interesting to note that one of the deepest sections of Seneca Lake lies just off the old Sampson Naval Base — now the state park — across the road from the Seneca Army Depot. Right where the old village of Kendaia was razed. And these depths also happen to be adjacent to the narrowest landmass between the two lakes — the isthmus of Seneca County. So, if there were any type of subterranean river connecting the two lakes it would be in that general vicinity."

"Uh huh," agreed Jake. He took notes in his research binder. "And that is how caves are carved — by underground rivers."

"Right. That's what the professors confirmed," said Joe. "But over millions of years. You see this whole area was once under a great receding ocean that contributed to the cave formation. There's more to back that up. Let me read from my notes here. Just a second. Okay. Seneca County sits on mostly a thick stack of sedimentary rock made up of various types of clay, gravel, shale, sandstone, and limestone. But there are two layers of this limestone strata that are most likely to have cave formations — the Encrinal limestone and the Tully limestone — both of which run directly below the Army Depot and are over one hundred and fifty feet thick in some areas. So, there you have it. The conditions are ripe for caves."

"Wow. Great work old chap," replied Jake, in an old English accent. "You sound rather impressive spouting out all those academic and scientific terms."

"Screw you Major!" Joe chuckled. "But seriously, remember when I took you to the Howe Caverns near Albany?"

"Yep, sure do."

"Well, that's what these academics said any cave network under the Depot would look like. Stalactites, stalagmites, flowstone, vast caverns, a snaking river, placid lakes, waterfalls, rapids. Basically very, very beautiful, but also extremely dangerous as well."

"Great," said Jake, snidely.

"So, what did you come up with on your end? Find anything out about those underground bunkers?"

Jake turned to the first print out in his binder. It was of a bunker floor plan. "Oh, I sure did. Matter of fact you could say I hit the jackpot."

"You've been holding out on me this whole time? Letting me ramble on and on?"

"Well, only out of respect for an elder," countered Jake. He received a guffaw from his uncle. "Just let me take you through the other evidence I found first. It's really very cool. Remember that story you heard about a well being dug on the base and hitting a current of water?"

"Yes sir. They added dye to it to check the direction of the flow."

Jake nodded. "Yep, well I confirmed it. It took place in 1941 when Army engineers struck an underground flow at a depth of almost three hundred feet. The location was north of the airfield near the old base incinerator. They placed a dye in it and the very next day the dye came out due east in Cayuga Lake — near Canoga. Go figure."

"Makes sense, since Seneca Lake is sixty feet higher in elevation than Cayuga Lake." Joe said. "And gravity would pull water downhill. So what about the freaking bunker? You're killing me."

"I'm getting there." Jake cranked the ignition of his SUV and pulled out of the parking lot. He headed back north up Route 96A toward the Depot. As he drove he explained his findings into his headset.

"Back in the early 1960's at the height of the Cold War, the Army hired an engineering firm out of Rochester to dig facilities for deep burial of highly toxic chemical munitions. That firm also received a secret directive if you will, to also dig underground shelters for base personnel in case of a nuclear attack.

"During the digging, a construction crew at the lowest level of the main survival bunker blasted through a limestone wall and ended up in a void at a depth of one hundred and eighty feet below the surface. They reported finding Indian markings on the cave walls, several arrowheads, and broken pottery. They informed their escort-handler, an Army sergeant who wrote up the report, and he ordered them to seal the wall back up with masonry blocks. That was it. The report was then filed in the commander's archives for all these years. Forgotten! But I now have the bunker number, the sub level floor plans and the construction report from 1963 in my hand, as we speak."

"Holy crap!" shouted Joe.

"It even shows exactly where that lowest level room is and which wall was penetrated. We are in business big time!"

"Damn straight Jake. Damn straight!"

"Plus, I was able to print off a copy of the cave map photo I took back at Lizzie's house. So we are all set. I've decided to head back up to the base right now to pull some recon of how I can sneak in and find that actual bunker. It just so happens to be in what's called the Q-Area — where the most highly classified weapons, including nukes, were once stored."

"Whoa! Hold on there," responded Joe with genuine concern. "Wait until I get down there to help you out."

"We're under the clock," said Jake. "I need to act alone. No offense but you're too slow. It's probably a matter of hours before Nero finds the cave entrance with his radar and his manpower anyway. Just trust me. Besides, the whole inner base area that Nero purchased is abandoned anyway. Not a soul around."

"Okay. Okay," said Joe, giving in.

"What I need from you instead is to go shopping again. There's lots of tools and safety equipment we're going to need. Then we can meet later tonight when you bring all the gear down. That's when we'll enter the bunker and try and locate the room in the report. But first, I need to establish the best route into the base without Nero and his boys noticing."

"But what am I shopping for now?" asked Joe.

"For our spelunking trip. What else?"

Site of Wilhelm Van Vleet's former homestead. Seneca Army Depot.

BASED ON HER map calculations, Anne Stanton had determined the most probable location of Wilhelm Van Vleet's original homestead was just beyond the railroads tracks inside the Depot's western outer perimeter fencing. Now it was a matter of finding out if any clue from the farm even remained from over two hundred years ago. Under her direction, Rousseau organized his eight security guards in a search party and for three straight hours the men trudged through mud and brush in a shoulder-to-shoulder line, desperately trying to locate any remnant of past inhabitation. But the past refused to reveal itself. The men grew agitated and sour. Even the weather refused to cooperate.

After such a gorgeous late November day with a high of sixty degrees, a line of squalls had moved eastward over the Finger Lakes showering the ground with drizzle. Soon, wind gusts kicked up to thirty miles per hour as thunderstorms approached under a heavy rain. The temperature dropped to the mid-thirties, threatening to turn the driving rain into ice. And while his minions endured the elements, Alex Nero kept warm and dry inside of his Hummer.

As night approached, the search party illuminated their target area with high-powered spotlights run by a portable generator. They outfitted themselves in cold weather gear to keep warm, donned radio-phones for communication, and snacked on power bars and coffee for energy. They inspected every log, rock, and terrain irregularity in several passes of a grid search pattern. On occasion, Rousseau rotated out an SUV patrol around the base perimeter road to ward off any troublemaking locals and to give his men a seated, heated rest.

As the rain finally turned to snow, their hard work suddenly paid off. One of the men tripped on several large stones laid out in a straight line. Clearing away dirt and brush, they revealed the corner of a stone foundation barely penetrating the earthen surface.

It was all that Stanton needed. She immediately repositioned the men two hundred yards across the field from the foundation and into a heavier wooded area. There they found a slight ravine about fifteen feet deep. Scattered down the sides of the ravine were thick, rotted, fallen oak trees of exceptional age. A trickling, two-foot wide brook flowed at the ravine's base in a westerly direction toward Seneca Lake.

Same time. Q-Area. Seneca Army Depot.

Major Jake Tununda's early evening reconnaissance of the Depot's northern Q-Area had gone much smoother than he had expected. To start out, he logged onto Google Earth with his laptop and zoomed right in on the north part of the Depot. The Yale Manor B&B was merely a mile from the Q-Area. He could clearly see, in high resolution, the sparsely populated farmlands surrounding the base. Picking a spot on the map to park his vehicle was rather easy.

He chose to motor east down Yale Manor Road and then turned south along the abandoned, weed-infested railroad tracks at the northeast corner of the base. With dense woods on one side and a farmer's tall hedgerow along the other side of the tracks, his vehicle was well hidden from any prying eyes.

Under cover of an approaching thunderstorm, with his M4 rifle slung across his chest harness and Rousseau's Browning pistol concealed in a side pocket, he disappeared into the woods. Minutes later, he emerged from the woods and stood before the chain link outer perimeter fencing bordering the base property.

It was only at that initial entry point, along the asphalt outer perimeter patrol road beyond the fence, that he felt his presence in jeopardy. He spotted an SUV in the distance through his riflescope. Undoubtedly, it was Nero's security team conducting a sweep. Fortunately, the patrol was too far away for them to have even noticed him. Within minutes the patrol disappeared back south of his position.

Had Jake tried to infiltrate the Depot when it was fully operational, when every conceivable weapon in the U.S. Army was housed there, he would have faced instant scrutiny from the Army. Overlapping defensive measures were designed to detect and kill him if necessary. The outer perimeter road, where he now stood, would have been patrolled 24-hours a day by jeeps mounted with .50 caliber machine guns and manned by a military police force of 250.

He now simply scaled the rusty fence and leisurely strolled through a tall grass field for about fifty feet. The grass then turned to gravel for another fifty feet where he met his next barrier.

There, at three consecutive rows of six-foot high barbed wire fencing, Jake faced his only true scare when a black and white striped Osprey swooped down on him after he startled her from her utility pole nest.

Back when the Depot was under full Army security, his same path through the grass would have taken him by hidden motion and audio detection devices triggering an immediate response from the armed guards. Once he approached he would have been illuminated by spot lights with bulletproof lenses. And that grass field he was on would have been maintained weekly to be no higher than six inches for a clear shot by the guards should anyone be crawling in. Had he even gotten past the fifty-foot wide gravel section with more crisscrossing surveillance monitors, he would have been confronted with how to cross the daunting line of three, 2,400 volt, electrified fences, topped and bottomed with coils of razor sharp concertina wire. One touch of the fence and instant death. Beyond that was yet another asphalt road patrolled with dozens more armed vehicles and MPs who shot first and identified bodies later.

Not willing to scale the three rows of barbed wire fencing this night, Jake simply clipped through the rusty links with his handy, all-purpose tool and slipped through. He rolled up each section of severed prongs back into its original position and secured them with carabiners so as not to arouse undue suspicion. He had now officially penetrated the Q-Area. And not a scratch was on him.

Inside the Q-Area sector were sixty-four igloo-type concrete bunkers resembling large grassy mounds. Arranged in five east-to-west parallel roads, they were labeled according to row and number. Jake found his target bunker with ease — the very first bunker of the very first row — A0101. It was one of the two uniquely oversized bunkers on the north side of the sector, their sole purpose being for protection of base personnel in case of nuclear attack.

The concrete 30-foot wide by 80-foot long bunker was buried under several feet of earth. Constructed under a barrel roof, the foundation of the bunker was ten times thicker than that of a typical residential home. The mound was almost completely covered except for its exposed entrance face. A set of double blast doors marked the only way to gain entry and they were large enough to drive a school bus through.

Protecting the entrance was a thick steel cage with double pad-locked gates. Fortunately for Jake, when he had arrived at bunker A0101 the locks weren't engaged and the double gates were wide open. In fact, none of the security measures on any of the total five hundred nineteen igloos on base were in place, according to the Romulus Town Historian. They all were left unlocked in response to local government safety guidelines prior to selling to a private enterprise.

Had anyone even thought of stealing a nuclear weapon stored inside one of these Q-Area igloos, the unlocking of these gates would have required them to hunt down the Depot's commander, who held one key, and the head of security with the other. Behind the gates, they would have found a 2,000-pound solid concrete block only moveable with a heavy forklift. Only then would they have access to the double steel reinforced blast doors. These doors were secured by two large locks the size of a heavyweight boxer's glove. Had they gotten these open, an electronic alarm would have then been tripped in the base security headquarters alerting the MPs of an unauthorized intrusion. Their response would have been fast and lethal.

And if the intruders had made it inside the igloo there were two more security features awaiting them. The first was a smoke generation system triggered by the monitoring station that would have produced a thick mixture of ammonium chloride smoke. Not only would it have filled the igloo with white smoke making navigation by sight nearly impossible, but the chemicals in the smoke also caused severe vomiting. And the second measure would have been the activation of a ceiling-mounted concertina wire system. The razor-sharp wire net would have dropped and snared anyone unlucky enough to be standing beneath it.

Finding everything disengaged, just as the historian claimed, Jake shoved open one of the unlocked blast doors and proceeded inside the pitch-black bunker. Turning on a flashlight, he observed that the igloo was completely empty. He pulled a brief recon of the large inner passageway vehicle ramp that led down to the underground survival facilities. Satisfied with his interior inspection, he immediately withdrew from the bunker, closed it up, and headed back to his vehicle.

Total recon time — one hour — to get in and out of the once impenetrable Seneca Army Depot.

MICHAEL KARPOVAGE

33

Thursday evening. Site of Boyd's marker tree.

ALEX NERO, Anne Stanton, and Kenny Rousseau stood together near the brook, observing the continued search. With spotlights illuminating the far side slope, Nero's men scoured the ravine for the elusive cave entrance. The ground penetrating radar equipment was also put back into use at the top of the ravine and immediately started registering positive hits of underground anomalies.

Stanton shivered inside her windbreaker, patting her gloved hands together as snow fell all around them. "It's got to be up there somewhere. All the clues add up. We came in on the south bank, where Boyd's cipher told us to go. It's the same side as the marker tree, according to Van Vleet's horseshoe story—"

"And we descended down into the ravine," added Nero in a gritty voice. "Boyd's directions clearly stated the cave would be on the opposite side, halfway up the slope."

Rousseau barked out orders for the men to focus their search in the middle area of the bank. Some slipped down the muddy slope while others found good footholds to steady themselves. The men were agitated and beyond exhausted.

"Maybe we should call it a night," suggested Stanton.

"Not on your life," replied Nero. He didn't even look at her.

It wasn't until an hour later and two hundred feet further downstream that one of the men came across something unusual as he cleared brush.

"I pulled up a piece of slate and found five rotted logs over here!" he shouted.

Heads turned his way as he stepped on top of the logs to test their strength. With a crack, the man disappeared into the earth. The logs disintegrated under his weight. A split second later, he popped his head and arms out and gave a thumbs-up signal.

"I found the cave!

Cheers went up. Lightning flashed in the clouds. Thunder rumbled. And the snow grew thicker.

Nero revealed a rare smile. He turned to Stanton. "The veil between our world and the underworld has been penetrated."

Lightning lit the sky once again. And to their north a single shotgun blast echoed through the air. It was masked immediately by another loud crack of thunder. No one's curiosity was roused.

But a minute later, as the group scrambled over to the cave entrance, an orange flash of light lit the clouds, followed by an enormous blast that reverberated a quarter mile to their west. The trees shook as a concussive wave swept over the search party. All eyes turned toward the airfield control tower where they witnessed a huge fireball rising into the sky.

Nero snapped his fingers. He pointed to Rousseau and his newly appointed lieutenant, the Cayuga, Mr. Makowa. He cocked his head toward the explosion and the pair immediately ran off to an SUV.

Q-Area. Seneca Army Depot.

After a hearty dinner rendezvous with his uncle where they finalized their hasty plans, Jake took Joe over to Depot. He parked out of view from the main road again. There they organized their new spelunking equipment, prepared survival backpacks, and armed themselves for the task ahead. Jake arrayed his weapons as before. Additionally, he strapped a firefighter's Halligan tool across his back. Joe lugged a sledgehammer, his deer-hunting shotgun, and he tucked away the other Browning pistol he took from Nero's dead security agents. Without further delay, Jake lead the way back onto the Depot's lands by following his same recon path in. He had to however, cut the outer perimeter fencing because his uncle was unable to climb over. Their mission started out smooth and both men were jacked with excitement.

Amid the high wind gusts, cracking lightning, and booming thunder they faced no security threats from Nero and his gang. Within twenty minutes, Jake stood facing bunker A0101 for the second time that night.

Suddenly, he spun around and switched off his flashlight. "Ssh! You hear that? Kill your light! Now."

Joe followed his order, plunging the entrance area of the bunker into darkness. Both men peered out toward the access road letting their vision adjust to the night.

"Footsteps," Jake whispered. He raised his M4 to his shoulder. "To my right, behind the bunker. Someone heading this way." He noticed Joe quietly setting down his sledgehammer and mimicking his nephew's move by raising his shotgun.

"When I say *Now*, we ID the target only. When I say *Fire*, we shoot to kill."

"Gotcha," replied Joe. His breathing became heavy.

They waited for a heart-pounding thirty seconds more as the footsteps crunched closer and closer. The wind surprisingly died down and rain transformed into snowflakes.

The footsteps stopped.

Jake quietly exhaled.

Silence for another thirty seconds.

The footsteps started again. The pace increased, now grinding the crumbling asphalt in front of the entrance. A shadowy figure appeared around the corner and approached the pair.

"Now!" shouted Jake. He lit the target.

Big brown eyes stared back at them.

The barrel of Joe's shotgun wavered. Lightning flashed.

"Lower your—" Jake ordered.

Too late. Joe pulled the trigger. A shotgun blast ripped from the barrel. The report intermixed precisely with the sound of thunder.

Never flinching from the wild slug that zipped by its head, there stood in defiance, a majestic, broad-chested, white-furred buck. More thunder rumbled overhead as if to accentuate the presence of such a noble creature. Heavy white snowflakes fell around him as he stared back at the two men. His large brown eyes glowed in Jake's flashlight beam. The master of the herd snorted and raised his snout. His pink nose sniffed the air.

Jake counted ten points on the antlers. His flashlight shook. Joe took several deep breaths. Realizing the significance of the white buck's appearance, each man stood mesmerized. The buck raised its front hoof and stomped three times and snorted again. He then turned and simply walked away.

As the deer slowly disappeared, Jake's knees became weak. "The ghost buck," he stated. His dream had come true. But was its appearance some sort of omen or a sign of good?

Joe seemed to answer his thoughts. "They say that those who rest their eyes on the white ghost buck will have magnificence bestowed upon them. Oh Great Spirit, I'm glad I missed."

Regaining his composure, Jake turned to the entrance blast doors and grasped one of the handles. "Come on. Let's get inside. Your shotgun blast may have roused Nero's troops." He slid the door open with a heavy grunt. The creak of rusted metal made a high-pitched squeal as snow swirled inside the black void.

The men grabbed their gear, with Joe squeezing inside first. Jake slowly closed the door behind them, but suddenly he heard and then felt a chest-rumbling sound from outside, off in the distance. It was reminiscent of battlefield artillery fire. More thunder? He cocked his head. Or was that the famous Seneca Drums he had just heard? He couldn't decide. Too many weird things were happening. He just needed to keep moving. Shrugging the sound off, he shut the door and turned to face the dense black interior of the bunker.

The pair became engulfed in a whirl of cool, stale air as their flashlight beams pierced the cavernous, empty concrete room. Stretching eighty feet to a great, cracked semi-circle of concrete forming the back wall, they lowered their beams to the floor to find the vehicle ramp angling down.

"Follow me," directed Jake. His voice boomed through the chamber as he led the way across the empty expanse and over to the entrance of the descending ramp. He pointed his flashlight down the concrete plane, showing his uncle how it spiraled around a corner. "This ramp is like one you'll find in a parking garage. We take it down six flights to the lowest level. Pace yourself."

Troop E Romulus Station.

Rae sat alone in her quiet office, awaiting yet another call from her superiors. An evidence envelope sat empty on her desk, as she twirled the Cranberry Marsh Indian broach between her fingertips. She couldn't help but wonder how such a small piece of jewelry had caused so much havoc in recent days. Deep in thought, she paid no attention to another flash of lightning outside her office window.

But instead of hearing the accompanying thunder, Rae experienced a horrendous blast that shattered her windows. She was sprayed with broken glass. She screamed and flipped backward over her chair, still clutching the White Deer Society emblem. Not sure what had exploded outside, she wobbled to her feet and shook off the debris. Blood dripped onto her sweater from several superficial cuts on her face. Without realizing it, she had pocketed the broach in her pants. In a stupor, she rushed out the back exit and stepped outside, just in time to witness a small mushroom cloud lift into the air not two hundred yards from her station.

She gasped.

Huge orange balls of flame rolled through black gushing smoke where the uppermost levels of the Depot's airfield control tower once stood.

Movement at ground level.

Miraculously, a figure stumbled from the first floor of the burning building. It looked to Rae like a large set man carrying some type of container. He turned and Rae saw that his back was on fire. The man dropped the can and clutched at his back, spinning wildly. The container on the ground suddenly burst into flames. It was a gas can.

The arsonist!

Spurred to action, Rae ducked back inside her office to retrieve her coat and cell phone. She then slammed opened a tool closest and grabbed a pair of bolt cutters. Running back outside at full sprint, she dialed 9-1-1 on her way. Arriving at the newly installed chain-linked gate, she positioned the bolt cutters around the lock and squeezed. With a ping the lock snapped off. She dropped the tool and swung the gate wide open so responding emergency vehicles would not be hindered. As she stepped foot on Nero's new sovereign territory she made the connection with the emergency dispatcher.

"Send fire and rescue to the Depot airfield." She caught her breath. "The control tower just exploded." Another deep inhale and she ran toward the arsonist who had now dropped to the ground. The man started rolling to douse the spreading flames. He screamed.

Rae spoke again in her phone. "Male victim on fire. Male victim on fire. Possibly an arsonist." She slipped the cell phone into her pocket, dropped to her knees, and flung her coat over the burning man's back and head. She patted him down while fighting his twists and turns.

Once the flames were extinguished the man's screaming subsided to whimpers. Rae tried to relax him as he lay facedown in the wet grass, arms sprawled out to his side. She couldn't help but notice his hands were covered in fragments of burned latex gloves.

Except for the middle finger of one hand.

The tip of that finger had been bandaged over. Anger welled in Rae's chest. Her lip curled. With all of her might she rolled the overweight man onto his back to get a clear look at his face in the bright firelight. She flinched.

"Bob Wyzinski? What the—" Her words never made it out as the supposedly flu-stricken veteran deputy sheriff cold-cocked her in the mouth. Tiny flashes of white sparks filled her blackened vision. She slumped over with a groan.

The arsonist cop got up on his knees to finish her off, but the barrel of a pistol stared him in the face. He froze. Rae rose to a sitting position with one hand grasping her Glock. Her other hand, she balled into a hidden fist and with all of her might she punched the cop with a clean connection of hard knuckles. Wyzinski's nose fractured upon impact. He fell back on the ground. Rae slugged him twice more in the nose and finished him with an elbow to the jaw, knocking him out cold.

With a bloody smile and heaving chest, Rae stood up, keeping the weapon aimed at Wyzinski's head. She still couldn't believe the elusive arsonist-dog killer was a dirty cop she had spent many a law enforcement scene with — including Cranberry Marsh. It boggled her mind that this was one of their own, albeit a deputy sheriff.

A glance at the coat he was wearing and the rip at his elbow sealed the deal. She holstered her weapon and reached for the handcuff holder on her waist. She unsnapped the flap and in a quick fluid motion she twisted Wyzinski's arms behind his smoldering, flesh burned back and snapped the cuffs on his wrists.

So it was Wyzinski all along, thought Rae. Unbelievable. Questions whirled in her head as she slowly put together all the puzzle pieces amid the roaring backdrop of the burning tower. Why the anti-Indian motivation? Was he acting alone or on behalf of some local extremists?

She fumbled inside her pocket for her cell phone, elated that she bagged the arsonist in the act. But now it was her turn to face the business end of a gun barrel — a sawed-off shotgun. On the other end glared a beaten mask of a face with light blue tattoos under each eye. That was the last image Rae remembered as an unseen thump on the back of her head dropped her where she stood.

The tattoo-eyed thug was already on his two-way radio with Nero. He pushed the transmit button. "We've got some lard ass over here, unconscious. All burnt up. There's a gas can nearby. He probably lit the building up. And, ah weird, he's handcuffed too."

"Say again," Nero demanded over a static-filled radio.

While repeating the message, Rousseau was handed a silver ID badge by his counterpart, Mr. Makowa. He had found it while frisking the woman he just knocked out. Makowa then showed Rousseau a Glock service-weapon he pulled from her holster.

"We've got a female cop here too," said Rousseau. "Ah, she's with the state police. Looks like she ran over from their station. Anyways, we knocked the bitch out. She was armed and trespassing."

"What is this woman's name?" asked Nero.

"Rae Hart, says her badge."

"Bring her to me. Leave the man behind."

Kendaia cave entrance.

With a pain-filled moan after having cold water splashed on her face, Rae emerged from her blackout and found herself flanked by two burly men she could hardly see in the darkness. The guards shook her for a response, grabbed her under the armpits and lifted her off the ground. The back of her head pounded as she tried to figure out exactly where she was and what had happened. Under wobbly knees, she leaned into her captors to regain her balance. Through blurry eyes she saw a scene of moving shadows pierced by flashlight beams. She gathered she was near a stream in a wooded ravine. Was she still at the Depot? She heard fire sirens in the distance. But who the hell hit her? And where had they come from? She had gotten a good look at the tattooed face man with the shotgun — obviously an Indian — but he had definitely taken a recent beating. Was he one of the murderers of The Mouth during Nero's gauntlet recording? And where's Wyzinski? Her weapon? Cell phone? She realized they had taken everything, leaving her dressed only in her turtleneck sweater, jeans, and boots.

A silhouetted figure approached under crunching leaves. A wave of confused panic swept through her as she thought she would be executed. Her heart lurched as a flashlight beam struck her in the face. Flinching with pain, she turned her head to shield her eyes.

"Have any good dreams, Rae Hart?"

Recognizing the raspy voice of the man behind the light, Rae's panic changed to rage. Her edgy voice accosted him. "Assault and kidnap of a law enforcement official. You are in deep shit, Alex Nero."

"Honey, I've been in deep shit all my life," replied Nero, inching closer. He moved the flashlight under his chin to illuminate his face in a grotesque shadowy glow of red, framed by long strands of hair. He grabbed Rae's chin and squeezed her jaw, their defiant eyes locked. "You think I care about roughing up some pathetic state police bitch trespassing on sovereign territory? Ray Kantiio should have aimed higher when he popped you."

Seething with anger Rae spit in his face.

Nero shoved her head back and wiped his cheek with a sleeve. "That's right. I have no qualms about doling out Haudenosaunee justice. Just ask your daddy. Didn't he take a bullet in the head?" Nero belched laughter as he pressed Rae's forehead with his middle finger.

With cat-like reaction Rae broke free from her captors and lunged at Nero. She caught him with a right uppercut squarely under the jaw. Nero's head lifted upon impact, his jaw slamming shut, biting his tongue. He was momentarily dazed, but kept standing. Rae's guards grabbed her and slammed her to the ground with a faceplant. Nero merely threw his head back and laughed again, spitting blood. He walked up and placed a muddy boot on her head.

"Ahh, my feisty little trophy."

"Eat shit," replied Rae, in a muffled voice.

Nero bent down and clenched the nape of her neck, pressing her face deeper in the mud. His cancerous whisper grated like sandpaper. "Your cowardly father took my mother's life, so I ordered his hit as payback. It's the ancient way of our people, an eye for an eye."

Spitting mud, Rae grunted a ruder obscenity aimed at his deceased mother.

Nero motioned the guards to stand her back up. He then slapped her face with a forehand and then a backhand and then another forehand. Mud splattered after each powerful slap. Nero then wiped his hand on her shirt. "Watch your mouth young lady."

"What do want from me?" mumbled Rae, her head slumped down.

Nero lifted her dirty face. "Now that you're a good girl, let's talk about you trespassing on sovereign land. You will have to be punished for your criminal activities. I'm thinking a little community service should be a fair, lenient sentence. What do you think?"

"Whatever, you piece of shit."

Nero ignored her insult. "I'm thinking you're going to be my guest on an underground excursion." He pointed with his flashlight to a small cave opening just up the creek bank. Several of his security men stood at the dark gaping hole. Nero's beam panned back to Rae. "You're going to be my little Miss Guinea Pig leading the way inside that cave. And if you're a good little piggy I may have mercy on your soul. I might even let you go. But if you're a naughty little piggy I'm going to take much pleasure in raping you, slowly torturing you to death, and then scalping that nice mane of yours for my collection. And no one will ever find your body down there. So, please be on your best behavior, prisoner."

A big bull of a man walked up to Nero, a short-barreled shotgun in a holster strapped to one thigh, a long dagger on the other, a Beretta 92 silenced pistol holstered at his armpit. He was decked out in hiker's clothing, had a backpack, and wore a spelunking helmet with mini spotlights. Rae recognized this tattoo-eyed warrior freak as the one who pointed the sawed-off shotgun at her over at the burning control tower.

Anne Stanton stood right behind him. Rae noticed she was not armed, at least not visibly. Stanton caught Rae's eye and frowned with feigned anger, then gave her an ever-so-subtle wink and twinge of her eyebrow to let her know she would be offering help. Rae breathed a sign of relief.

The large man told Nero his men were all set to go in.

"Thank you Kenny," gruffed Nero. "Keep six men back here as a rear guard. Have them monitor the fire scene. I don't want anyone venturing this way. Keep pulling routine patrols around the base too. There are probably more arsonists out there."

"Yes sir," acknowledged Rousseau.

"And tell them to be on the lookout for that bastard Army soldier Tununda. I know he's out there somewhere."

Rae cracked a smile at the corner of her mouth.

"Then I want you, Makowa, George, and Stanton going in the cave with me," continued Nero, throwing a thumb over his shoulder. "The pig here is taking point in case we run across any booby traps. Get her a helmet with a light. Move out!"

Same time. 180 feet below Bunker A0101.

"I'm over here!" shouted Jake. He flashed his light.

Joe stumbled to the end of the long, dark underground vehicle ramp and collapsed against a pockmarked concrete wall. He set down his gear then shed his backpack. Sweating profusely through a reddened face, he reached for his water bottle and chugged freely. He and his nephew had descended the winding ramp one hundred and fifty feet below the surface. They passed six sub-level bunkers all barricaded with locked double steel entrance doors.

Jake had explained along the way that the upper two levels were reserved for the lower ranked base personnel and their women and children who once lived at the base housing in Romulus. The next two levels were designated for storage of survival perishables and equipment, and the lowest levels were designated for the upper ranking officers, communications, and weapons storage.

"You okay there?" asked Jake. "I didn't bring an automatic electronic defibrillator you know."

Joe barely answered through heavy gasps. "Just need a minute."

Jake had arrived several minutes earlier at the lowest bunker level. He was in the middle of prying open the locked double steel doors at the entrance to the sub chamber. The dark gray doors were stenciled with faded white letters reading *Officers Only*.

"Bastard just won't budge," grimaced Jake. Again he wedged the crowbar end of his silver Halligan tool between the door's locking mechanisms. Used extensively in the fire and rescue service, Jake added the Halligan to the list of their necessary spelunking equipment because of the heavy locked interior barriers he encountered during his recon. As a multipurpose tool for prying, twisting, and striking, this stainless steel bar consisted of a forked claw on one end, and a wedge and curved tapered pick on the other. It was also the proven breaching tool of choice he had issued to his combat teams when raiding houses in Iraq.

Jake pried at the doorjambs, heard something snap, and with a screech one of the well-rusted doors popped open. The Halligan fell to the floor with a loud clang.

"Yes! Let's go!"

"My God, give me a break," bitched Joe. He was still huffing as he watched Jake illuminate the interior of a new chamber.

"Come on man," Jake said impatiently. He picked up and slung the Halligan over his back. He then pulled out a dog-eared copy of the bunker floor plan and pointed ahead down an ominous-looking hallway. "We're almost there. This is the weapons storage section. The room we need is at the very end of this hall. There's a shitter off to the side where the cave void is supposed to be walled up."

With shaking legs, Joe gathered up his gear.

Before entering Jake took a moment to snap a digital photo of the entrance with his trusty little camera. He grasped his M4 rifle and flashlight and proceeded in. "Christ, this is like a concrete coffin," he announced. His crisp voice bounced off the crumbling walls and low ceiling of a long, wide concrete tunnel. Rusted pipes, electrical conduits, stained cracks, and empty light fixtures filled with spider webs marked the dreary passage. Several open doors to small empty rooms split off from the main access tunnel. "How'd you like to live down here?"

"I'd go insane," replied Joe, dragging a bit behind.

"I'm thinking they probably stored their small arms and ammo in some of these rooms. God knows what else."

Joe grumbled.

The tunnel suddenly came to a dead end at another set of double doors. These were secured tight with a padlock. Jake jiggled the lock, inspected the old rusted clasp it was attached to and smiled. He then positioned his flashlight against the wall in the corner and directed the bright beam on the lock. With a flash of silver he swung the pick end of his Halligan upward, catching the lock clasp perfectly from below. With a bang, the clasp and padlock easily flew free. Jake snatched up his light and pulled the doors open just as his uncle arrived. Joe shook his head with a smirk.

"What?" Jake said, with a smile. "Let's just say I've got a knack for breaking and entering."

Whereas the other unlocked anterooms were completely bare, this one, measuring the size of a single-car garage, contained six large wooden crates of exceptional age. Beyond the crates, against the back wall, stood dilapidated rusted metal shelving holding various paint buckets, containers, and other sundry items covered in dust and thick spider webs. Jake panned his flashlight beam to the right of the shelving and centered it on a wooden door with a pealed sticker of a toilet on it.

Joe panned his light over the crates and found they were labeled with *To Be Destroyed*. He frowned. "Hey, check these out." He walked up to the closest crate.

"What have we here?" asked Jake, his curiosity piqued as he joined Joe. Each of the rectangular crates measured approximately four feet high by seven feet long. He noticed the crates swung open from a side hinge. Handing his light to his uncle and slinging his M4 on his chest harness, Jake took the Halligan off his back and jammed its wedge under a side slat. He pried. The rusted setting nails popped with ease. The crate's sidewall freely swung open.

Both men bent down. Inside they found a perfectly preserved World War II-era motorcycle sealed in a clear, long-term corrosion inhibiting cosmoline coating.

"Holy shit!" exclaimed Jake. He instantly recognized the make and model of the motorcycle. He tapped a white five-pointed star painted on an olive drab fuel tank. "It's a U.S. Army Indian Scout, a model 841. They stopped making these in 1944. Only about one thousand were ever made."

Joe whistled. "It looks like it's fresh from the factory floor."

"Supposedly, all the surplus bikes were destroyed after the war," noted Jake. He ran his hands across the frame. "They would have been sent here to the Depot and melted in the incinerator. I bet these were set aside for someone's rainy day. Wow, look at this leather seat." He pinched the waxy seal and easily pulled a rubbery chunk off, exposing the true leather underneath. The seat was in pristine condition. He pulled some more of the sealant off the chrome engine parts and front tire, revealing more of the motorcycle. "My God, this is priceless. Come on, let's check out the other crates!"

Within minutes they had pried open the remaining crates, exposing five more Indian Scouts in the same excellent condition. Although yet another great historical find, Jake didn't want to waste time enjoying them. He pressed onward with their main mission and went to the bathroom door. "Come on," he urged his uncle from across the room. "It's time to hit the head."

Joe couldn't resist a jibe. "All hail the porcelain God."

Jake snickered then turned the old doorknob and let himself in. He took a few steps before starting down a short flight of concrete stairs. At the bottom was a small closet-like room made out of gray cinder blocks. A rusted porcelain sink and crude steel toilet were the only furnishings. The bathroom door opened from behind. More light filled the room as Joe entered, whistling, looking up.

"Watch your step," warned Jake.

Too late. Joe tripped on the first step and fell.

His flashlight and sledgehammer tumbled through the air. Then his large frame slammed down hard against the concrete steps with a groan. Something cracked. His shotgun jammed against the wall, the barrel bent. Joe rolled down another step and banged his wrist, got hit in the elbow with his sledgehammer, and then turned his ankle before coming to rest at the bottom of the steps. Jake was already at his side holding him steady. Joe moaned through fluttering eyes.

"It's my fault," apologized Jake. "It's my fault. I'm so sorry. Oh man, what have I done?"

34

Below the Depot.

PRISONER RAE HART noted that the slippery, winding cave passage was remarkably clear of obstructions as she led Nero's entourage further below the surface of the earth. A half hour into their subterranean trip, the rocky trail remained in a northerly direction even as it increasingly sloped downward. Rae took her time to carefully illuminate the way ahead as the group descended deeper into the dark new world. Although never losing focus on a chance for escape, she became somewhat fascinated as the journey progressed. It was clearly evident that the route had been maintained over time as larger boulders, shale, and debris had been moved off to the side, allowing a clear avenue on the uneven stone surface. They experienced tight crevices and ceilings so low they were reduced to a crawl. Remarkably, the temperature was much warmer than the outside air. It seemed a constant fifty degrees or so but very damp.

Rae gingerly pushed onward, making sure not to twist an ankle or worse, run across any ancient anti-intruder booby traps. Crumbling shale cave walls soon changed to a smooth yet wet limestone surface marked with ancient man-made images. At several intervals along the way she had even observed the notorious white deer and snake symbol painted on the walls. Nero and Stanton stopped the group whenever these symbols appeared. They consulted an old map in a protected cover. Rae could only assume this as being some type of cave map with the symbols acting as an ancient wayfinding system.

The passage then started revealing actual artifacts of the past Indian culture. Rae stepped beside rotted cornhusk baskets, old wooden boxes, clay pottery, and used fire pits.

After ducking under an outcropping of rock, she emerged into a narrow chamber the size of a tennis court. She panned her dual helmet lights up the rising ceiling and held her breath as the room towered fifty-feet above her. The rest of the spelunking party pushed in behind her amid bouncing flashlight and helmet beams. They stood side-by-side under the vaulted ceiling, Anne Stanton to Rae's right and a coughing, sweating Alex Nero on her left. A slight draft of air pressed against their faces.

Stanton gasped. "My God, look at this place. It's beautiful." Mr. Makowa echoed her thoughts as he moved passed her, mouth agape.

The ceiling was adorned with a half dozen icicle shaped stalactites formed by dripping calcium salt deposits. Directly below the tapering spears were stalagmites protruding up from the floor surface in a hardened wax-like flow of sparkling colors. Two of the forms had actually connected into a petrified-like column of flowing minerals. Makowa stepped over and ran his hand up and down the column.

Transfixed by strange shapes dancing in the shadows of his helmet light beams, the other guard, Mr. George, walked over to a wall. "Mr. Nero," he asked. "You want some more additions to your scalp collection?" The group turned toward George. He held his helmet beams on a wall completely covered with scalps of hair. Each scalp had a White Deer Society symbol painted over it. What that meant, nobody had a clue.

"Don't touch a thing," ordered Nero.

Stanton and Nero proceeded down the slippery cave floor toward the center of the room. Their eyes went ablaze as their lights panned over a marketplace of ancient Iroquois weapons. The overwhelming inventory scattered about revealed war fighting bows and feathered arrows, blood-stained war hammers and chipped tomahawks, spears, daggers, swords, muskets, and powder horns. Stanton even spotted what appeared to be a Viking helmet.

"Some sort of weapons cache," Nero surmised.

Stanton knelt beside an old wooden crate and extracted a tattered

French infantry officer's blue uniform jacket and white sash. It came complete with the French Army symbol of the Fleur de Lis. She ran her eyes up the brass buttons and found a hole in the chest with a dark red stain. She placed the coat back in the box. "A weapon's cache that would never see the light of day," she mumbled.

"Explain," said Nero.

"Well, white deer were sacred and supposed to be protectors of peace for the tribes within the confederacy. So maybe whoever brought these items down here also despised war, the instruments of war, and trophies of war. Maybe this chamber is a place where Iroquois war items were hidden for good, to never be used or celebrated again." She shrugged.

Nero cocked his head at her, coughed, ignored her and continued on toward the far end of the chamber. Two dark cave openings appeared. Above each was a wooden false-face mask. Each was painted a dark red, eyes bulging, nose bent, mouth smiling. "Get over here," he gruffly ordered. "We've got a fork in the trail and I can't tell where it is on the map."

As Nero's party explored the room, Rae remained alone near the entrance, drinking water and buying time. She had kept her eye on Nero's top enforcer Kenny Rousseau, who had also remained slightly back. She caught him in her peripheral vision viewing some cave paintings. Rae realized this was the first good chance she had at escaping back up the passage to the surface — and freedom. She took a quiet step backward, hoping to ease her way back out without being noticed. That also meant killing her headlamp beams. As she reached up on her helmet to switch off her lights she caught movement from Rousseau. She glanced over. His light beams lit her up, his sawed-off shotgun leveled at her head.

"Go ahead. Give me a reason," he taunted.

Rae sighed, her first attempt foiled. A large paw soon clutched her around the neck, shoving her forward. "Move it, pig!" grunted Rousseau.

"Hey, check this out!" shouted Mr. George from behind several thin stalagmites, which formed prison-like bars. He moved his cigarette lighter over the end of a long stick jutting out from the wall. It was bunched up with rolls of dry grape vine. Flames spread quickly over the wood coils, casting one side of the chamber in an eerie orange glow. "We've got ourselves a torch!" He pulled it out of the wall and held it in front of him.

"Looks like they're all over the room. Light this place up," ordered Rousseau. He looked around, found Makowa rummaging through a basket, and barked an order for him to help out. He pushed Rae ahead to meet Nero and Stanton at the far end of the chamber. They were trying to decide which route to take next. Rousseau shoved Rae against the wall and joined his boss.

"Left or right passage?" asked Rousseau, looking up at the false faces over each tunnel entrance. He glanced down at the cave map over Nero's shoulder.

"Haven't the foggiest," replied Stanton, as the room lit up behind them. She looked back and noticed a half-dozen flaming torches lining the walls.

"I'm thinking we just follow the terrain and keep heading down," speculated Nero.

"The left passage seems to climb up, while the right descends," added Stanton as her helmet beams penetrated into each cave entrance.

Suddenly, a low boom emitted from the right cave passage, followed by three more cannon-like rumbles.

"What the hell was that?" shouted Makowa.

George chimed in, waving his burning torch. "Sounded like thunder."

"It's not thunder, you ass," chided Rousseau. "We're a good one hundred and fifty feet below the surface."

"It's the spirits of underworld warning us not to come any closer to their prize," said Nero.

"You're so full of shit," retorted Rae, leaning against the wall, her arms folded across her chest. "That's what the locals call the Seneca Lake guns. We hear them all the time. It's nothing more than your evil spirits having a case of natural gas build up and letting one loose!" Her dirty, bruised face revealed a white, full-toothed smile and a taunting rise of her eyebrows.

Stanton held back laughter. Nero caught her quivering grin. Rousseau, George, and Makowa also snickered at the remark. Embarrassed at the cop showing him up in front of his minions, Nero lashed out at Rae with the back of his hand. She tried to duck, but he was too fast. He caught her in the mouth with a crack, instantly drawing blood on her already fat lip. Makowa sprung up next to her with a drawn Glock, trying to make good for his boss.

"Who the fuck asked your opinion?" Nero boomed at Rae. He then grabbed her by her long auburn hair, twisted her head, and shoved her forward inside the right side passageway. Her helmet banged against rock. "Get going through there!"

Rae stumbled through the dark hole, tripped over a rocky hump, and fell to her knees. She tried getting up, but Makowa had followed right behind, booting her hard in the backside, telling her to get moving. Rae squealed in pain and tumbled ahead, busting her knees again on the rocky surface. As she fell face first, she unknowingly severed a thin fiber cord triggering a crude mechanism hidden in the sidewall.

Makowa again stood over her, waving the Glock. "Get your ass up."

He caught the full force of the booby trap as three crude spears from each wall sprung out and punctured him through his upper body. Suspended in mid air, Makowa looked down in shock at the six razor sharp spear tips penetrating his coat and pants.

Rae rolled onto her back and looked up as blood squirted down onto her. Shocked that it could have been her skewered on the trap, she lay frozen at the sight above. Makowa screamed down at her, then lost the grip on his pistol. Rae snatched it up, realized it was her very own service-weapon they had taken from her earlier. She squirmed forward out from underneath his legs.

Flashlight beams and a torch flame moved inside the tunnel entrance. Nero and his gang ran in, stopping before the booby-trapped barrier Makowa had formed.

Rae rose to her feet and dashed ahead as the chainsaw ripping of an automatic submachine gun burst out from behind the screaming cage of death. Bullets ricocheted off the limestone walls in a shower rock fragments. A shotgun blast then rang out as Rousseau joined in.

Rae instinctively ducked as an explosion of rock blew out next to her head. Another blast from the shotgun and the top of her helmet caught a spray of buckshot knocking the helmet forward over her eyes. She banged into the wall but managed to raise her re-acquired Glock behind her and fired off three wild shots to keep her attackers at bay. Their return fire stopped.

Taking cover around a corner in the passageway, Rae bent over and caught her breath as Makowa's wild screaming continued. She felt a sting on her upper thigh. Was she hit? She stood up and patted her thigh for a wound. Nothing. She slipped a hand inside her pant pocket and was completely surprised when she felt what was causing the pain. Pulling out the Cranberry Marsh silver broach, she smiled. She had totally forgotten she stashed the broach when the control tower blew up. And it had even slipped past the frisking Nero's thugs had given her. She placed the little good luck charm back in her pocket and ejected her service weapon's magazine clip, checking to see how many rounds she had left. Thirteen.

Another blast from Rousseau's shotgun smacked the wall next to her. She switched off her helmet lights for better cover just as Rousseau yelled out a prison-yard obscenity.

For the next twenty agonizing seconds all Rae could hear was Makowa's throes of agony until finally his cries became a whimper. She stole a glance back from around the corner and saw Makowa's head bow down on his chest, his light beams shining on a pool of blood at his feet. Rousseau and George were busy trying to dismantle the body from the booby trap in order to get by. Nero barked orders at them to hurry up.

After an unwitting escape, Rae was happy to be alive and armed once again. But she also realized she was stuck ahead of Nero's group and had no chance of getting back topside. She flicked her helmet lights back on and turned down the unknown passageway.

To her dismay, she almost stepped into a deep hole. Steadying herself against the walls, her helmet beams revealed a wide shaft about fifty-foot deep with a corn-fiber knotted rope ladder leading the way down. She had no choice but to go in and to make it fast before her would-be killers overtook her. Hoping the ancient rope ladder still had enough strength left she grabbed a knotted rung and stepped into the abyss.

Same time. Bunker A0101. Sub-level six. Toilet room.

"What are you thinking? I can't just leave you here," said a distraught Jake. He had just finished a makeshift splint for his uncle's ankle and a sling for his arm and wrist. Joe simply moaned as he sat against the toilet room masonry wall.

After the fall, Jake had diagnosed all of his uncle's wounds. He had injured a rib, probably broke his wrist, smashed his elbow, a high ankle sprain, and a very sore back. Plus, his shotgun was useless as a weapon.

"I can't go on, but you must," Joe insisted.

Jake shook his head. "That's crazy. This thing is over. I've got to get you to a hospital. Maybe we can start up one of those motorcycles and I can ride you back up?"

"I don't need a friggin' hospital. I need you to bust down a wall to see if this damn cave even exists."

"What if it does? Then what?"

"If the cave is there then you need to head in — alone — and not worry about me. I'll mess around with one of those motorcycles and see what I can do by the time you get out."

"Really?" said Jake. He stood up with hands on hips. "And what if I screwed up and there is no cave?"

"If there is no cave behind these walls," Joe tapped with his knuckles. "Then I suppose our next bet is to get you back down into the Cranberry Marsh well."

"Agreed." Jake pulled out his crumpled bunker floor plan. He flipped the page over and read the construction crew report one last time to verify which wall supposedly held the cave void behind it. He nodded, stuffed the paper back in his pocket, and grabbed the sledgehammer. "If there is a cave, then I'll continue with the mission only after I get you to a hospital."

"Fine. Just hit the damn thing!"

Jake swung his demolition tool about knee high. It hit with bone-crushing force. A masonry block cracked in half. Joe covered his eyes from the shower of concrete fragments that sprayed all over him. Jake swung again, blasting more of the block away. As the dust cleared, he noticed solid limestone in its place. He cursed.

"Go a little higher," directed Joe.

Jake hit the wall at waist level and crunched through another block. Two more swings and the block disintegrated, inward. To his astonishment the limestone surface was absent. Instead, he peered into a dark void. With a racing heart, he stood up and hammered away at a half dozen more blocks at waist and chest level. He blasted away a hole large enough to stick his head and shoulders through. White dust swirled in the dimly lit room as he stuck his head in and inspected what lay beyond. Just as the construction crew from the 1960s had reported, there, on the floor among the masonry chunks were several shards of broken pottery and an arrowhead. He panned around the walls with his helmet mounted light and found some strange cave paintings on the stone wall. Jake pulled back into the toilet room and looked at his uncle with a smirk. "The cave exists. There's Indian paintings on the wall."

Joe grinned, then sighed with relief.

And from the void they suddenly heard the terrifying echoes of a man wailing in death. They froze, chills shuddering through their bodies. Their smiling faces changed to looks of horror. Was it a ghost spirit? A burst from an automatic weapon then echoed from deep within. A shotgun report followed. A firefight was raging. More gunfire. Silence. Another shotgun blast echoed their way.

Jake moved quickly, demolishing more blocks to widen the hole. He stuffed his backpack, Halligan tool, and M4 rifle through, then squeezed his bulky frame in too. He told Joe to hold the fort — that he was going in to check out what was happening.

"Jake, if you come across a young lady with blonde hair, named Anne Stanton, please make sure you protect her at all costs. She's one of us."

Jake shook his head and bit his lip, pissed that his uncle held back on him again.

"She's the mole inside Nero's organization," Joe added. "I'll explain everything once you get back."

"Fine," Jake said, firmly. He the disappeared into the dark unknown.

In the caves.

THE ROPE HELD fine as Rae jumped down onto a rocky surface. The impact of her boots echoed across a darkened area she perceived as very large. She peered ahead with her helmet beams as an enormous cavern opened before her eyes. She held her breath. Directly in front of her was a tall row of connected stalagmites and stalactites forming a glistening forest of solid columns. Beyond, the cavern widened into a maze of rolling limestone humps, flowstones, and more icicle-like cave structures.

She heard a noise up above her in the shaft. Peeking up she noticed a faint glow of light spreading. They were coming down.

She moved quickly down a worn path, carefully shuffling her way between the natural columns and limestone outcrops. Her head was filled with questions. Were there more booby traps? Was there another way out of here? She only had one set of batteries in her helmet, a container of water, a gun, and no food. She couldn't keep running forever. As soon as her helmet light gave out she was all but done. She kept her head down on the trail, trying to determine clues of past visitors to make sure she headed in the right direction. Hell, any direction away from Nero. She felt dampness and cool air upon her face, then shouting from back at the shaft entrance. Nero yelled her name. She turned, a feeling of panic welled up inside of her. Tears tugged at her eyes.

Turning back around, a black hole appeared at her feet. She skidded a boot on its edge, tossing broken shards of stone into its gaping cavity. Her arms flailed helplessly as she lost her balance and fell forward. She reached out for something to grab onto and luckily caught a protruding rock to stop her fall. She pulled herself up and trudged ahead, eyes on the ground, heart pumping at full capacity.

Same time. Approaching the Weapon Room.

Jake hustled down a twisting cave corridor toward the last sounds of the firefight. With a backpack and Halligan strapped across his back and his helmet light shut off, he held his M4 rifle at the ready. Its rail mounted flashlight provided the thinner, targeted light beam he desired. A strange, disturbing feeling overcame him as he mentally switched back to combat survival mode once again. The rugged passage turned into a downward spiral. He narrowly squeezed through a bottleneck then made a sharp ninety-degree turn.

And stopped dead in his tracks.

His trigger finger twitched, almost shooting the skull face staring back at him. He inhaled.

Apparently it was a booby trap victim from many ages ago. All that remained was a skeleton in rags skewered on the tips of six spears that looked as if they had shot out from cracks in the walls. The victim wore several necklaces of beads and wampum over a buttoned red shirt, sleeves rolled up. Each of the skeleton's wrists held brass bracelets. Its bony fingers were adorned with silver rings. One hand clutched a burnt out torch. A black leather belt held up green trousers wrapped around an exposed pelvis, the belt holding a tomahawk and dagger sheathed in leather. Knee high black leather boots rounded out the victim's attire.

Jake noticed a deerskin pouch hung from a shoulder. He quickly perused its contents. He found several silver coins with British markings. From the clothing and the coins, Jake judged the person as being from colonial times. And from its jewelry and weapons possibly an Indian. Who knew what drew the victim to venture down here though. Might be the same reason Jake was risking his life? He used his Halligan tool and severed the tips of the spears on one side, freeing the skeleton to collapse in a heap of bones.

A cautious passage later and Jake met a warm orange glow. He emerged into a tall but narrow chamber illuminated by burning torches. He panned to his immediate left and noticed another passageway. A creepy looking false-face mask hung over its entrance. He panned right and followed his rifle barrel up into the expanse of the room. All types of ancient weapons were strewn about. It was a military historian's dream. He told himself to keep focused. He continued up there under a vaulted ceiling of sparkling icicle-shaped stalactites sparkling in the light.

Clearing the room, he let his rifle hang vertically down on his chest harness. He pulled out a paper copy of the cave map. Not sure at all where he really was since he came into the cave network at an unmarked location, he looked for a sign or symbol that could possibly match the room he was in.

A shout echoed from behind him. Weird, it sounded like Nero's voice. Jake whirled around, pointing his weapon. Another garbled voice, Kenny Rousseau's for sure. It clearly came from the passageway on the right. He pocketed the map and eased his way back to face the right tunnel corridor.

He went in.

Not ten feet ahead Jake spotted a body slumped to the side, this one definitely a fresh kill — from the firefight he assumed. But upon closer inspection he saw spear tips on broken shafts protruding from the body. The victim had died in the same type of trap as the skeleton in the previous tunnel. Moving the head with his boot, Jake saw that it was a man. Looked like one of Nero's guys. From the pool of fresh blood he was probably the one screaming just minutes before. Spent 9 mm brass casings and several red shotgun shells littered the ground. Jake lifted his M4, its beam and barrel pointed ahead. He noticed fresh pockmarks of limestone on the walls, probably from the shootout. But who had they been firing at? Maybe Anne Stanton, the mole?

He found three more bullet casings just before a tight bend in the tunnel, someone using the corner as cover. Swinging around, he found himself on the edge of fifty-foot shaft, complete with a crude rope ladder leading down. The ladder swung slowly, just used.

"Rae Hart! I will take your scalp!" shouted Alex Nero. His echoing voice rising from the same hole.

Rae? What the hell was *she* doing down here? Nero was after her? Jake clenched his teeth. He reached out for the rope, tested its strength, found it was good, and stepped off the edge in a careful descent. With a quick rappel down, he hit bottom and switched off his rifle's flashlight.

He stood in sheer darkness. The blackness was so intense he could not even see his own hand in front of his face. There were no flashes of anyone's light beams whatsoever. Where had Nero and Rousseau gone? He stood and listened. Nothing stirred, but something large loomed in front of him. He turned his rifle light back on.

"Whoa!" A wall of crystal-covered columns stood in his path, a huge cavern just beyond. He stepped forward and was hit with a draft of cool air mixed with burning wood, probably from torches, he figured. He stopped and panned his weapon left and right. More icicle-like cave features ahead, plus a narrow, twisted trail skirting misshapen hulks of limestone. He trudged onward.

He encountered open holes or fissures, dense black drop-offs in which cool air rose from the depths. He could tell people had just passed through from a freshly discarded chewing gum wrapper.

A shotgun blast boomed up ahead.

A woman screamed.

"Here Piggy, Piggy, Piggy!" echoed Rousseau's voice.

Jake's heart lurched.

In the cavern.

Caught off guard when Rousseau had fired his shotgun, Anne Stanton had screamed in surprise. Nero cut her a stern look then asked Rousseau if he hit Hart.

"Just missed her!" Rousseau answered. "George, take point, I've got to reload. Stay on the bitch."

Clutching an UZI submachine gun and chewing gum in an open-mouthed, cocky manner, Mr. George smiled as he took the lead position on the assault. He noticed flashes of light dancing upon the far cavern wall ahead. Depressing the trigger of his automatic weapon, he sent a chattering burst of bullets in toward the light. The light went dim. He moved in, wondering if he nailed his target.

As he swaggered closer, he sang out a familiar law enforcement television reality show tune, but with a twist. "Bad girls. Bad girls. Whatcha gonna do? Whatcha gonna do when they come for you?"

He blew a bubble.

BLAM.

A bullet cracked over his head. He ducked. Gum stuck to his cheek.

"That's what I'm gonna do!" echoed Rae's voice.

George responded with another deadly crescendo of fire. When his wall of 9 mm rounds smacked the cave rocks near Rae, sparks and stone fragments ricocheted all around. Rae gritted her teeth, ducked low, and crept forward. She felt her way through the dark and out of his line of fire. Another burst, more intimidating taunts, and Nero's henchman moved even closer.

Stumbling on hands and knees she felt a mist of cool air in front of her and heard the sound of rushing water. She switched on her lights briefly and found she teetered on a rock ledge with a drop off of about five feet. Machine gun fire ripped the air above her as she flipped over the ledge.

She landed inside another high-ceiling cave, this time with a fast-moving twelve-foot wide underground river flowing across her path from right to left. Debris was littered all over the level floor surface. She noticed battered driftwood, blackened logs, and even fresh weeds. But she also saw a torn Nike sneaker, a broken fishing pole and reel, clothing, an assortment of beer cans, and other modern-day garbage. She panned her helmet beam into the water, but couldn't see bottom. To her upper right the river seemed to originate from under a towering cliff wall. Just under the small falls shooting from the cliff was the partially decomposed carcass of a black and white dairy cow. Rae shook her head, shocked and confused.

She heard shouts behind her. She had no time to contemplate how all of this junk had made itself into this cave. She looked around and found she had no choice but to head left, down river. She paralleled the strong torrent of water along the debris-strewn bank until the river dead-ended and disappeared under another cave wall. There, a built-up dam of waterlogged wood and litter formed a mound pushed up against the wall. Rae noticed several more skeletons, some dismembered, but definitely human. One was even in an advanced stage of decomposition and still partially clothed. Could these be some of the countless missing drowning victims from Seneca Lake?

Shouting came from the cave ledge entrance behind her.

Rae needed to move, or die. She had to cross the river. It was her only escape. The mound of wood and bones seemed like it was stable, in fact there looked to be a rickety narrow wooden footbridge underneath holding everything up. She held her breath and lumbered across, crunching bone and branches under foot until she reached the far side. She stole a glance back up toward the rock ledge where she had entered. Approaching flashlight beams lit the entrance. Then something unusual caught her eye. A small black object the size of a racquetball was tossed through the light. It bounced once with a metal clang, giving Rae the only clue she needed.

She flattened herself behind a limestone hump and covered her head as the grenade exploded in an ear-shattering blast. Hot deadly shrapnel zipped off the walls and sprayed the water. A BB-sized piece of hot metal lodged in her left forearm. She grunted in pain. One of her helmet lights shattered. Her ears rang. The cave filled with gray smoke.

Kenny Rousseau and Mr. George jumped down off the ledge and plunged into the smoke. They blindly sprayed the area with shotgun and submachine gun fire. Nero and Stanton climbed in right behind them. Nero produced his Glock pistol and joined in with the wild firing squad. Beams of white light, amid Stanton's flaming torch, bounced in every direction as they advanced through the swirling smoke and crash of exploding gun barrels.

Rae remained flat as the spray of lead tore up the rocks all around her. When the firing ceased she heard the sounds of weapons reloading. Time to leave. With just one helmet beam now guiding her every step she got up and ran for her life.

Rousseau and George both saw the flash of light through the smoke — about fifteen yards away, off to their left. Fumbling to reload their weapons as they pursued the light source, they never saw nor heard the river of water obscured in smoke directly in front of them. Their next steps sent them tumbling over a large piece of driftwood and face first into the cold rushing current. With muffled shouts their heads went under. Their bodies were caught by a strong undertow. In an instant, their still-glowing helmet lights traveled toward the mound of debris and disappeared under the cavern wall.

Same time. Approaching the river.

Jake's pounding heart felt like it leapt in his throat as he heard what was definitely a grenade exploding. He watched as several helmet beams disappeared down into a hole, followed by a womanly figure holding a burning torch. The gunfire then started again, in heavy volumes. It was a classic urban combat tactic of clearing a room. Toss in a grenade, enter immediately after it detonates, then sweep the room with non-discriminating fire. Basically, fire first and ask questions later.

Jake flicked on his rifle flashlight and made the best possible time he could on the treacherous cavern path. Would he be too late? Again?

He finally came to the lit opening where gray wispy smoke trailed. He turned off his light. Flickering reflections of orange and red flames met his eyes about five feet down as he peered over a rock ledge. Without the slightest hesitation he jumped down — his rifle poised to fire.

River chamber.

As the grenade and gun smoke dissipated, a hoarse blood-curdling scream of pure rage shot from Nero's mouth. He had watched his two bodyguards simply vanish in the river that emerged before his eyes. From across the stream, somewhere in the darkness, he saw the faint glow of light and heard the rising laughter of a woman. He walked forward through debris and litter and stood at the edge of the river looking both ways. Anne Stanton approached him from behind and tried to speak. Nero silenced her.

Boots hit the floor behind them.

They spun around to face Jake Tununda's M4 assault rifle.

"YOU!" roared Nero. He shook with demented fury.

"Good to see you too," winked Jake. "Drop the weapon in the water or *die right now!*"

Nero's jaw muscles pulsed. His face turned red.

Jake took two steps closer. "Do it *now!*"

With grinding teeth, Nero flung his Glock into the dark water. "How did you get here?" he asked in a low, fury-etched voice.

"I'll ask the questions," replied Jake. "Where's Rae Hart?"

"She's across the river," pointed Stanton. "Somewhere over by those rocks at the far end of the cavern. You can barely see her light."

"RAE! It's Jake Tununda. Are you okay? You can come out."

Jake heard female laughter from the darkness. Or was it crying? He cocked his head, confused.

"Rae, it's me Jake!" he yelled again.

"Die Nero!" Rae screamed. She fired off a round. The bullet struck Stanton's torch, knocking it out of her hand. Stanton squealed. Jake ducked instinctively, losing his aim on Nero for a split second.

Nero seized the distraction and plunged headfirst into the river. Underwater, he switched off his helmet lights and disappeared into the blackness. Jake leveled his rifle, flicked on his rail light beam and fired several bursts where he saw Nero go in. Nothing. Then he turned and aimed his rifle at the blonde haired woman behind him. Her eyes grew large. She threw her hands up in surrender.

"Don't you move an inch," he ordered. The woman merely nodded. Jake spun back around and followed the river in the direction of its current. He waited for a head to pop up. As he ran, he unexpectedly dodged debris scattered about until finally slipping on a dead lake trout clipped with an orange tag. His legs split, feeling like he pulled his groin, but he kept upright keeping his focus on the river in case Nero surfaced. Nothing. He approached a wood and bone-filled pile against the cavern wall. The river disappeared underneath, sucking downward. Nero was nowhere to be seen. Jake hustled back to the woman, her hands still in the air.

"Where did he go?"

"I don't know."

"Where's Kenny Rousseau?"

"He fell in the water too."

"Are there others?"

She nodded her head again. "Yes. Another man, Mr. George. He fell in with Rousseau. They both just disappeared in front of our eyes. They didn't see the river in the smoke."

"Who are you?" Jake spat, anger in his eyes.

"Anne Stanton. I'm the director of Nero's collection," she replied. She trembled with fear. "I'm actually on your side. Please don't kill me, sir. Please."

Jake's eyebrows rose momentarily. "Why is Rae Hart down here? Why are you trying to kill her?"

"I'm not trying to kill her," pleaded Stanton, her chin quivering in panic. "I'm unarmed. Nero and his men kidnapped her back when the Depot's airfield control tower blew up. They forced her to come down here. I had no choice but to go along too."

"What? The control tower blew— What are you talking about?"

"I, I'm sorry. There's so much to explain."

"Shut up and lay face down, arms and legs spread apart." Stanton immediately complied. Jake knelt down over her, pressing a knee into her back to keep her pinned down. He switched off her two helmet lamps then killed his own rifle rail light again. The only source of illumination was the burning torch on the ground, a good ways away. He patted her down and found no weapons.

"Rae!" Jake shouted again. "It's Jake. For real. Nero's gone. Do not shoot! It's me."

Rae fired off another round from her Glock. The slug smacked a rock near the torch. Jake saw the flash of the muzzle this time, marking her location just twenty feet away across the river.

"God dammit Rae! It's me, Jake. Stop shooting!" His voice boomed this time.

"Jake?" shouted Rae, in a confused tone.

"Yes! It's safe. I'm here to help you."

"How do I know you're not working for Nero? How can I trust you? You've held back on me this whole time."

"The truth is I'm working for a Seneca clan mother who heads a secret Iroquois society," he shouted. "We're called the White Deer Society. Nero is our sworn enemy. I'm trying to stop him from getting an important crown that we protect." Stanton squirmed underneath him. He pressed his knee harder in her back. "The crown is down here in these caves somewhere," he continued. "Okay? That's the truth. Now please come out."

Jake saw a flicker of light pierce the darkness, then a white beam turn his way. "Where is Nero?"

"He and his men fell in the river and disappeared. I'm here with this Stanton woman."

"Okay! I'm coming back over," Rae yelled.

Jake sighed.

Stanton grunted, trying to shift her body under Jake's weight. "We've got to talk."

"Oh, I'm sure we do," replied Jake. "I was warned about you. Let's just wait until Rae gets over here."

Same time. Waterfalls chamber.

Alex Nero's biggest gamble paid off — he was still alive. Banged up, but still breathing, as were his men Kenny Rousseau and Mr. George. They had fished him out of a deep pool of swirling water after he too rode the underground river and small waterfalls beneath the cavern wall. They pulled him up onto the limestone bank of a small cave. The cave was dimly lit by one of their hand-held flashlights propped against the wall.

Nero coughed and looked up with a smile. "I knew it," he rasped. He rolled over on his back, his chest heaving. Besides some abrasions on his arms and legs, a bloody slice on his cheek was his most serious wound. If not for his helmet staying on during his risk-all underwater escape from Tununda, he would have probably died from a rocky head bashing.

Rousseau unstrapped Nero's dented helmet, the dual lights completely shattered. His and George's were also in similar shape, already discarded up on the bank.

"Lucky roll of the dice," Nero gasped. Wet strands of his long gray hair stuck to his bruised face. He looked up at the stream of white water that shot him out from the top of the rock wall.

"Got that right," said the crooked-nosed Mr. George. He held his arm and limped up on the bank to grab the flashlight.

Nero looked about the cave. Broken branches, weeds, and garbage were strewn about. Ancient horizontal water lines marked flood levels on the limestone walls. "You lose any gear?"

Rousseau grunted and wiped away the wet hair plastered flat against his forehead. The wound from the gauntlet had opened up again. Blood trickled down across his brows. "George lost his Uzi and I lost my shotgun. I still have my Beretta and a hunting knife." He produced the six-inch dagger in one hand and a silenced pistol in the other. "And we have our backpacks, two working flashlights, extra batteries, and food. That's it."

"My pistol's gone too," replied Nero. He sat up, shedding his backpack and pushed back his wet hair. "Any grenades left?" he asked, wiping away blood from the gash on his cheek.

"We've got three," said Mr. George.

"I take it that bitch is still alive or you wouldn't be here," asked Rousseau. He helped his boss stand up. "We heard gunfire up through that passage after we got out of the water." He pointed back toward the waterfall at an opening leading upward.

"Hart's still alive," Nero said. "And that Army freak Tununda came outta nowhere — armed with an assault rifle. He probably wasted Stanton. Doesn't matter though, she's expendable."

"So, we've got three grenades and one pistol," Mr. George remarked. "Tununda's got a rifle and the bitch has her Glock."

"But we're in the lead," said Rousseau. "Let's get moving."

"Wait a second," remarked Nero. "You could hear gunfire you said?"

"Yeah, why?"

"Give me a grenade," ordered Nero. "And follow me. We've got unfinished business."

36

River chamber.

RAE STEPPED ACROSS the debris footbridge, her Glock lowered in front of her. Her shirt sleeve was pushed up, forearm dripping with blood from the shrapnel wound. She pulled off her helmet and let it drop at her feet. She looked a wreck. Her face was battered and dirty with several cuts. Her long hair was snarled with sweat and mud, her clothes wet and grimy.

Jake met her near the burning torch. In the flickering light Jake gazed into her weary eyes. She collapsed into his strong arms and buried her head in his shoulder. He hugged her tightly.

As they pulled apart he looked down at her arm, inspecting the severity of the wound. He told her it was minor, that he would bandage her up. She laughed. Then out of the blue he leaned in and kissed her. She responded initially by pulling away, but his lips were soft, wet, and simply felt good. She gave in, yearning for more.

Pressing her mouth tight against his, a low pleasurable moaned escaped from her throat. She held the back of his neck with her fingers. He threw his arms around her waist, shoving her up against the cave wall. Their kiss was deep, breathless, and long. Finally, it was Rae who broke the lock.

"Wow," she whispered, catching her breath.

"Tell me about it," said Jake, clearing his throat. "Ahh, okay then. Well then, um, shall we get back to business? We've got find out where this river empties out. We have to see if Nero and his boys are alive."

"Lead the way soldier!"

"Wait, where's that Stanton woman?" Jake asked.

He and Rae looked all around.

"There," pointed Rae, back across the river, in the same general area where she had just been hiding. A faint light beam reflected off the bullet-ridden limestone walls. Jake raised his rifle and peered down the scope. Her illuminated helmet appeared in the crosshairs of his M4 scope.

Stanton turned. "Hey lovebirds! I'm over here if you're done. There's a passage headed down, hurry up!"

Jake lowered his weapon. Rae strapped her helmet back on and grabbed the burning torch. The pair scurried back over the river to meet Stanton at the top of what looked like a limestone spiral staircase leading down into a black hole.

Stanton faced them. "I remember seeing something like this on Nero's cave map. This river empties into some new chamber." She gestured to the crude staircase. "He and his men are probably down in there, their bodies at least."

"You think they're still alive?" asked Jake, fumbling in his pocket to pull out his own copy of the map.

"I hope the hell they aren't," said Stanton.

"Here, I've got a copy of that map. It—"

Stanton chuckled. "I figured you would. Let me show you where I think we are."

"Not so fast," said Rae, grabbing Stanton's arm. "She's got some explaining to do first."

"Yeah, apparently you and I have a common employer," quipped Jake. "Miss Lizzie Spiritwalker ring any bells? How about my uncle, Joe Big Bear Tununda?"

Stanton sighed deeply. She nodded her head.

"We'll talk later," ordered Jake. "Let's get down there and find the bodies first." And then, in what seemed like slow motion, he saw movement in the shadows a few steps down around the bend in the stairs. He raised his M4 just as a grenade flew by his head. His feet seemed glued, he couldn't move fast enough. It was as if he were in a dream sequence. He watched as the metallic ball of death hit a rock behind him and bounced straight up, making a clinking sound as it hit.

"GRENADE!" Jake reached out with his right hand. His movement now in fast motion, his adrenaline jacked to its fullest. Afghanistan flashed through his mind. He snagged the grenade in mid-air, clutched it for a split second like a baseball player on a double play, and tossed it toward the river. "GET DOWN!"

Jake knocked the legs out from under both women just as the grenade plopped into the water. It detonated just under the surface with a muffled blast of red-hot shrapnel slicing through a torrent of water. The spray showered the trio.

Jake stood up first, dripping wet, rifle to his shoulder, beam aimed down the spiral steps. His old forearm wound tingled. He charged in and fired as he advanced. He heard men shouting in front of him, women screaming behind. Shadows danced, lights bounced, bullets cut the air and ricocheted as his trigger finger worked his rifle's magic. Down a series of naturally carved spiral steps he hit bottom. A small waterfall spilled to his left from a wall. It emptied in a pool of black water. Three damaged spelunking helmets sat on a narrow rocky bank littered with more garbage. He saw movement ahead — three figures racing inside another cave passage. He took a bead on the last figure and pulled the trigger.

Waterfalls chamber.

The first bullet ripped through Mr. George's backpack and into his back. It punctured a lung and exited through his stomach. George threw his hands in the air with a grunt, his flashlight dropped, bounced off the rocky bank, and rolled into the river. Pain shot through his body. His knees weakened.

Jake's next bullet struck a shoulder blade and redirected upward through George's neck, severing an artery. The third round cut clean through the spinal cord. George's vision went black. His knees buckled. The next round turned his head into an exploding watermelon. His lifeless, blood-spewing body slumped face down with a dull thump.

"Son of a bitch," mouthed Rousseau. He was staring back at George from just inside the new passageway.

"Let's go! Leave him," ordered Nero, from further up the tunnel. But Rousseau realized that George had on the backpack with the rest of their food and extra flashlight batteries. He needed to retrieve it. Rousseau pulled the pin of the second grenade and tossed it back into the waterfalls chamber, just over George's limp body. He took cover back inside his tunnel.

Same time.

Watching another grenade roll his way, Jake calmly took three steps back up the spiral rock staircase and sought protection around a curve. The grenade exploded in a deafening roar. Shrapnel ripped through the room and took chunks of limestone off the walls. Smoke instantly filled the chamber. Jake switched off his light. Rae and Stanton piled into him from behind.

"Oh my God, are you alright?" asked Rae.

"Fine. You two okay?"

"We're good," replied Stanton.

Jake peered around the corner into the smoky chamber.

THWACK. THWACK. Two muffled shots struck the wall near his head.

Jake pulled back. "Kill your lights! Kill your lights!"

The women complied, Rae stomping furiously to extinguish the torch she carried. The chamber went pitch black.

"Silenced pistol," Jake whispered from a kneeling position, his M4 shouldered, eye on scope. He looked back around the corner.

A light flickered from across the way. It came from just inside a far passageway. There was movement near the downed body. Through a smoky haze, Jake zeroed in with his scope. A hand reached out from the passageway, fumbling with the dead man's backpack.

CRACK! CRACK! CRACK! Three rounds smacked into the body with dull thumps. The hand pulled back.

"You dirty son of a—" screamed Rousseau, but his voice was drowned out by another burst of fire from Jake's M4. The next rounds struck just inside the passage where Rousseau was taking cover. Rousseau turned his flashlight off.

Jake pulled the trigger again, but heard metal on metal. His magazine was empty. He threw a switch and dropped his magazine. "Reloading," he whispered.

Rousseau heard the empty click sound too. Flashlight back on, he made another attempt at George's backpack. He was met by a loud blast from a pistol. A bullet struck the cave wall over George's body.

Standing just above Jake, Rae held her smoking Glock steady. While Jake reached into his pocket for another full-metal jacket, she sang out a familiar tune in defiance. "Whatcha gonna do? Whatcha gonna do, when they come for you?"

She received a rage-filled bellow for her efforts. She had flicked Rousseau's switch. Reloaded, Jake rejoined her. They waited for the thug's next move.

THWACK! A round impacted the wall near the pair. Although Rousseau's aim was off, Rae backed away and sought cover behind Jake. The darkened stand off continued.

Jake whispered. "I wonder if that's The Mouth's silenced pistol?"

"How do you figure?" asked Rae, squatting behind him, her hand gently holding his waist.

"We had a little get-together at Conesus Lake. They had that same pistol. Hit me in the head with it."

"I knew you were there, dammit!" she replied, whispering in his ear. "We had a report of a gunshot in that same area Ashland had circled on his topo map."

"Hey Clown Face? That you over there?" Jake goaded out loud. "Got any glass in your ass?"

THWACK! Another wild round cracked Jake's way.

"Make your move you little prick," Rousseau yelled back. "And I'll shove another grenade up your ass!"

Jake responded with two bullets aimed at the voice.

A minute went by as they waited for Rousseau's counterattack. Then two more. The clock ticked.

"What are we going to do?" asked Stanton. "What if he has more grenades? We can't go in there."

"There's something in that backpack they want," said Rae.

"I'll take point," whispered Jake. "Stay here. I'll tell you when it's clear." He moved into the pitch-black chamber taking each step with care not to stumble on any debris. The sound of his steps were masked by the waterfalls spilling into the pool. He watched for any flicker of light ahead where Rousseau was last seen.

Nothing. No light, no sounds from the far passage as Jake inched closer. It took him a full minute to make it to where he felt the bloody body of Mr. George. He flicked on his rifle's flashlight and immediately pointed the weapon into the passageway where Rousseau had been.

Empty.

Jake covered the tunnel in a kneeling position, eyes glued to his scope. The narrow cave passage traveled straight and far before his beam dissolved into darkness.

He whistled back toward the women and announced, "Clear." As they took their time getting over, he checked the area around him for any grenade booby traps. He did the same with Mr. George's body and the bloody backpack.

Nothing.

When the women arrived near him, he resumed his posture, covering the cave tunnel. He told Rae to check inside the backpack. She flicked her headlamp on and unzipped blood smeared pockets. Inside she found several packages of flashlight batteries and energy candy bars.

"It's going to suck for them when their batteries run out," said Stanton. She and Rae stuffed the precious items in their pockets.

"Miss Stanton," Jake said, never taking his eyes off the scope. "You've got some explaining to do. Now's a good time."

Stanton sat down with a sigh and leaned back against the rock wall. "Alright. I'm Miss Lizzie's granddaughter…"

Jake blinked. "What?"

Stanton continued. "She recruited me years ago when my mother took no interest in the White Deer Society. I moved from Atlanta and went to college near the reservation. Lizzie weaned me to become the head of the secret society as a direct matrilineal next of kin once she passed away."

She spoke softly. "When we learned Nero was the direct descendant of Atotarho we needed to keep a close watch on him. I positioned myself to enter his organization as an undercover operative. With my non-Indian looks, expertise in the field of archaeology and preservation, I landed a research position for his collection. When his mother died I became director. I gained his trust. And that's when he told me he knew of the secret mark of the society — the deer and snake symbol. He had learned it from his mother just before she died. He ordered me to keep an eye on anything that was even remotely associated with it. That's when we knew what he was really after. The Crown of Serpents."

Rae piped up. "Ahh, so that's this ancient artifact thing you all are after. This crown."

"Right," replied Stanton. "It's what we are sworn to protect."

"And what I unwittingly got myself stuck in!" mentioned Jake.

Stanton shrugged. "You were meant to be."

"I guess there are other forces at work," said Jake.

Stanton nodded. "When that news report came out of an Indian grave being found in Seneca County, along with a piece of jewelry with a deer and snake symbol on it, I had no choice but to inform Nero. I needed to show him that I was legit. But secretly, our society was seeking the crown too — and the cave that would lead us to it. Because we lost that location as of 1779."

"When Sullivan's troops burnt Kendaia," added Jake.

"Exactly," agreed Stanton. "And then the discovery of Thomas Boyd's journal blew everything wide open."

"Wait, wait," said Rae. "Boyd, he's the one who hid the British gold at Conesus Lake, right."

"You're catching on," replied Jake. He lowered his rifle to give his arms a rest, but still kept his eyes on the passage ahead.

Stanton nodded. "Yes, you see, it turns out Thomas Boyd was the last one who knew of the location of the cave that leads to the crown. He wrote about it in his journal. Once Nero read that journal at Old Fort Niagara he bought it on-site. And then he told me straight up of his ultimate grand plan to find Atotarho's crown or die of cancer trying."

Rae laughed. "Let's grant the latter wish."

Stanton continued with her story. "He gave me full access to the journal. We just had to decipher the Masonic encryptions to find out. At that point, I knew I had the clues to find the crown, protect it, and stop Nero at the same time."

Jake nodded. He stood up and raised his rifle to look down the scope again. Rae just shook her head in bewilderment.

Stanton spoke faster. "Because of my research on McTavish's rifle, Nero sent Ray Kantiio down to Pennsylvania to steal it. But I didn't know that at the time. And that's when I heard of Ashland's murder."

Rae rubbed her chest where the two bruises were. She gulped.

"But Ray failed. Nero had him beaten to death in some gauntlet ceremony. Little did he know that I tape recorded it and I immediately went to the state police with the evidence. I had everything I needed to take that bastard down and send him and his thugs back to jail. And then the whereabouts of the crown would be safe as I continued the search."

Jake took his eyes off his scope and glanced at Rae. Her eyes widened and she nodded, confirming Stanton's account.

"But the elders — Spiritwalker and Big Bear — kept me in the dark about your initial involvement, Mr. Tununda. I didn't know who you were at first. Just as they didn't tell you of my role, I take it."

"I didn't know who you were until I stepped foot in these caves. Big Bear is sitting in an underground Depot survival bunker as we speak, waiting for us to come out. He told me to protect you."

"And I need to protect you too, as the star witness against Nero," said Rae, softly placing a hand on her shoulder.

"You got here from the Depot?" a confused Stanton asked Jake.

"Smashed a hole in a wall of a bathroom six levels below ground. A cave tunnel was hidden behind it. Found out about it in some old Depot construction reports. It was a lucky break. I came in just after your firefight, where one of Nero's guys got skewered in that booby-trap."

"That's when Rae escaped," Stanton added. "But listen Mr. Tununda, I knew you were out there meddling in Nero's affairs because your name kept popping up. I knew you had to be related somehow to Big Bear."

"Tell me about it," said Rae.

Stanton stood up. "After I demanded, the elders finally told me who you were but Lizzie wanted me to keep on researching where the cave entrance was on the Depot. She said my information would have been relayed back to you in that regard, but everything moved so fast."

"Yeah, they ambushed us at Lizzie's house last night," added Jake.

"I heard what happened," replied Stanton. "I know what Lizzie did." Her eyes darted to Rae then back at Jake.

"I tried to stall," pleaded Stanton. "Honest. I thought the state police would sweep in and arrest Nero. But when I was doing my research in Ovid, he text-messaged me the deciphered code to the cave. He threatened my life if I didn't produce again." Her voice wavered and cracked. "And I knew he wouldn't tolerate failure. Just look at what happened to The Mouth. I am truly sorry I caused of all this. I am. I bit off more than I thought I could handle." She bowed her head.

"I've got something to show you and Jake," said Rae. She reached inside her pocket. "I think this little charm protected me so far. I want you to have it." She gave the broach to Stanton, who all but cried when she saw it. "I've got *this* back and it's all I need now." Rae raised her Glock firearm.

"Nero has the other broach, the one from Luke Swetland," Stanton stated. "He's wearing it around his neck."

"I doubt it's going to protect him," replied Jake, turning back toward the cave tunnel. "Not when we find him. Let's move out!"

MICHAEL KARPOVAGE

37

Chamber of the Crown of Serpents.

NERO AND ROUSSEAU hit a dead end. The long, twisting passageway they had been following for several fast-paced minutes had just stopped at a pile of rocks. The pile was stacked about three feet high in a shape reminiscent of a human figure. Nero glanced at his cave map to figure out where he was. Seconds later, he picked up the top rock on the pile. It was a skull-shaped boulder balancing on a long, flat rock used as the figure's arms. He noticed something behind the sculpture. He smiled greedily and kicked over the rest of the rocks.

Behind the pile was a stone slab leaning on-end against the wall. Sure enough, a tiny white deer and snake symbol was painted on the slab's surface. Nero easily moved the stone to reveal a jagged, tube-like passageway dimly lit in a silvery-blue light. His heart raced.

He crouched low and directed his flashlight ahead. Wasting no time, he entered first on hands and knees. "After you get in here, turn around and reposition the slab the way we found it," he whispered back to Rousseau. "Then set the last grenade against it with the pin ready to drop as soon as the slab is touched. Booby-trap it."

"My pleasure," Rousseau smiled.

A few minutes later Nero crawled out from the snake-like cave fissure and collapsed in exhaustion on the ground. His flashlight rolled away a couple of feet ahead of him. Its white beam illuminated a smooth, gray shale floor shrouded in an iridescent fog. By the time Rousseau caught up to him, Nero had managed to recuperate and catch his breath. He stood up and retrieved his flashlight, spit some flem from his dry aching throat, and peered ahead in the bluish chamber.

It was astounding.

They had entered into a beehive-shaped grotto about forty feet in diameter. Hovering just above the ground, a shimmering white haze permeated the lower reaches of the chamber. Painted around every inch of the smooth limestone walls were white deer and snake symbols that danced eerily in the light. They reached as high as the eye could see into a topless, chimney-like fissure of black. The flickering room seemed to have a hallucinogenic effect. It was as if the chamber was possessed with some form of life.

Nero pointed his flashlight toward the center of the room. Tongues of silver, blue, and white flames burned about three-feet high. They approached the flames like mosquitoes attracted to blood. Trudging slowly through flowing waves of chest high fog, they found that the source of the fire was contained in a boulder-lined pit bubbling full of a clear liquid. Nero cocked his head, realizing the flames radiated no extreme heat. Coolness rose from the water, its depths aglow in deep blue and silver shadows. Instead of smoke, milky white mist generated from the flames. Nero's flashlight suddenly pulsed. It grew brighter then dimmed. He shook it. It pulsed again then died. He switched it on and off to no effect. Setting the flashlight down, he and Rousseau happened to glance up.

Jutting straight up from the middle of the flames stood a long twisted wooden pole. At its zenith sat a large buck skull with blackened eye sockets. Long bright white antlers, branched in multiple points, extended from each side of the white skull. Nero stared at the buck skull, its hollowed eyes now seeming to blink alive. Or was it an illusion? And then the pole seemed to slither like a snake. He backed away, breaking his gaze, shaking his head from side to side. But he bumped into stone. The fog dissipated and then he knew immediately the grotto was actually a funerary chamber.

Positioned around the flaming pit, like spokes around a wheel hub, were three mummified corpses displayed on waist high stone slab tables. Raised several feet off the rocky flat floor, the ancient corpses lay flat on thick shale altars as if they were floating on clouds. Their upper torsos were wrapped in white deer fur shawls. The heads of the corpses were covered in wooden false-face masks carved and painted in an array of bright colors and hideously laughing expressions. Long, fragile white hair framed the bent-nosed masks. Inspecting each, Nero noticed two of the deceased false-faces had male features, while one seemed female in its characteristics. The corpse's highly preserved clothing, under their deer coats, revealed jewelry, wampum necklaces, and other accessories further denoting their genders. The bony fingers of two males, wrapped tightly with shrink-wrap-like maroon skin, held turtle rattles and eagle feathers. The female clutched a single corn-husk doll in one hand and a painted clay head the size of a baseball in the other. Rousseau reached out and touched the little head.

"Don't touch a thing," warned Nero. "There are other forces at play here. Spirits are here. I can sense them." He took a close look at the jewels around the corpses' necks, just under their masks. Silver broaches gleamed at their throats. Sure enough, the corpses wore the same wampum-bordered, hand-hammered silver jewel that he had around his neck, complete with a duplicate buck and snake emblem.

"Who are they?" asked Rousseau, his body already chilled to the bone from a growing sense of fear.

"I'm pretty sure they are the Founders," answered Nero in a deep garbled voice.

"Of the Confederacy?"

"Yes. The Crown of Serpents is close. It is calling me."

"This place is freakin' me out," muttered Rousseau, his head on a swivel. He waved his silenced pistol. "The deer are moving all over the walls. And these masks seem real. It's like this whole place is coming alive or something."

A muffled blast echoed from far up the entrance tunnel in. A man bellowed in agony.

Rousseau and Nero looked at each other smiling.

"Make sure they're dead," ordered Nero. "I'll search for the crown."

Snake tunnel.

Jake's old battle wound on his arm itched like a bad disease as he snaked through the twisting, dimly lit, smoke-filled cave tunnel. After setting off the grenade he had detected at the stone slab entrance, he screamed feigning injury. He then handed off his Halligan bar to Stanton so it wouldn't scrape in the tunnel and took the point position to confront whoever lay ahead. He was hoping a curious rat would come back to the scene of the explosion to check on its handy work. And then he'd dispose of the menace once and for all.

He gave Stanton and Rae instructions to remain behind, shut their helmet lights off, and to make no sounds whatsoever. With his rifle slung close to his chest, he breathed slowly, focusing on any sounds or movements up ahead.

Five long minutes later he heard a slight scrape just around a bend. A shadow cast on the low ceiling made the slightest hint of movement. Jake froze in the prone position, rifle butt tight to his shoulder, vision glued down his scope. Someone was definitely there. One person. He could even hear labored breathing. He waited for his soon-to-be victim to make the first move.

As the seconds passed, Jake wondered if the person just around the bend had another grenade. If one was tossed in his direction, he was simply dead meat. No matter about it. Should he proceed forward, make the first move instead? He became distracted. He needed to remain calm, think clearly, hold a bead on that corner. He shook the negative thoughts and peered ahead in the blue glow, trigger finger twitching.

Another scrape.

A shadow grew.

Let the rat come.

A forehead appeared slowly from around the corner, filling the cross hairs in Jake's riflescope. Then eyebrows and blinking eyes with blue tattoos under each.

Clown Face. Time to go to hell.

Trigger. Rifle blast. Slight kickback.

In Jake's scope Rousseau's head snapped back and dropped sideways on the ground. A black bullet hole appeared directly between his wide-open, frozen eyes.

"Rat poison," Jake whispered. "Works every time."

Chamber of the Crown of Serpents.

Soon after, Jake's female counterparts caught up to him in the tunnel and he helped the pair weave their way passed Rousseau's lifeless body. Jake had already searched it, finding a knife and Kantiio's silenced pistol. He took both then led the way into a hazy blue, dome-like chamber. Jake and Rae entered first, keeping their helmet and flashlight beams extinguished. Working in tandem with weapons at the ready, they hit the perimeter in a classic room sweep.

Seconds later they met at the far side. Jake confirmed, "Clear!"

"Ann!" shouted Rae. "Come in. Go to the middle of the room."

Jake and Rae also converged toward the center. They watched Stanton approach on the far side, mouth agape in wonderment. Jake ignored the three corpses on the stone tables. Instead, he walked through a calm misty fog to pinpoint the luminous blue light that seemed to keep the funerary chamber aglow. It was originating from a circular, rock-edged hole or pit centered between the corpse tables. He slowly panned his rifle up a knotty wood pole leaning out of the hole. A large, ten-point antlered buck skull sat a top the pole looking as if it would fall off at any moment.

Jake then peered deep inside the pit, his eyes following the twisted effigy pole down another eight feet to where it disappeared into a shimmering pool of bubbling liquid. On the surface flickered low silvery blue flames, their height no more than a oven burner gas flame set on low.

"Some sort of a natural gas well," he said out loud. Inspecting the pit closer he noticed a series of jutting rocks and crevices along the sides. The rough stairs led down into an open wider area under a shale lip. He detected a slight draft of air rising out of its depths. Strange, he thought, it felt cool against his face — no heat being generated.

"Probably the source of the Lake Guns," commented Stanton. She set Jake's stainless steel Halligan bar against one of the stone corpse tables. She then closely inspected the female corpse lying on the slab.

"These paintings are unbelievable," remarked Rae. She stood mesmerized by the shadow dancing of deer and snake symbols plastered all over the walls.

Jake ignored her. He looked up, his head cocked to one side, a frown upon his face. He was fixated at the ominous buck skull on the gnarly wooden shaft. Suddenly, the pole moved. It twisted. Or did it? Jake glanced back down into the pit. The flaming water rose slightly, causing the pole to shift.

"Mr. Tununda?" prompted Stanton, now hovering over one of the male corpses. "I'm going to hazard a guess, but I think these individuals are the three original founders of the Haudenosaunee Confederacy. Two males and a female."

"Deganawida, Hiawatha, and Jecumseh," stated Jake, stealing a glance back at her.

She nodded. "It was said by the Faithkeepers," explained Stanton, as Rae stood listening at her side. "That the three great ones wanted to rest together when they passed into the spirit world. That they wanted to provide the first line of defense from anyone possessing Atotarho's crown ever again."

"That means the crown is around here somewhere," offered Rae.

Jake agreed, watching the grave marker pole. It slowly righted itself as the churning, burning water rose another foot. Light pulsated from deep within the well's bowels.

"Or maybe it *was* here and Nero already found it and took another way out," added Stanton.

White swirls of fog crept out of the pit. Jake took a step back. "Shit. Did we miss an exit?" He looked around the room and then tried to switch his rail-mounted flashlight back on. It didn't work. He cursed and tried again to no avail. Giving up, he raised and panned his M4 out toward the cave walls.

"But there's no other way out of here," said Rae. She raised her Glock toward the perimeter too. "We already searched."

"Or is there?" refuted Jake. "Let's do a secondary search again near the walls. A little slower this time. Miss Stanton, take this." He pulled from his pocket the Browning pistol confiscated from Rousseau back at Lizzie's house. He handed it to her. "The safety is off. Make your shots count."

Stanton took the weapon without saying a word.

"Split up," ordered Jake. He stepped away from the corpse circle. "And turn your helmet lights back on."

"Mine doesn't work," said Rae. She walked out toward the chamber wall, her Glock leading the way. "I already tried it."

"Mine either," shouted Stanton, nervously pressing the on-off switch on her helmet. Her weapon was also raised, although within a shaky hand.

"Mine's malfunctioned too," said Jake. "And it ain't no coincidence."

"Not sure we need lights anyway seeing as how it's getting brighter in here," observed Rae from clear across the room. She continued to grope along, searching for signs of another concealed passageway.

"And the fog is getting thicker too," shouted Stanton. She searched an opposite wall.

Jake shouted back from his side of the cave. "The water in that pit has been rising too."

Stanton glanced back to the pit. Silver flames reached higher, their tips dancing with cyan blue tongues. The skull pole had righted itself completely and now stood vertical. Waves of milky blue mist spilled out of the hole causing the three corpses to look as if they were floating on air. And then something peculiar caught her eye.

"Oh my God! *Look!*"

The Crown of Serpents.

Rae and Jake spun around. And froze. Was it a hallucination?

Rising out of the flames and fog slithered a cluster of silver serpents. Flickering tongues darted from their open mouths. Their reddened eyes flashed like rubies. They hissed like boiling water.

Stanton blinked from across the cave. Her eyes must be deceiving her, she thought. Her head felt light. Cool air drifted upon her face. She blinked and looked again.

A muted Jake shook his head. Through the flames he saw Rae across the room. A look of horror filled her face as she stared wide-eyed, back against the wall.

The snakes had now wrapped themselves around the pole and were climbing higher. A human head started to take shape below the intertwining serpents. Flames rose higher in whites, blues, and purplish hues. Long, wet, gray hair intermixed with the hissing snakes. A shadowed face with silver glowing eyes emerged. Naked broad shoulders rose with wiry arms folded across a heaving hairless chest glimmering with a silver and wampum broach on a necklace. Dark wet pants clung to strong legs. A flash of light revealed the full figure.

Alex Nero.

One with the Crown.

Jake raised his assault rifle and centered his mark on Nero's chest. Stanton gripped her pistol and took aim. Rae was already in position, her legs spread apart with one hand grasping her Glock, the other cradling in support.

Nero floated higher. He seemed unreal. The Crown of Serpents was now at the same height as the buck skull. The snakes took a hold of the skull and shattered it in a smattering of bones. All that was left were two, multi-pointed antlers now clearly meshed as part the crown.

Nero stepped out of the overflowing well and onto the smooth shale floor. He looked physically bigger, stronger, and much healthier. He stretched his arms out in a God-like pose and slowly turned in a circle, announcing himself to his small captive audience.

"*I AM ATOTARHO!*" he announced in a clear, strong voice. His raspy coarse tone was completely absent. Suddenly, three flashes of white light shot from the pit. "Kneel down to me my servants or meet instant death!"

The three remained still, unsure how to handle what was happening.

Nero took it as defiance. "*NOW!*" he bellowed.

Stanton flinched with fear. She pocketed her weapon, kneeled, and raised her arms in surrender. But Jake and Rae refused to give in. From opposite sides of the room they acted simultaneously and depressed the triggers of their respective weapons.

Clicks followed.

They tried again. Their weapons refused to fire. Jake checked his chamber. A round was there. He aimed at Nero's head and pulled the trigger again. Misfire. Malfunction. Rae's Glock acted the same.

Nero's deep laughter echoed throughout the chamber. "Your modern weapons are useless against my power," he shouted. Wasting no time in dealing with the insubordination, he first lashed out at Jake, his strongest threat. Closing his silver laced eyes, he summoned his crown's newfound energy. He extended both arms and pointed all of his fingers toward his foe, then opened his eyes.

An invisible force tore through the fog. The jolt struck Jake like a concussive electrical shock. It knocked him backward, helmet flying off his head. He screamed in horrified torment, clutching the sides of his head while backpeddling and slamming himself into the cave wall. A frenzy of searing pain shook his body.

Nero roared with arrogant laughter. "Feel my power. I *am* the great wizard. I *am* reborn!"

Jake's head felt like it would explode as electrical energy heated inside his brain. He dropped to his knees and moaned loudly, slipping into semi-consciousness. In a moment, he went silent and fell flat on his face. His M4 rifle came loose from his harness and skittered on the slate floor. Swirls of white mist enveloped his motionless, depleted body as he disappeared in the fog.

Nero spun around and searched for the other defiant one — Rae Hart, symbol of the white law enforcement that had oppressed him all of his life. She had made her way around the cave perimeter toward the entrance tunnel and was just bending down to escape when he caught her. Nero screamed a war whoop as his supernatural power sliced through the air once again. He struck Rae in her backside with another jolt of invisible electricity. She screamed in pure agony as she was jarred against the wall. She then slumped silently down in the mist, disappearing.

Nero then looked around the cave for Anne Stanton, expecting her to still be kneeling in submission. He crouched and turned like a panther, his moves nimble and quick, searching for the last of his prey. He could sense her presence moving away from him, but she was nowhere to be found within the chamber. He figured she must have made her escape back out of the tunnel. He relaxed.

"You have served me well, woman," he muttered to himself, not willing to pursue her just yet. "I shall have my way with you later." He chuckled in a deep insane tone as long thin snakes groped his cheeks.

The chamber floor had now filled entirely with soupy whirlpools of fog. A rumble developed from the pit. Nero spun around to look. His silver eyes narrowed.

BOOM!

A gusher of water and flames exploded from the well. The wooden pole shattered into pieces. A overpowering baritone drum-like sound echoed through the room. Pieces of limestone slipped from the walls. The blast propelled Nero backward into the stone table of Jecumseh, the female corpse. His eyes fell upon the false-face mask of his ancient opponent. The carved, painted smile of the mask then came alive and transformed into a sinister grin. The small painted head she held in her hand twisted his way as her silver White Deer Society broach glowed brightly.

"JECUMSEH!" Nero roared. He spun his head in a moment of fright, buck antlers swooshing in the air, serpents flailing wildly. He backed off.

Another huge blast from the well blew him to his knees. He got up confused and stumbled over to the next corpse table. Standing over the male corpse, his eyes were drawn to the same silver broach around the mummy's neck. It burned bright. Skeletal hands moved, shaking the turtle rattle they held. Nero cringed in paranoia. He barked his other ancient nemesis's name. "HIAWATHA! No. You cannot be alive. No!"

Another rumble pulsated from behind him, this one much bigger. Nero leaped away from Hiawatha's corpse. Bent on leaving the chamber, he searched for the entrance tunnel but could not find it in the fog. He became disorientated. The snakes on his head writhed in animation. He then heard a sound behind him. A scrape. He spun around.

The remaining corpse sat up from its table, its silver broach burned hot.

Nero gasped. His chest burned. He clutched the broach hanging around his own neck and scorched his hand.

The corpse raised an arm, its bony fingers grasping an eagle feather. A deep voice spoke inside Nero's head. It uttered the ancient language of his ancestors, but he knew the meaning of the words. "I am Deganawida," the voice said. "You are not worthy to wear the Crown." The feather released from the corpse's clutch and floated away into the mist.

Nero turned in terror. He ran.

A flash of bright steel.

The Halligan.

Rae swung it like a bat, the single curved prong searching for flesh. She caught Nero high in the side with a rib-shattering crunch. Nero howled. Rae yanked tool from his body, tearing open a large gash that streamed with bright red blood and torn muscle. Nero fell to his knees.

Rae raised the Halligan over her head for the finishing blow. "Now you bow down to me!"

She swung again.

Nero dodged.

The tool clanged against the rock floor. Nero lashed out and knocked the legs out from under Rae. She fell backward and bounced the back of her head on the stone floor. Sharp pain shot through her skull. Stars twinkled in her eyes. She lost her grip on the tool. It clamored away.

Nero rose above her, hunched in severe pain. He stretched his shaking hands toward Rae's head. He focused his eyes — raging with a silver glow. His head of serpents quivered, their fanged-mouths biting the air.

The last thing Rae remembered was the silhouette of the crown against the bright backdrop of silver-blue flames. The outline of writhing snakes and two antlers marked her slide into darkness.

Jake careened into Nero just as his invisible shaft of energy shot toward Rae. It missed, bounced, and redirected against the cave wall. A large chunk of rock fell from where the blast struck. Another enormous gaseous boom suddenly shook the chamber. The concussive blast pushed the bodies of Rae, Jake, and Nero clear across the room. The three Indian corpses, however, remained as they were, seemingly untouched by the explosion of gas.

Tumbling, Jake and Nero groaned with injury, but both gathered enough strength to stand up and face each other. Nero's lips curled in rage. He showed white teeth as if to bite. The snakes on his head wiggled and hissed. He circled Jake and directed his silvery gaze into Jake's eyes.

"Once I finish plucking out your dreams I will steal your soul and enslave it for all of eternity. Then I will—"

Jake smashed Nero with a jab to the mouth. "Shut your pie hole."

Nero was taken aback at the quickness of Jake's strike and his audacity of defiance. He spit out a bloody tooth.

Jake mocked him. "You're not worthy to wear the Crown. Your orenda is weak. You're no God. You bleed. Just like a man!"

Nero countered with a backhanded slap across the Jake's face. The blow felt like someone hit him with a brick. Jake's head twisted to the side as saliva sprayed from of his mouth. He stumbled backward, knees weak, surprised at Nero's physical strength.

Jake shook off the blow then cautiously moved back to within arm's length of Nero. They circled slowly, sizing each other up. Jake reached into his pocket and pulled out Rousseau's knife.

"You fucking piece of jail trash," Jake taunted. He lunged and sliced Nero across the bicep.

Nero wailed as blood squirted out of his arm. He balled his fist in rage and swung a roundhouse. Jake blocked the punch, slashed with the knife again and sliced Nero across his chest. Nero grunted but countered with a hard fist to Jake's stomach, knocking the air out of him. Jake lost his grip on the knife. It scattered away lost in the fog. He staggered back, sucking wind, trying to breath.

CRUNCH!

A large rock smashed down upon Nero's crown. It struck his skull directly between the antlers, flattening a handful of serpents. Nero wavered a moment, his eyes rolled in a daze. He then dropped to his knees.

Jake looked up. Anne Stanton stood across from him, grimacing. She clutched a large boulder between her hands. Nero swayed from the blow, moaning in agony. Stanton tossed the stone and grabbed a hold of each buck antler to keep him from falling. Snakes tore at her flesh. She grunted in pain from their bites.

Breathing heavily, Jake jumped over and grabbed the antlers too. Razor sharp fangs dug into his hands.

"Pull!" he shouted.

They lifted as one.

Nero screamed and reached up, locking his hands around Jake's wrists to counter the tugging. The chamber pit rumbled again. The earth shook. Jake and Stanton regained their balance and pulled harder. Nero screamed. They gave one final tug.

The Crown of Serpents ripped free with a wet tear.

Jake released his grip and Stanton stumbled backward, holding the great treasure in front of her. The snakes immediately stopped moving before her eyes and froze into hardened silver. But on the bottom side of the crown hung long strands of gray hair and bloody meaty flesh.

Nero cried out. His hands searched the top of his head.

Jake looked at the pitiful man. He had been scalped clean. A bloody, hairless patch of skin and skull was all that remained where Nero had worn his short-lived crown. Nero screamed again, the silver fading from his terrified eyes. Jake could care less. He turned and searched for Rae.

She was already up on her feet, leaning against Jecumseh's funerary table. She pressed a hand on the back of her head to keep her wound from bleeding any further. She gave him a thumbs-up. Jake exhaled slowly, in pained relief.

The well behind her suddenly pulsated with light as water burped from its depths, the bowels rumbling again. Flames shot high in the air. Another explosion brewed from below.

Nero suddenly jumped up and bull-rushed Jake, knocking him aside. He made an unexpected dash toward Rae. She remained calm as the bloody bald wretch of a human being barreled toward her.

Jake shouted, "No!"

Nonchalantly reaching down into the fog, Rae found what she needed. Nero was upon her. She sprung up, gripping the Halligan tool horizontally, and then cross checked Nero's face with it.

Nero's jawbone shattered. His legs gave out. Rae stepped aside to let him fall. He stumbled like a drunkard and tripped into the pit with a flaming splash.

Jake ran over. Stanton followed, the crown still clutched in her grip. They looked into the well as Nero slowly submerged headfirst. Jake reached down through the flaming water and grabbed his ankle. The pit groaned. He saw light pulsate from below. A large bubble of gas rose from its depths. It would explode at any second.

"Take cover!" Jake shouted. He released Nero and dove for cover behind a corpse table. The two women followed suit. Stanton released the crown for just a moment as she scurried behind Hiawatha's table.

The chamber instantly went black. The trio went blind in pure darkness. A tremor shook the room. They waited for the blast.

Seconds ticked by but the explosion never came. Instead, they heard a strange flushing of enormous quantities of water down inside the pit. The room then became eerily silent. A light switched on. It came from Jake's rifle lying in the corner of the chamber. Another light flicked on, this time from a dropped helmet near the entrance passage. A third light illuminated from a flashlight left on the floor. In the splash of light the trio noticed the layer of fog had disappeared completely.

On hands and knees, Stanton searched the floor in front of her, groping to find the crown. But it was nowhere to be seen. "It's gone! The crown is gone," she cried. "It was just here!"

Jake scurried over and grabbed his weapon and the flashlight. Rae snatched the lit helmet then they both drew back close to Stanton and searched some more.

"The crown is gone," Stanton whispered.

"I thought you had it?" asked Jake. He looked at his hands and all of the snake bite wounds vanished.

"I dropped it in the dark," Stanton replied. "I can't find it. Did Nero take it?"

"Not a chance," replied Jake.

They walked over to the pit, Jake pointing his rifle in the hole. They stared down into emptiness. The pit was devoid of all flames, liquid, or any source of light.

"Nero's dead," said Rae. "He got sucked down that hole. There was no explosion to toss him out or he would be in this room."

"Flushed," Jake smirked.

"I'm getting the hell out of this place," said Rae.

"10-4," said Jake, still staring in the pit. "But first I need to check something out. I think I know where the crown might be. *We* need to know. To make sure it's safe. Give me some light when I climb in."

"Huh?" muttered Stanton.

"Oh no," said Rae. "You're not going down into another well."

"Oh yes I am."

Jake flung his legs over the edge and entered the pit. Hands pressed against the pit walls he scampered down the rock steps jutting from its sides. Below him was a bottomless black hole he refused to look into. Slipping slightly, he steadied himself on a firm ledge and peered under a rock lip to an open area in the wall. A silvery blue light suddenly illuminated his face. He smiled.

"The crown is down here! Everything's good." Jake squinted in the light and reached forward out of Rae and Stanton's view. He grabbed an item, inspected it with a grin, and hung it around his neck. The silver guardian's broach had found its new *rightful* owner. He climbed back up.

Pulling himself out, Jake told his two counterparts that the crown was indeed intact and safe down there under the rock lip. "It's in its own sanctum sanctorum." His backside was then suddenly cast in flickering blue and silver light emitting from the pit. He looked back. "I don't know how it got back down there. Maybe had some help here from our three friends." He pointed to the corpses. "But anyway, we are leaving it alone.

Our business is done here. This whole damn escapade is over."

"We have no choice," said Rae. "Look behind you."

The water had risen to the top of the pit again, bubbling and flaming. Wisps of white mist spilled from its surface.

"We are out of here," Jake ordered. "Let's find our gear before this place fills up with fog again. We've got a long, dangerous hike back and I've got an injured uncle to attend to. We'll deal with protecting the location of this place once we get back topside and sort everything out."

Toilet room.

Almost an hour later Jake squeezed through the hole in the toilet room wall and laid his rifle on the floor. The room was quiet. His uncle was no where in sight. Jake thought maybe Joe had attempted to make his way back up to the surface to seek help.

Jake helped the two women into the room and they collapsed in exhaustion without saying a word. As Rae and Stanton shared a bottle of water, Jake heard an odd sound up the flight of stairs, beyond the door. It sounded as if a can had been dropped. He stood up and directed his M4 rifle up the corridor.

"Big Bear?" he shouted. "That you up there?"

Silence.

Jake bounded up the steps two at a time and burst through the door. There, under a canopy of flashlight, sitting on a shiny Indian motorcycle, with a candy bar sticking out of his mouth, was Uncle Joe Big Bear. A gas can rolled at his feet. Jake lowered his rifle and sighed with joy. He smiled. Rae and Stanton appeared at Jake's side.

Joe smiled at the trio, just shaking his head with relief. He then stood up and pressed down on the kick-start bar with his good ankle. The motorcycle sputtered to life with a puff of gray smoke. Joe torqued back on the handlebar grip and revved the engine to full capacity. It roared like a tiger. His stomach shook with laughter. He revved some more.

38

The next day. Yale Manor Bed and Breakfast.

JAKE STOOD AT the burnt out Indian grave at Cranberry Marsh. Nothing remained. Not one remnant of the past survived the blackened carnage all around him. Charred trees and soot-covered branches lay at twisted angles in a pile. A burned firefighter's glove lay partially buried under a black rotted log. How can this be so real, Jake asked himself, his memory in a foggy haze. He hadn't even revisited this site since hearing of the arsonist attack. Then he heard something behind him. Laughing. Muffled laughing from underground. His eyes wandered to the large iron slab covering the limestone well where he had attempted to rescue the ill-fated Derrick Blaylock. The heavy slab moved. It lifted, then slid to the side. Jake saw a quick glimpse of bony hands. The hands then grasped the edge of the hole. What came next sent a jolt of fear through Jake's body. Silver snakes, alive with rage, emerged from the hole. They hissed and sought him out. Then buck's antlers. No, it cannot be happening again, Jake pleaded as a tormented, laughing face appeared at the rim. It cannot be. Alex Nero. Risen from the dead, silver snakes molded into his scraggly, long gray hair. Back from the abyss. The Crown was his once again. His glowing silver eyes moved wildly about. And then all went black.

Jake stood motionless in the shower stall, both hands pressed against the tiled wall to support his naked, bruised body. His throbbing head was bent low as he blinked his eyes and tried to wipe the dreamy horror from his mind. As hot water soothed his tight muscles, he moaned with a mixture of pleasure, pain, and sheer relief. Opening his eyes wide, he watched the water splash at his feet like heavy rain. He wondered at the meaning of the nightmarish dream that had roused him out of bed so early.

Nero laughing under the mask — his hair turning into snakes, it was all so vivid in the dream. Was it a dream? Jake shook his head. Maybe the ruthless bastard had survived, retrieved the mask, and somehow found an escape route up through hundreds of feet of limestone and ended up in the Cranberry Marsh pit. No, clearly this couldn't be, Jake tried to tell himself. That's impossible. But maybe it was a message or a sign or some sort of telepathic threat. Clutching the silver broach dangling from his neck, he willed the negative thoughts from his mind. Then all was well. He stepped out of the shower and began to dry himself off.

An inviting female voice murmured softly. "Hey soldier. Now that's the kind of uniform I like."

Startled, Jake looked up. There stood Rae, admiring his wet body with mischievous eyes. She was dressed only in a white robe. She leaned against the bathroom door and looked him up and down, smiling admirably.

Jake grinned. He dropped his towel and walked up to her. He untied her robe. "It seems I didn't tamper with your evidence enough last night?"

Rae opened her robe and pressed her warm naked body against his. She pulled him close and whispered in his ear. "Honey, you can mess up my crime scene any time you want."

On the bedroom nightstand next to a bottle of wine, Rae's cell phone blarred. She pulled herself away and uttered an obscenity at the bad timing. "I have to take it. Don't you move, mister. I'll be right back."

"Yes, ma'am," Jake grinned.

Sitting on the edge of the bed, she answered. "This is Hart. Uh huh." She listened to the caller and immediately smiled. She looked at Jake standing in the bathroom. He caught her glance and raised his eyebrows.

She listened a minute more then praised the caller. "Great. Nice work. Listen, I'm still resting. I'll be in later. Okay, goodbye."

"What are you so happy about?" asked Jake, entering the bedroom, the towel back around his waist.

"Bob Wyzinski, the arsonist. He just confessed everything. Looks like he acted alone. His motive was profit driven. Three months ago he lost his side business of a car-wash company up in Seneca Falls when an Indian-owned firm started competing against him. With credit cards maxed out and his marriage in a shambles he was already on shaky ground. After hearing an Indian was going to buy the Depot, then after the grave was found and you, of all people crawling out of that hole, he said he basically lost it and decided to act. Took it out on the Indians with fire. He did a little research into Indian symbology — thus the dog strangling — to send a message that it was war. But he said he never intended to hurt anyone. Really?" She looked up at Jake. "That good-for-nothing bastard is going to have a long time to think about that."

Her phone rang again. Rae rolled her eyes and answered angrily. This time her mouth fell open as she listened to the caller. "Okay, give me twenty minutes. Where is it again? At the end of Parker Road, got it." She closed her cell phone and bowed her head.

"What's going on now?" asked Jake.

Rae looked at Jake expressionless. "I was just told a badly beaten body, bearing a striking resemblance to Alex Nero, was just reeled in by some fishermen on the lake. Sheriff said the top of his head was scalped."

Jake's lips parted.

"Well, you want to check it out with me? Make sure it's really him?"

Jake shook his head. "I don't need to see him again. Besides, I've to get back down to Pennsylvania."

"Well, I'll ID the son of a bitch and close this case once and for all."

"I've got to ask," said Jake. "What lake did they find him in?"

"Cayuga Lake. Up near Canoga Landing," answered Rae, somewhat confused. Then her eyes grew wide, knowing why he asked. "That underground river really connects the two lakes then."

Jake nodded. "I guess so. We saw it for ourselves. Now we know it empties into Cayuga Lake somewhere way underground." He then grew incredibly silent.

Rae stood up. "You okay?"

Jake looked into her eyes. "Listen, that crown needs to remain a legend though, you know? Some things need to be kept secret, still as a myth." He touched the silver broach hanging from his necklace.

Rae nodded. "And a legend it will remain, Jake." She moved close to him and placed her arms around his neck. "I owe you my life. You can count on me keeping a secret." They embraced.

EPILOGUE

A FTER A THOROUGH examination of the Boyd and McTavish keg
contents by MHI, a team of expert coin collectors was called in to
assess the monetary value of the British coinage. It was determined that
because of the rarity and excellent condition of the gold Guineas, along
with the incredible story attached to them, that each coin could fetch up to
ten thousand dollars. The news made instant headlines across the nation.
But it was decided by Dr. Jacobson that the coins and other war souvenirs
were not to be sold for profit. Instead, MHI partnered with the Freemasons
and formed a traveling exhibition to tell the unique story to the general
public. And of course, on this successful opening night ceremony, Jake had
been assigned the lead presenter for the exhibition. He was an instant hit in
front of the famed American Numismatic Society in New York City.

Afterward, as the crowds thinned, Jake snuck away to wrap up some
unfinished business. He retrieved an item held by staff security, left the
building, and jumped on his Indian motorcycle for his two destinations
in the city.

His first stop was a visit to a close friend in law enforcement who was
also an expert scuba diver. Jake laid the groundwork for an MHI-funded
dive off the Painted Rocks in Seneca Lake. Their goal: Sullivan's cannon
of gold.

Next, he paid a visit to the state headquarters of the fraternity he had
belonged to since his first tour in Iraq. On the top floor of the Grand

Lodge of Free and Accepted Masons of the State of New York, Jake exited the elevator and proceeded to the end of the posh hall.

"Brother Tiler?" Jake announced, walking up to a distinguished man in his seventies.

The man stood up from his chair, guarding a closed door. The gentleman held an elaborate sword, hilt up, blade between his legs. He was dressed in a black tuxedo, silver vest and tie, and his hands covered with white linen gloves. He wore a bright white apron around his waist. The apron was trimmed and tasseled in blue and gold. Jake noticed the middle flap of the apron was pointed down, denoting the man as a Master Mason.

"I am Brother Major Robert Jake Tununda, a Master Mason from the Land, Sea, and Air Lodge Number One of Iraq. I seek admittance to the Grand Lodge on a matter of returning the remains of Brother Mason Lieutenant Thomas Boyd of the Continental Army."

"Brother Tununda, it is an honor to make your acquaintance," replied the Tiler, duly impressed with Jake's Class A Army dress uniform and his medals and ribbons. Among them, the Tiler noticed was a small pin with a square and compasses — the Mason's symbol.

Jake also wore an apron around his waist, but his was trimmed and tasseled in olive green, black, and brown, the colors of the military lodge he had been raised a Freemason in several years back while on duty in Iraq.

"We've been expecting you." The Tiler shook hands with Jake. In a very subtle motion both men repositioned their grip. They then performed several body motions only fellow Masons would know. "And the password?" asked the Tiler.

Jake leaned in close to the Tiler, mouth to ear, and whispered the secret password to gain admittance to the Lodge. The Tiler nodded and uttered the same word back to Jake. The examination was over.

Jake tucked under his arm a small wooden box he was carrying.

"I need to inspect the contents of that box before I ask for your admittance into the Lodge."

"Certainly Brother Tiler," replied Jake. He placed the box on the chair and lifted the cover. "Boyd's ah... scalp is there in the protective bag." He did not look in. "His remains are being returned to the Masons on behalf of the director of the Haudenosaunee Collection, granted with authority from the Grand Council of Chiefs. His scalp is to be added to his grave at Mt. Hope Cemetery up in Rochester."

"I am satisfied," said the Tiler. He then turned around and gave three sharp raps on the door. In a moment, three knocks were returned from within and the door swung open. A younger man in a similar tuxedo and blue and gold apron appeared. He held a staff topped with a metallic Masonic square and compasses over a half moon. Jake knew this particular symbol to be that of the Junior Deacon of the Lodge and the only member allowed to answer what was called the outer door.

"Brother Tiler," asked the Deacon. "What is the cause of the alarm?"

"Brother Major Robert Jake Tununda," announced the Tiler in a commanding voice so all inside the Lodge could hear. "Master Mason of Land, Sea, and Air Lodge Number One of Iraq, properly clothed and vouched for, seeks admittance to return the remains of Brother Mason Lieutenant Thomas Boyd of the Continental Army."

The Junior Deacon nodded. "Brother Tununda, I am so honored. Please enter and follow me." He motioned Jake inside and closed the door behind him.

THE END.

ACKNOWLEDGEMENTS

With thanks to David W. Corson and Eileen Keating of the Cornell University Library's Division of Rare and Manuscript Collections for their research assistance; to Cornell University Professor Art Bloom and Hobart William Smith Professor John Halfman for their suggestions and opinions regarding the truths and lore of the underground lake connections; to Lee J. Wemett for information on the history and legends of Hemlock and Conesus Lakes; to Dennis Money and Tom Klotzbach of Seneca White Deer, Inc. for providing information about the white deer herd of the Seneca Army Depot; to Seneca County IDA and Seneca Army Depot Base Project Manager Tom Enroth and Chief of Security John Cleary for the base tour and history inquiries; to WWII European-theater Army veteran Robert Lounsbery for allowing me use of his memoirs on the 666th Field Artillery Battalion and for details of his time spent on the construction of the Seneca Army Depot; to WWII veteran Harry Hunter Morgan for his history as a guard at the Depot; to writer, lecturer, and consultant Doug George-Kanentiio of the Akwesasne Mohawk Nation for his source information on the Iroquois culture; to Onondaga Clan Mother Ada Jacques for her clarifications; to librarians Margaret Anderson, Ann Sullivan, Barbara Kobritz, and Steve Massey-Crouch of Tompkins Cortland Community College Library for research assistance on Sullivan-Clinton campaign journals, the Luke Swetland memoir, and production assistance; to U.S. Army CW3 John A. Robinson for army protocol corrections; to Robert Spiegelman, author of *Fields of Fire*, for reference verification; to critical readers Lisa Karpovage, Thomas Karpovage Sr., Gene Baier, Chris Bissen, Kathy Zahler, Lisa Ford, Alexis Dengel, Sean Barry, Lauren Wright, Thomas Ventura, Kyle Downey, the late John Colella, Bootsy Colella, Phil Colella, Jen Drumluk, Gene Conrad and Shari Hurny for their wide ranging improvements; to Joan Notebloom, former Town Clerk of Romulus for her valuable insight; to Eric Lindstrom, Patrick Gillespie, and Peter Voorhees for passing on important Ithaca area information; to Tompkins County Historian Carol Kammen for providing local research sources; to Larry Turner, Groveland Historian, for clearing up inaccuracies in Boyd's ambush; to Bill Stinson and Steve Mount for lending me their rare copies of the History of Seneca County (1786-1876); to VW Tom Savini, Director of the Chancellor Robert R. Livingston Masonic Library of Grand Lodge in New York for inquiry into the Freemason's Code; to Karen D. Osburn, archivist for the Geneva Historical Society, for finding several articles in relation to Seneca Lake; to Luzerne County Historical Society and Northumberland County Historical Society for research assistance; to Sampson State Park Ranger Tom Watts, Sampson WWII Navy Veterans Association, Inc., and Sampson Air Force Base Veterans Association for their valued correspondence and knowledge on base structures; to Bill Hecht for his incredible effort in providing a free source of online information on the history, geology, and geography of the Finger Lakes as well as discussing the possibility of underground caves; to Cornell Army ROTC Captain Kurt W. Belawske for officer training course information; to Lt. Pete Tyler of the Ithaca Police Department as well as the New York State Troopers for answering my law enforcement related questions; to Al Heitmann for access to his property at Cranberry Marsh; to the Waterloo Volunteer Fire Company and the Seneca Falls Fire Department for honoring me with their service — sometimes literally under fire; to the office personnel at Sampson State Park for providing emergency relief from bee stings; to Stevi Mittman, author and TC3 instructor for her writing tips; to my fellow Masonic brothers of Hobasco Lodge No. 716 for their fraternity; a special thanks to Laura Galecki Kouns; and finally to my sons Jake and Alex for their inspiration.

Historical Timeline

1142 A.D.: Atotarho, the ancient Onondaga wizard, reigned the lands as a brutal murdering dictator. After a meeting with Deganawida, Hiawatha, and Jecumseh he suddenly reformed his ways. The evil snakes were combed from his hair and he emerged as a key founding figure in the birth of the Iroquois or Haudenosaunee Confederacy.

1779: By this year the Iroquois Confederacy had expanded into the mightiest empire in North America until it was almost entirely destroyed during the Sullivan-Clinton campaign of the Revolutionary War. The Confederacy still remains intact to this day.

September 5, 1779: American scouts of the Sullivan campaign rescued Luke Swetland in the Seneca Indian village of Kendaia. The Seneca had captured Swetland in Pennsylvania a year before. An elder clan mother spared his life and adopted him into the tribe. After the war, in his memoirs, Swetland wrote that the scouts, mistaking him for a Tory, stole a silver broach from his shirt and threatened his life. He also wrote of finding a secret cave in the side of a hill not far from the village, a place he took refuge during the cold winter months of his captivity.

September 13, 1779: American Lieutenant Thomas Boyd, a Freemason, along with two soldiers in his scout detachment, were taken prisoner by British and Iroquois troops during what is now called the Groveland Ambush. Mohawk Chief Joseph Brant, also a Freemason, allegedly received the secret Masonic hail sign of distress from the prisoner Boyd. Later that night Brant was called away on other duties and was unable to offer protection. Boyd was turned over to Freemason British Colonel John Butler and the Seneca warriors under Little Beard. The next day Boyd suffered the most heinous torture death of the American Revolution. A mystery to this day is, did the Masonic gesture actually occur and if so, why did Brant leave? Or did Brant and Butler knowingly betray a fellow Brother of the Craft, condemning him to death at the hands of the vengeful Indians?

Early 1940s: The U.S. government enacted eminent domain and acquired seventeen square miles of farmland in central Seneca County, New York for construction of the Seneca Army Depot and the Sampson Naval Training Base. Both bases were key weapons storage and training facilities during the second half of the 20th century.

1941: According to a construction worker and WWII veteran, during the Depot's construction a well shaft was sunk and struck an underground flow of water. Dye was added to detect the direction of the current and was soon discovered in Cayuga Lake to the east. Some say this is evidence of a real underground river linking the two largest Finger Lakes of Seneca and Cayuga. Others who have conducted research on this possibility have concluded it an absurdity.

Present Day: After the Depot became fenced in during the forties the famous white deer herd of the area was corralled and thus protected. They've since grown to become the largest white deer herd in the world.

*For more in-depth information, including background research, a photo gallery that follows the story, and interesting web links associated with the novel, please visit **www.CrownofSerpents.com**.*

Cover / interior book design, maps (except where noted) and illustrations by

Karpovage Creative, Inc.

designer • map illustrator • publisher

www.karpovagecreative.com

LaVergne, TN USA
10 January 2011
211792LV00004B/90/P

9 780615 281100